T0354905

The Industry

Koto

Order this book online at www.trafford.com
or email orders@trafford.com

Most Trafford titles are also available at major online book retailers.

Printed in Victoria, BC, Canada.

ISBN: 978-1-4269-1769-1 (soft)
ISBN: 978-1-4269-1770-7 (hard)

Library of Congress Control Number: 2009938458

Our mission is to efficiently provide the world's finest, most comprehensive book publishing service, enabling every author to experience success. To find out how to publish your book, your way, and have it available worldwide, visit us online at www.trafford.com

Trafford rev. 11/4/2009

North America & international
toll-free: 1 888 232 4444 (USA & Canada)
phone: 250 383 6864 ♦ fax: 812 355 4082

This book is dedicated to the Matriarch of the family
Victoria "Big Momma" Burley

Acknowledgements

I want to thank George Renaud and Anthony "Black Face" Walker, for all of their assistance and support. Without them this project wouldn't have been possible.

I also want thank my mother, Demetrie "Ye Ye" Howard and my Pops, Stephen Howard, I couldn't have finished this project without their financial support, encouragement, love and support.

Prologue

Chad Stevens, General Manager of the Syon Music Group, straightened his tie for what seemed like the fiftieth time. The Golden Boy of Syon bounded up the stairwell in deer-like fashion from his twenty-fifth floor office.

He inwardly smiled at the irony of his current predicament. How many times had he preached to his minions and staff about being punctual, having good work habits, and taking the initiative? Now, here he was, late for an important meeting with the company's top brass.

Chad glanced at his gold Rolex in midstride as he climbed the stairs. It was "9:20, not good," he admitted. How the hell was he going to explain being twenty minutes late for the most important meeting of the month? As he hustled to the meeting he begins to think what to say! Should I tell the truth? "Well, Sir, you see, I was getting my knob polished. Bill Clinton style, by my new secretary's intern." What? Yes sir, she is black, sir with an ass like the women in the 'Luke' videos sir, and a pair of lips that gave my Johnson insomnia when I laid the head down on them.

Hell no! He'd be out of work and collecting unemployment before lunch. He had to think of a suitable lie. If I just could've kept my dick in my pants Chad thought. But the perks of his job fed his insatiable appetite for women, especially fine black women. Chad was not prejudiced in that area. He liked them no matter what color of the spectrum they fell under, but something about the sisters made his dander rise.

Chad really didn't feel bad about being late. After all, he brokered multi-million dollar deals for brunch, lunch, dinner, snack, even after snacks, on a daily basis. His penchant for finding and cultivating music entrepreneurs into fat ass paychecks for Syon was renowned throughout the company. That's how he earned the name "Golden Boy."

Chad entered the thirtieth floor from the proposed fire escape route flat out running. He barely mumbled an "excuse me" to the staff members that he'd ran through like tackling dummies on a football field.

"Slow down, ass hole."

"Hey, watch what the fuck you're doing," someone yelled.

It went in one ear and out the other, as Chad rounded the hallway on his tiptoes trying to maintain his balance.

He checked his watch again; 9:25.

When Naudia first entered his office, it was forty minutes to 9. After his seemingly short trip to the galaxy called ecstasy, Chad opened his eyes to the reality of a clock that read 9:15. Damn, that girl was good!

Chad skidded to a complete stop in his Gucci loafers in front of the conference room's double mahogany doors. Panting like an overworked Camel in dry desert heat, Chad attempted a last minute effort at composing himself. He ran his fingers through his tousled hair, and straightened his tie once again.

"Fuck!" he sighed, attempting to muster a veneer of confidence. "Here goes," he told himself, as he stealthily entered the conference room.

The feeling of being late was awkward to Chad, because under normal circumstances, he would be the first to arrive and wait on everyone else to show. To make matters worse, he had a plane to catch in an hour. After its magnificent start, his day was unraveling.

Chad's plan of sneaking into the meeting unnoticed went to shit when someone cleared their throat, bringing attention to his tardiness.

The president and C.E.O. of the company, Morten Stillwell, cut his presentation midsentence as all eyes diverted to Chad.

Chad felt completely stupid. He felt as though he were in the middle of a Southwest Airlines commercial where everyone just wanted to "get away."

Morten Stillwell smirked at Chad.

As Mr. Rodgers would say, "Can we say embarrassing, boys and girls?"

"Well, gentlemen, we have a special guest amongst us. What a pleasant surprise! Our knight in shining armor has decided to grace us with his presence, he snidely remarked. "On behalf of the Syon music group, and I do speak for everyone present when I say that we are truly, truly, flattered to have you take time out of your busy schedule for us," he continued, as snickers and giggles arose.

His embarrassment complete, Chad tried to explain.

"Sorry, sir, my um ... my schedule ... um ... Well, ... I'm going to have to ... um ... You see, sir, a last minute problem surfaced with one of the labels, sir." He lied sheepishly.

Chad fidgeted and once again straightened his already straight tie.

The snickers and giggles turned to full scale laughter, as the president looked at Chad closely and rolled his eyes.

"What the fuck was so funny?" Chad wondered to himself.

Tommy Nguyen, a longtime friend of Chad's, pointed his Monte Blanc at Chad's exposed cum-stained black briefs.

Chad looked down and noticed his dilemma. He flushed red as he hurriedly turned back toward the doors.

Chad stormed from the conference room with gales of laughter taunting him from behind.

Stalking to the bathroom, he seethed with rage.

"Fuck them," he thought. "Let them ass kissing do-boys laugh. They won't be laughing after the end of the year and I broker this 450 million dollar deal that will net this company $1.2 billion in seven years. Then we'll see who's laughing when I become president," he thought. "The scenery will be much different then. Fuck em all."

BOOK ONE: INDUSTRY MONEY

Chapter 1

Friday
March, 2003
Beaumont, Texas (Beaumont Federal Correctional Institute)

The March breeze, after serving 10 years in the federal prison system, was a welcome relief to Kiwan Rush as he stepped into the fresh air as a free man.

The sun was high and the humidity was thick, even for Texas. Kiwan didn't notice nor did he care about the weather, as long as he was out of prison. Happy that his recent nightmare was over, Kiwan surveyed the parking lot in search of Amin, his youngest brother, who'd promised to pick him up upon his release.

Kiwan looked at his Casio watch, which he purchased while incarcerated. His brother was officially 25 minutes late, typical, he thought! That is one thing that time didn't change, Amin has always been selfish and only did things in his own time!

Mildly disappointed, Kiwan sat on the curb, in front of the prison doors, with his meager belongings. Visitors attempting to visit their loved ones passed Kiwan as he resumed his search of the parking lot.

"Waiting on baby brother huh?" a voice inquired from behind.

Kiwan looked over his shoulder to see who was speaking. Carl Littrell, a computer hacker and embezzler from Dallas, who was released on the same day, stood with his property and release papers behind Kiwan. Carl had been caught embezzling 30 million dollars in federal money from his savings and loan investment bank. For his crime against the U.S. government and its precious economy, Carl received 18 months in a federal prison. Kiwan Rush, on the other hand, had been imprisoned for one kilo of cocaine that didn't belong to him, receiving a sentence of 122 months. He often reflected on the irony of life's little mysteries.

"Yeah, man, I'm waiting on my baby brother."

Kiwan had once stopped Carl from getting his ass kicked by a disgruntled black inmate who just so happened to had just finished watching "Mississippi Burning" on TV, and Carl just so happened to be the nearest white boy who the inmate could take his anger out on. Ever since, he and Carl had been associates of sorts.

"Well, I see my wife pulling up. Would you like us to take you to the bus stop or something?" Carl asked.

"Naw, man, he'll show. He's just busy more than likely, he'll be here," Kiwan said with more conviction than he felt.

"Okay bro. Well, you have my number, right?"

"Yeah!" Kiwan answered, gritting his teeth. He hated when white people tried to use the word 'bro' in reference to blacks. They seemed to always use it in an exaggerated manner.

"Then call me sometime. Especially if you need anything," Carl told him, walking out to meet his wife, who stepped from around a new Lexus 430, looking sophisticated in a Kim Basinger type of way.

Kiwan watched as Carl gave his wife a long, slow passionate kiss after she squealed in the delight of seeing her man. Life was a muthafucka, he thought. He wondered how many years he would have gotten had he been in Carl's place and had embezzled $30 million? Carl had once confided in him that the government never did recover the entire $30 million. "Life," he thought, shaking his head.

Kiwan retrieved a copy of "The Coldest Winter Ever," by Sista Soljah from his property, and hadn't read a page before he was rudely interrupted.

"Rush, you can't sit there!" came the voice, shattering his thoughts, from behind. Kiwan didn't bother to acknowledge the voice. As far as he was concerned he was a free man and could do whatever he pleased. Well, anything that didn't violate his three-year federal parole stipulations.

The guard walked around to face Kiwan, standing over him as he continued to read. Kiwan finally placed the book next to him gently, face down, and looked into the officer's face inquisitively, as if to ask, *May I help you?*

"Did you hear me?" she asked. "The warden said that you couldn't sit there and wait for your ride; he said that you could either come into the visitor's lounge and wait, or we can give you a ride to the bus station in town."

The female was one of the most "police-ing-est" black officers in the entire prison. She was the type to oppress her own kind just to score brownie points with her supervisors, always trying to prove that she'd do her job. But she went too damn far. Kiwan knew of a few brothers who she'd fucked over for no reason, and he reveled with the opportunity to cuss her ass out.

"Man, fuck you and the warden!" he spat, as he rose to his full height of six feet, three inches. He weighed right at a solid 225 pounds and had a chiseled physique from years of basketball.

"Uh, excuse me?" she asked, rolling her neck.

"You heard me, bitch, you been running around here treating the brothers like shit, and like your shit don't stink. But I'm free now, and I'm here to tell you that if you don't get out of my face, I'm gon mop yo ass across this concrete. I'll make sure I scrape all the black off your ass, then you can be white like them folks you always sucking up to."

She stood there speechless, as Kiwan looked angrily down at her. She positioned the radio to her mouth to call for help when it appeared. A white stretch Lincoln Navigator pulled up to the curb, distracting them both.

The truck came to a complete stop in front of Kiwan. Now his curiosity was piqued, as he tried desperately to look into the back window through the dark tint.

The driver's door opened and what appeared to be a giant stepped from the truck as it rocked from the shifting of his weight. The driver of the limousine stood every bit of seven feet, Kiwan noticed, as he rounded the truck to open the door for Kiwan.

The man had fire red hair and red freckles all over his tan skin. He was an imposing figure and Kiwan would not have liked to be on this man's "shit list." He looked very, very violent.

"You Kiwan?" the man asked curtly. Kiwan couldn't even speak, instead nodding his head as a means of communication.

"Tony," the big man stated, without even offering his hand. Kiwan noticed that the man didn't even have his two front teeth.

The giant named Tony then walked to the rear of the truck and opened the passenger door.

A beautiful appendage with a white sandal at the foot and a platinum ankle bracelet appeared from the truck.

"Damn!" Kiwan thought. He wondered what the rest looked like as his mouth hung open in anticipation. Kiwan noticed the manicured toenails and beautiful polish on the woman's feet. He could tell just from her feet that she had a lot of taste and class. But what did the rest look like? He wondered.

His wait was short-lived, as her feet hit the pavement; she stepped from around the door. Kiwan was not disappointed. The woman was stunningly beautiful. She had an exotic look, the kind of look reserved for runway models.

Kiwan took in the woman's air, an air of money, and the power that comes with a woman who knew how to use her femininity. At first glance, she appeared Oriental, but a second glance prompted Kiwan to determine her to be some type of mixed breed. She was too shapely in figure to be anything short of black, he surmised. She wore a linen peach-colored short set and sported white Gucci shades, which she removed to get a better view of Kiwan.

"Nigga, pick your lip up, dang!" she stated playfully.

The security guard who was standing next to Kiwan giggled.

Kiwan frowned up. "What'd you say?" he inquired, addressing the beauty queen.

Giggling, she said, "I told you to pick your lip up and close your mouth before something flies in. Your shit was just hanging down like duhhh ..." She taunted. Kiwan wanted to be mad, but he couldn't help but smile. She was pretty and had a sense of humor, as if her beauty didn't matter to her. He immediately took a liking to her. He was ashamed at himself, though, for openly ogling her. Not very smooth, he thought.

"My name is Prescious," she introduced herself, extending her hand to Kiwan. "You must be Kiwan, Amin's brother. I've heard a lot of good things about you."

"Yeah," he said, grabbing her soft hand and lightly shaking it. Damn, it felt good to be out and to just hold casual conversation with a pretty woman without having people looking in your mouth – he missed that.

Kiwan couldn't help but be attracted to her and he knew instantly that she was attracted to him. Things shouldn't have changed that much in ten years to where he couldn't read a female's body language, he figured. If so, he was in a world of trouble.

"Damn, your brother didn't tell me that you were so big, ya know," she commented, eyeing him up and down. She then looked at Tony, who went rigid, or maybe that was just Kiwan's imagination playing tricks on him.

"Well, I ain't seen my brother in ten years, ya know!" Kiwan said, mimicking her.

"Hold on a sec," she told him, as if she'd just thought of something. Kiwan watched Tony from the corner of his eye as Prescious reached back into the limo. Her backside immediately caught his attention. 0 hell yeah! He thought, noticing how fat in the ass she was. The girl was definitely mixed with a black person somewhere. A black man will always leave his mark. Noticing the way her ass shook in her loose-fitting shorts, Kiwan could tell that she either didn't have on any underwear, or she had a g-string on. Either way, it turned him on.

Prescious retrieved what looked to Kiwan like one of those flip phones that he'd seen his sister-in-law with on one of her many visits, except Prescious' phone had a small attachment at the bottom.

She flipped open the face of the phone. The phone chimed as it was activating itself for use. Prescious looked at the LCD display screen, punched a few buttons, then spoke into the receiver. "Call boss man," she chirped.

After a few seconds, Prescious smiled at the screen and held up a finger as if to say, hold on. She handed the phone to Kiwan and instructed him to hold it at the bottom. "Don't block the camera," she told him as he adjusted the phone in his hand.

When he looked into the screen, Kiwan saw his brother Amin in realtime TV. "Well, I'll be damned!" Kiwan exclaimed. "Where the fuck you at, man?" he asked.

"What's the deal, big brah? How does it feel to be out of that motherfuckin' cage, Nigga?" Amin yelled. "Nina! Look, it's your brother-in-law," Amin informed his wife over his shoulder. Kiwan couldn't see her, as Amin filled the screen, but he definitely could hear his sister-in-law.

"Let me talk, baby, let me talk," She was pressing, with her diamond-clad hand tugging her husband's shoulder.

"Hold the fuck up," he yelled shrugging off her hand.

Kiwan was so glad to see his brother's face, after so many years of not seeing him, that he'd forgotten that he was angry with him.

"Say, listen Amin. I appreciate the fact that you did the limo thing for ya big brah, but damn, dog, it would've been cool had you picked me up yourself instead of sending someone else to do it."

"Come on, man, chill out," Amin told him. "I was planning to scoop you up, but something important came up. I'm in the middle of an important business meeting as we speak. Bear with me, baby! Enjoy what you see for the rest of the day," Amin winked. "I'll get with you later. Precious will take care of you. I gave her a stack of chips for you, and she's got the credit cards. Go shopping, spend some loot, enjoy yourself, nigga," he advised.

"I'll see you later on, and then we'll ball together. I'm a show you how it's done in the 2000 and 3, you ain't seen shit yet. This is just the tip of the iceberg, baby!"

"Awight!" Kiwan conceded, thinking that it couldn't be too bad. After ten long years in the joint, he deserved to blow off some steam, he felt. Plus he needed to be fed, fucked, sucked, and tucked! His time was due.

"One," Kiwan barked into the screen, signing off with his brother.

"One," came the reply from Amin before the call was disconnected. Kiwan was temporarily satisfied after not having seen his brother in person for so many years. Of course, he'd read the magazine articles, seen photo spreads and layouts, and had even talked to him on the phone extensively throughout the entire stretch, but it just wasn't as good as seeing his face in person.

Prescious sucked her teeth, breaking Kiwan out of his reverie. He handed her the phone back. Tony moved to get Kiwan's belongings off the curb.

"Look, man, you don't have to kick it with me if you don't really want to," Prescious told Kiwan, shifting her weight to one leg, fidgeting with the antenna on the cell phone. "But if I must say so myself, I can be damn good company when I want to be," she told him, blushing.

Kiwan caught the hint. "Let's ride," he said, climbing into the limo.

"Wait a minute, Rush," the female officer said. Kiwan had forgotten that she was standing there.

"My name is Nikki, not bitch," she rudely stated. Obviously offended by the tongue lashing Kiwan had given her.

"Who cares, B-I-T-C-H!" Kiwan yelled over his shoulder, climbing all the way into the limo.

Prescious smacked him on his ass playfully, before she climbed in behind him.

"Ooh, a bad boy!" she kidded, giggling. "I like that in a man. If it ain't rough it ain't me," she finished.

Kiwan would later come to realize just how true those words were.

Chapter 2

The private G-4 jet soared amongst the indigo blue skies toward its destination of Houston's Hobby Airport. The scheduled flight would've been non-stop from New York to Houston if the emergency meeting with Syon's General Manager hadn't received precedence due to mitigating circumstances. The meeting prompted a 30-minute layover in Atlanta to accommodate Chad Stevens and his assistants.

Amin Rush, CEO of Murder One Records, one of the biggest independent rap labels in the dirty South, didn't mind changing his flight plans to accommodate the executive and his lovely assistants, especially the young, cute, mocha colored sister. Giving them a lift to Atlanta would give the CEO an opportunity to call up Lil John and the Eastside boys about contributing some tracks to his upcoming project.

Amin was used to the hustle and bustle of the industry after seven years in the business. Having just come from New York on business concerning his new "Kotto" clothing line after thirty minutes of sleep from prior meeting on the West coast, another thirty minute nap from an unscheduled layover would be a Godsend.

Besides, Chad claimed to have an important proposition to discuss with Murder One.

Kiwan's phone call had interrupted the flow of the discussion between the two companies. Chad, grateful for the interruption, used it to gather his thoughts and regroup as he excused himself to go to the lavatory.

The Murder One's staff and entourage were currently occupied with their everyday routine of returning phone calls, responding to important two-way pages, organizing interviews, scheduling appearances, dividing up studio time, and engaging in the perfect amount of bullshit amongst the crew members who held no real duties concerning the daily activities of the company.

To Chad, it was an awkward, but necessary place to conduct such an important meeting. He was in a race against time to implement his plan before the flow of the fickle Hip-Hop industry changed directions again. Chad knew that with the industry you had to get on board the train of current events before it lost steam.

For Amin, this was his preferred field of battle. Any general would tell you that he'd rather choose his own field of battle than have it dictated to him. Especially when dealing with the sharks of the music business.

What worked on Amin's nerves, throwing his concentration off, was the way his wife, Nina, parked her ass in front of him and crossed her legs, looking squinty eyed. She had a way of glowering at him with her jade green eyes that made him feel naked and exposed. It was as if her eyes cut a path directly to his heart.

A native of Puerto Rico by way of New York, Nina Rush had not been a happy woman in the last five years, ever since her husband's independent label was picked up by Syon with a record $200 million deal. With an attitude like "Hoe!" Amin knew that his wife's patience was wearing thin with the industry and the strain that it was placing on their marriage. She definitely let it be known every chance she had. He wondered what kind of bug she could have up her ass, now! Anything was liable to have set her off; there was no telling with her.

Amin felt that he was the classic case of a man who'd paid too damn much for what he had. The money, the homes, the cars, the jewelry, the women, entourage; none of it was worth his marriage or the rift in his family. He was so wrapped up in the industry that he didn't have the foggiest idea of how to give it up. Music controlled his very essence in more ways than one. Like a powerful narcotic, Amin was hooked. The industry was his life and his life was the industry.

"Idie Amin," as he was known throughout the business, had carved out a niche for himself and his entire family. Amin had gone from playing the drums in his Jack Yates high school band, to making and selling beats from his home studio, to the vast empire laid out before him. Although his story was no different from any other rags to riches saga, Amin knew that hard work and hustle was not the major factors that contributed to his rise in fame. One turn of fate could've put him and Nina in prison for three lifetimes! Of course, he had a past. Of course he had skeletons, and of course, he paid dues to amass and maintain his fortune. But what kind of credit plan was God running? How much would it cost him on the back end? Though times had been rough as well as sweet, one thing in his life remained constant, and that was his wife and the love she'd given to Amin and his daughters, Kayla and Kya. Ever since their college days at N.Y.U., Nina had been down like four flat tires.

Nina's foot draped daintily over her leg and rocked as if it had a mind of its own. That was his wife for you; she tried to remain cool and ladylike at all times, even when she wanted to go the fuck off! He could tell at the exact moment she decided to confront him. A glimmer shone in her eyes, a twitch in the corner of her mouth was a dead giveaway.

"I don't know what the fuck you sitting there, thinking about it for, talk to me, don't just look at me crazy," he told her. Trying not to put their business on front street, Amin lowered his voice an octave or two. She remained silent, crossing her arms over her chest. She changed her mind just that quick. Must be serious. "Fuck it," he thought. "I really don't have time for this bullshit." Frustrated, he rose out of the leather captain's chair to walk away.

Amin had never hit his wife, nor did he like to fight; walking away had been his temporary solution to their seemingly permanent problems.

Nina snatched Amin back down by his wrist, snagging the band of his Jacob and Company watch. All he could do was to shake his head as he watched his $50,000 watch hit the floor.

"Nah, muthafucka; ain't nowhere to run on this plane," his wife hissed. "Wherever you go, I follow, because you gone hear this shit!" she scolded, her eyes blazing green fire.

Amin sighed. This shit was beginning to take its toll on him. He'd thought plenty of times of leaving, but he knew that she wasn't having that. She'd made it clear plenty of times that death would come before divorce; his death, not hers! And he truly believed her. His father had warned him that a woman who would do anything for you bore watching, because she would do anything to you. "What, Nina?" he conceded, seeing no other way out than to confront the situation head on. His personal cell phone rang as Amin prayed it was Kiwan again.

"Let the muthafucka ring, dammit," she demanded. Amin just looked questioningly at his wife, wishing that Chad would hurry his ass up. What could be taking him so long anyway? "I know this muthafucka ain't taking no shit on my plane! In the middle of a meeting that he deemed important for me to alter my flight plans; sucka must've bumped his head."

"Talk, Nina. What's wrong with you?" he asked, his brow furrowing in agitation.

"Everything is wrong, Amin. I cannot take too much more of your shit. You gon have to do better than what you're doing." She stressed the last, on the verge of tears. "I love your dirty drawers, Lord know I do, I've put up with the late nights in the studio, the video shoots, being out of town for weeks at a time, but I will not put up yo trifling ass bringing home no fuckin diseases," she hissed, pushing Amin in his face.

Amin's reactions almost got the better of him as he poised to slap Nina, catching himself at the last minute. Nina didn't falter, waver or divert her gaze.

"Nina, you got me fucked up," he growled, trying to maintain his composure in front of his crew, hoping that no one was paying attention to them. "I ain't got a mothafucking thing" he told her, without the conviction required to convince her, least of all himself.

She continued to glower at her husband, tears welling up in her eyes. They both knew he was lying. The problem was that Amin really hadn't shown any signs of a disease and that in itself was a bad sign. He fucked up this time.

"I just got a call from my gynecologist, Amin. She found traces of gonorrhea in my culture," Nina revealed, tears bursting through the frail dam of bravado that she'd managed to put up. "Gonorrhea!"

Now Amin was really confused. Relieved that it wasn't anything more serious, but confused all the same. He wasn't burning or having any discharge, there's got to be a mistake.

"I ain't got no damn gonorrhea!"

"You got something, Amin, I really do hate you sometimes, man, how could you do me like that?" she whined, her hands covering her face, embarrassment setting in. She sobbed uncontrollably in the confines of the jet.

Nina's emotions must have permeated the air because all eyes seemed fixed accusingly on Amin. He wondered had anyone heard what she'd said, as the heavy feeling of guilt started bearing down on his broad shoulders.

Ayanna Vincent, Amin's personal secretary, who also happened to be his wife's best friend and confidant, left her seat to comfort her distraught girlfriend. Being blind didn't seem to deter Ayanna in any way, as she made her way to Nina with little effort and no help. "Come on, Nina girl, help me to the bathroom," Ayanna insisted.

Nina rose from her chair across from her husband, doing her best to regain her composure. She straightened her cream-colored Fendi suit jacket and took Ayanna by her outstretched hand, leading the way to the plane's restroom.

Chad finally exited the restroom as Nina and Ayanna made their way down the aisle. Chad, his secretary, her assistant, and Amin's lawyer Tisha Russel returned to their original seats to resume the discussion they started before the drama began.

Amin was still caught up in his thoughts. He knew that he should've been embarrassed. He wasn't, and he wondered what kind of man he was becoming. The hustler within told him that he didn't have time to be embarrassed. As it had done in the last five years, his business concerning the label came first.

"Now where were we?" Chad asked, crossing his legs, and steepling his fingers. Chad tried to convey a comfort that he didn't feel.

"What, ... Oh ... Umm ..." Amin stuttered, snapping out of his trance-like state. He looked over at Tisha, who was busy rifling through some paperwork. "Well," Tisha said, "Chad was bringing us up to speed on his proposal," she said, without looking up. Tisha found what she was searching for and handed it to Amin, as she pushed her tortoise shell glasses up on her button nose.

Amin held a copy of the distribution contract that elevated Murder One onto a professional playing field in the game of Rap and Hip-Hop. The file was three inches thick.

Tisha Russel, a product of the streets of New Orleans third ward, a Masters in Economics from Texas Southern, and a law degree from Harvard, had come highly recommended in the industry to Amin from several sources. Together, he and Tisha had negotiated the deal of their lives in Murder One's third year of business. Deals of such magnitude were unheard of in the industry back then. Now they were poised to make Murder One the largest independently owned black label in the world, with the ability to keep total control of its master tapes. If Murder One could exercise its option at the end of its five-year contract to purchase the masters to the ten albums released under Syon's distribution, then Murder One would be totally independent, needing only major distribution for its future projects. Being in control of his own masters was a dream, which if it came to fruition, would allow him to retire. Then he would be able to enjoy the things he'd worked so hard for.

The hustler in Amin loved this part of the game. This is what made the business sweet and addicting to him. Like a heroin addict who needed to get over the sickness of the drug before he could enjoy the high, all Amin had to do was get past the preliminaries and foreplay of the deal so he could enjoy the high of grinding. The money and the power were just perks of the industry that came secondary to him. It was about the hustle, the grind, the get money part of it that gave him a hard-on. He got off on the feeling that he was handling his motherfucking business. He focused on the Golden Boy of Syon, as he leaned back into the plush leather, trying not to crease his bubblegum blue velour jogging suit. It was a prototype from the designer in New York. Amin was without a doubt in his element.

"Here's the thing," Chad said, addressing Amin. "Syon has been very pleased with the relationship between Murder One and the company, especially with the returns on the projects and artist that Murder One has invested in. But frankly," Chad hesitated, searching for the proper words without offending the C.E.O.

"Frankly, Amin, Syon is rather concerned with the success of the last album under the contract." Chad's gray eyes glinted as his head shook from side to side. "Murder One hasn't had a platinum release since the "Lady Black and the Hit Squad Compilation," and that was almost two years ago. Now we know that's not due to marketing or promotions. Our research shows that it's just not marketable or the type of sound that the industry's buying that Murder One is releasing."

Amin listened, showing no emotion, keeping his eyes locked with Chad's. Chad smirked.

"You see, Amin, the industry is like a choosy lover, as we all know, and right now that bling-bling shit is playing out. People are tired of hearing about gripping grain, rolling 24s, or how much your diamonds shine, unless it's club music. In my opinion, your beats and musical talents are being wasted. Your production skills on remixed tracks and the tours have been your bread and butter for the past year, am I right?" Chad asked rhetorically. They both knew that the answer was yes. "In this business if you don't keep reinventing yourself, then you're a dead duck in tall grass, capiche?"

Amin remained nonchalant, maintaining his tact, a lesson from his mentor, Black Jack.

"Now what I'm proposing to Murder One will take the industry by storm. This idea will take the sound of the dirty South worldwide," Chad announced with a wave of his arms, looking off into some invisible scene into the future. The bullshit and foreplay was over, Amin thought, and now came the hustle.

"Now Syon is looking to pick up an up and coming independent label from Houston. The talent at this label is great. The sales are off the chain without any major distribution. They shipped one million units in just two months, and for an indie that is outstanding. Just think what major money, and major distribution, could bring."

"You're speaking of Ruff House, correct?" Tisha asked. Chad nodded. Amin's jaw twitched the first crack in his stern veneer. "Your point?" Amin barked.

"Syon is willing to disperse a $450 million deal for a 12-album, seven-year term if Murder One will ally itself with Ruff House and create one label. Each company'd still be able to operate independently when dealing or signing any new artist and their projects, but the current roster of talent on each label and their projects would fall under the Syon umbrella," Chad finished.

Four hundred and fifty million dollars was a nice chunk of change for 12 albums, Amin thought. Syon must really believe that the marriage between the two camps would work, but Amin knew different.

"Hell mothafuckn nah!" Amin yelled, creating complete silence on the jet. "It ain't happenin, Cap'n. You got my camp fucked up, 'lil' daddy. The feud between me and Romichael Turner is real, not some publicity stunt, not some movie or book. The shit between us is real. Nope, it won't work."

"Hear me out. I'm aware of the beef between Amin Rush and Romichael Turner," Chad exaggerated. He'd only heard rumors of the beef. "This merger would be perfect for the industry and your company. You know the industry inside and out, you can bring the talent at Ruff House to the pinnacle that they're capable of. Romichael has a pipeline to some raw and potential superstar talent. Where he finds them, we don't really know, but word is, that he's signing them while they're still in prison, just on their reputation. If they're close to parole or discharging their sentences, he signs them. Plus he has a hookup on the parole board in every region that allows him to swing votes in his favor. He gives them a light signing bonus for commissary money, gets them paroled, and puts them in the studio as soon as they're released. If they turn out to be shit, then he releases them from their contracts, only out a couple of grand. But the talent he's accumulating over there is tremendous, and they are producing."

"Nah!" Amin repeated, shaking his head so hard that his chain and pendant threatened to put his eye out. "I don't like the way he handles his business," Amin told him. An understatement to say the least. Amin hated Romichael and everything about him. Amin also knew for a fact that Romichael was still into pushing dope, and he wanted no part of it. He suspected Chad knew it too, which would be all the more reason to pair an up and coming company with a reputable, already established, veteran company: image.

"This business devours its young if they aren't protected, Chad, and I protect mine. I keep them happy, and that way we all make money and keep money, because there's definitely enough to go around. I even set up a small retirement for my artist, for when their careers come to an end," he added.

"Yeah, yeah, your methods are renowned in the industry, and I applaud what guys like you and Russell Simmons have brought to the table. It's innovative, and the industry needs that, but ... Amin, your artists have lost their hunger. You're coddling them. They're getting lazy," Chad argued. "They know that 'Idie Amin' their Lord and savior will come to their rescue. You can't possibly continue to make money that way. The competition will eat you a-fucking-live!" Chad screamed. "Syon is just giving you the opportunity to reinvent the label, put another two or three hundred million in your stock," he persisted.

"Don't forget to mention putting money into Syon's stock as well, making you look good, and slaving my ass like a scoliosis-having Hebrew for another seven years," Amin countered. "It ain't about the money no more. You got me twisted with somebody who needs it, because Amin Rush fo sho in the fuck don't. I came into this game with my own bread and if I didn't have Rap or Hip-Hop I'd still have bread," Amin flung the contract in Chad's lap. "All I want is the right to exercise my option to buy my masters at the end of the five-year contract, as it states in the renewal clause. Page 110, Chapter 12, sub-clause D-4, line three," Amin rattled from memory. "If, after we purchase our masters back from Syon, and they still want to remain our distributors under a new, non-masters owning contract, then cool, if not then fuck you in ya ass!" Amin stressed.

"Wait a minute, Amin," Tisha interjected. "We might want to consider ..."

Amin shot Tisha a glance that would refreeze ice. She instantly shut up.

"What, everyone must be deaf up in this bitch," Amin ranted, losing his cool. "I said no, end of discussion, anything else?" he asked Chad.

Chad blanched under Amin's tirade. Amin was going to fuck up his plans. This was supposed to be a simple deal. Why was Amin being so stubborn? This was another opportunity of a lifetime for him.

"Alright, Amin," Chad exhaled, deciding to switch tactics.

"I feel where you're coming from," Chad soothed. "But what you have to start thinking about is that in order to fulfill your contractual obligations and to exercise your option to purchase your masters outright, that the numbers on your last album under us have to meet or exceed the platinum mark, and that's before the end of this fiscal year. That option can be overlooked with the inception of this deal."

"Ayanna!" Amin called out. "Bring this muthafucka some Q-tips, because evidently he don't hear too good."

Giggles emitted from the Murder One family.

"Be sensible," Chad persisted. "The entire industry knows that Murder

One isn't so hot right now. Club Music and Gangster rapping is coming back, especially with the slow methodical bass-filled beats from the South. I'm offering you the chance to re-establish the new South. You'd be right up there with some of the best if you could pull this off, and Syon has $450 million that says you could do it ... And Amin ... the entire industry is watching you on this one. If you pull away from the table cold turkey other major distributors might be tentative to do business with you. Then where would you be? Distributing with money from your own pocket. That could put you in a bind, just ask some of the industry's best," Chad advised, a smug look on his face.

Amin covered the distance between he and Chad like a streak of chained lightning. He grabbed Chad's lapels on his shirt, snatching him to his feet.

Both men were eye to eye,

Tisha screamed in fright as Amin's bodyguards moved in to intercede. Chad's secretaries jumped over their seats.

"Are you threatening to blackball me, bitch?" Amin hissed through clenched teeth, spittle flying from his mouth. Damon, one of Amin's personal bodyguards, stepped in between the two men, forcing Amin to let go of Chad before he did something that he might regret.

Chad was unfazed. He knew that he'd struck a nerve with that move. He felt the momentum of the game shifting into his half of the court. Chad fixed his ruffled shirt. "It seems that your lack of judgement in business has also affected your perception in verbal conversation. I said no such thing," Chad stated calmly.

But the threat had been made and the implications were there; one just had to read between the lines. Chad was saying, "Work with me or else!" and everyone knew it.

"Fuck Syon!" Amin retorted. "We can find distribution elsewhere." He stressed it with little certainty, before storming off to see about his wife. As far as he was concerned, the meeting was over.

The pilot announced their approach into Atlanta and requested that all passengers return to their seats and fasten their safety belts.

"Good," Amin thought. "Get that muthfucka off my plane before I do him bodily harm."

Devastated by Amin's reluctance, Chad had a few tricks up his sleeve. If Amin wouldn't play ball, Chad would move on, but Murder One records would pay dearly; he would see to that. His dream of becoming Syon's next president was all that mattered to him.

"Mr. Stevens?" his young secretarial assistant inquired. "Are all C.E.O.s in rap that crazy?" she wanted to know.

"Nah! Just him and Sugga Man," he joked. On second thought ... they really were kind of special in the temper department.

Chapter 3

This bitch is crazy! Kiwan thought. This crazy mothfucker had the nerve to ask me, out of all people, was I gay? The girl had class, but she didn't have an ounce of tact. She better be glad that I'm a changed man, because ten years ago I would've kicked her ass, he thought. Gay! She had to be the biggest fool since the wide mouth mule.

Kiwan tried not to let the comment bother him too much, as he and Prescious walked through the Beaumont Central Mall amidst the cornucopia of sights, sounds, and aromas of food and baked goodies. But Kiwan couldn't help it; the question bothered him despite the fact that he'd been ignoring stupid shit for years. Coming from a woman, it was different. Not to mention one as pretty as Prescious. He was going to fix her ass, he concluded. He had ten years of stress built up and she was going to be the receptacle of that energy in the bed.

"I don't mean gay, I mean, like ... You know bisexual, because ten years is a long time to go without any pussy," she told him.

Kiwan gritted his teeth and bit down on his tongue. He gave her an exasperated look. She actually had no clue that she was antagonizing a viper, he thought. The blank expression on her face spoke volumes. She actually expected him to answer that stupid shit.

Kiwan just shook his head and laughed. He'd forgotten what his sister-in-law had told him on one of her frequent visits. The women of today were ten times more brazen than they were ten or eleven years ago, she'd told him. Now that was a bold statement coming from a New York native, and a Puerto Rican to boot. So he just decided to let the matter go. Thank God the ringing of her phone intruded on the awkward silence. Kiwan figured that the girl must be somewhat important because in the hour that he'd known her, her cellie had not stopped ringing. She held clipped and one-sided conversations, issuing instructions to the unseen parties on the other end. His keen senses were threatening to go into overload as he took everything in. He still couldn't believe that he was walking amongst the free after all those years. He watched the people converse and interact with one another as he began to appreciate something so simple as shopping.

Kiwan was anxious to get the hell out of his prison clothes, but marveled at the idea of having an abundance of choices in trying to decide what he wanted to wear. Prison had robbed him of such simple freedoms and he was as giddy as a three-year-old at Christmas. Kiwan made up his mind to just try and, relax; his brother was right, he was well-deserving of a little pampering.

Prescious hadn't understood him, but he never really expected her to. She'd been downgrading the mall since their arrival, saying that it was too country and raggedy; complaining that there wasn't even a Gucci or Prada store.

"You trippin," she'd whined earlier. "Man, we could go to the Galleria or Katy Mills when we get back to H-Town. Why would you want to go to this raggedy-ass mall?" She'd asked him.

Kiwan searched for a shop that he could relate to. The patrons in the mall kept glancing and peeking at him and Prescious. At first he figured that they were looking at his odd manner of dress, but the more he thought about it, the more he came to realize that it was his sassy escort that commanded so much attention. She stuck out like a sore thumb in the small metropolis. He eyed her again as she chattered on the phone. It was her look of young innocence and exotic beauty, along with her strut. With each step she exuded sex appeal; with each step her ass shook, announcing that she didn't have on any underwear. A g-string maybe, but definitely no panties, he'd concluded.

Prescious thrived on the attention. She knew that she was being watched and became coquettish as the object of attention. After all, her sex appeal had served her well in her line of work over the years, she thought, as she ended her phone conversation.

"I'm sorry, Kiwan," she said, her voice filled with femininity. "This business is demanding, somebody always needing a favor," she said as she turned off her phone and returned it to her purse. "Have you found anything yet? Because I'm telling you, this mall ain't shit."

"Naw, but I tell you what, how much money you got?" he asked, deciding to handle her just as brazenly as she handled him. He knew that she didn't understand kindness.

"Your brother told me that money was no object. He said that anything you wanted to do was fine with him," she assured him.

"Anything?" Kiwan asked, raising his eyebrows. He wanted to see how far 'anything' went, as he pulled her close, putting his arm around her and resting his hand in the small of her back.

She timidly looked up into Kiwan's eyes and blushed. She was beautiful when she blushed, he thought.

"Anything," she softly said.

No other words needed to be said as Kiwan grabbed her by the hand and stalked toward Tony and the limo.

Chapter 4

The colorful airbrushed mural on the side of the tour bus was an attention getter, to say the least. The mural read, "Ruff House Records," and consisted of a picture of Ruff House's hottest artist, who, at this very moment, was on his way to platinum status with his latest album, "The last are breathing."

A native of Dallas, Patrick "Monster Pat" Williams, was Romichael Turner's first prison protégé. He was Ruff House's featured artist, the pinnacle of the entire program. He was the general of the camp where the artists were concerned.

To Monster Pat, a $200 thousand tour bus was a far cry from the rundown prison Blue Birds that he'd become accustomed to while doing his eight year bid. But rapping was rapping and rapping was his life, no matter where he rapped or whom he rapped for. Pat didn't care; he just wanted to be heard. His voice is all that mattered. His displayed passion is what carried over into his unique style of flow. Patrick's flow, a syrupy baritone, showcased a lyrical flow that was edified by his gangster influenced Southern diction, and set him apart from the rest of the rappers. That and his guidebook of ghetto life stories had his star rising fast. Pat was known throughout the Texas prison system talent show circuit for ripping the mic like a Monster, hence his name. As his reputation grew from prison farm to prison farm, so did his following.

Finally, word had gotten to one of Romichael's henchmen, through his incarcerated brother, about the talent and potential of Patrick Williams. The rest, as they say, was history. Upon Pat's release, Romichael immediately took him in and put him in the studio. Pat didn't even have a chance to return to the East Dallas projects in which he had been born and raised, before Romichael conjured up and implemented the idea of soliciting talent from the prison system. Monster Pat became the intermediary between Ruff House and the incarcerated artists and was given free rein to put together his crew of "Headbusta's" as the rambunctious group of ex-con rappers was appropriately titled. Each artist brought a different style of flow to the table, which created a gumbo of success. With the proper production and promotion in the rap game, Romichael knew that you couldn't help but come out on top. At least that was what Romichael was banking on. But no business was without its risks and minor setbacks. Already coming to the end of a five-state, twelve-city tour, and the Ruff House camp had encountered its share of drama, mostly stemming from internal rivalries within the company, born from Monster Pat's recent attention, on his solo project. Romichael had been neglecting E-dubb and a couple of other artists from his 5th Ward neighborhood. Jealousy had reared its ugly head in the camp, causing numerous fights, arguments, petty competitions and major drama. Romichael didn't mind a little internal competition, but when it got to the point where it interfered with business, then he had to put his foot down, as was becoming the everyday norm.

The tour bus carried the Ruff House clan to its final destination of the Spring Break tour. Baton Rouge would be the final stop before heading back to Houston. The "Third Coast" tour had been a success in Romichael's point of view. He knew that in order for a new artist to sweep the nation, he had to control his own backyard first - ergo the tour in the dirty South. This move would prove to be pivotal in the career of Monster Pat, and for the longevity of Ruff House. With every city they entered they were greeted with a sold-out crowd and over 5,000 spins on the radio, all of which brought Ruff House under scrutiny, as the independent record label was being courted by almost every major distributor in the industry.

The customized tour bus headed Westbound on 1-10, 45 minutes from Baton Rouge, when Romichael awakened with a start. The yelling, screaming, and hollering coming from the buses saloon caused him to jump up from the bed, hitting his head on the ceiling.

"Fuck!" he cursed, wondering what the hell was going on now. He'd already decided to skip the summer tour, as he rubbed his head, trying to get his bearings. He searched the room for his clothes to see what time it was.

Clad only in his silk boxers, Romichael was starting to get pissed. He'd left explicit instructions not to be disturbed until they reached Baton Rouge. He found his watch amidst his crumpled clothing and shoes at the foot of the bed. His companion's cocktail dress and lace panties lay next to his garments, reminding him of his promiscuity after last night's concert. Damn shame, too, for the life of him he couldn't even remember the girl's name.

Hell, nah! This couldn't be right. He rubbed his eyes, not sure he was reading his watch correctly. Yep! Just like he thought, 8:35 p.m. Now he was really pissed. They were scheduled to be at the radio station at 6 p.m., and had a mic check at the club for 7:30, not to mention the concert that was supposed to start at 9. That would mean that he'd been sleeping for fifteen hours straight. How the hell did that happen? No more syrup for me, he concluded, as he stormed toward the bedroom door. The bus was still rolling and shouldn't be, he thought, as he headed for the commotion to raise some hell of his own.

He flung open the door, banging it hard against the wall. No one in the crowded cabin of the bus noticed, as the group of rowdy, pussy hungry hoodlums was jeering at and rooting on two females performing a seductive striptease to Lil John and Usher's new club hit, "Yeah!" The crew had been so loud that Romichael didn't even notice the music until he opened the door. They were whooping and hollering, throwing money, and smacking the two women on their asses. The women shook, bounced and gyrated to the bass-filled music as Romichael trudged to the front of the bus. "I should've rode in the Hummer," he thought.

The crew pretended not to notice the half-naked C.E.O. continuing with what they were doing.

"Stop the muthafucking bus! Pull this bitch over," he yelled to the driver.

So out of control, no one even took notice of the bus coming to a complete stop. Romichael cut the music.

"I thought I told you muthafuckas about pulling these busted ass bitches off the street. And why the fuck we ain't in Baton Rouge yet?" he screamed.

An incessant knocking on the door of the tour bus interrupted Romichael's tirade. He opened the door as Corey, his right-hand man, and Flip, his bodyguard, boarded the bus with the assumption that there was an emergency. Why else would the bus have pulled over? They were late as it was. Both men were perplexed as to why Romichael was at the front of the bus in just his boxers.

"Flip! Man, you and Corey be bullshittin, why the fuck we ain't in Baton Rouge? We was supposed to be at the fuckin radio station two hours ago!

Where is that punk road manager at? He knows better! That's your boy, Corey!

What type of games you niggas playing with my money?" Romichael went off.

"I know, Ro," Corey attempted to explain. "But my boy Keith wanted to make a quick stop in New Orleans while you were sleep, to see his kids, since we were making good time. Then his baby momma flipped out on the fool and started throwing a fit, so the tender dick muthafucka stayed! We left his ass, and you know how these niggas are, man, you can't let these fools out of your sight. They don't know how to act. These stupid muthafuckas always trying to push up on every hoe they see."

"Yo momma stupid!" one of the rappers called out.

"Man, suck my dick," Corey yelled, trying to determine who made the comment.

"If you got a dick, it don't belong to you, it's borrowed contraband, and you need to give it back to who it belong to," came the reply. The entire crew burst out laughing.

"Oh, so now I got to find another road manager?" Romichael continued. "That still doesn't explain these funky ass bitches, where did they come from?" he wanted to know. "Who let them on?" he asked, eyeing the crowd.

Nobody answered, as Monster Pat snickered. The Purple Haze they'd gotten from Florida was doing a number on his vision as he watched the pudgy C.E.O.'s cellulite shake as he spoke. Romichael stood six feet, but his chest and stomach were covered with the testimony to his good living. Pat didn't think that Romichael even knew what a set of weights looked like. Pat tried to keep a straight face, but couldn't help it. Romichael reminded him of a bell pepper with feet; no! Better yet, he reminded him of that purple thing, "Grimace," that starred in the McDonald's commercials.

"Oh, it's funny, Pat? Huh? I wonder if the shit would be funny if I put all of you funky muthafuckas of the bus?" he fumed. It was a bluff that he'd used before. Everyone knew that he was full of shit. He had too much money tied up into the rappers. But the niggas who were just freeloading were in trouble if he did ever decide to make good on his threat.

"Fuck it!" he concluded. "Get these tramp ass hoes off my mothafucking bus!" he demanded. His face muscles were taut and twitching with his rage.

"I ain't going nowhere, you got me twisted. I'm here with Monsta Pat," one of the women shouted. "Yous a lie, bitch! Big Dave brought you on," Pat denied. "Man, fuck that hoe, bitch got too many stretch marks on her stomach, probably got twelve kids or some shit," Big Dave announced, his comment eliciting more laughter from the buzzed crowd.

Romichael frowned. The last was enough to push him over the edge. "This bitch must've lost her fucking mind; who did she think she was talking to," he thought. He lost all self control and reverted to a page from a chapter in his life that he was trying to close. Quick as chained lightning, he reached out and grabbed the girl by her braided hair, pulling her into the fist that burst her nose like a Gusher's fruit chew.

"Ooooohh!" someone yelled.

"Ahh! the girl screamed. "You broke my nose!" she cried, blood gushing like from an overheated radiator. She cried in vain to dislodge Romichael's hand from her hair, swinging wildly.

"Bitch, I don't know who tha fuck you think I am! But i'ma sho yo punk ass," Romichael hissed, spittle flying from his mouth.

"Wait, wait, okay, alright, man, please, just let me put my clothes on!" she screamed.

Monster Pat couldn't hold it in any longer. The scene was hilarious. He rolled with laughter watching the half-naked Romichael and the naked girl tussling. The whole entourage was as high as a light bill in the Texas summer heat. Pat's fit of laughter caught on to the rest of the crew as they decided to egg Romichael on.

"Don't forget about the other hoe, Ro," someone yelled out.

The woman in question, watching her friend catch the short end of an ass whipping, tried to run to the back bedroom of the bus.

"Grab that other bitch, Flip," Romichael demanded, as he punched the belligerent and struggling woman in the stomach. The woman cried out, doubling over in pain, as her voluptuous breasts swung wildly. Big Dave ran up and started scooping his money up.

Someone clipped the fleeing girl from behind. She fell face first, her hands full of money. She was unable to break her fall, and her chin split and she bit a hole in her tongue as her face cracked on the parquet floor of the bus. Flip grabbed her ankles and started dragging her, leaving a trail of blood.

Romichael led the way as they slung both women into an overgrown patch of weeds on the side of the interstate.

Headlights illuminated the fiasco, as the instigators watched, falling from the bus in hysterics. The women screamed and cried in a fit of panic. They did not want to be left on 1-10 butt naked with no money, no ID and no means of transportation. Gales of laughter was all that they were left with as the caravan moved on without them - clouds of dust and diesel fumes were the last they saw of the Ruff House "Headbustas."

Romichael was furious. Nodding his had like a rabid bobblehead doll, he thought of the money he was about to lose because he'd decided to cancel the show.

"The show is canceled!" he screamed. "Fuck Baton Rouge you muthafuckas just gon have to miss this show. Ain't gon be no parking lot pimping tonight. Nobody's getting paid. You muthafuckas done fucked up now. I'm gon have to start putting my foot down because ya'll don't understand plain English. I'm going to have to start fucking with y'all paper like y'all fuck with mine."

They were heading straight back to Houston, Romichael decided. "I've hustled too hard for mine to be just giving it away," he mumbled, as he stormed back to the bedroom, trying to slam the door off the hinges. A hot second later the door flew open and another naked female came stumbling out. Her clothes hit her in the face just as she fell flat on her ass. "What tha fuck did I do?" she whined, the door slamming shut again.

Behind the closed door of the bedroom, Romichael couldn't help but laugh, as his cell phone and two-way pager alerted him of incoming calls.

He snatched the cell phone off the battery charger, ignoring the two-way. He knew it would be the promoter trying to get in touch with him about tonight's concert.

"What?" Romichael barked into the cell phone.

"Mr. Turner, how's it going with the tour?" Chad Stevens asked.

"What's up? Who dis?"

"It's Chad Stevens from Syon. We need to talk, Mr. Turner, In person. I have something to discuss with you that you might find interesting."

Strange, Romichael thought. The general manager of Syon calling him, in person, this had to be good!

Chapter 5

The hallway lights illuminated the entrance to the suite at Harrah's Hotel and Casino located in the French Quarter of New Orleans' business district. The suite instantly became pitch dark again, as the two heated bodies that threatened to fuse together from the passion-generated heat slammed the door shut while engaging in frenzied and passionate kissing.

Hands groped, tongues danced and talking was obsolete as fires were ignited within the two willing participants.

Prescious' tongue tasted sweet and fruity from the five Amaretto Sours that she'd drank in the casino while Kiwan shot craps.

Kiwan hadn't had a drink of hard liquor in years, so the two mixed drinks of Hypnotic and Hennessey had his mind reeling. He was buzzed, relapsed and ready to break Prescious' back, he thought, as his manhood began to respond to the heated action and to Prescious' moans of pleasure.

"Ain't got no rubbers," Kiwan said, planting soft kisses to the crook of her neck.

"Keep some," she informed him.

"Oh, so you stay ready, huh?"

"Yeah, to keep from getting ready," she huffed, her breath catching in her chest when Kiwan lightly licked in her ear and inhaled. Most men exhaled with the heated air from their breath, but when you inhaled cool air would invade the space you just licked, giving a cool sensation that tickled in the right spots.

"Oooh, urn, where'd you learn to do that?" she asked, groping Kiwan's crotch through his recently purchased Versace slacks.

"I forgot," Kiwan moaned, feeling the need to lose all of his self control. "Where's the bed?"

"Don't know, can't see shit," she said, ripping his new Versace dress shirt, buttons flying everywhere.

"Damn, hold down, mommi, that was a new shirt," he told her.

"Shhh ... I know, don't sweat it, I'll fly you to New York and buy you ten of them," she told him, planting a kiss on his open mouth, resuming the tongue sparring session. Prescious came up for air after what seemed like an eternity.

"Hold on," she said, fumbling around for a light switch. "Let's find that bed!" she told him. Her two-way pager rang like an angry cell phone as she found the light switch. The bright lights illuminated the spacious and immaculately decorated suite, as Kiwan shielded his eyes from the harsh lighting.

The suite was extravagantly decorated with antique furniture, with gold and silver fixtures, and hand embroidered drapery.

"I'm not even going to answer that," she told him, ignoring the incessant ringing.

Kiwan marveled at the opulent suite as he noticed a complimentary bottle of champagne and fresh flowers in the suite's kitchen. And to think that just this morning he had awakened in a six by 10 foot cell, he thought.

Prescious booted over, rubbing her ass into Kiwan's crotch and then unstrapped her sandals. She kicked her sandals off, picked up her Gucci bag and sashayed across the floor barefooted like she'd been there before. She dropped her belongings on the French-styled love seat.

"I love the way marble feels under my feet," she commented, dropping onto the sofa.

"Don't worry; they'll be in the air soon." Kiwan grinned.

Prescious ripped open her linen blouse, picking up where they left off, as she leaned back into the sofa, jutting her chest out. "Is that a promise?" she wanted to know.

"That's a fact, shawty!" he told her, removing his Now and Later burgundy alligator loafers and silk socks.

"You cleanup nice, daddy," she told him, giggling, letting down her water wavy hair that had been in a ponytail all day.

"Yeah, you got taste, Miss lady," Kiwan commented. Precious had just picked his clothes out from Neiman Marcus two hours ago.

"Show me how much you appreciate me by coming over and stripping for ya girl!" she suggested. "Hell, be like R-Kelly and pull a switcheroo, take it all off," she demanded.

"Well, aren't we just so damn demanding?"

"I'm a freak behind closed doors, daddy. I know what I want and demand what I need. I stopped being shy when I lost my virginity," she told Kiwan, undoing her buttons on her shorts and snatching them down her legs, flinging them past Kiwan1s head with a kick.

"Now stop talking; you know you been wanting some of this pussy all day," she assured him. "You and Mercedes need to be acquainted with one another."

"Who's Mercedes?" Kiwan asked, hoping that maybe she had a girlfriend who was about to join in on the soiree, making it a full-fledged menege-a-trois.

"Come meet her; she's ready to open her store of love anyway!" Precious offered, spreading her legs wide, her g-string sinking into the soft folds of her dripping wet womanhood. "She's been blowing wet kisses at you all day."

"Ooh, hold up," she said, startling Kiwan as she spotted a Sirius satellite radio in the cherry wood entertainment center. She jumped up and ran to set the mood, as she turned the radio to the all R&B station. Luther Vandross crooned about how a house was not a home, as she then went to dim the lights. Before she sat down, she opened the heavy drapes to allow some of the moonlight to penetrate the suite.

"Awight, we ready now," she allowed, resuming her open-legged pose on the sofa.

"Not yet, boo," Kiwan stated retreating to the kitchen to grab the bottle of champagne. He fumbled around for an opener in the kitchen drawers until he realized that the cork twisted off.

Precious was eager for a good fuck. It had been a while since she'd been fucked correctly, and she hoped that Kiwan was not a waste of muscles and testosterone. Her legs shook with anticipation. She'd been a real bad girl and deserved to be punished, she thought, giggling, feeling tipsy from the earlier drinks.

Kiwan rounded the kitchen's wet bar with his shirt open and the bottle of champagne in his hand.

"Hold up, baby, let me look at you a second. You look too good in the dim light," she told him as her estrogen level immediately rose just looking at Kiwan's chiseled prison frame.

"You sure you not gay, or bi...?" she teased.

Kiwan stopped and struck a dapper pose, whirling around for her.

"I see you're into pain, you're just making it worse on yourself," he quipped.

"Yeah, sweet pain," she retorted. "What you gon do, shove that bottle in me?" she grinned.

"Nah, maybe next time," he said, easing over to where she sat, gently setting the bottle of bubbly on the wood and glass coffee table.

He eyed Precious and rocked with the music, as he slowly removed his shirt.

"You not gon dance for me daddy?" she pouted.

"Can't dance, mommi," he lied, as he kept his pace steady, continuing to undress. He stood over her and unbuckled his slacks. Precious gently ran her hands up and down his stomach. Losing patience, she eagerly helped him undo his slacks as she became curious about what his daddy gave him. She ripped his shorts down to his knees, exposing his semi-erect phallus.

"Nice, daddy," she smiled, fondling it, bringing it to full attention. Kiwan's mood returned, seeing Precious so eager. He knew that there would be no slow lovemaking tonight. Nothing but "thug lovin," he surmised.

Precious quickly inspected his phallus with the practiced eye of a pro with admiration. Kiwan didn't even notice the cherry flavored condom between her fingers as she nimbly rolled it on him with one smooth motion. "Shit!" he exclaimed when she took him into her mouth. She had his undivided attention and he momentarily forgot his mission.

He removed himself from her mouth. Precious looked up, perplexed "Whass up" she asked.

"Shut up," he instructed. "I'm driving this Mercedes," he assured her, snatching her up from the sofa, kissing her hard on the mouth again. She moaned as Kiwan was reassured that he was correct when he suspected that she liked it rough.

He tore her bra off from behind her back, and slung the useless material across the room. Spinning her around suddenly so that she faced the sofa, Kiwan roughly bent her at the waist. He admired the view from the back as he became even more aroused with the fact of Precious submitting to his will.

Her ass was so fat! Kiwan had her bent over and he still couldn't see the g-string that ran down the crack of her ass.

"Good lawd!" Kiwan thought, as he pulled the g-string out and moved it to the side, inserting his crooked index finger into her wet Mercedes.

"Oh, shit, Kiwan!" she hollered, as he dug hard into her vaginal canal, passing over her g-spot, trying not to scratch her with his fingernail. She arched her back and responded by opening her legs a little wider, wiggling a bit on his groping finger.

"Damn, you got some fat ass fingers," she told him. Kiwan smiled as he poured the chilled champagne across the middle of her back and watched it drip down the crack of her ass. She squealed and tried to raise up as Kiwan held her steady with a forearm across her spine and deftly guided himself in from behind.

"Some things you never forget1" he thought. He went deep inside of her as arched her back from the penetration. She cursed up a storm from the pain and pleasure of it all.

Kiwan pulled out a bit and started working her with short circular jabs that had her trying to back up all the way on him. But he would not allow it. He was teasing her and they both knew it. The champagne fizzed and bubbled, tickling her clitoris as Kiwan pumped.

"Oooh, muthafucka, I'm cummin," she cried. "Oh, daddy you making this pussy cum already," she insisted.

"Oh, Oh, Uh cuuummminn ..." she yelled, letting the entire floor of the hotel know and obviously not giving a fuck, Kiwan thought. This, however, was music to his ears, as he went deeper, starting to pump harder and long stroke at the same time. He stroked harder as Prescious' body rocked and responded with multiple orgasms. She became sloppy wet as Mercedes began to smack and blow wet kisses at Kiwan. He knew that it was good to her when she tried to buckle and lie flat while he was pile driving the pussy. She tried to ease her way down so she wouldn't have to support herself and allow Kiwan to handle his business. But Kiwan would not allow her to bow down under pressure.

The crack about his sexual preferences continuously ran through his mind. Every time she tried to sag, he would dig his palm in her ribs as he held her up with one arm under her diaphragm. The pain would immediately stiffen her back up.

Sweat began to drip as Kiwan worked her from behind. "Damn Kiwan, you taking ... all ... my ... pussy ... and ... you ... ain't ... saying ... shit," she panted, trying to look over her shoulder.

"Too busy to talk," he told her, steady pumping. He slacked up a bit as the inevitable feeling of release threatened to end his assault on Mercedes. He was starting to see colors behind his eyelids. He refused to let her off that easy, by cumming too quick. Kiwan wanted her ass walking bowlegged for a couple of days as he was about ready to change positions.

Prescious felt him swelling inside of her and knew that he was slacking up so as not to cum right away. She left one hand on the back of the sofa and reached the other underneath her, between her legs. As Kiwan slowed his pace, Prescious took his scrotum into her hand and gently fondled it. She worked his balls in slow circles, kneading them like dough.

The move caught Kiwan unawares. An electric sensation shot from the back of his knees to the top of his head and back down to his toes, as the colors swimming behind his lids intensified. He knew instantly that he'd lost it and it was a lost cause to fight the sensation.

"Damn baby ..." he screamed and started speaking in tongues he never knew existed.

"Oooh, bitch ... you ... cheated," he cried out.

Satisfied with her handiwork, Prescious grinned and reached back, grabbing the base of his shaft and milking it.

"Definitely not gay," she decided out loud.

Kiwan could do nothing but smile.

Chapter 6

A common misconception about players from Texas is that they are countrified and low. Ballers from out of town automatically assume that if you're from Texas then you know how to ride a horse, but Corey Long, Romichael's right-hand man, had never in his life seen a real live horse. In his line of work, Corey was a well-traveled man. He'd been to many different states, and cities; partied from California to New York and back down to Miami. Corey lived the infamous life of a known drug dealer. For 10 years the U.S. government had been trying to build a drug conspiracy, tax evasion, or any kind of case that would send him away for the rest of his life. And through his travels, whether to party or fleeing from federal indictment, Corey Long came to the conclusion that there was no place like the South, preferably his hometown of Houston. A bonehard product of the streets of Houston's Fifth Ward, Corey had been selling drugs since age 10. His first crack sale had been to his father, But Corey didn't know it at the time.

He could remember like it was just yesterday when he was hustling rocks in Brewster Park, chasing cars. Back in those days he ran around so much that most of his profits went to buying tennis shoes. He chuckled to himself remembering how the girls used to call him dirty instead of Corey. He would have on raggedy, oil-stained t-shirts with holes in them, hand-me-down high-water jeans, and brand new tennis shoes.

He was a sight for sure. And ugly! He knew that he was ugly back then. His nose was too big, his teeth were bucked; lips big and pink; he knew that he was hurting! But now, now things were different. Times had changed and the tables in life had definitely turned. Black as the Ace of Spades, young Corey Long had grown to be a true player in every sense of the word. He'd grown into his Afrocentric features, which were considered ugly when he was younger.

Now, instead of oil-stained shirts, Corey wore Camel-haired shirts. Now, instead of hand-me-down high-water jeans, Corey wore tailor-made slacks, and his shoes; well, he never wore the same pair twice, unless they were 'gators.' Times had indeed changed. Instead of running after cars trying to hustle dope, now he was being chauffeured whenever he felt the need. And the same girls who used to call him names, tease him and throw paper at him in class damn near shit in their pants when they would see him in the club, escorting one of the many Hip Hop divas or actresses listed in his little black book. Corey loved to keep R&B hoes on their knees! A woman had to really be different to catch his eye. He'd graduated long ago from the average 'hood rat.' He left women like that to the younger ballers. If a woman wasn't a star in the industry or on her way to being a star, Corey just wasn't interested.

But tonight was the exception! There was something about the cat-eyed sister in the VIP section of Club Max that piqued his curiosity. She was as dark complected as him, but on one of his trips to the men's room, he'd noticed that she had blue eyes. Not contacts, but real blue eyes! And she was svelte, model thin, with a touch of class. Corey instantly knew by her mannerisms that she wasn't from Texas. What really got him was the fact that she seemed to have an agenda, no matter what she did, as if everything she did served a greater purpose. She wasn't mingling, socializing, dancing, nothing! She was just there and had an air or inapproachability about her. The brothers who did approach her were batted down with few words, a wave of her hand, a feminine shake of her head and much tact. Corey was actually enjoying watching her work. But something didn't set right with him about her, because if she didn't want tape bothered, what the fuck did she come to one of the hottest clubs in Houston for?

The VIP room on the second floor of Club Max was not crowded on this particular night. The dreamy mood was enhanced by the black lighting, soft glows of reflected light against the white clothing, slow groove R&B music from the human-sized speakers, and two cognacs that Corey had already downed in the private booth that he and Flip occupied.

The burly bodyguard had his six foot, six inch, three-hundred pound frame slouched back in the booth with a parking lot, miniskirt wearing, bopper in his lap. Corey couldn't see Flip's hands as he watched the girl squirm, but he could just imagine what was really making her giggle.

Genuine's "Tell Me" soothed the club's elite ballers, providing the perfect music to Mack to, as Corey watched the dark-skinned, blue-eyed sister at work again. He chuckled, as he thought about going over to her to see what was popping tonight. He thought better of it; he was there on business. He could play later! Corey watched the action in the haze of the cigar and weed smoke-filled room. Glow sticks bobbed and weaved in the air as if they were being carried by some unseen phenomenon.

The man Corey was there to meet entered the VIP room, sticking out like a Chevy in a fleet of Mercedes. The way he was dressed, the way he walked, everything about him was wrong. While everyone else had on ultra chic urban and casual wear, this clown had on a shitty brown suit, blue and yellow tie and some wing-tipped runover looking shoes that had for sho' seen better days.

The light from the hallway was a stark contrast to the surreal setting to the VIP room, as the fool stood in the doorway surveying the room without letting his eyes adjust from the two different atmospheres of light.

"Flip. Check this fool out," Corey brought to the bodyguard's attention. "Get rid of that bitch and go get that sucka," he instructed starting on his third cognac.

As Flip sauntered over to meet the man, Corey decided to take a peek in the blue-eyed sister's direction, and to his surprise, she was gone. Strange! After being under federal watch for so long, Corey wondered if the bitch was the law. Then he thought better of it because he knew when someone was watching him, and she hadn't looked his way all night.

Flip returned with the nervous little man. The man wouldn't even sit down right away. Corey snapped at him as he adjusted the frameless spectacles on his nose. "Man, sit tha fuck down!"

"Look," the agitated man said. "I really am not supposed to be seen with you in public. I don't know why I even agreed to meet in a place such as this," the man worried, looking around, drawing even more attention to himself.

"Look, muthafucka," Corey barked. "You're the one who said that you wanted to talk, so talk! If it's that important, we can leave, but don't stand up there looking stupid, wasting my time."

"Well, we don't have to leave, but ... You know, we need to talk ... uh ... speak in private!" Corey didn't like the man, but he had to tolerate him. If it wasn't for him, he and Romichael would've been locked down tighter than frog pussy years ago. He liked to antagonize the man though, make him feel uncomfortable.

"Follow me, then," Corey clipped, rising suddenly from his comfortable seat, startling the already timid man.

Corey weaved his way through the intoxicating aura of the lounge, past half-naked women and codeine sipping players who were putting in early bids on whom they'd be leaving with later that night. It used to be a ritual with Corey when he first started having money in the game.

Corey led the way to the bar, walking around the seated men and women to a dark corner next to the bartender's entrance, where a hidden door led to a liquor closet.

When the bespectacled man finally entered, Corey turned on a small light and leaned against stacked crates of longneck Budweisers.

"I'm listening," Corey told the man, pulling out a silver cigar case with gold inlays. He pulled out a blunt and fired it up, purposely pulling hard to exhale the weed smoke in the faint-hearted man's face.

"I don't know how I got involved with you and Romichael," the man said, shaking his head. "You two are the worst."

"You don't say that when you're getting those briefcases full of cash," Corey noted, exhaling clouds of the pungent weed smoke around the man's head. "Now, did you come here to complain or did you come here to talk? Complaining is not your strong suit, now, is it counselor?" Corey snidely remarked.

The man fidgeted a little before speaking, Corey wondering how the hell this little piece of shit coward thought he would ever make district attorney.

"Okay, listen. My source inside of Murder One tells me that Syon is trying to blackball their distribution, but it doesn't matter because they are going to jockey for the National Caucus of Afro-American Millionaire's seat, but I assure you that Ruff House will occupy that seat on the committee. The committee will perform an extensive background check on all executives of each record label, but don't sweat it, because I'm in control of that. I'm sure Murder One is clean, and I assume that Ruff House is, also," he inquired with a raised brow.

Corey smirked, and the man continued. "The committee just doesn't want any nefarious activities concerning the record label to surface later on and taint its image," the man warned him.

"Our books are straight," claimed Corey, enjoying his smoke.

"Nevertheless, just your names and images in the community and with the authorities raise a red flag. Even despite your- clean records, I can handle all of that. Just keep your noses clean for the next six or seven months. No hanky panky!" the man chided.

"Oh, believe me, we don't even begin to hold a candle to you in that department," Corey laughed. Both men knew exactly what was being hinted at. Every man had his weaknesses and the assistant district attorney standing before Corey was currently paying dearly for his. Romichael and Corey were making sure of it. The man cringed a bit at Corey's laughter.

"Just make sure that we get that committee seat; if not..." Corey let his words trail off.

"If I complete this task, will I be able to get the tapes?" the naive little man asked. "The originals?"

"Oh, sure, counselor; you can get the originals now if you'd like, but we would still keep our copies for insurance and security purposes."

"Then why am I even bothering to do this? Will you cretins ever leave me alone?" the assistant district attorney screamed.

"You better lower yo mothafucking voice," Corey calmly told the irate man.

"I'm tha muthafucka you don't want to see upset," he warned. "Let's just say, that with this favor, Romichael has agreed to drastically minimize your duties." Corey laughed once again.

The little man stormed from the liquor closet back into the VIP lounge, as Flip entered the liquor closet.

"You awight?" Flip asked Corey.

Corey nodded as he puffed on his blunt. "Let me hit that, dawg," Flip asked, reaching out for the fragrant, cigar paper-rolled joint. Corey exhaled the smoke and almost choked. He beat his chest in an attempt to clear it. "Hell naw, nigga, you ain't washed your hands, playing all in that ole nasty bitch's pussy under the table. That boppin ass bitch; ain't no tellin how many niggas she don let fuck," Corey told the giant man, frowning up.

"Here," he barked at Flip who looked hurt by the remark. "Kill it; I don't wan no more."

The two men exited the club as Corey, known amongst Houston's night denizens, greeted and spoke to a few acquaintances on his way out. His extroverted personality served him well as he patted women on their asses, kissed their cheeks, and gave a few other ballers he knew some dap.

They made their way to the front of the valet line as Corey gave the valet his slip to retrieve his candy blue-green V-12 Aston Martin Vantage. It was the same one in Jay Z's "Me and My Girlfriend" video with Beyonce.

The infamous Southwest Gorillas had the 'Red Line' out that particular night, and had the VIP line backed up. The 'Red Line' was about 20 candy red painted vehicles that were all equipped with 22-inch rims or better. It was their M.O., and when they were all together, despite some of them being incarcerated, that was the way they liked to roll. The Gorillas, an up and coming rap group/rap label, were the pride of the Southwest side of H-town. Every member of the group had his own, no one wa4eing carried. They kept it all in the family.

"Look out, Corey, when you gon hit your load up with the candy red baby," one of the members named Monk asked, diamonds from his mouth casting shiny reflections of light.

"Nah, that ain't me, baby; that's for you boys on the South, that's y'all's thing," Corey winked, as the valet drove up to Corey in his car.

An extinguishing light in a 500 Benz parked in the adjacent parking lot of the club caught Corey's eye. Someone had just turned off a light and was sitting in the car.

Corey feigned curiosity in his rims, as he walked around the car pretending to inspect them. He wanted to see if whomever was in the Benz would sit there. After a walk around, Corey took a glance over his shoulder.

"What's wrong, dawg?" Flip asked.

Corey didn't respond as his focus was on the Benz. The car started after a moment. As it was leaving the parking lot, Corey got into his car. He decided to sit still a moment to let the car pass. Flip tipped the valet a twenty and hopped in.

"Let's go, fool!" Flip anxiously demanded.

"Wait!" Corey barked.

As the platinum Benz rolled by Corey noticed the blue-eyed beauty behind the wheel. Strange, he thought, as he made a mental note. Strange, indeed!

Chapter 7

"There is just no reprieve for a gangster," Clyde Rush thought. He wondered if the chase of money and notoriety was worth it. But the cold-hearted gangster inside always reminded him that this was all part of the game. "And this too, shall pass," he thought.

To his kids, peers, associates and prison guards he was known as "Daddy Bo," Third Ward's finest. The city streets of Houston's Third Ward have known no greater hustler, no finer gambler, and no gangster as legendary as Daddy Bo!

In his five by nine foot cell he concentrated and plotted the future of his family like a game of chess. The next few months would be crucial for himself and his family. The move at hand would catapult Murder One Records and the Rush clan into entertainment history and would set the stage for a new millennium of business for the black race. He considered his time in prison as a blessing in disguise and he used his time wisely. It was a constant reminder of how, when you think that things could be no worse, they can and do progressively worsen.

Clyde Rush didn't live the life of luxury, although he had accomplished financial prosperity. He provided his children with what they needed because of all he had accomplished in the streets. He considered leaving the streets years ago, but why? He could think of no valid reason. He owned his home, several businesses, vehicles, and real estate. Third Ward had been good to him; everything he owned was provided by the street of the Trey. Why should he leave?

Yes, Third Ward was a declining urban neighborhood, which had seen better days, but Daddy Bo grew up there and raised his family there. Everybody cared for and loved lived and died there. So he would never leave the Trey, as the Old Gs called it. He had faith in the Trey, faith that the neighborhood would rebound. Hopefully, it would rebound for the greater good of the people who still lived there. It was now rundown, raggedy, dirty and crime infested, but it was home.

There was too much black tradition and heritage to let go. Texas Southern University, the Thurgood Marshall School of Law, Jack Yates High School, the Wheeler Avenue Baptist Church, not to mention the first and last "Original Frenchy's Restaurant." Yes, indeed; Third Ward contributed to its share of black history. It had survived Martin Luther King, Medgar Evers, Malcolm X, the Black Panthers, Jesse Jackson and Spike Lee. The Trey had also produced its share of notable blacks: Debbie and Phylicia Allen, Clyde Drexler and Thurman Thomas, just to mention a few. However, more notably was Daddy Bo and his sons, the trendsetters of Houston's, maybe the entire Hip-Hop and Rap music scene.

There were things that the public knew about his family and things they didn't know. Everyone had some type of baggage and skeletons in their closet. Few people knew that Amin Rush had amassed millions through the drug trade. Few knew that his wife Nina was connected in the New York and Philadelphia streets. She was connected so well that she could move massive amounts of cocaine, marijuana and heroin, all of which was supplied by Daddy Bo's ace boon coon, Keith Vincent, better known as Black Jack. Not many were aware that his children's mother was an ex-prostitute turned junkie, who died from AIDS years ago, nor the fact that Daddy Bo himself was addicted to heroine years ago but had kicked the habit. These were some of the obstacles and secrets his family had to overcome. Daddy Bo wanted to remove the stigma so his grandchildren and great grandchildren could have a solid foundation. He felt they at least deserved that much.

Today was the day, the start of it all. Kiwan was to come home and would immediately take his place at the head of •the family. Daddy Bo's was sentenced to aggravated life for attempted capital murder, he was trying to protest one of his own. He had gone up against a highway patrolman and the patrolman lost. Deep in his heart he felt that he would not live long enough to make it out or prison alive. He felt that the burden was on Kiwan to lead his brothers and the rest of the family into the future. Daddy Bo was a strong believer that every family always needed a strong backbone.

All the money in the world could not exonerate Clyde Rush from the attempted capital murder charges. He was a black man in Texas, who had gotten caught unaware and out of his element. No city council member police chief, mayor or judge in the city of Houston had enough juice in Jefferson County to get him out of this mess. The hick county was one of friendship and kinship. It was about who you knew, not what you knew. He'd even made the mistake of hiring a big city lawyer to represent him, which did not sit well with the hick county judge. His lawyer pleaded temporary insanity by a fit of rage but that did little to evoke sympathy from a jury of twelve rednecks. They wouldn't, nor did they want to, understand a father protecting his child after he was shot by a trooper. All they saw was a black man with an extensive criminal history who nearly killed a white police officer. In the state of Texas there was no such a thing as a "reformed gangster" or "retired thug," wards used by the prosecution to describe Clyde Rush.

The jangle of keys brought Daddy Bo back to reality. Some one was coming down the run. To think about it, it was too quiet to be midday in prison. "Where was everyone?" he thought. The run on the Darrington Unit was never this quiet. He stuck his mirror out on the run to see who was coming. It was his daughter, a guard on the unit, a daughter only he and one other person in his immediate family knew about. He had taken care of her all of her life and kept her out of his other life style. He did not want to subject her to the cruel, harsh realities her half-brothers had to face. One day they would know their sister but that day was yet to come. She had grown up in a Missouri City middle-class neighborhood, the first place black folks moved to when they got a little money and wanted to get out of the inner city. She knew who her brothers were but they didn't know her. She was independent and did not care to live in her brothers' shadows. She wanted her own and Daddy Bo didn't blame her one bit. At 22, she was ready to take on the world. She was a stunning-woman with intelligence.

"Hey, old man," she greeted as she strolled up to his cell. Daddy Bo's cell was the last one on the run and if you didn't live back there you didn't belong back there. He didn't have a cellmate because he had been able to pull some major strings. That made it easier for him to conduct his private business.

"What you know good?" she smiled. "You feeling awright today?"

"Shit, you make an old man happy just seeing your pretty face," he spoke proudly.

"Stop it," she said, blushing. Her ebony skin glowed as she stood on the back of her bowed legs in her TDJ uniform. "My momma always said that you were the most charming man she'd ever met."

"Ahhh, your momma's lying; she was infatuated with the Old G image. She was young and impressionable," he told her, dismissing her comment with a wave of his hand. Daddy Bo rose from his bunk to his full height of six foot, three inches. His daughter was almost as tall as he was. One had to look closely to see the resemblance. Only three individuals knew about the two of them at the prison. They did not have to worry about any conflict of interest being raised in regard to her job.

Daddy Bo kissed his child on the cheek through the bars. "Uggh, you need to shave," she told him playfully.

"I see you have a few whiskas yourself," he said, laughing. She pinched him through the bars.

"Where is everybody?" he asked.

"Oh, yeah, they're having the basketball tournament on the rec yard," she said "That's right; I knew that you wouldn't take no stupid chances not my baby," he said. "Well, you know that I get off in two hours and that today is my last day. wanted to see you before I leave and I bought you some stuff to make sure you are okay before I go," she whispered.

"Look, sweetheart, you know that your old man is gonna be fine," he spoke in a very low but audible voice.

"I know, daddy, but I want to make sure," she said solemnly, tears in her eyes.

"Don't start that shit, girl," he told her. "You are just like your momma; sentimental and shit! You gon make me cry and gangsters don't cry," he smiled.

"Shut up, Daddy," she said, pinching him. "Stop making fun of me."

"Miss Brown!" someone yelled from the picket at the opposite end of the tier. "Are you okay ... Do you need 27 cell rolled?"

"I'm fine, I'm talking to Rush. Holler at me if the sergeant comes," she yelled back. "Here, Daddy," she said, handing him three markers from her pocket and a small Motorola flip phone. She pulled out two lighters and some Zigzag rolling papers along with the cord that plugged the phone into a lighter socket. "I brought your phone. I recharged the battery and brought the cord so you can fix it to plug into your radio to recharge the battery. There are some first class tickets to Pluto from the land of Purple Haze in these markers; it should be four ounces," she said. "That should last you until my home girl Christi comes back to work so don't smoke it all in one day."

"I start my new job tonight and I'm going to miss ya. I'll be back in six months. Don't get into any shit while I'm gone," she kissed him and turned to walk away. He said, "Yeah," almost choking up.

"Go on and handle your business and be careful. I still don't understand what kind of office job would have you working at nights" he said.

"Well, Daddy, apparently this music company does a lot of business in its studios at night. Nobody really records music in the day," she said.

Daddy Bo knew his child and he knew that she was lying to him, but why? Didn't she know that he would understand whatever it was she was doing? "Okay, lady, you know who to get in touch with, right," he asked skeptically, as if she had forgotten.

She cocked her head back, placed her hands on her hips, and said, "Oh, I got this, Mr. Man. Damn, give a nigga some credit! After all, I did learn from the best," she taunted.

"Yeah, I guess you did. Now go on, I'll see you later. I'll call you tomorrow to see how the job went."

The affection and concern that his child was giving him made him want to cry. There was no greater feeling than to be loved and cared about, especially in this type of environment. She would be alright, after all she was a Rush. His blood ran through her veins. She didn't have any choice but to be all right, he thought.

Chapter 8

Right now, life just couldn't get any better than this, Kiwan thought, as his sweat-soaked body collapsed on the azure satin sheets.

"Ooooh nigga, you gonna get some dap for that," Precious wearily told him. She lay flat on her back, staring at the ceiling as she brushed her damp mane from her face. Both of them were too taxed to move.

Kiwan could think of no better way to wake up on a Saturday morning. After a night filled with barbaric sex, he decided to fill his morning with some passionate lovemaking. Kiwan was amazed at Precious' stamina. She gave just as good as she got, and best of all, she never dried up. She stayed wet with back-to-back orgasms. Kiwan could fall in love with a pussy like that. Nah, on second thought, he was tripping. His first shot of pussy out of the joint and now he was thinking marriage. To make matters worse, he knew nothing about her other than her name, that and the fact that her cell phone stayed ringing. Not to mention her two-way pager.

Precious barely drug her body from the comfort of the bed as she got up standing on wobbly legs. Kiwan watched her from behind as she sauntered bow legged into the bathroom. Damn! that girl's ass was fat.

Kiwan was still amazed by his current predicament. "What should I do today?" he asked himself. He clasped his hands behind his head, thinking of what to do next. He was like a child at Disney World trying to decide what ride should be visited next, which new wonder should be discovered.

"Vegas!" he blurted aloud.

"Excuse Me?" Precious asked, appearing at his side with a glass of water and a warm, soapy face towel, dropping it on his chest.

"I was thinking that we could hit Vegas tonight," he informed her, caught up in his new agenda as he took the glass of water. "Thanks."

"Not hardly," she told him, bursting his bubble.

"Why not?" he wanted to know.

"Oh, man, where tha fuck is your condom?" she drilled, looking at his exposed, cum-covered phallus. "Shiiit, we used all of them muthafuckas last night."

With an exasperated look, Precious rolled her eyes and slapped her forehead.

"Oh, nooo!" she whined, plopping down on the bed next to Kiwan, her exposed breasts swaying seductively.

"What tha fuck you tripping for, I ain't got nothing, you got something" he asked curiously.

"I wasn't worried about that," she fussed. "What if I get pregnant, fool; I can't have no damn babies right now! I'm enjoying my career and my job. Why didn't you say something? I thought you put one on this morning!"

"Don't yell at me, shit, you can count, can't you? You knew how many rubbers you gave me. Shit I thought you knew we ran out, so when I started this morning I figured since you didn't say nothing you was on the pill or something," he said.

"I was, I mean, I am," she pouted. "I just haven't taken any in a couple of days. I've been flying from Cali to Miami, then back to Texas to pick you up before I even went home. I didn't get a chance to bring them because I didn't think that I'd be gone so long."

As she explained animatedly, Kiwan got aroused again. He giggled while sipping the water. Precious looked at him, wanting to know what was funny and redirected her gaze to what had his attention, noticing his manhood at attention.

"Oh, hell no, nigga, you tripping. I'm wore out for real," she said. "I'll give you some head or something, but you ain't getting no more pussy. I'm already walking bow legged. I'm about to go soak my cat in the hot tub now," she rattled on, her hair twirling as she shook her head.

"Awright, well, just clean it off for me," he chuckled.

"Uh!" she huffed, taken aback, feigning indecisiveness. "I like your nerve," she scolded, picking up the towel. She dutifully cleaned Kiwan off while scrutinizing his member.

"Your thing has a big Darth Vader helmet," she teased.

"A what?"

"You know, the head," she giggled. They both laughed.

"The better to have you climbing the walls with," he came back.

"Boy, you're a trip," she told him, hitting him with the wet towel.

"Prescious?" Kiwan spoke all of a sudden with a seriousness from out of the clear blue.

"Yes?" she asked, her coal black eyes lighting up at the sound of her name

"What's up with you?" he inquired, handing her the glass of water. "I mean, you know, what's your story?"

"Why?" she asked, a solemn look passing over her face. Kiwan knew that she has just put up a shield.

"I'm curious, ya know," he smiled.

"Look," she said, standing up with the glass and towel in hand. "I'll fuck you, I'll suck you, hell, I might even give you a little asshole if you know how to coax me into it, but don't ask me about my personal life because I'm not looking for a man," she informed him. "What we're doing is kicking it, enjoying ourselves; no regrets, no strings. It is what it is. I fucked you because I wanted to, that's all. Let's not make this more than what it is. Let's keep it simple, daddy."

She turned and walked into the bathroom again. Damn! Kiwan didn't like what she said, but he had to respect it. He couldn't help but feel like she'd just checked the shit out of him, after effects of a slowly dissolving prison mentality, he figured.

After a few minutes Prescious called Kiwan into the bathroom to rub and wash her back for her. As Kiwan washed her back, he decided to just climb in behind her instead of sitting naked on the cold marble tub.

The bubbling water almost gave him the same pleasure that the mysterious woman in front of him had the past few hours. Prescious had scented candles, compliments of the hotel, lit and strategically placed around the bathroom. The mood proved to be too much for Prescious as she hugged herself and gently started crying.

Kiwan dropped the bath scrungee into the water and gently kneaded her neck muscles. "It's all right," he assured her.

"No," she cried. "I didn't mean to snap at you, but it's just that ... aw, hell, you wouldn't understand," she told him.

"Try me,'" he dared her. "I'm a hell of a listener, and I don't judge,'" he assured her, trying to coax her and make her feel comfortable enough so that she'd talk to him.

Her phone rang in the bedroom. Grateful for the excuse for not having to allow her wall of feelings to be penetrated, Prescious anxiously stood dripping wet and hopped onto the fluffy, white imitation bearskin rug to answer the phone. She had broken the spell.

"Fuck it!" Kiwan thought. He didn't know why the fuck he was so interested in knowing more about this woman, anyway. OK; he lied; he knew why, it was because she reminded him of himself. Her eyes held secrets. His father had told him long ago that the eyes were a gateway to a person's soul. They were always the first thing to give a person away. Hell, everybody had secrets, he thought. Lord knows he definitely had his share.

A few minutes later Prescious strutted back into the bathroom with a tray of marijuana and cigars in one hand and her cell phone in the other. "It's for you," she said; handing him the phone, his hands still wet. She carefully sat cross-legged on the rug that covered half of the blue marble floor of the spacious bathroom. Setting the tray in front of her legs, she skillfully began to prepare a blunt.

"What's up, Amin?" Kiwan asked, thinking that it was his brother calling, since they hadn't checked in since yesterday.

"Well, well, if it ain't the busy bee working his jelly, on the move, spreading his honey," the voice responded. Kiwan immediately knew who was on the other end of the phone.

"Pop!" he yelled, with the excitement of a two-year-old. "What's cracking in the land of Oz? And how in the hell are you calling me?" he wanted to know, snapping to the fact that TDCJ didn't allow its inmates to use the phone unless there was an emergency, and even then you needed to call collect. Kiwan knew that cell phones didn't take collect calls.

"What, you think that you youngsters are the only ones with game? You must've forgot who was on the other end of his phone," his father capped. "I invented game. It don't stop because your old man is on lock."

Kiwan watched Precious eye him seductively while he was on the phone. She licked her lavish tongue out to produce adhesive for the cigar paper. She turned him on with every stroke of her tongue!

"What I want to know is what the hell you doing in New Orleans?" his father quizzed.

"A little R&R, pops; don't you think I deserve it?"

"Well, I'm surprised that your brother hasn't called you by now, cursing you nine ways to Sunday. When I spoke with him a few minutes ago he didn't know where the hell you were. He said that Tony hadn't even called in," Daddy Bo informed him, referring to the elephantine-like bodyguard. "What'd y'all do to old Tony?"

"Shiit, Tony went to his room drunk with some broad from the casino last time I saw him," Kiwan admitted.

"Well, I'm expecting to see you in visitation on Sunday. We have a lot to discuss," his father told him.

"Pops, I'll be there bright and early with bells on. Just make sure I'm on the list," he advised, eyeing Precious as she lit the blunt.

"One more thing, Ki. You know that gal you with is MIA, don't you?"

"Naw, what you mean?" Kiwan wanted to know.

"What I mean is this - that girl you with is head of the Murder One public relations team, and she's supposed to be working on the company's image, not on you," Daddy Bo told him.

No wonder her phone kept ringing. Damn! Kiwan wondered why she didn't say anything as he watched the weed take effect on her.

"A word to the wise should be sufficient," his father chided. "Business first, pleasure last."

"Awight, I'm on it, old man," he responded despondently, not wanting Precious to know that she was the topic of the conversation.

"Don't sweat it, though," Daddy Bo told him. "Your brother ain't tripping. He wouldn't dare deny you anything, anyway. That's why I'm telling you, so you don't abuse that. You know how he feels; anything Kiwan wants, Kiwan gets. The burden of guilt alone permits that. But that broad should know better; she should've told you. She's normally about her business. She's plugged in with everybody in the industry from Def Jam to Death Row, even Rap-A-Lot. In the entire time that we've been in business, she's never failed to be invited to any important or pivotal industry function. Believe me when I say that she has connections. Just giving you a heads up, playa! See you in the morning. One."

"One!" Kiwan responded, hanging up the phone.

He handed it to Precious, who was occupied fogging up the bathroom with the thick-pungent weed smoke. She was relaxed, leaning back on her elbow, blowing clouds of Purple Haze.

"Blow me a charge, daddy?" she asked, slowly sitting up.

Kiwan stepped out of the hot tub, his manhood at full attention. "Awight."

Precious locked in on the full salute of his thoughts and said, "Fuck the charge, and let me blow you."

Chapter 9

Amin hated phones. Then again, he knew he couldn't live without them. He'd just dozed off again after speaking with his father from prison when the phone started ringing again. If he would've been at home Nina could've answered it, but the disease thing had her stressing. So Amin decided to spend the night in his loft instead of returning to the hostile environment of his own home. He was tempted not to answer the phone and to just let it ring, but in hopes that it was his wife calling, he peeked at the caller ID from under his down comforter.

The name on the screen read a Monica Jackson. Amin tried to jog his memory of having met a Monica Jackson. He came up blank. Plain curiosity at how she could have his private unlisted number made him answer.

"Lo?" he answered, in a husky sleep-filled voice.

"Damn. No warm reception for your future partner? Hell, you need to sound a little more excited when I call." The voice on the other end criticized with obvious sarcasm. Amin immediately became wide awake.

That voice, he'd know that voice under water, Amin thought. He couldn't believe that this punk muthafucka had the nerve to be calling his house as he removed the phone from his ear and stared at it in shock and disbelief.

Amin almost hung up until Romichael shouted in his ear. "Don't hang up, bitch, we need to talk."

"That's strike, one, lil daddy, yo momma's the bitch!" Amin retorted icily, trying not to get too emotional. Every time he thought about Romichael his blood pressure rose.

"Look, fool, I didn't call you to get into a debate or play the dozens, because if my memory serves me correctly your mother was the real hoe, if you want to go there," Romichael dug, adding fuel to Amin's raging temper.

"One of these days I'm going to get sick of your little bitch ass and bury you," Amin shot back.

"Ahh, you doing it like that on the phone, you could get indicted for that," Romichael laughed. "And, I assume you mean buried like your cousin."

That hurt! Amin's cousin, Gary, had been killed in a drug deal gone bad back when Amin was starting his freshman year in college. Word on the street was that it was Corey from the Fifth Ward who'd done it, but since Corey worked for Romichael, they assumed that Romichael had wanted Gary dead.

For what reason no one knew, but back then the South Side of Houston didn't get along with the North Side, you were taking your life in your hands when doing any type of dealings with people not from your own side of town. Gary had known better, but when drugs are your livelihood and there being a shortage in the city, he'd taken the risk and suffered the consequences. The childish North Side against South Side beef had been quelled a bit but back then it was serious, dead serious. If Amin hadn't of been in college in New York, he would've helped Gary out by hooking him up with his connection, but then again if his aunt had a dick she would be his uncle. We can't change history, but you can write your own future, he thought.

Amin gritted his teeth in an attempt at maintaining his composure. He wanted to hear what Romichael had to say.

"You got five minutes, and then I'm hanging up," Amin instructed. "And how did you get my home number?" he asked as an afterthought.

"Fuck that. You worry about what's irrelevant," Romichael chided. "What is relevant is the fact of you turning down Syon's offer. What's cracking with that?"

Amin was far from stupid. He knew that Chad called Romichael and discussed the deal with him. But the strange thing was the fact that Romichael was actually calling him about it. Amin knew that Romichael wanted to be picked up by a major label and he figured that Syon's offer had been the best. Amin deducted two things from Romichael's phone call: one, this was very important to him, and two, it was important to Syon. This information elated him. He definitely wasn't going to do the deal now!

"First of all, I don't owe you an explanation, playa, and secondly..." Amin started.

Romichael cut him off in midsentence. "You know, this is the second time that you have cut me off concerning business. I'm starting to get the feeling that you don't like me much, homie! Business is good in my camp. We could do well together. You need to stop harboring grudges about things that's out of your control. I didn't have anything to do with your cousin getting killed. You need to move past that shit. Even the issue with Ayanna, I don't have any animosity toward you or your clique behind that incident, not where money is concerned," Romichael explained.

His plea fell on deaf ears. Amin had his mind made up.

"Look, man," Amin broke in. "I don't understand the language you speaking. What do they call that, shawt money talk," he cracked. "When your paper grow up, call me back," Amin told him, about to hang up.

"You think that NCAAM seat gon save you?" Romichael blurted. "Believe me when I tell you that I got that seat on lock."

This was an unexpected blow to Amin. He was shocked speechless. How the fuck did Romichael know about the committee seat? That didn't make any sense. Not only that - how did he know that Murder One was bidding for the seat?

"To be so smart, man, you're really a stupid sonofabitch," Romichael said.

"I don't give a fuck about that deal with Syon. I've got bigger fish to fry. If I did care about it, I wouldn't be calling you about it. You're too emotional.

"That's the difference between us. Your time to shine has come and gone, fool; that's just the way business is, man," Romichael stressed.

That did it for Amin. "Motha fuck you in your fat booty, bitch ass nigga! You wanna play the game in the big leagues, then we gon play for keeps," Amin screamed. "Now you trying to fuck with my livelihood. That's strike three, chump. Suit up, bitch, cause we going to war!" he hollered, slamming the phone onto its cradle, busting it into fragments of wires, diodes and plastic.

"Muthafucka!" he shouted. He did not need this right now. Amin was glad that his father couldn't see him right now. He knew that Daddy Bo would be upset. Romichael had gotten Amin out of his character. He was hotter than a black iron skillet frying catfish. His emotions ran unchecked and Daddy Bo had warned him about being too emotional. Black Jack would've put him in time out like the two-year-old he was behaving. But he couldn't help it with Romichael. They had crossed paths on unfriendly turf too many times. What Amin was trying to figure out now was how in the fuck did Romichael have that information about the seat concerning Murder One? That was the $20 million question, he figured, as he scrambled to find his cell phone. He needed to start making calls. And he made a mental note to get his number changed.

Chapter 10

The candy platinum Navigator with silver tinted windows and 23-inch Luxor rims cruised the parking garage of the Galleria Mall shopping complex. "Forget it," Nina thought. She exited the garage and decided to valet park the Navigator in the Neiman Marcus parking lot.

Just as she pulled in front of the valet stand her cell phone rang. She punched the function to speak hands free through the speakers of the truck. "Yes, Moochie?" Nina answered. She already knew who it was. The red vested valets ran up to the truck to open the doors of the Navigator. The silver mirror tint didn't permit a view inside of the truck, but a truck like this must have a big tipper behind the wheel, they thought.

Nina and Ayanna opened the doors of the truck, but neither moved to exit. Nina donned a pair of Gucci shades to hide her tear-swollen eyes.

"I thought we agreed that you weren't going to pull this shit on me anymore?" Moochie's voice pleaded through the speakers in mock irritation.

"Damn that shit, Moochie, I don't need a bodyguard everywhere I go. I need space sometimes. I'm not famous, Amin is," she fussed." Well, infamous.

"We've been through this before," Moochie reminded her, trying to have patience. "It's not about you being famous. I was hired to do a job, so I need to be allowed to do it. If I lose this job then I will be homeless, and if I become homeless then I go back to committing robberies, then I'll go back to prison. Do you want me to go back to prison?" Moochie asked in mock sadness.

"Nooo!" Nina stressed, playing the game with her bodyguard.

"Well, then, cooperate with me, please. Plus you're Amin's heart. If anything happened to you he'd have to be buried with you," Moochie coaxed, appealing to her sense of loyalty to her husband.

"Paleeease!" Nina said, smacking her lips, and rolling her eyes. She looked at Ayarha, who just smiled.

The young valets stood impatiently, waiting for Nina and Ayanna to exit so one of them could park the truck. They were already jockeying for position inside the door of the truck. Nina smiled at the boys. She motioned for a young Oriental boy who was getting bounced around like a pinball amidst the other burly teens. The other boys looked disappointed as they sauntered back to the valet stand to await another charge.

"That nigga's heart is between his legs," she remarked as she and Ayanna giggled.

"Where are you now," Moochie asked, wanting to get to the point.

"You make me sick, Moochie. Stay at home for a change. Go fuck around with dem dum groupie bitches that you fools mess around with," she scolded upset now, her heavy Puerto Rican accent becoming more pronounced the angrier she got.

"Calm down, calm down," he lulled. "We go back too far for you to flip out on me like that. I thought that we were better than that?"

"You're right," Nina conceded. "I'm sorry. Don't pay attention to me boo. Ayanna and I are at the Galleria Mall," she told him solemnly.

"Awight. Cool. I'm getting dressed now. I'll be there in another thirty or forty minutes. I'll call you when I get there," he told her. "Oh, and Nina."

"Huh?" she replied, digging through her purse for a twenty to give to the valet. Seeing that she didn't have any small change, she gave the teen a fifty instead.

"Let's not do this shit anymore. My nerves are already bad," he wanted her to know.

"I love you too, Moochie," she cooed and disconnected the call. Ayanna laughed and adjusted her Chanel shades. Nina stepped from the truck and walked around to help Ayanna. When the other valets finally noticed that she was blind, they rushed over to help.

"No, thank you, "Nina told them."I got it," as she guided her down with just her hand.

It wasn't often that the youths got to see two beautiful sisters in one workday, and they were eager with the opportunity to please. One young brother wouldn't take no for an answer. He stepped forward anyway, taking Ayanna's other hand and helping her down from the truck the rest of the way.

"Thank you, baby," Ayanna blushed.

The two women strolled away arm in arm into the department store, leaving a group of slack jawed testosterone filled teenagers ogling them.

Nina and Ayanna were not in the mall for a leisure stroll and glamorous day of shopping. Nina was there to meet an old friend and sorority sister from her college days at NYU, who'd called her Out of the blue asking that they meet. Her sorority sister, Nya Phillips, said that it was important and vital to Murder One's future that they meet up. Nina suggested the Galleria.

At first Nya had been reluctant to meet her in public for fear of there being a conflict of interest with her new job, but then she acquiesced, deciding that even if her employer, by some remote chance, happened to bring up the meeting between she and Nina, she could chalk it up to happenstance.

Nina was excited about seeing her old friend, and had kept Ayanna up for half the night reminiscing on her days at NYU as a Delta. The other half she was bashing, cursing, sobbing and screaming about Amin, in that order. Ayanna had stayed the night with Nina because she had been so distraught and almost inconsolable after hearing from her doctor. She'd left Amin at the airport, not wanting to ride home with him.

Nina didn't want to believe that her marriage to the only man she'd ever really and truly loved was coming to an end. But she couldn't in good conscience remain in an unhappy situation and raise her daughters, not for all the money in the world. That was just it, she thought. She had been there in the beginning when there was nothing. She had been instrumental in helping acquire the money needed to realize her husband's dream. It was his dream to start a record company and to be a producer; all she dreamed of was true love. His dream had come true, hers was still lingering in the wind. Sure she loved her husband, but was that very same love requited? Her husband had always been charming and a flirt. The signs of infidelity had always been there, she just chose to ignore them. Maybe she was crazy! At least that's what everyone had told her growing up. Even her parents. They'd always said she chose the wrong men. All of her boyfriends had wound up either dead or in jail, until Amin. And if Amin kept it up, she would kill his ass herself.

The women strutted through Neiman Marcus with a purpose, bypassing the lures of the perfume counters and signs announcing their extravagant sales.

Nina sported a pink, skintight, Baby Phat halter top with a matching pink miniskirt, a pair of pink Air Force Ones with no socks, her long caramel legs speaking of unimaginable pleasures at the end of the golden road.

Her long coal black hair cascading past her shoulders, Ayanna, on the other hand, had managed to squeeze her 5' 2", 135-pound frame - measuring 34-24-37 - into a size 6 Apple Bottom jeans and a rhinestone Knuschitt spaghetti strap halter top with the back out. The jeans were a stretched fit accentuating every outstanding curve she had.

Both women were oblivious to their beauty. If you asked Nina if she knew how beautiful she was, she would tell you that her thighs were too fat, ankles too big, arms too short, and her face was too round. To make matters worse, she thought that her teeth were too big for her mouth. She was constantly begging Amin to get them all filed, and he swore that he would divorce her if she defiled her mouth like that.

Ayanna was a tad different. If you asked her about her beauty, she'd say that she was just pretty, which was far from beautiful, and that she needed just a tad more height.

Each woman was beautiful in her own respective way, according to who was asked and their preferences, but both women turned heads as they stepped through the threshold of Neiman Marcus into the bottom level of the Mall's promenade.

"How does your girlfriend look?" Ayanna wanted to know. She loved description. Being blind made her a stickler for descriptive details about everything she asked about.

"Damn, A, it's been about seven years since I've seen her, but the last time I did see her she was modeling part-time for Donna Karan to pay for college. The girl was rail thin. But one thing that I know for sure hasn't changed, her smooth, coal black skin and blue eyes," Nina described.

"Blue eyes, girl, real blue eyes? Is that really uncommon?"

"It is in really black women, girl. Usually you only see it in bright women, and Nya is gorgeous."

"Someone that different has to be really striking," Ayanna commented.

"She was in college," Nina quipped. "Ooh, Ayanna, girl, when we come back through here remind me to stop."

"Not another shoe boutique!." Ayanna guessed. "Every time we're together in the mall I end up buying two or three pairs of shoes. Shit. I haven't wore the same pair of shoes twice in over a year," Ayanna retorted as Nina laughed at her friend.

They were walking past the ice skating rink heading to the food court before they were stopped by two young professional looking brothers in expensive cut suits, who were waiting outside of Chili's to be seated.

"Excuse me," one of the guys hailed, stepping in front of Nina, impeding her forward progress.

"Yeah, excuse you," Ayanna snapped, not appreciating someone abruptly walking into her space.

"Well, hold up, lil bit, I didn't mean to upset you. My friend Darrell and I were getting ready to have lunch and we would love to have some beautiful company," the man flirted. "Our treat!"

"First of all, my name is Ayanna," she politely told him with the nastiest disposition she could muster up. "Secondly, I make six figures a year, and if I was hungry I would eat, I don't need a man to do nothing but fuck me correctly, and half of you can't even do that!" she hissed.

The man was shocked into slackjawed delirium, but quickly recovered. "Where is your broom and hat, you evil ass woman?"

"In my purse with my Mace and my gun," Ayanna declared, the sarcasm not lost upon the man.

"Excuse my friend," Nina said as the man's friend Darrell interceded to help his boy out. "Come on, Anthony, man, they don't feel like being bothered," Darrell added.

"Damn straight," Ayanna shot back.

"She's not normally this way," Nina excused for Ayanna. "She's blind and doesn't like people stepping in her way," Nina explained. "We were already on our way to lunch, but thanks for the offer," she said, trying to pass.

"Well, hold on a sec!" Darrell said. "My name is Darrell Smith and this is my partna Anthony," he introduced, offering his hand to Nina.

Taking off her sunglasses, Nina took his hand and shook it gracefully, her green eyes sparkling.

"Damn you're pretty," he stammered. "And so is your friend Ayanna. Do you both model?" Darrell asked.

"Nooo," Nina cooed, turning lobster red.

"Do you mind if I gave you my number so you could use it whenever you feel the need for food or some company? Hell, I'll even let you treat if you want," he said tactfully.

"She's married," Ayanna blurted out. She wasn't cutting slack; a cock-blocking pro.

"Really," Darrell said, noticing the five karat Marquis cut diamond on Nina's wedding band. "Damn," he thought, "that is a ring!" He wondered what the hell her husband did, but he didn't inquire for fear of setting Ayanna off again. She was already five minutes past hostile.

"Well, I don't mean to pry but you seriously don't look happy," he told her. "Your eyes are red and puffy, like you've been crying all night - not that it detracts from your beauty - and if you were mine the only tears you would ever cry would be tears of joy," he spoke matter-of-factly. The comments caught Nina by complete surprise.

"Girl, let's go," Ayanna pushed. "We better hurry up, too, cause, I can already hear your panties falling down," Ayanna capped. "Next thing you know you'll be hollering about, oh, it was an accident, Amin! I don't know how it happened. My panties just fell," she mimicked with an impersonation of Nina. "Standing there all quiet and shit. Girl, what's wrong with you, you was getting ready to take that fool's number and Amin was going to kill both of us," Ayanna fussed, pulling Nina forward, bumping into patrons walking the mall.

"No, I wasn't Ayanna, shut up!" Nina answered.

"Girl, please, you can tell that lie to somebody else. I know you, shiit, you're probably beet red, you been blushing so hard," Ayanna quipped, knowing her friend.

As normal, the two women left hearts of the opposite sex longing in their wake as they headed to their rendezvous.

"Why was you so mean to those two men, A?" Nina wanted to know.

"Girl, you know good and damn well that we don't want no stiff ass, polite, bourgeois, turtleneck wearing muthafucka. We like those thugs, those roughnecks, those penitentiary bound ass niggas, tha dogs! We like going through the drama," she preached, exaggerating her movements to emphasize her point. Nina knew that her friend was just acting silly to cheer her up. That's why she loved Ayanna, because Ayanna never got wrapped up in her own feelings. She would always try to help others, no matter what mood she was in. Come to think of it, Nina had never seen Ayanna down or in a funk, with the exception of her split with her husband. Ayanna had always kept the family in good spirits.

"And anyway, my boo is home, now, so I'm going to be the first to get that dick that's been out of action for ten years," Ayanna added.

"Girl, you crazy. I forgot that you and Kiwan used to be sweethearts. But I hate to bust your bubble, I think you'll be sloppy seconds on getting that dick," Nina informed her friend. "Amin sent Prescious to pick him up with Tony, and we all know what a hoe that girl is."

"Damn," Ayanna blurted, mildly irritated. "Well, seconds aren't that bad. I wasn't in a rush to get a hysterectomy anyway, with my little ass, because that boy is working with something," she smiled deviously.

Nina shook her head at her friend. She wondered what would she do without Ayanna. She would've definitely lost it a long time ago.

As they approached the downstairs food court of the mall, Nina began searching th4ables for her friend. She scanned the entire area with military precision and eyes like a hawk. She began to feel a sense of nostalgia at the thought of reuniting with Nya.

She swept from left to right as she and Ayanna carefully made their way through the wrought iron eating tables.

"Damn, it smells good in here," Ayanna commented. "I'm getting hungry now. Girl, go see if you can find Darrell and his fool ass friend, "Ayanna kidded. Nina burst out laughing.

"Hey, Soror!" a voice called out from behind Nina. She instantly knew who it was before she turned.

Both women threw up their dynasty signs in unison and gave each other the customary greeting. After they embraced in a hug that seemed to last for, what seemed to Nina, an eternity, the women stepped back at arms length for an appraisal of one another.

"Damn, you look good," Nina was the first to compliment. And Nya really did look good with her long jet black hair pulled back into a neat French roll that accented her long graceful swan-like neck. Already standing at 5 feet, 9 inches, her blue suede riding boots put her at an even 6 feet. With her matching stone washed Enyce blue jean outfit, Nya put one in the mind of a Hip-Hop urban cowgirl, minus the hat. Void of any makeup with the exception of a deep raspberry lip gloss, Nina admired Nya's ebony beauty. In college when the two women stood side by side, people would immediately be reminded of salt and pepper, literally. Both women wanted to ask each other a million questions.

"Are you still modeling, girl?" Nina quizzed.

"Hell, no girl, when I moved to Cali, I just sat around and let my booty get big so that I could get a part in a movie," Nya admitted.

"Did you get it?" Nina asked.

"Hell, no, the part was already slated for Vivica Fox, but at least I got some exposure," Nya explained. "Is this your friend?" she motioned at Ayanna.

"Oh, excuse me, where are my manners Nina blushed."This is my best friend and my shoulder now, she took your spot. This is Ayanna, Ayanna this is the Ebony Queen that I was telling you about, and Miss Nya Phillips."

The two women shook hands as Nya had just taken notice of Ayanna's infirmity. "Yes, girl, I'm blind, but far from handicapped."

Ayanna put out there before Nya could ask, picking up on the fact that she had just noticed.

"Girl, pay no attention to this nut," Nina commented, as they took a spot at the nearest empty table. "She's also my husband's, personal secretary at the record label, and trust me, she don't miss a thing."

"That's good, because the reason I looked you up was to give you all a heads up about something concerning your label."

"Yes, you said something about that on the phone, but you didn't go into detail," Nina said, all of a sudden serious.

"Okay, listen, I have to start from the beginning," Nya confided, scooting her chair closer to Nina. "But first I have to tell you that no matter what, after we go our separate ways today, this conversation never took place. Agreed?" Nya asked sincerely. They both agreed in unison.

"Good, because I'm trusting you guys with my livelihood," Nya added.

"Girl, what is it? Is it that serious?" Nina wanted to know.

"Yeah, yeah, yeah," Nya waved her question off, not wanting to lose her train of thought. "But I'm going to let you decide, first. Let me tell you. You see, when I left NYU in our third year for Cali, you know that I had stars in my eyes to be in the movies. But when that shit didn't work out, I went ahead and got my B.S. Then a couple of years ago, I ran into some old sorors in Cali for a conference of some sort. Anyway, Katrina said that she'd gone to your wedding when you and Amin had gotten married and she was telling me about you and him starting your record label and moving to Texas. Then I started reading about Amin in the magazines and stuff. Eventually, I got a job with this law firm and they ended up relocating to Texas. I started to look you up back then, but I had so much going on in my life," Nya sincerely admitted.

Nya had regretted leaving New York and her friends but she needed to chase her dreams. Nina had just met Amin about two years before she'd left and the three of them had become close. Nina, not having many friends, felt abandoned by Nya, she knew, though Nina had acted happy and nonchalant about the situation. Nya knew her friend was devastated. But Nya knew that she had Amin and that theirs was a true love, after all, Amin was the only man at NYU to break through

Nina's rough Spanish Harlem facade. They all vowed to keep in touch, but the cross nation separation proved too formidable.

"I was just trying to work and live, Nina, and I didn't want to rain on you and Amin's parade. I was tired of pity parties," Nya told her, her blue eyes delving deep into her old friend's very essence. The look Nina returned said enough: she understood, but she hurt none the less.

"Well, anyhow, this lawyer I worked for left the firm and took me with him. He now handles the personal and business agendas for Congresswoman Charlette Cunningham and her new NCAAM committee," Nya said, dropping her dilemma like the bomb on Hiroshima.

Each woman at the table suddenly felt the weight of the problem all at once. The tension became thick enough to choke an elephant, especially affecting Ayanna, who knew the importance the seat on the committee had on Murder One's future, and thus on the Rush family.

"So that means I'm in a position to help you and Amin," Nya tentatively told Nina.

"Damn," was all Nina could say. She tried to digest the information and calculate an outcome as to what this meant for Murder One at the same time. As sick as she was of the industry, she still wanted Murder One to succeed. Nina knew that Nya was putting her job in jeopardy just by being there She was violating the trust of the people that she worked for. If Nya was caught or probably even suspected, more than likely that would be the end of her career.

"There's more," Nya added. Nina's eyebrows shot up with suspicion.

"Someone in Amin's employment is leaking information about what Murder One is doing to the Congresswoman's son, Dexter. Evidently Dexter is affiliated with Ruff House, somehow. Last night I followed Dexter. He was supposed to meet with the lawyer early Friday and he got there late, so when he arrived I heard him prepping my boss on Ruff House attaining the NCAAM seat over Murder One because he was going to make sure of it. Then he asked my boss how to get to Max's. He said that he was going to get his party on. But I thought that strange for an assistant D.A. Besides, if you are the partying type, how is it that you don't know where one of the hottest clubs in H-town is? So by me not having a social life of my own, I decided to go get my groove thang on and see what was poppin. Right before the club shut down, he met with two guys from Ruff House. According to the bartender, she said that their names were Corey and Flip."

Nina looked at Ayanna, who was nodding her head. "Flip is Romichael's bodyguard, and Corey is his dooboy!" Ayanna informed them.

Nina knew Daddy Bo's long-range plan to use the NCAAM seat, to expand Murder One's influence, and how important it was, to the Rush family. On one of her visits to her father-in-law, he had filled her in on the company's long-term agenda. Daddy Bo knew that a wife needs to feel needed and wanted in order to assure her loyalty. He knew his son's shortcomings with Nina and that communication was one of them. So Daddy Bo kept her abreast of the situation and most other important issues.

Daddy Bo was a wise man and his plans always glorified his means. Nina stayed loyal and, true to her husband and family. Since Amin had a phobia of visiting jails, Nina opted to step in and support Daddy Bo and Kiwan. She'd visited both on a regular basis and would take the kids so that they would know their uncle and grandpa.

"So do you have, any idea who it is?" Nina asked.

"No," Nya admitted, "and Dexter didn't hint at it. But that's not the worst of it, girl. There's more," Nya said solemnly.

Nya saw it in her friend's blue eyes. She was 'trying to decide if she should cross the line about something. But the line had been crossed by her just meeting with Nina.

Nya thought a second while Nina and Ayanna remained silent. They didn't want to push her. Nya decided to forge on.

"Nina," Nya spoke, breaking the silence. "I have to ask you a serious question and how you: answer the question will not sway my decision to help or deter my actions from this point on, but I need the truth." Nya looked down at her long fingers. "And I want you to know that I'm not here to judge you, I'm just trying to help. We are friends before anything else."

"Listen, girl," Nina interrupted. "We've been friends a long time. If it weren't for you I would've never gone to college, never pledged, never would've met my husband nor would I have my kids. I owe you a lot,

Nya! I owe you the truth if nothing else, so ask me. I won't lie, whatever it is," Nina sincerely told her friend with tears in her eyes.

That gave Nya the courage she needed to ask her friend her personal business. Nya leaned forward before she asked, "Is Murder One on the up and up? Have they been tainted by any illegal activities in the past?"

Nina knew what she was asking and tried to exhale her built up tension in one strong breath. Nya was inquiring about the drug money. The money that she and Amin made from her transporting drugs from Texas to New York. How much did Nya know or want to know? Nina's shield of caution immediately went up. Was this a trick? After all, she hadn't seen her old friend for years. Nya could be there to help or there to hurt. Who knew? There was no way of telling.

Nina got claustrophobic all of a sudden. She couldn't speak even if she wanted to. Her cell phone was her saving grace. It broke the emotional link that stretched between the women.

"Moochie, where are you?" Nina blurted into the phone before she could even open the LCD screen up. She hadn't even bothered to look at the caller ID screen good.

"I see that my beautiful daughter-in-law is, up to her old tricks again," Daddy Bo teased. "What's the reason this time for dumping Moochie? A shopping spree, a day out with the kids, or are you catting around on my baby boy?" he asked playfully.

Nina was so relieved that she burst into tears. Sobbing into the phone she greeted her father-in-law with a tear-filled greeting. "Oh, hey popi," she cried. The conviction of her guilt and confusion on which way to turn from the position that Nya had put her in, had her body racked with sobs.

Ayanna reached for her friend's hand, knowing how emotionally drained that she already was. She grabbed Nina's phone and explained to Daddy Bo a little of the situation between Nina and Amin and how strained she was before Moochie walked up on the scene.

Nya was confused, patting Nina's hand and asking what was wrong before Moochie spoke. "What's poppin?" he wanted to know as he and two of Ayanna's male cousins from the third Ward stood threateningly, seemingly ready for whatever.

"What tha fuck's wrong, Nina?" Moochie asked when he saw that she was crying. Upon seeing her bodyguard, Nina jumped up and hugged him, crying on his shoulder. Everyone was confused but Ayanna. She knew her friends.

Having hung up the phone with Daddy Bo, Ayanna defused the situation quickly. "She's alright, Moochie, just take her to the truck. We valet parked outside of Neiman Marcus." She abruptly turned to Nya, reaching for her hand. Nya extended her hand to Ayanna as she watched her friend walk off.

Nya wondered what really had upset Nina. Ayanna pulled her close and spoke in her ear. "She and Amin are having problems," Ayanna whispered. "Give me your number so I can call you, then we can all meet up later," Ayanna assured her, squeezing her hand and giving Nya a hug as a gesture of a friendship formed.

"Alright," Nya said, reaching into her purse for a card. "Make sure you call me, girl, I want to make sure she's okay."

Ayanna stuck the card in her back pocket as her two cousins, who were being groomed by their uncle Black Jack to leave the streets alone, escorted her to the Navigator.

Nya watched in dismay. She wondered if any of them carried weapons. Even worse, would they use them to protect the Murder One family?

Chapter 11

Amin gazed out of the picture window of his studio apartment. The loft style penthouse took up the top three floors of a converted warehouse that his father had given him as a wedding gift his last year in college. The warehouse was located in downtown Houston, adjacent to Minute Maid Park. In 1997 the building had been placed smack dab in the middle of a real estate war to consume all property surrounding the proposed site for the new baseball field. If Clyde Rush hadn't of had influence with the mayor's office as well as the city council, then Amin would've lost the property. So it held dual sentimental value, because to Amin, it was like his father had given him the building twice. Out of all the properties and real estate that he'd acquired throughout the years, as well as his personal residences, this was his favorite one. He'd made a home away from home in the converted building.

He gazed out of the window from his office again and tried to make out who it was that the Astros were playing. From the looks of it, they were engaged in battle with the Colorado Rockies, but Amin couldn't be sure unless he retrieved his binoculars.

His loft had set him back a cool $5 million, but had been well worth every penny to Amin. The split level styled loft contained eight bedrooms, six full and two and one-half baths, a media room, music studio, playroom (nicknamed the Bath Boom Room,) a gym, game room, all formals, and a library with an adjoining office. Black art from the Shrine of the Black Madonna and from an up and coming black artist by the name of Oscar Banks, who happened to be in prison with his father (and the man was an artistic genius), adorned his walls as well as did African sculptures and artifacts. It was his personal space, which Nina and the kids hardly ever invaded. Hell, he couldn't even remember the last time his wife stepped foot in his penthouse. She actually thought the penthouse belonged to Black Jack. Amin never told her different. Amin always needed a space to call his own.

He leaned back in his calf skin leather executive swivel chair and took a deep breath. Things were piling up; the more money he made, the more problems he was faced with in his endeavors to keep it. This was not what he had expected when he started the company seven years ago. He assumed that he would be able to enjoy his money as he made it, but it was a constant hassle to keep the vultures away. Now he didn't have time for anything anymore, least of all himself. He was spreading himself too thin. The only problem with that was the fact that he actually enjoyed it. Could someone please explain that? He shook his head in frustration of trying to figure himself out. At the age of 27 there was not much in plans for life that he still needed to accomplish. Actually only one thing remained, and that was to see his father home.

Amin thought back and marveled at how it all began. He tried to think of the time that he was the happiest in his life.

It finally dawned on him that his high school years were the happiest times. Life had been so simple then. No money, no real responsibilities, nothing but his family and the love that the three men shared. The public assumed that he had it made; they thought that his life was a cake walk. But what they didn't know and didn't realize was that had it not been for his family and their sacrifices, none of his accomplishments would've been possible. His family was the nucleus of his success. Especially Nina! She had definitely made everything possible, not to mention Kiwan. Amin didn't know whose sacrifice had been the greatest. Both individuals made it possible for Murder One to exist. He owed a lot to them both.

He stared out the window into Houston's twilight, seeing but not seeing. His mind spun a reel of rewind as he thought back to one of the biggest mistakes he'd made. Or was it a mistake?

Koto

A young, hardheaded youth coming up in the streets of the Dirty Third, Amin was easily influenced by the changing fads and trends as most teenagers are. What made Amin different and had possibly saved his life, were his love and ear for music, which his father discovered in his son and encouraged at a young age.

Young Amin could pick up any instrument aid teach himself how to play it. Once he learned how to play it, he could play any song just by listening to the notes. The piano, the guitar, the saxaphone, even the drums; all were instruments that the young musical genius learned to play on his own. The only problem was that the young knuckleheads in his neighborhood frowned on his talent. They weren't into such sissyfied things. They were into selling crack, smoking weed, skipping school, shooting dice and aspiring to pimp hoes! So Amin grew up wanting the same things, or at least pretending to, and fighting much of the time when he followed his true love of all things musical.

Time and time again his sexuality had to be defended against the young roughshod hoodlums of the Trey. Now he was good at two things; knocking muthafuckas out and playing music. Not one time did Amin have to run and get his older brother, Kiwan, even when the other youths would gang up on him. The stubborn streak that he'd earned from his mother would manifest itself and young Amin would lie in wait for the perpetrators one by one. His brother and father would have to find out through various other means, having gotten so used to Amin coming home with busted lips, bruises and black eyes.

Amin watched his older brother by three years grow up leading his neighborhood comrades in whatever they could get into, from fistfights with other neighborhoods at school functions to full fledged shootouts. Though both brothers were solidly built, Kiwan was the athlete of the family. He excelled in all sports. Basketball just happened to be the one sport that seemed better suited to the young lefty that Kiwan was.

By the grace of God, Kiwan made it out of high school alive, despite his life shortening rambunctious behavior, which he'd displayed throughout junior and high school. Kiwan had fooled his father with dynamic SAT scores, which had helped him earn a full-fledged basketball scholarship to Rice University. After injuring his ankle in his sophomore year, the highly recruited guard turned to a past-time that plagued many inner city youths who fell short of glory on the playing fields: Kiwan turned to selling drugs.

Since Black-Jack had been in the drug selling business for some years, Kiwan went to him seeking the secrets of the trade. Seeing that Kiwan could not be deterred from his decision, Black Jack gave him three pieces of advice. Number One, never shit in your own back yard. Number Two, stay low and stay humble; make yourself as small of a target as possible. And last but not least, if you're going to hustle and do wrong, hustle to get out of the game, not for the glory and fame! He was told that if he kept to those principles without compromise, that he would be successful in the game, with moderation.

So Black Jack put Kiwan down with the game that had started the ball rolling for himself, allowing him to become a millionaire. Through Black Jack had been selling drugs for years, he rarely if ever had seen any. It had gotten to the point where he saw nothing but cash.

Already street savvy from hanging around his father's after hours club, Kiwan learned to manage his affairs well. He would never touch the product himself and whenever dealt in small quantities. He would get young coeds from TSU who needed extra money to deliver his packages to his out-of-town customers in small Texas towns and in Louisiana. All the while that Kiwan conducted his business, Amin watched and took it all in, the two following a sad cycle of street life that Daddy Bo wanted to see end.

Daddy Bo, an old street hustler himself, knew of his son's actions. He neither condemned nor did he condone what his sons did. His only warning to Kiwan had been to save some money. "Always pay yourself," he would say. "Be ready for the repercussions of what you do. If you can't pay the band, don't dance," he'd warned.

Kiwan never understood the logic behind his father's words until years later when he was sitting in a prison cell on lockdown.

What else could Daddy Bo say? He'd hustled all of his life while his sons had watched. From the gambling houses to the whorehouses that their father maintained, they had seen it all. But one thing their father did, throughout his addiction and all, Daddy Bo always took care of home first. They may not have had the best, or may not have had it all, but they had everything they needed. Their father had always kept money turning, making it work for him, hustling less and less as the years passed and his bank roll grew.

Through the streets came the connections and through the connections came the opportunities. Daddy Bo was clever and shrewd in all of his business dealings. Neither he nor Black Jack had been flashy or ostentatious with their money. They kept themselves and their families with the necessities they needed, only indulging in clothing.

Sacrifices turned into investment, investment turned to profit, and profit turned into opportunity. Along with the money came the power of the game. Daddy Bo called it resources. Clyde Rush undoubtedly used his resources every time he saw fit, providing himself with information on investments that would turn a quick profit.

With diligence and hard work, Daddy Bo established a name for himself as well as for Black Jack. The two men turned "Daddy's Cafe" into a profitable after hours joint as well as a popular bookmaking spot, even, for police officers.

Growing up around such an atmosphere, Kiwan and Amin learned everything they needed to know about life and business. They held an educational jump start on the game that no college PhD could ever provide. Young Amin watched first-hand how the knowledge paid off for three men that enshrouded his life; his father, his brother, and his mentor, Keith Black Jack" Vincent. These influences played a major part in Amin's future decision- making process. Without his mother there to balance his education, Amin fell victim to his environment as most young men often do.

Although Amin felt that he was ready for the next stage in his life, he somehow held on to finish his last year in high school. He'd been offered several band scholarships. Grambling, Southern, Texas Southern, Prairie View, Florida A&M and other universities with reputable bands had besieged young Amin with full scho1arhip offers. But Amin had other plans. He settled on going to NYU, of all places. Shocked wouldn't describe the reaction that his father and brother displayed upon finding out his decision.

Why so far from home, they both wanted to know? Amin indulged them with an excuse about studying classical music to broaden his musical horizons. Supporting his sons in whatever they decided to do with their lives, Daddy Bo reluctantly conceded to his baby boy's decision. There was a method to Amin's madness that Daddy Bo and Kiwan would later find out about the hard way.

A change began in Amin that his family had been oblivious to. He started to want more, to control more, to have his own without the shadow of his father and brother. How could he ever be his own man if his brother and father catered to his every want and need? What kind of man would he become then? All of these questions shaped Amin's decision after touring the campus of NYU during spring break of his senior year in school. After finding out that kilos of cocaine sold for almost twice as much as they did in Houston, he needed little else to convince him that the opportunity to establish his own foundation in the drug trade was at his fingertips. It was never about the money with Amin; it was always, always, about the hustle! Money was just a tool to be used as his key to open a door to a fleeting sense of freedom that he longed for.

After convincing Black Jack of his scheme, he was able to procure five kilos of cocaine on consignment. It didn't surprise Black Jack that Amin had come to him; actually, he'd expected him a lot sooner. Scretly, Black Jack had conferred with Daddy Bo beforehand and both men had agreed that if Amin was not able to get what he wanted from them, he'd just find it somewhere else. They knew the determination and stubborness that young Amin possessed.

When the day came for Amin to pick up his package, something he thought that he was doing on the sly, he borrowed his brother's Suburban to pick up his future from one of Black Jack's many stash houses.

That very same day was the day that Kiwan had been planning to ride to Atlanta for that year's annual Freak-Nik. Daddy Bo, Moochie, and two of Black Jack's nephews, Dominick and Brick, had all planned to take the trip with Kiwan. Anxious to hightail it to Atlanta, Kiwan had warned Amin to hurry up so that they could hit the highway. In his haste to appease his brother, Amin left a packaged kilo in his brother's truck. He didn't realize that the kilo was missing until they'd left. Too afraid of the repercussions of his actions, Amin kept quiet and hoped that they would make it back without noticing.

Amin knew a fact of life that a familiar saying summed up. "Hope in one hand and shit in the other, then see which one fills up the fastest!"

Deep down he knew that he should've paged his brother to let him know, but he couldn't bring himself to do it. His family would never believe in him again. He would never attain his freedom. "What kind of man would he ever amount to if he couldn't, handle his business?" an inner voice asked. So he allowed himself, or rather willed himself, to forget about it until they returned. That one mistake almost proved fatal to his entire family.

The crew of Third Ward's finest made it virtually trouble-free to Atlanta, enjoying immensely the activities and attention of young, available, sexy vixens that frequented the week-long party from every state in the country. But on the way back their luck ran out as soon as they crossed the state line. A Texas department of Public Safety trooper pulled them over in Jefferson County, just outside of Beaumont.

Unknowingly the victims of racial profiling because of his tricked-out truck, Kiwan and crew pulled over. It was the five heads, sparkle of the rims and glossy paint that attracted the attention of the hick officer. Immediately profiling his suspects as drug dealers, the officer had every intention of searching the vehicle.

Though Kiwan suspected that the officer was tagging them and labeling them because they were black, he knew that he didn't have anything to hide; at least that's what he thought!

After running a check on Kiwan, who was driving, and requesting for backup, the officer asked all of the men to step out of the truck.

With the arrival of the backup, the hick cop's backbone stiffened with bravado derived from so many years of wielding a badge. Upon searching the vehicle, the officer produced a cellophane wrapped square package that all of the men against the truck immediately knew to be cocaine. Before the handcuffs could be placed on the crew, Kiwan went completely off. He swore that he'd been set up! Irate and argumentative, when the officers tried to subdue him, Kiwan became violent.

After all was said and done, Kiwan ended up in the hospital with multiple gunshot wounds, and Daddy Bo was severely beaten after beating into a coma the officer who'd shot Kiwan.

The other members of the crew interceded to break up the melee, but were too late to save Kiwan. Moochie wanted to kill but had to be refrained when the sirens from the other assisting officers converged onto the scene.

It was a story that broke Amin's heart after hearing it from Erick, who beat the assault case when Daddy Bo was convicted. All five men had originally been charged with assault on a peace officer. After Kiwan copped to a 144-month federal sentence for drug possession, his assault charges were dropped. Daddy Bo ended up with an aggravated life sentence for attempted capital murder, while the officer had yet to come out of his coma. After the two main convictions, the prosecuting attorney decided to drop the cases on Moochie, Dominick and Erick. But the weight of the guilt had never dropped from Amin's shoulders.

Chapter 12

"What's going through that devious mind of yours, baby boy? Black Jack asked Amin, breaking him out of his reverie.

Surprised at hearing his mentor's voice, Amin swiveled away from his unique view of downtown Houston, oblivious to the tears racing down his face.

Black Jack noticed them right off but had enough tact not to let on. "Damn," Amin said, wiping his eyes. "I didn't even hear you come in, I was so far out of it," he confessed.

"Yeah, I came up from the club. The door was open," Black Jack told Amin.

Murder One Records owned a club called, "Flip Mode," which took up the first three floors of Amin's building. The Flip Mode was Black Jack's personal pet. He treated and handled the club with kid gloves. Having been in the entertainment business for over thirty years dealing with Houston's nightlife, Black Jack had quickly turned the club into the most exclusive downtown night spot in the city. The numbers that Flip Mode did on a nightly basis were astronomical. Every single night, the club turned at least 200 heads down at the door due to capacity laws.

Saturday night was always Sex in the City night at Club Flip Mode. It featured the controversial DJ Portia Surreal, who spun the turntables topless. So Black Jack always got an early start on the Saturday night crowd. Besides, tonight was a special night. Tonight was about business. Tonight, Murder One would officially issue its proposal for the NCAAM seat.

Black Jack entered Amin's sanctuary with his suede Bally loafers, drink in hand, and money on his mind. He slow strolled, careful not to waste any of the Chivas Regal on Amin's hardwood floors, or Oriental rugs before taking a seat. He knew that something had been bothering Amin, but he wanted to let him come out with it when he was ready.

"Tonight is the big night, young blood! I'm taking Andrea with me. She's about ready," he assured Amin. "She's the smartest one in my bunch," Black Jack admitted, referring to all of his nieces and nephews that he'd adopted, since he was sterile and couldn't have children.

"I think you're right, that girl is something else. I remember when she was running around in pigtails and shitty diaper," Amin laughed.

His laughter was forced. He knew that he was suppressing feelings that were bound to come out in negative ways if he didn't get them off his chest. His normal confidence and veneer of Big Bad CEO was shaken with the uncertainty of Murder One's future. Amin sighed deeply; he needed a blunt.

Black Jack and Amin had agreed that Black Jack would be the one to address the committee on Murder One's behalf. They both knew that he was better suited to address the conservative and bourgeois crowd of affluent businessmen and women.

"Shit is getting hectic," Amin admitted somberly. "I'm actually to the point of where I don't know what tha fuck to do," he confessed in an exasperated tone, throwing his hands up in frustration.

Black Jack leaned back, jacked his slacks before crossing his legs and just shook his head. He took a swallow of his drink before forging ahead. Amin marveled at how the 53-year-old could look so well preserved, with his distinguished looks and head full of black wavy hair, only slightly graying at the temples.

"Look at you," Black Jack exclaimed in his usual cool demeanor. "Look at all you have accomplished for yourself and your family in the ten years that your brother has been away. Don't you think that you have punished yourself enough?" Black Jack inquired, rhetorically, pausing to sip his drink.

Koto

Amin looked into the wise eyes of his mentor. Black Jack had informally adopted Amin as his own son after Daddy Bo had been sentenced.

"Nobody's judging Amin but Amin," Black Jack assured the younger man. "Niggas in the streets do the things that niggas in the streets do once you elevate your game to the next level, leave the bullshit and take what you can use with you. You're not confused on what to do. You know what you need to do. It's just a point in your life where it's time to elevate your game to the next level and you're having so much fun that you don't want to go. That's understandable, but a wise man knows that nothing is forever" his mentor stated.

"Tha money, tha broads, tha power! You've been there, you've done that, let that shit go. You've had a head start in the game of life that many people don't get. Not only that, but you have actually capitalized on it. Move on. You can't be in the light forever. Tha background is the dwelling place of wise men," Black Jack said with a smile. "You used to be tha pimp young blood, now you tha hoe. You're letting tha money pimp you. Take your father's lead and take care of home first," his mentor told him, sipping his drink. Amin felt exposed. Black Jack's words cut deep. Then again, the truth always did.

Chapter 13

The fawn-colored stretch Maybach Benz pulled up to the gates of the luxurious estate belonging to Congresswoman Charlette Cunningham. The limo slowed to a crawl as it entered the oak tree lined, circular, pebble stoned drive that fronted the Congresswoman's River Oaks estate.

A young vibrant Andrea Vincent, a product of the inner city slums of Houston, didn't look at the stately home in reverence or awe; her response was simply that the Congresswoman had good taste. Andrea had become used to the finer things in life the last few years as Black Jack had begun to indulge his relatives with the luxuries he'd denied himself as he built his empire.

Black Jack was always impressed with his niece. She displayed a wisdom well beyond her 16 years that Black Jack assumed came from his cultivation of her young life. Though her brothers and sisters knew different, they knew that Andrea, also known as A-dray, paid attention to details. Her mother had told her long ago that the details in life are all that mattered.

A doorman awaited the two guests as the driver exited the car to open their door.

"Are you nervous?" her uncle asked, puffing a Cuban cigar?

A-dray looked at her uncle as if he were a dog that had just shitted on her brand new fur coat. "Moi?" she said, placing an immaculately manicured hand on her chest. "You mean that you would ask me if I am ready? Me, the heiress to the Murder One empire, the future owner and CEO, the first black woman who will own, operate, and control a multi-million dollar label herself? Unk, those are my people in there. They know me. They sympathize with me. We're here," she said, imitating a gesture from the television show "Martin," where he waves two fingers back and forth as if to insinuate eye-to-eye contact.

Black Jack chuckled at his niece. She was his pride and joy, he thought, as he snuffed his cigar and placed it in a humidor. She always made him smile.

Dressed, to the nines in some of his most elegant and dapper attire, Black Jack stepped from the Maybach with his niece as if he'd been born of money. His 3 karat diamond cufflinks sparkled in the amber lighting of the floodlamps in the Congresswoman's yard. His elegant attire was totally fitting, as he was decked out in a charcoal grey pinstriped Armani suit, a matching fedora with a red peacock feather, grey alligator boots, and his signature ebony wood, gold-fisted walking stick. His outfit had the perfect touch of gentlemanly class. At this moment he was the picture-perfect candidate to grace the cover of Ebony or G.Q. Magazines.

The vision of loveliness that was A-dray complemented her uncle to the tee. Her butterscotch colored skin was enhanced by the plethora of red freckles that accentuated her strawberry red hair. She stood a hair taller than her older sister, Ayanna, and her slender body only hinted at the development that would soon grace the grown woman. The strapless red evening gown didn't quite make it to her knees.

You would think that in the revealing split that ran up the side of her gown along with the matching satin strapped stilletos - more appropriate to a woman of much more practiced elegance and sophistication - would be betrayed by an occasional misstep, a stumble brought by her youth and innocence.

But not A-dray! She strutted in a way that let everyone know that, Hey! the queen has arrived; I belong.

The couple was met and escorted through the foyer by the tuxedo-clad doorman to the greatroom, where the other guests mingled.

Observing the decor of the mansion, Andrea had to reassess her earlier observation of the Congresswoman having good taste. The details! Just by studying the decor and color scheme of the house, A-dray knew that she would not like the Congresswoman on a personal level. Her business demeanor was yet to be scrutinized.

The other guests engaged in light conversation as the conservatively dressed Congresswoman circulated around the room playing the ever-gracious hostess. Champagne floated freely on trays, caned by bowtie-wearing youths who, to Black Jack, looked to be fresh out of high school. He had to remind A-dray not to pick up a glass of wine, lest he break every bone in her lovely hand. She just laughed.

Black Jack just couldn't help but be amused by his niece. He was proud of all his nieces and nephews, all of which he'd adopted, even the ones with no ambition or drive. He respected the fact that they didn't want anything out of life. He couldn't understand it, but he respected it. Black Jack had always wanted kids, but the codes that he lived by never allowed him to settle down with any of the women that surrounded him. Besides him being sterile, the streets never gave him an opportunity to live the type of life that having and raising children required. It wasn't until later in his life, when he'd somewhat slowed down that he'd decided to adopt his brother's kids. He adopted all seven of them, five boys and two girls. Ayanna was the eldest, followed by Dominick, then Brick, Tray, Willie, JaMarcus, and A-dray, the baby.

Yep! He and Daddy Bo had come a long way, he thought, as he scrutinized the crowd of affluent Afro-American millionaires. Andrea was right; one day she would take the lead and hold the reins of the family's future, and hopefully by then his sacrifices as well as Daddy Bo' s would have been worth the risk. As it stood now, none of his or Daddy Bo's kids would ever have to work. They were trying for grandkids and great grandkids, and that would take a legacy. Only one as big as the Kennedy's would suffice. Was that too far fetched a dream? Was it unthinkable? He'd thought so at first until Daddy Bo convinced him other wise. Now look at them; they were at the threshold of that very dream. Thirty years ago he would've never thought it possible. Too many things got in the way of blacks and their dreams.

"We as a people limit ourselves and put limitations on our achievements before they're even thought out! Hell, we need to start thinking bigger! Shoot for the stars and you just might hit the moon," he mumbled to himself.

Koto

Keith Vincent was not the media hound or public figure head that his younger protégé, Amin, was, but Black Jack was familiar enough with the media to recognize some of the richest and most powerful blacks in America mingling in the room. A few faces he recognized from the Ebony magazines yearly update on the 100 Most Powerful African Americans article.

The Congresswoman spotted the newest arrivals and cordially made her way to Black Jack and his niece. A-dray gave the Congresswoman a little credit as far as the ambience was concerned. The music of Sade wafted softly through the greatroom, creating a light and classy mood.

"How do you do, Mr ...," the Congresswoman subtly asked, offering her hand to Black Jack. "Vincent," he finished, gripping the diamond-dripping hand of the smartly dressed Congresswoman. She could pose for a graceful picture in the Dark & Lovely rinse commercials. Her stately gray hair was pinned into a neat grandmother bun. The only thing missing, A-dray thought, was a pair of wire framed spectacles and she would look exactly like the granny on the package of the "Mothers Cookies," only black.

"And you are representing ..." the Congresswoman asked, "Murder One Records," A-dray finished, reaching to shake the Congresswoman's hand. "Nice to meet you, Congresswoman Cunningham. My name's Andrea. I secure the position of Assistant Vice-President of Operations at the label, and this is my uncle, Keith Vincent, Co-owner of the label. We're fans of your achievements in Congress and I have aspirations of following in your footsteps one day," A-dray revealed to a shocked Congresswoman. Her uncle grinned.

"Really?" the Congresswoman asked in mock fascination, as A-dray took her by the arm, guiding her into the crowd so that Black Jack could walk around, mingle and breath a little.

A few women cut their eyes in his direction, but Black Jack's interest ran deeper than social. He was on a mission to familiarize himself with the crowd to get a feel of the group as a whole. It was simple. Once you looked as though you belonged, the next step was to just act as though you belonged, which is exactly what he did.

As he scoped the room, it didn't surprise him to see Romichael Turner and his cronies. What did surprise the old gangster was the sight of an ancient nemesis of his by the name of Duck! What the fuck was Duck doing here? As Black Jack assessed he situation with the speed of a number's runner, he thought it a logical move for Romichael to be teamed up with Duck.

Duck was an old Fifth Ward hustler who, like Daddy Bo and himself, mastered the game in the business of drugs. What made Duck the outstanding member of that fraternity was the fact that Duck was also a one-man Murder Incorporated. Duck was a hit man from the old school. Drugs had just been a hobby to him. Of course, Duck had supposedly hung up his gun belt, but rumor had it that he still dabbled in wet work every now and then.

The Ruff House representatives were, Romichael, a known drug dealer; Tony "Duck" Harris, known murderer; that dumbass Flip, Romichael's bodyguard; and what did that spell for Murder One, Black Jack mused? TROUBLE! Big trouble! they had to be teamed up for financial purposes. Black Jack decided to gravitate over to them, maybe to gauge what reaction they would have to his presence.

"How you doing, Black Jack?" a lovely voice asked from his immediate right. He spun around to face the most dynamic blue eyes that he'd ever seen. He casually looked the woman up and down. She wore a black cocktail dress with a spaghetti strap that tied around her neck. Her ebony skin held a sheen that no lotion on earth could provide. Only genetics could bless a person with a glow that lustrous.

"I'm sorry, but I just don't remember ever meeting you?" he stated inquisitively. "Must be my age," he told her, offering his hand to her.

"Well, I'm a friend of Nina's and Amin's. We all went to NYU together. My name is Nya," she informed him, lightly shaking his hand. Black Jack smoothly leaned over and kissed her hand, causing her to softly blush.

"Nyaaaa?"

"Oh, I'm sorry, Nya Phillips!" she blurted.

"Well, I'm delighted to meet you, Miss Phillips. I must tell Nina that I saw you." Something nagged at Black Jack concerning Nya, but he couldn't quite place his finger on what it was. He was actually too preoccupied with Romichael and Duck. Tonight would be very, very interesting, and he was anxious to see how everything played out.

Just as he was excusing himself from Nya, the Congresswoman got everyone's attention and announced that it was time for dinner.

Let the games begin, Black Jack thought.

Chapter 14

"What tha fuck are you doing here, Amin?" Nina asked from behind the security chain of the washroom door in surprise. Amin had just pulled up to their Clear Lake estate and tried to enter his home from the five-car garage, but found the security chain in place on the door.

Nina had heard him pull up and ran to keep him out. She was still upset at her man. Her emotions were in disarray. She was pleased to see him, but not happy about it. Every nerve in her body tingled.

"Can I come in," he humbly asked. With the door cracked, Nina could smell the fragrance that her husband wore. It was Calvin Klein's Obsession for Men, a present from her on his last birthday.

"No, Amin," she cried hoarsely. It took every ounce of strength she had to deny him. "Not tonight; you need to go to the doctor first," she told him.

"I've already been to the clinic, Nina, I just left."

Nina didn't know if it was love or curiosity that prompted her to open the door, but she found herself doing it with no reluctance. When she opened the door her husband held a plain cardboard box in his arms. Nina looked into the box and melted. Inside were two Sharpei puppies with purple bows on their heads.

"Awwww..," Nina cooed, lifting one of the whimpering, wrinkled puppies out of the box and nuzzling it to her face. She hugged her husband tight as her stomach did flips. After six years of marriage, Amin still gave her butterflies. "Amin, I'm still pissed at you. We need counseling," she said, choking up, looking into Amin's eyes. "I need counseling, Amin. I … I … just, I just don't know anymore," she told him, her emotions in turmoil. She wore one of her husband's dress shirts and was nude under it. Her legs shook. She put her hand on her thigh to try and calm her frayed nerves and to stop her leg from jumping.

"I know, I know," Amin hurriedly spoke, trying to calm her. He led her through the massive house and into their bedroom, where Nina had been sulking. Amin noticed a glass of wine on the night stand while her favorite group "Jagged Edge" played on the bedroom stereo. He gently sat the box with the puppies in it on their huge, custom made, four poster, mahogany sleigh bed. It was larger than a king sized bed and had hand carved Egyptian hieroglyphics adorning the wood.

Amin took his wife in his arms. "I'm sorry," he whispered in her ear as they swayed to the music.

"Yeah, I … I know you're sorry, nigga," she cried and pounded her fist on his chest, tears flowing freely.

"The doctor said the gonorrhea was masked by all those penicillin pills that I've been taking.

"Shhh," Nina cut him off with a manicured finger to his lips. "Later." She let herself drift to a nice place, a place where the love she received was equal to the love that she gave.

Amin hugged her close and a fire raced up her spine, one that she almost didn't recognize, one that so often gave her the strength to do what needed to be done back in the day when they were saving their illicit monies to start Murder One. A tingle that had kept her focused during those lean years.

"Are you going to the party later on tonight for Kiwan?" her husband asked softly, his face in the crook of her neck, trying to hide his tears of shame.

"Wouldn't miss it for all the bare asses in Africa" she giggled.

Chapter 15

The cranberry red BMW 760I pulled into an empty pump at the Exxon station on the corner of Fondren and West Bellfort on the southwest side of Houston.

The 22-inch chrome rims continued to spin despite the fact that the car had come to a complete stop. Behind the wheel, Monster Pat had just extinguished a chronic stick, the remains of which would fit on the head of a matchstick. Pat did not believe in wasting good dope.

When the passenger door opened and Monster Pat's homie, Kayron Lewis, stepped out, the bass that had shaken the foundation of the Exxon, combined with the treble, highs and mids from the car's system, produced the quality sound that the $40,000 audio system was intended for.

A cute young dark-skinned vixen, who happened to be pumping gas into her Toyota Camry at that moment, started moving, swaying, then eventually dancing to a 'screwed' and 'chopped' version of Ludacris' unreleased song, "Splash Waterfalls." Being the clown that Kayron was, he walked right up to the girl and started dancing behind her while the gas pumped. Not one to miss an opportunity, Kayron decided to dance instead of pay for the gas.

Monster Pat stepped from the car, laughing at the antics of his friend. "You a fool, boy!" Monster Pat yelled to his friend over the thunder of the bass.

Though the female didn't know who in the hell she was dancing with, the gaudy and extravagant diamond inlaid jewelry that each man wore did nothing to hurt their cause.

As extroverted as Pat was, he felt content to watch. He didn't want to blow his high as he noticed twilight settling over the city of syrup. He looked at his diamond-bezeled watch, noting that it was already 8:30 p.m.

When he returned from paying for his gas, Kayron had the parking lot pimping in full effect. He had the young, dark-skinned woman jammed up on the back of her car already. He had her 'skinnin and grinnin,' so Pat knew that Kayron was straight in whatever game he was spittin at her. Pat knew that when a woman didn't shy away from you invading her space, and she smiled as you talked, then she had definitely already made up her mind that you were somebody that she'd sleep with.

"K-boogie," Pat called out, pointing to his watch as he filled his gas tank. There was an industry party tonight that Pat did not want to miss. The girl from Murder One, Prescious, was throwing the party and every artist, groupie, and anyone even remotely involved with the industry, and some that weren't, within a 1,500 mile radius was going to be there.

Pat loved the industry parties. They were combinations of orgies, network summits, and car shows. He couldn't picture himself doing anything else other than rapping.

Kayron programmed the woman's phone number into his cell phone and took a quick picture of her with his camera phone for his digital rolodex. He then sauntered back while Pat sat in the car, sipping on a longneck Bud. Pat felt good; he was ready to party. They had one more stop before the festivities could begin.

Pat eased the BMW out onto the ever busy West Bellfort Boulevard. He crossed over Fondren, headed to one of his best friend's house. After two lefts off of West Bellfort, Pat entered a residential neighborhood that seemed to be hiding from the rest of the city. It was a stark contrast from the hustle and bustle of the overcrowded business district that ran the length of West Bellfort. If you didn't pay any attention, you would never know that the quiet, tree lined streets of Westbury Manor lay just two blocks from one of the busiest streets on the southwest side of Houston.

When Pat turned onto his friend's street, he lowered his music a tad. The short street was a cul-de-sac that allowed Pat to see his partner outside the front of his house with his candy blue and chrome 1300 Suzuki and two Great Danes watching him.

Lemmie Brown, otherwise known as Sleepy, was one of Monster Pat's best friends. They had befriended one another in prison on the Coffield Unit. They were two men with different backgrounds, different beliefs and different lifestyles that had been brought together through the harsh oppression of prison. Not only that, but they were both talented artists in their respective fields who bonded through respect for one another's art. While Monster Pat was known for his aspirations and talents as a rapper, Sleepy was an aspiring author and poet who had made a lot of money in white-collar criminal activities.

Sleepy had been Pat's ear and inspiration while they were on lock, as well as Pat having been Sleep's. Sleepy was supposed to be going to the party with Pat.

Sleepy's house was the two story brick home at the very end of the street. He could stand in his garage and see anyone who turned onto his street. Pat pulled right up to the edge of the driveway, but didn't pull in.

He didn't want to hit the Hiabusa by accident. He'd never hear the end of that one!

The two Great Danes stood alert and erect beside their master, as if waiting on his assessment of this new development. The dogs know that this was their domain and they didn't take kindly to intruders. Every other time that Pat had visited Sleepy, they were in their kennel in the back yard.

"What's tha damn deal?" Pat asked, stepping out of his ride. "You ain't dressed yet fool? I thought you were going to ride with ya boy tonight. You know I don't know how to get to Clear Lake, "Pat addressed his friend, who was looking at him crazy.

Actually, Sleepy was looking at Kayron, but Pat couldn't really tell because Sleepy's eyes were hooded and lazy, so sometimes it was hard to tell. That's how he got his nickname, because he was sleepy-eyed.

"You hear me talking to you, you cock-eyed muthafucka?" Pat hollered at his homeboy.

"Who that fuck is that with you?" Sleepy asked, stern-faced. Though he was strictly legit now, Sleepy still lived by the rules of the game. He didn't like people to know where he laid his head.

"Man, that's my nigga K-boogie out of East Dallas. I flew the fool out here today so he could kick it with us. I'm trying to show the fool a good time, get him out of those projects for a week or two, ya know, get him away from the dope selling. He wanted to see how you boys in the 'H' do it." Pat spoke in an exaggerated manner, trying to appeal to his boy's ego.

Sleepy smiled. Pat was his boy; he should've known that his homie wouldn't violate by bringing just anybody to his house. One just couldn't be too careful nowadays.

"Well, tell him to get out, fool, where your manners at?" Sleepy asked, needling Pat. Both of them loved to cap on one another and crack jokes. "You know you a woman anyway, you should have that hostess shit down pat," Sleepy joked.

"Aw, fuck youu!!" Pat said, and motioned for Kayron to go ahead and get out of the car.

Sleepy went around to the side of the house and locked his dogs behind the gate. The dogs stayed at the fence whining and barking; it seemed to Pat as if they were upset about being put up and wanted back out.

"You going or what?" Pat still wanted to know.

"Nah, man, Zarina done popped up over here. She talking about she want to head to the movies."

"Movies? Man, you gon miss this party for some ole bitch ass movie? You lying, nigga, what you got going? Seriously," Pat stressed. "I don't see her ride, what she come over here on, that motor cycle?"

"Hell, naw," Sleepy pulled out a small remote and lifted his garage door with the press of a button. Parked next to his 2003 Vette was the Ford Expedition that he'd bought for Zarina.

"Oh!" Pat exclaimed. "Why she park her shit in your garage, fool? And where is your Navigator and your slab," he asked, referring to Sleepy's tricked-out 92 signature series Lincoln Town Car.

"Man, my shit at my momma's house," Sleepy told his friend in an exasperated tone. "This bitch always park her shit in my garage and close the door. She calls herself being slick. She nosy as fuck. She trying to find out who I be having running in and out of my house. If it wasn't for us having a child together, I would've been checked that hoe."

"Fool, tell that bitch about herself," Pat prompted. "Nah, fool, she got a right to know who comes and goes because of our child," Sleepy responded. "I can understand her concern. She thinks I might have all them hard headed hoodlums runnin in and out of here with my child running around, cause that's the way I used to live when I was 17. But I'm a grown man now, fool, twelve years behind bars will do that to you. You should know. But you and I both know that her motives run deeper than that," Sleepy said, giving his friend a knowing look. "She trying to see what hoe's I got mobbing through here."

"Man, that's how them bitches act," Pat stressed, getting into the topic. "You can't pay them funky hoes to do right by a nigga when he get locked up, then when he get home you got to pay them bitches to leave you alone. That's bullshit!"

"I ain't tripping," Sleepy said. "I play all these hoes from a distance. I don't have time to trip; I let them trip by they gotdamn self. I got a daughter to raise."

Just as he spoke of his child, she came sauntering through the garage door looking for her father.

"What, Dymond?" Sleepy asked, addressing his child. At 13, she was his spitting image, except for being two shades brighter. He could tell that she didn't really want anything. She just liked being around her father after having missed out on having a relationship with him for the last twelve years of her life.

"Ain't nobody out here but grown men, take your ass back in the house," he instructed, before she even got out of the garage. She stuck her bottom lip out, did an about face and stalked back into the house.

"She just like her nosy ass momma; her momma probably sent her out here to see what I was doing. I got $100 bet that her momma come out here in the next two minutes," Sleepy offered, reaching into his pocket, pulling out a wad of cash and peeling off a bigface hundred dollar bill, dropping it to the pavement. Pat knew better than to take the bet, but Kayron didn't.

No sooner had Kayron's hundred hit the ground did the garage door to the house open again. When a tall and voluptuous woman stepped out, Sleepy and Pat burst out laughing. Sleepy snatched his money off the ground in mock aggravation as the mother of his child sashayed out to his side.

Kayron and Pat couldn't help but gawk. Zarina was an Amazon, literally. She stood every bit of 6' 2" barefooted, with the shape of a real life blowup doll. Her curvy hips bordered on being completely round and complemented the medicine ball sized ass that screamed to be released from the low cut azure jeans that held it prisoner.

Her breasts had to be at least D-cups, but looked moderate when compared to the outsized proportions of the rest of her body. Her low cut halter revealed a flat and tattooed belly, highlighted by a pierced belly button. Even her wide nose, which at the moment was flared in what Sleepy knew meant she was fixing to go off, would be huge on a woman of a lesser size. Her dyed auburn hair was braided from side-to-back with the overflow pinned up with a banana clip. Her full lips were tinged in a burnt orange to match her tangerine halter.

"Lemmie Earl!" she called out. Sleepy hated when she called his first and middle names out like that. She got that from his mother who would do that when he was in trouble. She would call his name out as if it were one long word.

"Whaaaat!" Sleepy yelled at her, as she stood over him, looking down on his 5'8" frame. Zarina stood on the back of her legs with her hands propped on her hips, trying to strike an intimidating pose. Pat didn't know about intimidating, but she sure in the fuck looked feminine and sexy despite her size. She was turning him smooth the fuck on! Looking at her ass, he had to fix himself before he let it be known what was going through his mind, he thought. Luckily he was wearing some baggy pants. It made it easier for him to play it off.

"What's wrong with you? What tha fuck you yelling for?" she asked, pretending her feelings were hurt.

"I'm talking Zee, what's up?" Sleepy inquired, continuing with the hard approach.

"The movie starts at 9:45," she informed him.

"So?"

"We still going?"

"Naw, we can go tomorrow. I got to show Pat how to get to Clear Lake. It's an industry party tonight and he don't know how to get there," Sleepy said.

She tightened her lips and shook her head in a frustrated manner. Everyone could tell that she was pissed. Sleepy knew what was next. She was getting ready to throw his daughter in his face.

"Well, what about your child. You know that she was looking forward to going to the movie,'" Zarina told him as if it were the news of the century.

"I said we'll go tomorrow. She can wait until tomorrow. I'm not staying at the party, anyway, I'ma just show him how to get there. I'ma take my bike and he gon follow me. I'll be back in an hour. We can go bowling or something. Just be ready when I get back," he insisted.

"That's fine!" Zarina huffed, and walked back into the house.

When Zarina closed the door behind her it was as if all three men breathed a sigh of relief, all at once. None of them wanted a scene, especially Sleepy. He still held the psychological scars of being incarcerated for twelve years of his young life. Having been locked up at the age of 18 for robbery, doing eight years, getting released for nine months; then going back to prison for counterfeit money and check forgery for another four years. He didn't take being put out on front street well. His attitude about things like that, having evolved some, still needed work. His favorite saying was that "God is not through with me yet!"

"Man, you gon miss the party for real?" Kayron asked. "You gon pass up the chance to mingle and rub elbows with all them groupies and stars?" he wanted to know.

"Trust me, man, that shit gets old, black," Sleepy told Kayron. "Ask ya boy Pat, if you been to one, you been to them all. It just goes hand in hand in his line of work. For me, I would just be going just to be going. It wouldn't benefit my career any," Sleepy confided.

"Fuck that," Pat chimed. "I want to go to this bitch. This is a Murder One party. Ain't no telling who flew into town for this muthafucka."

"What do you do for a living?" Kayron wanted to know. Sleepy smiled.

"That punk write books, and that cross-eyed motharfucka is pretty good!" Pat interjected.

"Yeah, I run my own publishing company, too!" Sleepy proudly admitted. "That's what your boy here needs. I keep telling the fool he needs to start his own label. Ain't shit like being your own boss. Working for yourself keeps an ambitious man from losing his hunger to get more out of life, cause ambitious people are their own worst critics. But this nut just want to rap!"

"Shiiit, that's all I need to do is rap," Pat admitted. "I'm like a pimp, and rap is my hoe. If I don't rap then I'll die. I keep it pimpin for real. It's pimp or die with me for life," Pat yelled, and the ever-alert dogs howled in response, adding their chorus to Pat's hollered feelings about his God-given talent.

"I keep telling Pat that shit," Kayron blurted out. "I tell that fool all the time that we need to take some of this dope money I got and do something with it. It don't do no good in my safe," he cracked.

"You better clean that shit up first; them feds ain't bullshittin. They cracking down on all these labels behind that shit. Those hoes hate to see a nigga come up and get out tha hood," Sleepy stated. It was a sore subject with him because he knew that America was hypocritical when it came to that type of thing. He and Pat had plenty of conversations about it late at night when they were behind bars. Prison was where their dreams were born.

"Because you muthafuckas ain't no Bill Gates, Paul Allen or Michael Dell. Them muthafuckas were computer hackers. They used to steal money from big business accounts, invest the money and put it back before anyone was the wiser," Sleepy claimed. Pat knew how militant his friend could be and wanted to get to the party early before they ended up standing out there all night.

"Yeah, yeah, man! We'll talk about that shit later," Pat blurted out, ready to go. "I would like to get to the party early before all of the groupies are taken."

"What you tripping on?" Sleepy asked, cranking up his chromed out bike. "You getting ready to go platinum, fool, even though your money ain't reflecting it," he smirked. "You still popular enough to fuck off your name," Sleepy sarcastically told his friend, walking to the garage to retrieve his helmet and riding gloves. "Besides, what groupie would pass up the chance of hitting a rap star in the ass with a strap on? Everybody in Texas know how you get down," Sleepy laughed.

Kayron couldn't help but bust out laughing, despite his best efforts to hold it in.

"Aw, shut up, you punk muthafucka! I know your cross-eyed ass used to try to suck them dicks, but you kept missing your mouth and poking yourself in the fucking eye," Pat shot back, imitating Sleepy struggling with an imaginary dick, then poking himself in the eye. "Damn, I missed!" Pat joked.

They all fell out laughing, rolling on the ground at Monster Pat's acting skills. It was something that could actually be pictured.

"Maan, you a retarded sumabitch!" Sleepy laughed. "Just make sure you keep up11' Sleepy told him before strapping on his helmet.

"Just lead the way," Pat told him. "Ladies first" he finished, hopping into the V-l2.

Chapter 16

The expensive dining room table seated sixteen adults comfortably with room to seat more. The custom-made marble and glass table with 18 karat gold fixtures embedded into the marble was exquisitely set with silk hand-woven place mats, fine bone china, silver and gold eating utensils and crystal flutes and wine glasses at each setting.

The guests of the meeting, Ruff House and Murder One Records representatives, flanked the Congresswoman, who sat with regal elegance at the head of the table. Finished with the main course of the meal, bypassing dessert, her aides rushed to retrieve the necessities for the night's meeting.

Stuffed to the gills on the lavishly catered meal, Black Jack wondered how all of the pretentious and bourgeois muthafuckas would act if he let loose a loud and nasty fart? He smiled inwardly at the thought. Although he would never do such a thing (mainly because he was just too cool for that type of shit), he laughed to himself nonetheless just thinking about it. He hated the fact that so many of his people could come together and be so fake. Half of them were probably one generation removed from the ghetto! And they had the nerve to pretend to be doing him a favor by allowing him to be there. Though it had not been said verbally, their actions conveyed the 'I'm better than you because I have almost a hundred million dollar portfolio' attitude very clearly. Little did they know that Keith Vincent himself was worth close to $150 million, not counting his stock in Murder One. The game had been good to him and Daddy Bo.

The food he'd just consumed had actually relaxed him a bit. He'd enjoyed the catered meal of baked 'barnyard pimp' (chicken)) collard greens, mashed potatoes, broccoli and rice casserole, candied yams, green beans with new potatoes and onions, and homemade honey buttered yeast rolls. He couldn't even think about trying to eat any of the pecan and cheese cake with vanilla ice cream that was about to be served.

A-dray had finished eating long ago and was being baited into conversation by the blue-eyed lady that Black Jack had met just an hour ago. But A-dray had a mission and would not fall short of what she had to do and was cordially ignoring the lady. A-dray's focus was on the Congresswoman and her every move as she imitated the Congresswoman in mock adoration.

The Congresswoman was clearly smitten with A-Dray, having taken time away from her social obligations prior to the meal to explain some of the intricacies of being an African American female in a predominantly white male occupation. The thought of youth adoration was evidently a concept that the Congresswoman could get used to. Black Jack was tickled.

Tonight was pivotal point in Murder One's future. Tonight, Murder One would take advantage of a once-in-a-lifetime opportunity. Tonight, Congresswoman Cunningham and her National Caucus for African American Millionaires Committee was holding an open session for the two record labels in hopes that one would profit the committee and its cause by. allying itself with the NCAAM. Tonight each record label would make its pitch in an effort to acquire the offered seat.

The newly formed committee, which boasted a membership of the most prominent and influential group of African American millionaires in the U.S., was hellbent on redirecting and eventually controlling the concerted economic muscle of the black dollar.

The Congresswoman and a few of her friends had formed under a corporate umbrella after research and demographic studies were performed in reference to when, where and how the black dollar was spent in the U.S. Other than the necessities of life, most African Americans squandered their money on things that depreciated in value over time, like jewelry, clothing, music, liquor, late-model automobiles, and beauty products. African Americans weren't investing in land, gold, silver, agriculture and natural resources, things that gained and increased in value over time. So the Congresswoman and her committee decided to pool their money, resources and power in an attempt to direct and control the power of the black dollar through an alternate Wall Street, so to speak. The NCPAM would be the parent corporation of many subsidiaries that would branch into every aspect of business relating to the markets that benefited from the black dollar. Overall, the black dollar economy comprised thirty-two percent of all retail monies spent. That translated into billions of dollars each year. With that type of money and power, the committee hoped to be the voice of a race of people who'd been ignored and exploited for so many years.

It coincided with a longtime vision of Daddy Bo's and included his long-term goals for his and Black Jack's families. Daddy Bo's lawyer, a member of a prominent black professional ski club called the Ski Jammers, had heard whispers of the newly formed committee on a trip to Mt. Crest de Bute in Colorado. He brought it to Clyde's attention during one of their many meetings concerning his appeals. Daddy Bo immediately insisted upon receiving any information the lawyer could dig up on the Committee. Through various channels the lawyer was able to verify the committee's existence and aims. With strategically placed inquiries, Daddy Bo's lawyer was able to attain a plethora of information on the Houston-based Congresswoman's committee and its agenda. An added jewel to the cache of information was the discovery that the committee wanted to ally itself with a reputable record company and would offer the owner, or owners, a seat on the committee's board.

Rumor had it that the committee needed an independently owned record label with no ties binding it to the five major labels - BMG, Syon, Universal, Warner Music and EMI-Capital - to head a pre-funded distribution operation that would not conflict with the interests of the majors.

The Congresswoman wanted everything black-owned. The committee wanted no outside influence of white corporate America to reach its corrupted tentacles in and taint what they hoped would be the unchallenged voice of Black America. They were quietly gaining strongholds in corporate America and knew that if they were exposed to the wrong money men, their dream would be killed even before it would begin. The committee knew that music was the avenue to its youth. In a constructive context, music could be used as the vehicle needed to bridge the generation gap and stand as the voice used to empower today's youth for tomorrow.

The only obstacle was image. The committee was concerned with the image of the label and its executives. Not so much the sexual and violent images that today's artists portrayed through their music, because that could be worked around, but the image of the company as a whole and the foundation it stood on. The committee knew that the stench of drug money - its bloody beginnings, its ties to inner-city feuds, its sickening grasp on the youth of black America - was rumored to be at the bottom of many young moguls rise to the top of the Hip-Hop and rap industry. The committee would choose a record company that, first, was Houston-based so the committee could keep tabs on its dealings; that owned all of its masters; that was established and showed longevity and the potential to generate profit; and most importantly, that was free of scandal and with no ties to drugs and their corrupting taint) not to mention the negative publicity that went with them. The Congresswoman did not want a problem on her hands.

She knew that any label worth its salt would be involved with one of the five major labels in some way, shape, fashion or form, and that in the public's eye, the Hip-Hop and rap industry seemed to be synonymous with the criminal element. A few things could be overlooked, but not many, and certainly not those that would validate the misgivings of much of America, which viewed blacks in general and black business in particular as being based on drugs, gambling and prostitution. The fact that so many white fortunes had been built on similar unsavory enterprises was now lost in the avalanche of white-washed history.

The committee had done its homework, coming up with four possibilities from H-town's music scene. Out of 272 independently owned record labels registered in Houston, only four companies even remotely came close to what the committee was searching, for. Those companies were Rap-A-Lot, Wreck Shop Records, Murder One Records, and Ruff House Records. Out of those four, two were exed off the list after further consideration.

Rap-A-Lot was the first to be scratched due to an extensive federal investigation stemming from Rap-A-Lot angering a Florida senator, who took exception to the label repeatedly voicing anarchistic and controversial views. They were before their time.

Wreck Shop Records had been scratched simply because they'd just signed a long-term contract with one of the majors. Murder One was a tentative candidate at best. They were exiting a five-year contract at the end of the year with a major and had yet to procure their masters.

Despite the allegations about Ruff House's CEO, Romichael Turner, concerning his illicit activities, Ruff House was the front runner in the race for the seat. Both companies stood to gain billions as well as the influence of the Congresswoman and her committee, so she had to choose wisely.

Unbeknownst to both parties, the Committee already had an investigation going, delving into the histories and backgrounds of each company.

As the servers asked about dessert, the aides set up a portable podium at the head of the table next to the Congresswoman. Romichael looked at Black Jack and winked. If Black Jack would've been thirty years dumber, he would've shot Romichael in his bitch ass face for having the nuts to even play him close.

As he sat there, surrounded by good food, opulence and people to whom the struggle and violence of the streets was unknown or long-forgotten, Black Jack thought of the twisted road and events that had made Turner such an enemy of the Murder One family.

From the beginning of Romichael and Ayanna's relationship, Black Jack had seen through Romichael's facade. He'd only tolerated the punk because of Ayanna. She was so in love with Romichael at the time, that in her eyes he could do no wrong. So Black Jack had kept his misgivings to himself and advised Amin and her brothers to do the same. They would just wait the sucka out. They knew that Romichael just wanted to exploit their influence and clout.

Romichael had become 'hood rich' like they had, but had been too careless in his flash, which prompted the feds to swarm all over his ass. He'd been desperately trying to find a means to legitimize his drug empire and silence the storm the feds had started. Romichael had figured that Ayanna was his ticket, and that by marrying her, a law student with a connected family, he'd gain full access to their circle.

But Black Jack and Amin had quickly closed that door in his face, declining all business propositions Romichael had brought to them. Romichael had even gone as far as to offer both men a stake in his men's club, The Midnight Run, which turned a nice annual profit. Maybe that's where Duck had come into the picture, Black Jack mused. Maybe Duck was the reason that the feds had backed off Romichael. Could Duck have that kind of stroke, Black Jack wondered? It was possible; Duck had been in the game long enough. After all, Duck ran in the same circles as he and Daddy Bo, so it was possible.

Where Amin's reasoning for not wanting to ally himself with Romichael was strictly personal and connected to his cousin's murder, Black Jack and Daddy Bo were simply about business. Romichael was too much of a loose cannon and couldn't be controlled. He was too greedy, therefore would present a problem in the long run. So to keep from having to kill Romichael, it was just best to let him do his own thing and not get involved. It was simple economics with the older men, unlike Amin, who was still young enough to be ruled by his emotions. Besides, Amin had blown his opportunity to kill Romichael without any drastic repercussions last year. The time to kill him had come when Romichael and Ayanna had gotten into a fight and she'd stormed out of the house and to Club Flip Mode, which was hosting a semi-private fashion show.

Romichael had not been content with allowing Ayanna to have the last word and had followed her. Being midday, club security was lax, allowing Romichael easy access to the club behind Ayanna. An irate Romichael had snatched Ayanna from a booth in mid-discussion with Nina, determined to get her home by any means necessary. Nina rushed to get Amin from his office, where he'd been discussing business with his bodyguard Damon and Dominick, Ayanna's brother.

Despite putting up a good fight, Ayanna was dragged by Romichael to the lobby of the building where he was met by Amin and his crew. Romichael was beaten unmercifully by the men and had to be hospitalized. Left for dead, he'd been taken to Herman Hospital. No charges had been filed against Amin or Romichael when the event was replayed to officials.

That had been Amin's chance. After that incident, Romichael hired a team of gun toting, small minded clucks, who he paid to do his bidding and protect him.

Black Jack returned to the present and smiled at the lucky muthafucka, making a mental note that if the game didn't catch up to Romichael and leave him in a grave, Black Jack would have to find a safe and efficient way to kill him himself.

"Ladies and Gentlemen," the Congresswoman announced in her husky voice, "may I please have your attention. The twelfth monthly meeting of the NCAAM is being brought to order."

The Congresswoman stood ramrod straight and brought the meeting in synch with her graceful and queen-like presence. She efficiently took control of the meeting, outlining the committee's responsibilities and agenda in graphic detail for the benefit of the visiting parties. Next, she moved on to any old issues that the committee needed to address.

A budding actress on the stage of life herself, A-dray felt that this performance was staged for their benefit rather than being an actual meeting. The Congresswoman addressed all issues with the practiced ease of the seasoned orator. Finally, timed with Murder One's introduction, the Congresswoman's aides passed around a proposal package done by Ayanna to everyone at the table with the exception of Duck and Romichael, who sat there dumbfounded, wondering if the lack of their materials was intentional.

Andrea had prepared for two months prior to this meeting. It was her time to shine! The intro was her cue to proceed to the podium as the Congresswoman introduced her.

As A-dray took the podium, she used the old tactic of clearing her throat to gain everyone's undivided attention before she began. The Congresswoman found it amusing and laughed.

"Thank you, Congresswoman Cunningham," A-dray began. "First of all, I would like to say that it is an honor and privilege to be amongst some of the brightest business minds in the African American race, not to mention some of the richest," she joked. Spatterings of laughter speckled the crowd as she reined in the remaining butterflies in her stomach.

Her eyes strayed to Romichael, who gave her the most irking smile she'd ever seen. He capped it off by licking his disgusting tongue across his lips. She wondered again, not for the first time, what her sister had seen in his perverted ass. That was all the boost she needed to get over the hump. Her hatred of Romichael propelled her forward. A-dray took a deep breath and continued.

"On behalf of Murder One Records and myself, I would like to thank the committee for the opportunity that they have given us. We fully comprehend the power and prestige that this committee retains. We identify and agree with the strong voice, the ideals and the ideologies set forth to better the African American community by this committee," she articulated, gaining momentum. "We also realize that with much power comes much responsibility. Murder One would like to exhaust all of its resources to assist this committee in shouldering some of that responsibility, starting with the youth in our community."

"Hip-Hop, as we know it, is here to stay whether we like it or not. It is affecting our culture innumerous ways, some positive, some negative. It is change, nonetheless, and unless that change is geared toward ultimately all positive endeavors, then the: dreams we dream for a better tomorrow as well as actions of this committee will all have been in vain."

"I personally am fond of a saying that my uncle taught me at a young age, and it's that 'It takes a village to raise a child.' If our forces are combined, ladies and gentlemen, we will become that village!"

A-dray's pitch gained intensity as she progressed. "Now if you will, would you please turn to page two of your packets?"

As she detailed the proposal of Murder One, mostly from memory, you could see that she had the audience captivated. Details, she thought, winking at her uncle, who beamed with the pride of a father seeing his firstborn child delivered.

Andrea went through the information with surprising ease and speed. She didn't even think. It all came from memory as she detailed Murder One's financial statement and six-year sales projection with and without the committee's distributional assistance like a veteran financial advisor. The amazement leaped from the faces in the crowd; even Romichael was impressed. Her final trump card was played when she announced that Murder One was making a $20 million contribution to the Committee's children's fund, which sponsored charter schools that provided a quality education to inner city youths.

Even the Congresswoman was proud and she didn't even know A-dray. Her entire presentation took twenty minutes, from start to finish. The ovation was a standing effort as Andrea took her seat and Duck was introduced on behalf of Ruff House. Duck knew that he could not even begin to compete with Murder One's presentation, only hoping to sustain his audience's attention in the wake of such a gargantuan performance by the 16-year-old.

Duck felt dwarfed by his paltry speech, having been assured already that the seat was in the bag by Romichael. Duck felt absolutely stupid having been caught so unprepared, a fact that didn't go unnoticed by the Congresswoman and her NCAAM committee.

Afterward, the Congresswoman recessed the committee pending a fifteen-day investigation on each company. Both parties knew that there would be an investigation and neither was worried. Each company was prepared for anything the committee could dig up. Little did they know the investigation had begun much earlier.

Afterward, reclining all the way back into the luxury of the soft leather of the Maybach's seats, Black Jack relit his Cuban cigar. "You did good, kid, I'm proud of you," he confided in A-dray. "I knew you could pull it off."

"You better know it," his niece snapped. "I worked hard, now I needs my pay," she added, letting her street roots manifest themselves through her mannerisms, now that it was just her and Black Jack.

"What pay?" Black Jack asked in his normal cool demeanor. "Your butt better be happy I feed your fat ass. You eat more than all my kids," he joked.

"Yeah, right," A-dray giggled. "Your cheap ass is going to pay tha kid, starting with that position in the company you had me fronting with tonight," she demanded.

"Well, you did do good, and it does seem as though you're ready. I guess you do need a little bit more responsibility, seeing as how you're getting ready to graduate high school and all. I guess a good job would do you some good, but that vice president position is fictitious, so you can't have that one. However, I have one that is perfectly suited for you, and it even complements your qualities and talents," he offered.

"Ooh! What is it?" she asked excitedly.

"A mail sorter," he laughed.

Chapter 17

Amin Rush and some of his closest friends sat around his penthouse and kicked the shit. They had a chain of hydro-blunts being passed around the room to each person, listening to some old school Frankie Beverly and Maze, all the while entertaining three females from California who were in town performing a stage play at the Wortham Theater.

Amin was tired! Literally, figuratively, emotionally, spiritually and any other way that ended in 'ly,' he thought. He was worried about Kiwan, still not having heard from him or Prescious since his release. Luckily, Tony had called him and informed him of their whereabouts, but they still should've been back by now from New Orleans. Amin didn't want to keep calling and checking up on the man, making it seem as though he didn't trust them, but he couldn't help but worry! He could just imagine all of the shit he'd be into after doing a ten-year bid, then being released with virtually unlimited resources at his fingertips. He would be missing in action for months before he decided to finally return home.

"Yo, Amin," someone called, breaking through his heavy thoughts. Amin looked up from his seat on the sofa through drug-addled eyes at his friend Poo-Poo. "What time does the party start tonight?" Poo-Poo asked, not even bothering to look up from the game that he and his friend Chris were playing on the Playstation 2 that was hooked up to Amin's 61-inch plasma screen TV, enhancing the already surreal graphics to epic proportions.

"I don't know, tha muthafucka don probably already started," Amin barked, looking at his watch. "What I do know is that you need to get yo mothafuckin feet off my coffee table," Amin warned. "And turn that pussy ass shit down," he added, shouting and rising from his relaxed position to refresh his drink.

One of the tantalizingly gorgeous women met him before he could take three steps. "Let me get that for you, Daddy," she offered, taking his drink for him. Amin couldn't even remember her name, yet here she was in his private pad and walking around in her bra and panties smoking weed. They had all gotten comfortable pretty quick. This was how he always fucked up and got in trouble. He'd been blessed so far to not have gotten a paternity suit slapped on his ass.

"Thanks, boo," he told her as she winked at him. Amin was determined not to fall short tonight.

"Who you riding with, Poo-Poo?" Carlos, another one of their patnas, asked.

"I don't know," Poo-Poo blurted. "I just know I'm a little too fucked up to be driving," he admitted, his $22,000 diamond and platinum dental work glaring back into the living room from its reflection in the TV.

"I do know one thing," Amin announced. "Non of you cats are rolling with me."

"What tha fuck we waiting on?" Chris asked. Quincey, who had been involved in an intimate conversation with one of the women up until that point broke in, saying, "I ain't got to roll with you, Amin, just let ya boy get the keys to the Modena, please!"

"Nigga, you must be on some stupid juice or something. You got me fucked up," Amin-stressed. "Your funky ass already wrecked my fucking bike, which I spent almost $20,000 customizing. You think I'm gon let you tear up my $250,000 car? Naw!" he said, shaking his head. "You got me twisted, black."

"Aw, man, stop whining," Quincey retorted. "That's why you pay them white folks insurance, for shit like that. I told you I'll buy you another one just like it," Quincey offered.

"Fool, that ain't tha point. Tha point is that you rolling my shit, and when people find out who that stuff belongs to, if something happens, the first thing they wanna do is sue me," Amin fussed, receiving the drink from the long-legged fawn colored Californian, who sat in his lap after handing him the drink. She knew what she was doing, plopping her soft ass right on the head of his dick as she wiggled around pretending to try and get comfortable.

"Ya know, that could be a rap song," Poo-Poo stated in his drug-induced state of euphoria. He was the clown of the bunch and always showed his ass when they hung out, but the boy was funny.

"What could be a song, fool?" Carlos asked, encouraging Poo-Poo.

"Yeah! Can I get the mothafuckin keys to the Nodena, please," Poo-Poo rapped.

"Shut tha fuck up!" Chris warned Poo-Poo, cutting him off. "You blowin my mothafuckin high," he told him, as everyone giggled.

Amin jumped up, dumping the girl roughly on the couch, as she smacked her mouth in mock irritation. "What's up?" she wanted to know.

"Nothin," Amin lied. He looked around his loft at his custom furniture, black art, nice possessions and noticed that something was out of place. "Tha damn thugs!!!" he thought, as he watched them playing, bullshitting and attempting to talk the females into fornication. They'd all grown up together from elementary fighting, playing and fucking the same neighborhood freaks from running home to running trains the crew of men in his home were his boys through thick and thin. He could never have turned his back on them, no matter how much money he'd made.

Daddy Bo had always reminded him to never forget where he'd come from. Although he often tired of being the big brother, always being the responsible one in the crew, Amin knew that he needed his friends just as much as they needed him. Most of his crew continued to engage in their destructive behavior. Those that weren't employed by Murder One in one capacity or another continued to live the street life and he could do nothing but respect that, and to counsel against the most destructive acts. He had told them all at one point or another, that he would not tolerate their drug-dealing and car-jacking and other violent acts to endanger Murder One, that if they ended up in prison he would stand by them and support their families, but that they all had meaningful employment with the Rush family, if that's what it took to get them off the street. It's just that they were all raised in the streets and needed the adrenaline rush the street life provided and many were unwilling to suck Murder One's tit.

But his love was unconditional, no matter what they chose to do or how they wanted to live. He sent thousands of dollars every month to his boys on lock. They kept a list of everyone from their part of Third Ward down with them that was on lock, and pooled together every month to send them money, pictures, and reading materials. Amin even started a carpool service with his own promotional vans providing rides to different units around Texas. It was his way of saying, "To all the strugglers, keep struggling no matter what, the rain won't last forever!"

The promiscuous female from Cali puffed on the blunt and passed it to her girlfriend who was in a heavy liplock with Quincey at the moment. She rose from her seat and whispered in Amin's ear. Chris snatched the blunt from Quincey's companion, who was just holding the damn thing. Carlos watched his friend from the corner of his eye as Amin brushed off the woman's evident sexual advances. He knew his homeboy well enough to know that something was bothering him, but he didn't know what.

"Hey, lil momma, let me holla at you a second," Carlos addressed the female pouting on Amin's arm. She ignored Carlos, continuing her pursuit of Amin. Carlos didn't want to cause a scene so he stood up and announced that it was time to get ready to leave, they were going to head to the party. Amin could wait on Kiwan and bring him later. It was getting late already. Carlos instructed the women to get dressed.

"Yeah, I'm ready to go get my mothafuckin party on!" Poo-Poo hollered. "Where is Ayanna? She think she too good to get with a brotha, wit her fine ass."

"Poo-Poo, Ayanna don't wanna be bothered with yo thuggish ass. Nigga, you sell dope for a living, she got a law degree, what you gon do for her but get popped then write her talking bout she can come see you cuz she on your visitation list?" Quincey chided. "And you ugly than a muthafucka," Carlos chimed in, as if on cue.

"Yeah, I might be ugly, but she blind, she don't know how ugly I am," Poo-Poo stressed, as he stood and stretched his legs. Everybody had to laugh at that one, even Amin.

Amin took his cue from Carlos and stepped out of his loft; into the foyer that held his private elevator. There was also a security desk in the foyer that was manned 24 hours a day, seven days a week. This prevented anyone who wasn't supposed to be on the top floor from just barging into Amin's loft. The private elevator led to the lower floors as well as the VIP room on the third level inside of Club Flip Mode. The first three floors of the building consisted of the club and the suite of offices that Amin and Black Jack worked out of. The next two floors held apartments and empty storage space, where Amin and Black Jack put old equipment and furniture that they didn't need or want. The apartments were kept for out-of-town guests, artists, or anyone in the family in need of a place to crash. The apartments saved him tons of money on hotel fees whenever his entertainment and promotion company brought acts into town to perform at the Toyota Center or the club.

There was also a door that led to a stairwell and fire exit that connected to the adjoining building. The building next to Amin was also owned by Murder One and doubled as a parking garage for the club as well as the company's personal vehicle storage. Murder One kept its fleet of limousines there along with its tour buses, promo vans, trucks and assorted vehicles. Black Jack and Amin kept their personal collection of vehicles on the gated top two levels of the garage, or at least those that couldn't be stored at their homes. At last count Amin had over 30 cars and trucks, some classics; 12 motor cycles, including a T-rex trike made by the Ruff Ryders.

Damon and one of the other members of the security staff stood at the desk watching the security cameras. After the incident with Romichael the entire building was covered with cameras, which were strategically spaced. The cameras even monitored the street and sidewalk in front of the building.

Amin walked to the stairwell entrance and crossed the walk that connected the two buildings. Upon entering the top level of the garage, Amin switched on the lights, illuminating two of his most recently purchased vehicles, which had been delivered last week.

Sitting under the fluorescent lights of the garage was a brand new 2004 burgundy Cadillac Escalade EXT and a 2004 coal black Corvette C-6. Both were customized with rims, audio and video equipment, custom interior, paint and personalized plates. The Escalade featured 23-inch Spreewell rims, 7-inch TV screens in each headrest, a 10-inch screen dropping from the roof with one in the dash, DVD and X Box equipped with white ostrich-skinned interior, with burgundy piping and the name Ki-one monogrammed into the headrest as well as on the personalized plates. The Corvette was similarly equipped, with tan ostrich skin interior. Amin had the dashboard and dials redone in chrome and cherrywood. All in all Amin had spent close to $275,000 on both vehicles. He hoped his brother would like his gifts. Guilt played a major part in the mixed emotions that stirred within the pit of Amin's stomach.

How do you show your appreciation to your brother who sacrificed ten years of his life for you? What do you say? How in the hell do you even begin to make up for a mistake like that?

Even though Amin had visited neither Kiwan nor Daddy Bo during the last ten years, there was not one day that went by where Amin didn't think of both. Maybe he was just too young to understand his own feelings? Maybe not! Amin couldn't even in a million years, fathom the thought of going to visit either one when he knew that it was all of his fault that they were incarcerated. It was an emotional scar that worked to motivate him to be successful in public and tear him down behind closed doors.

He spun one of the shiny chrome rims on the Escalade as he watched his reflection chopped up by the spinning metal blades.

The motor on the automatic door opener for the crash gates was activated by someone, diverting Amin's attention. Curious, he rose up and started walking down to the lower level of the garage to see who would be pulling in at such a late hour. Maybe Nina or Black Jack was returning with A-dray from the NCAAM meeting. Because if it was Nina, then he had to rush and get those freaks out of the loft. He was in enough trouble as it was. As he rounded the corner he prayed that it was Black Jack and not Nina.

Tires screeched on the slick pavement as the Navigator driven by Tony came flying around the turn up the ramp. Tony hit the brakes on the limo at the last minute, bringing the truck to a halt just inches from Amin. The hydro-weed had Amin's reflexes in freeze frame and he could do nothing but look crazy with his mouth agape. Amin was so high that he didn't even realize how close he'd just come to being as flat as a 20-year-old can of Coca Cola.

"Yo! You betta slow that muthafucka down, you dam fool!" Amin screamed, realization finally dawning on him seconds later. Tony frowned at his boss. Amin was scared shitless of Tony, who happened to be a distant cousin of his mother, but he would never let Tony know it. Tony was as loyal as any of his crew. He was always serious, never smiled, and he hardly said a word. Tony was the only one of his bodyguards who didn't carry a pistol. As big as he was, he didn't need one. The black gloves he always wore and his size were deterrence enough for any would be heckler or crazed fan.

Before Tony could even park the limo, Kiwan had jumped from the back of the moving limo and embraced his brother in a hug strong enough to bring a grown man to his knees. Both men shed tears of joy. It had been a long time coming for the both of them, and the long-awaited reunion surpassed any feeling that either man had experienced in their lives.

For Kiwan, memories of his little brother growing up flashed before his eyes. "Damn, it's good to see you, baby boy," Kiwan said softly, almost choking on a sob trying to escape his throat.

"You too, big bro, I see you with your buff on," Amin complimented.

Tony parked the limo, and he and Prescious got out with a slew of shopping bags. Neither of them wanted to disturb the touching scene of the two brothers reuniting.

The rambunctious crowd of Third Ward hoodlums could be heard way before they were seen. "Yo man, where he at?" someone yelled. The acoustics in the garage provide a nice, loud echo.

"There they go, yo Kiwan, what's up, baby?!" Chris yelled as the group of friends rounded the corner.

"Ki, what up dog?"

"Holla at your boy, Ki?" Everyone was excited, talking at once. The group gangrushed the brothers, hugging, high-fiving one another and giving dap to Kiwan. They were genuinely happy to see one of their soldiers in the struggle free from the system. They all vied for Kiwan's attention. All of them had a million questions to ask.

"Yo!" Amin yelled, getting everyone's attention. "You mothafuckin niggas gotta jet, you fools crowding my space," Amin joked. "We gotta party to go to," he stressed.

"Oh, no!" Kiwan protested. "Nan, I gotta go see pops in the morning, and I'm tired as shit. I got sleep on my mind."

The crew cracked up. They knew that there was no sleep in the music industry. There was always something to do. Parties, studio time, business meetings, and more parties. Not to mention the marathon sex. There just wasn't enough hours in the day for sleeping.

"Maaan ... get off the bullshit!" Poo-Poo told Kiwan.

"Yeah, Cuz, ain't no such thing as sleep in the business, man," Chris added. "Especially at night. There's always work to be done in the form of partying."

Someone handed Kiwan some Ecstasy pills. "Take these, fool. You'll be aight in a few."

"Oh, I almost forgot," Amin remembered, reaching into his pocket, pulling out a long rectangular jewelry box. Kiwan took the gift from his brother and opened it. He was almost blinded by the diamond encrusted platinum "Murder One" logo pendant on a 32-inch platinum chain.

"That's the family crest, big baby," Amin said as Kiwan removed the necklace from the box. When he placed it around his neck everyone cheered as if Kiwan was being bestowed knighthood at King Arthur's round table. They hugged him again, patting his back amidst a chorus of welcome home's.

"One thing fo sho," Qwan said. "If a fool out tha hood don't have this," he announced, holding up his pendant and chain, identical to Kiwan's and everyone elses in the group, "then they ain't part of the clique."

Chapter 18

The X pills were taking effect on Kiwan. His system had been without any drugs or alcohol for ten years. Their entourage proceeded through the streets of downtown Houston. They were five cars deep with the burgundy Escalade in the middle, providing protection for Kiwan and Amin.

Kiwan watched as the lights blurred by, although he didn't seem to be going that fast. Everything seemed surreal and the neon lights in the truck amplified the entire scene. They were riding with the windows down and the moon roof opened as the crisp March breeze ruffled Kiwan's tan "Nautica" short set.

"How do you feel?" Amin asked as he turned down the music with the remote control. They were jamming a mixed tape with the best of Notorious Big and Tupac screwed. Only in the city of Houston. The entire feeling and aura of the night intensified Kiwan's high. Damn! He never felt better in his life. But he couldn't tell Amin because for some reason his jaws would not open for him to speak. He just nodded his head. Amin just smiled; he understood because he had been there on numerous occasions.

"What do ya think of my girl Prescious?" Amin asked his brother.

"She awight," Kiwan said as he looked out of the window.

"I've known her since NYU. She was always cool but not New York material. After she found out I was coming back to Texas to help run the family business she begged me for a position. It was as though she was running from something. I knew the feeling, so I was feeling for her. I had the dough so I brought her along and it turned out to be an advantage for the company," Amin said as though explaining. Kiwan knew Amin well and old habits don't just die, Kiwan thought. He knew that when Amin got nervous he rambled. After all these years, he still rambled. Kiwan smiled; how ironic that he was beginning to feel as though he never left home after being gone for ten long years.

Amin was still rambling when he said, "Kiwan, I wanted to let you know that the sacrifice you made was not in vain and I'm so sorry for not being able to visit you and Daddy Bo. But the guilt, man, was and still is eating me alive. I couldn't stand to see the two of you behind bars ,knowing that I caused it."

Yeah, thought Kiwan; he knew it. Kiwan also knew that this had to be heavy on Amin's heart, and so he didn't speak. He just let Amin get it all out.

"But everything is okay, big bro. I'm working on getting Daddy Bo's sentence overturned so that we can all be home together. But until that happens, you are about to know how royalty is treated. You are about to see firsthand what true freedom really is. We can go anywhere, buy anything, and do damned near anything that our heart's desire. Can you feel what I'm telling you, man?" Amin said, still rambling.

"Yeah," Kiwan answered, "but where are we going?" The caravan was headed down 1-45 South toward Galveston.

"You'll see, it's a surprise" Amin turned the music back up as the truck filled with slow, screwed-up methodical bass from Tupac's Machiavelli album. The song, "Me and my girlfriend," flooded their ears. Kiwan sat back and enjoyed the ride. Five minutes later, he nodded off. When he awoke they were in Clear Lake. Kiwan knew because he loved Clear Lake. Before he got popped on that bogus dope charge he almost had enough money to buy a home in Clear Lake. Well, he shouldn't say bogus because he did sell drugs. He looked at the situation as a blessing; it could've been worse. He could have gotten much more time.

Amin turned down the music as they hit the Clear Lake city limits. He had a pistol in the truck and didn't want to get pulled over even though he had a license to carry it. If they were stopped and they ran

Kiwan's name they would know that he shouldn't be in the car with a pistol. He could get a minimum of five years added to his current sentence. They headed down NASA Rd. 1, crossed the overpass into Kemah, came to the second light and made a right down a major road that Kiwan missed the name of. For some reason, something told him to pay attention to the route they were taking. They traveled down the highway a couple of miles and came to an intersection that turned off the highway. The sign into the neighborhood said Dead Something's Landing. He'd missed it trying to learn the route. They traveled through the neighborhood passing some prime water front condos and town homes and came to the huge waterfront housing area, stopping at the gated entrance.

"Man, where in the fuck are we ... What are you doing?" Kiwan asked.

"Chill out, fool, we are going to a party at a friend's house. You can say that we are close like brothers," Amin said, smiling and joking as he got out of the truck and stepped into the guard shack. Kiwan watched as his brother began pointing and explaining. He motioned at all of the vehicles, then motioned back toward the gate. The guard, who was white, shook his head as if to say no and proceeded to pick up the phone. Oh shit, he's calling the cops, Kiwan thought, as he watched his brother buck up to the man. Damn, this fool here is tripping ... Kiwan was getting nervous. I bet he's got a pistol in his truck, damn fool. Then it hit him that this was HIS truck and the truck was in his name! Kiwan frantically went to search for the pistol in a blind panic. We going to jail for sho in these white folks neighborhood, he thought. Finding the Glock under the seat and stepping out of the passengers' side of the truck to the back of the lake, he hurled the pistol as far as he could throw it. All of his friends started getting out of their cars.

"Yo, what the fuck you doing, Ki?" Poo-Poo asked, laughing, smelling like weed and Obsession cologne. "You look scared as a muthafucka."

"Shut up, man, what the fuck it look like I'm doing," Kiwan told Poo-Poo. "I'm getting rid of the gun before the laws come. Mighty white in there is calling the Po-Po!" he motioned toward the guard shack.

"Naw he ain't, man," Poo-Poo laughed, irritating Kiwan.

As Kiwan looked at him, he thought that Poo-Poo was always instigating some shit.

"Yo brother got a house back there and the rent-a-cop in there is new. He's just verifying with his company. They do this shit every now and then, man. You was lookin like a straight up ho, man, throwing that gun away," Poo-Poo laughed, imitating Kiwan throwing the pistol away for the added affect of humor it caused, the crew erupting in laughter. But Kiwan didn't think it was funny. When Poo-Poo spun back around to face Kiwan, Kiwan hit him so hard on the jaw with a left hook that he lifted him off his feet. "That's for calling me a ho," Kiwan said as everyone stepped in between them to stop the fight. But there was no fight to breakup because Poo-Poo was out cold.

"Yo Ki ... man, you know how Poo-Poo is. You didn't have to hit tha boy," Quincey said.

"Yo Quincy, man, don't run up on me," Kiwan said softly, while turning toward him. "Just pick him up and take him to the hospital and while they are wiring his jaw up teach him to have some respect for his patnas," Kiwan said, getting back in the truck.

Amin came out of the guard shack and noticed them picking Poo-Poo up from the embankment. "Yo man, why that nigga always gettin so fucked up that he can't walk straight. That's the shit I'm talkin about, I can't take these niggas nowhere. He did the same shit in Cancun. Take his ass home," Amin yelled, climbing into the truck, closing the door, then easing into the neighborhood as the security guard opened the gate.

"See, big bro, that's how ya homeboys act when they get a little money," Amin said.

"Un-huh," Kiwan muttered, leaning back into the softness of the leather. "Yo friends, not mine!" A black Navigator peeled from the entrance and headed to Clear Lake Memorial Hospital as the rest of the caravan entered the gated community. Kiwan marveled at the way the community was lit up at night.. It made for a picture-perfect setting to a Beverly Hills Cop sequel. The architecture displayed in this community ranged from Mediterranean, to conventional, ranch and Spanish-style villas. This is a beautiful neighborhood, Kiwan thought.

They traveled deep into the community, turning corners and following curves. The deeper they went the larger the houses got. They came to a four-way stop sign and made a right onto a street named, "Palm Rush." It was a cul-de-sac with only four houses on the street. The street wasn't very long but one thing in particular got Kiwan's attention; the two houses in the middle of the cul-de-sac. It was the way they were built in an asymmetrical position to one another with an elevated glass encased walkway that connected the two houses. Amin drove to the circle in the cul-de-sac and entered the driveway on the right. The gate swung open to reveal a massive circular driveway crowded with expensive cars and parking valets. Kiwan noticed close circuit cameras mounted in many different places for security.

"Nice house," Kiwan said to his brother as they proceeded past the commotion to a five-car garage that veered off to the left of the house, which was situated almost directly under the walkway.

"You really like it?" Amin smiled.

"Yeah," his brother stressed, "but how can you party in the place you live? You've got to maintain some form of privacy."

Amin squinted his face into a frown and stared intently at his brother and laughed. "Yo, I don't live here. This is your crib!" Amin told him. He then pointed to the house that was joined by the walkway, "and that is Daddy Bo's crib. Daddy Bo had this place built a couple of years ago after he and Black Jack procured all of the lots on the street. I just use his place as a get away spot sometimes. Your place is for parties," Amin smiled. "Black Jack lives over there." He pointed to the first house on the street. "Whenever he's out here fishing, anyway. The other house belongs to the company but is vacant right now."

"Palm Rush Street. I should've guessed," Kiwan said, shaking his head.

"I told you, big bro, that money ain't shit. I have many problems but money ain't one of them. Let's go. This is your coming home party," Amin said.

The gesture almost moved the big man to tears as he and his brother shut the garage door and entered the long hallway that led into the house. The mood quickly turned festive. As they entered, the first thing Kiwan noticed was the music. Ludacris' "Move Bitch," was reverberating through the entire house. As he was walking through the hallway he almost tripped over a pair of legs. There were two of Murder One's rap artist getting their knobs polished by a couple of groupies. "Damn ..." Kiwan said aloud, trying to get their attention. Nobody moved, blinked or attempted to stop what they were doing. Kiwan instantly thought of Prescious and wondered where in the hell she was.

"Pay no attention, just keep stepping. Welcome to the industry," Amin told him as they entered the massive ballroom. Kiwan shook his head in amazement as his question of Prescious' whereabouts was immediately answered. She and Nina walked in from the double doors of the kitchen.

"Hola Poppi, mi cunado," Nina yelled to Kiwan, rushing to hug him. "Look at you, so cute, jefe de jefe," she told him.

There was no other woman on the planet that could make six foot six inch Kiwan Jovan Rush blush. Nina Rush was the only woman that could get next to him. She knew how to stroke his ego.

Amin went back in the hallway, addressing his artist. "Yo, as many empty rooms as we have in this muchafucka, you niggas got to set it out like this?"

"All the rooms are full! Even the bathrooms," one of them said.

"Fuck that, take that shit outside in your cars!" Amin demanded. "The owner of the house is here and he don't know y'all like that, so jet," he yelled. "Have some respect." The naked women scurried for their clothes sucking their teeth at Amin. "Yo, and teach those bitches some manners."

He went back into the ballroom where Nina was catering to her brother-in-law. She grabbed him by the arm and whisked him off to show him around his house and to mingle with his guests. Most of the crowd was from the old neighborhood and the south side of Houston, as well as some of the elite talent in the music business out of Houston's local music scene. There were also some of the Rap-A-Lot family as well as some executives from the Def Jam Down South crew.

The atmosphere was a mixture of formal and casual, a blend of partying and networking. There was plenty of music, drinks, drugs, food and sex. As Kiwan and Nina made their way to the staircase, a tray of golden colored marijuana passed him. He had never seen that before. "Acapulco gold," Nina said, seeing the look on his face and knowing he was curious.

Nina introduced Kiwan to a group of models from her agency and they all wore halter tops that had "Kiwan's Girls" written in rhinestones across their breasts. She also kept a photographer on payroll and the brother hadn't missed a beat. The entire thing was becoming too much for Kiwan, who had less than three hours of sleep since his release from prison.

"Here, take these," someone said, handing him some pills over his shoulder from behind. He looked and it was two yellow and black pills. "Yellow Jackets," the voice said. "They will help revive you." Kiwan turned around to thank the person and was surprised to see his childhood friend.

"Moochie!" Kiwan yelled and grabbed the man in a fierce bear hug. "Man, I thought that you had a life sentence," Kiwan said as he looked his childhood friend up and down. Moochie looked good. He and Kiwan were the same height and build, both of them had taken good care of themselves physically. Moochie was dressed from head to toe in Gucci. He had on a sweat suit that was black and silver with platinum and diamonds shining everywhere.

"Shit, your brother had plans for me! He hired an appeal attorney for me and he arranged for me to give back my life sentence. I had served six years on Darrington with Daddy Bo at the time my appeal was granted. They gave me time served and I walked!" Moochie was smiling from ear to ear, happy to see Kiwan and to tell him the story of his good fortune.

Growing up poor was common in the Trey but nobody begged. Everybody had a hustle, everybody except Moochie. Even kids had ways of getting money in the Trey. One day Moochie kept begging for Kiwan's candy and they ended up fighting all the way home from school. When Daddy Bo found out Kiwan got the worst ass whipping of his life, and from that day on Daddy Bo was Moochie's surrogate father. Since that time Kiwan and Moochie were like brothers.

But later in life Moochie found his trademark hustle. Everyone in Houston from the north to the south side; from Greenspoint to Missouri City - everyone knew that Kevin "Moochie" Butler was a stone cold-blooded killer. When Moochie entered a room it was as if it was the parting of the Red Sea. No one wanted to bump him, step on his shoes or offend him in anyway. Moochie had that killer instinct growing up. He would never back down from anyone, but under Daddy Bo's tutelage he learned to control his rage. He learned to command respect instead of demand it. Daddy Bo taught him that to make people fear him was not good because he would always have to watch his back.

"Damn, it's been too long," Moochie said excitedly.

"You look good, man," Kiwan said, smiling in amazement. "What are you into now?"

Moochie dug into the t-shirt under his sweat suit jacket and pulled out the Murder One pendant. "I'm your sister-in-law's personal bodyguard. When she let me," he said, cutting his eyes at Nina, who was busy yapping to a dark-skinned sister.

"I should've known. Man, a lot of things have changed since I left," Kiwan said in amazement.

"You ain't seen the half of it. Wait until we go on tour or jet setting in the summer time, hitting all of the industry parties! Especially parties thrown by Puffy, Suge or Snoop. This is mild compared to how wild it gets on the West Coast," Moochie bragged to his friend.

Mild? Kiwan looked around him as if he had just taken notice of the scene. Half naked women, music blaring, free flowing liquor, drugs. He couldn't imagine a party getting any wilder than this, but he guessed that with money anything was possible and those boys had major paper. They were papermade and with much paper comes much power.

Damn! That looked like Eve over there, Kiwan thought as he floated off in the direction of what looked to be his favorite female rap star. Amin appeared and startled him.

"Let's go, baby, I got something that I need you to be a part of."

"Wait a minute man; is that Eve over there?" Kiwan asked, looking in her direction.

"Yeah, yeah! Ain't no tellin who you'll see at a party that Prescious put together. You'll see her again at the album release party," Amin said, ushering his older brother in the opposite direction. They headed through the kitchen and out of the patio doors. They walked through the atrium outside of the kitchen and headed down a walkway that lead to the boat slip behind the house. A 130-foot yacht was docked to the pier.

"Man, don't tell me that you bought me a yacht too! Man, this is too much," Kiwan told his younger brother.

"My, my aren't we just full of ourselves! The yacht belongs to the company, fool. This is where I chose to hold a last-minute meeting tonight. This will give us the privacy we need," Amin said, shaking his head.

"Well, excusssse the hell out of me!" Kiwan said as they both burst out laughing.

They boarded the yacht as they passed Tony, standing there like a Greek pillar in the Parthenon.

Chapter 19

The 130-foot Miora yacht was tastefully decorated in hues of blue and mauve. The Queen Donetta, named after Kiwan and Amin's mother, had brass and mahogany accents throughout the decor. Ayanna and Black Jack sat comfortably in the saloon of the yacht, drinks in their hands, when the brothers walked in down the stairs from the deck.

When Kiwan entered the saloon of the yacht behind Amin, Black Jack stood to give the young man, whom he had played an integral part in rearing, a hug.

"Long time no see, boy!" Black Jack said, giving Kiwan a sturdy pat on his back. "You look damn good, son. We all missed you, especially this one here," he said, motioning to Ayanna.

Ayanna held out her hand for Black Jack to help her up. The anticipation of being around her old flame after so many years was written all over her face. As Ayanna arose from her seat, Kiwan stepped forward to give her a friendly embrace.

"Damn, nigga! You ain't seen me in ten years, give me a mothafuckin hug. I don't want that friendly shit, like you just met me," she fussed feeling his reluctance through his body language.

Kiwan stepped into the embrace and lifted the petite woman off the floor, spinning her wildly. Ayanna giggled. "Now that's what I'm talking about," she said. "Trying to hug me with yo ass all poked out," she fussed. "Now put me down so I can look at you!"

Where others had vision, Ayanna saw through her fingers. When Kiwan put her down, she stepped back and placed her hands to his face. She gently cupped his face, then slowly moved down to his chest and arms. Kiwan chuckled as she lightly squeezed his muscular biceps. "Nice," Ayanna commented as she moved slowly to his flat stomach. Kiwan felt weird as he stood there with mixed emotions about his ex-girlfriend. With a devilish grin Ayanna abruptly patted Kiwan's crotch.

"Girl!" Kiwan yelled as he jumped, his head almost hitting the ceiling. Everybody laughed at his response. As hard as it was for Kiwan seeing his high school and college sweetheart, he couldn't help but still feel butterflies in his stomach where Ayanna was concerned. He wanted to be bitter at her for falling off on him during his ten-year bid, but couldn't. In the beginning, her letters an support were what had gotten him through the days full of rage and despair. She'd promised him that she would be there for him. She knew the circumstances under which he had been confined were not his fault. She'd said that she understood! But in the end, she'd left, taking with her a piece of Kiwan's heart. Ayanna had been the only woman that he'd truly loved, other than his brother, Donetta.

"Come on, ya'll, let's get this party started," Amin said, ushering everyone to a seat.

Ayanna grabbed Kiwan's elbow and sat next to him. "If she wasn't blind, I would push her ass down," Kiwan thought, "grabbing on me like I'm her man, or as if she'd been down with me the entire ten years. Stop it, Kiwan," he thought, "she didn't owe you shit. She deserved to live her life, too, just like Amin. Maybe one day somebody will sacrifice for me, so I can get my life together," he concluded.

"Awight," Amin spoke, clapping his hands together for added effect. Kiwan jumped again! Amin smiled; he knew that Kiwan had drifted off to la-la land for a second. "Listen, Ki, let me put you up on game about why we're here," Amin explained to his brother. "Sometimes the three of us get together and have a 'trey-sixty.' A trey-sixty is a meeting of the minds, big bra. Me, Ayanna and Black Jack, sometimes Nina, but lately she's been tripping," Amin exaggerated.

That comment evoked an, "Oh, paleese," from Ayanna.

"Shut up, you," Amin said to her. "Anyway," he continued, "we get together and strategize after our monthly departmental heads' meeting, but sometimes we get together when something important comes up, like now," Amin pointed out. "The shit that Syon is trying to pull and with us trying to get that committee seat, we had to come together to decide the best course of action for the company. So where are we now concerning our masters?" Amin directed at Ayanna.

It was like switching on a computer when it came down to business with Ayanna Vincent. She switched roles instantly. Her posture stiffened, her etiquette became professional, and her mannerisms became distinctly different. Kiwan watched her intently.

"Okay, guys, here's the situation. I've been over this twice with Tisha. She says that Chad was correct in his statement that only a multi-platinum album will produce the number of units needed to fulfill the masters' clause in the contract. The good thing is that the clause doesn't specify that the artist has to be signed under the parent company, only that the numbers have to be distributed through the parent company," Ayanna smiled.

Amin jumped from his seat as if he was shot in the ass with a Desert Eagle 44 magnum. Black Jack and Kiwan eyed young Idie Amin suspiciously; they knew that he'd just had a revelation.

"Ayanna, are you thinking what I'm thinking?" he asked, pacing in front of the group.

"If it has anything to do with fucking Syon out of points for the next album I am," she sung out.

"Okay, okay, stay with me here, y'all. Follow me and hear me out," Amin said excitedly.

"Spit it out!" Black Jack said, a bit out of character, his surprise revealed in the way he dug into his pocket for one of his cigars while one still burned in the humidor in front of him.

"Yeah, here's the deal. Syon will benefit in every way if we fulfill this masters' clause. It's like this - if we do produce a multi-platinum album under the Murder One label, then they get to distribute it, make money, and they get money off the back end because they are the parent company. Though it's on a percentage basis, they still make out like fat rats because then we have to negotiate a price for cash pending the worth of the master," Amin explained, the wheels turning almost faster than he could explain.

"Now, let's say we don't do platinum numbers. Here's where we get fucked, because our distribution and label deal will be up. Without our masters we will be on our own without any royalties from the music that established this company. Then in essence we will be back to square one, trying to shop for a major to carry us. If we re-sign with Syon or anyone else, for that matter, then we still will be operating under another parent company without our masters," Amin said while pacing.

"Sit down somewhere, Amin, you making me nervous and dizzy and I can't even see you. Pretend we're at Syon in the board room discussing the price for the masters," Ayanna advised.

Ayanna was right, Amin thought. That was the main reason she was his personal secretary. She'd taught him a lot of correct business etiquette that she'd learned in law school. As hyper as he was, he took a seat, continuing to analyze the situation.

"So here's how we'll work this," Amin continued. "Ayanna, first thing tomorrow get with Tiffany Reed about ..."

"Tomorrow is Sunday, Amin," Ayanna reminded him.

"I wouldn't give a fuck if tomorrow was Easter Sunday, get her ass on the phone first thing in the morning. Why do you think I pay the woman $70,000 a year to head up the A&R department? If I wanted to wake her ass up out of the grave she better get up and ask what took me so long. If she don't like it she's fired, I'll give A-dray her job, I bet she'll make an extra day in the week if I asked her to," he stressed.

"All right, Amin, I get your point, please continue," huffed Ayanna.

Kiwan and Black Jack laughed. Amin was a muthafucka to work for when it came to business. He'd read the "48 Laws of Power" too many times Black Jack thought. It was a book that Daddy Bo had recommended to all of them.

"Awight, call her and tell her that we are going to go ahead and sign her young friend, K-flex," Amin instructed, fully in his element.

"Hold up!" blurted Kiwan, who'd been silent up until then. "What K-flex? You don't mean the young K-flex from Southpark with the platinum album out, 'Can't stop, won't stop?" Kiwan asked.

"Yeah, that's him," Amin proudly answered.

"I thought he was signed to Arista?" Kiwan wanted to know.

"He is!" Amin exulted, showing his pearly whites. Kiwan just shrugged his shoulders in resignation. He just let it go.

"I'll explain it to you later, big bra, but let's just say that he was uncomfortable in his present contract and I had to do a little regulatin for the dude because Tiffany knows his mother," Amin explained, with his chest puffed out. Kiwan just nodded his head; he got a picture of what his brother meant.

"Yeah, I get it. You think you Suge Knight or somebody," Kiwan laughed.

"Or somebody," Black Jack chuckled.

Amin shot his mentor the evil eye, as he puffed on a newly lit cigar. Black Jack had advised Amin to stay out of that situation because it could backfire on the company if somebody got hurt.

"Don't pay me any attention, man, I'm just from a different school. I would've done it differently. You can't save everybody with a fucked up contract. You'll be trying to save most of the industry," Black Jack voiced.

"Anyway," Amin continued, ignoring Black Jack. Very rarely did they disagree, but Amin had felt something with K-flex. He prayed that his intuition turned out to prove right, because only Cod knew that he'd made too many mistakes in judgement in his life.

"Listen, Ayanna, tell her to get in touch with K-flex, and make a note to Tisha to call Arista and get ahold of his manager. Also, shop around to the other four majors and ask about distribution set ups. I'll ask Tisha to see if she can line up a distributor in case we don't get the seat."

"Oh, we'll get the seat!" Black Jack stated with confidence and a smirk.

"So what we'll do," Amin continued to explain, "is we'll sign K-flex under our Murder One entertainment company, which cuts Syon out of the loop on them making money on the back end. The label deal that Murder One has with Syon has no bearing on the entertainment company. Those are two separate companies. We'll just get Syon to distribute the product and by the time they realize what we've done, the royalty checks will already be printed," Amin said, grinning like a cat still tasting the canary in his mouth.

"So you actually think they won't notice the small discrepancy," Kiwan asked.

"I seriously doubt it," Ayanna spoke. "We've done good business with them in the past with no problems. It would be something they wouldn't expect from us. Actually, I like the idea," she agreed.

Everyone in the room agreed. "Now what about this committee seat thing," Kiwan asked with genuine curiosity.

It was Black Jack's turn to put on a devilish grin. "The old bitch is trying to play hard. She's trying to throw us off, but I know better, I've been around too long. She's got something up her sleeve," Black Jack said.

"Why do you say that?" Ayanna asked.

"Well, dig these blues," he explained, sitting up a bit. "Here she is, a powerful Congresswoman, with virtually unlimited funds and resources, right? She introduces herself to me then pretends like she doesn't know who the fuck I am. Now that makes me think that either you're not on the ball as well as you appear to be, or you're playing with my fucking intelligence, or you're hiding something! Either way, it raises my suspicions."

"Could be nothing, could be something," Amin deduced.

"Maybe," Ayanna quipped.

"Find out!" Amin exclaimed.

"Another thing," Black Jack added. "Who tha fuck is this Nya chick?"

Chapter 20

The sun filtered through the haze of the early Sunday morning fog. The money green late model X-type Jaguar, with peanut butter colored leather interior and shining chrome 18" rims, pulled into the parking lot of Dot's Cafe. The small cafe was located off the 1-45 feeder, just past the Woodridge exit and catered to the late night and breakfast crowds. The driver of the Jaguar parked facing the freeway, and she cased the surrounding area for anyone tailing her. The restaurant parking lot provided the perfect view of the area, a panoramic expanse of parking lot and freeway. The feeder produced traffic in only the Southbound direction and she sat pretending to dig in her purse while actually scoping out cars as they passed. The parking lots to the left and right of the cafe were both empty.

Satisfied that she hadn't been followed, she exited the Jag in a haste to enter the cafe. As she came upon a black 600 Mercedes Benz parked directly in front of the door, occupying a handicapped parking space and with personalized plates that read "Sxy-Dex," she slowed. Keys in her hand, she skirted as close as she could to the car without stopping. The sharp metal key bore into the glossy paint and dug a gash neatly down the side of the Benz, and Prescious never broke stride. She loathed the owner of the car, wishing his front page obituary in the Houston Chronicle on a daily basis.

"Trick ass nigga!" she muttered. The crowd inside the cafe was a mixture of Hispanics and blacks. The Sunday morning rush crowded the front of the cafe and a long line of hungry patrons awaited their pre-church breakfast.

Prescious weaved her way through the crowd to the bustling waitress podium. "Excuse me!" she called out to the young Hispanic waitress that was preoccupied with a seating chart.

"Jes?" the waitress responded, without looking up from the chart.

"I'm with the Cunningham party," Prescious announced, her head on a swivel. The waitress abruptly looked up and spoke to another, older Hispanic waitress in Spanish.

"Oh, excuse me!" Prescious called out again, losing her patience.

"Ma'am, ju can just go look, we no seat by reservations," the elder of the two women spoke in her broken English.

Prescious abruptly turned on her heels and stalked off. The smell of freshly brewed coffee, eggs, frying bacon, onions and fried potatoes wafted through the cafe as Prescious walked around in search of her date.

Heads turned at the sophisticated beauty of the young vixen, despite the fact that she felt as if she looked rough due to her busy week. She was used to the life by now after seven years of ripping and running in the industry. After the party ended this morning at nearly 5 a.m., Prescious sped through the 45-minute drive from Clear Lake back to her condo, took a quick shower, changed clothes, fed her fish, and rushed back out to meet up with this asshole by 7 a.m. She did it all routinely, but not before popping a Black Molly to help her through.

Prescious tried not to think about the fact that she'd become addicted to speed just to further her career as she spotted the person she came to meet. She tried to look poised and confident to give herself the courage to confront the sadistic muthafucka.

Dexter Cunningham, assistant district attorney of Harris County and only child of Congresswoman Charlette Cunningham, spotted the beautiful mixed breed woman walking toward him. He stood to greet her, showing off in his off-the-rack suit in a pose he thought was cool.

As she drew nearer to the man her breath quickened and her feet became lead-like, but she forged on. She knew she had to get this over with. This had to stop. Dexter was slowly killing her. He had an iron grasp on her that she needed to break. Tears started to well up in the corners of her eyes as she reached him and he rudely stuck his tongue down her throat. He was rough with Precious, as always, grabbing and kissing her as if he were claiming possession. Precious wanted to throw up! His breath stank of the coffee he'd been drinking.

"So pretty," he complimented, stroking her face softly. She recoiled from his touch, looking around, noticing the envy on some of the faces of the men in the cafe. She sat down nervously in the booth across from Dexter. He smoothed his tie and unbuttoned his jacket, removing it to get more comfortable now that Precious had arrived. "Were you followed?" he asked while sitting back down. "I watched you pull up and I didn't notice anything strange," he told her, eyeing her suspiciously because of her silence. He rested his hand on her knee under the table and she instinctively knocked it off.

"Bitch! What is your problem this morning?" he hissed through clenched teeth.

Precious looked down at her silverware and fidgeted with her fork, resisting the urge to stab the shit out of him. "I want out Dexter, I want out now!" she blurted out in one rush of breath.

Dexter was taken aback by her outburst. He narrowed his black, beady eyes before he spoke. "You're kidding, right?" he squeaked in an attempt to intimidate her. "Let me tell you something, you tramp ass bitch," he scolded, his voice increasing in volume.

"Are ju ready to order now, meester?" the waitress wanted to know, her pen and pad poised.

"Un, un ... no, no ... give us a minute," he said, startled by the sudden arrival of the waitress.

"Ohkay," she said and sauntered off to resume her duties.

"There is no way out, you stupid bitch, not now, not later, not ever! Lest you forget and bite the hand that kept you out of prison," Dexter hissed with malice. "You didn't forget, did you love," he asked, reaching across the table and grabbing her chin. He lifted her head so their eyes could meet.

"No," she replied sternly, trying her damndest not to cry. How could she forget. At the tender age of 16, Precious Daynette Williams had been a professional hooker. She had been working for a pimp who went by Day-Day, and who had her working the resorts in her home state of Hawaii.

Never having known her father and with a Hawaiian mother who as strung out on crack, it was easy for a young girl, attracted by the lure of fast money and easy living, to fall victim to the cursed venom spat at her by a man who thrived on young souls.

Dexter met Prescious on one of his sabbaticals outside of the mainland. He loved to travel to different tropical islands and indulge his more primitive natures. Dexter was a freak. Upon being introduced to Day-Day in Honolulu's flourishing nightlife, the assistant district attorney, just out of law school, would always order girls and await them in his room to act out his freaky desires.

That was when Prescious entered Dexter's life. Despite all that she'd been through; it was the worst day of her entire life. Young, innocent, with her entire life ahead of her, her potential was spotted by Dexter who, like Day-Day, wanted to exploit that potential for his own personal gain, only in a different manner. Dexter fell for her on the very first night after sodomizing and abusing the young girl, subjecting her to cruelties and degradations she couldn't imagine. But it came with the job, or so she was taught. Dexter offered to take her from the life, but Day-Day had warned her that men would come from the mainland and promise her the world, men who wanted to steal her away from paradise just to put her in hell!

Those words rang true for Prescious even to this day. Not one to be rejected, least of all by some young prostitute, Dexter left his card with her in the event she should change her mind. He was clearly taken with Prescious, and specifically asked for her whenever he came back to Honolulu, which was often.

Day-Day knew that he had a gold mine in Prescious. He not only pimped her, he also used her to run drugs from Hawaii to California, figuring that her youth would bypass authorities.

Their luck ran out one day when Prescious was apprehended at L.A.X for interstate trafficking. She was caught with four kilos of heroin strapped around her waist. She tried frivolously to contact Day-Day, who always had another woman follow and watch Prescious. He knew of her situation 15 minutes after it happened and decided to completely disassociate from her.

The young Prescious' only hope was the phone number on the business card that she had accidentally kept in her wallet. The card read Dexter Cunningham, attorney at law, Ny. NY. The attorney practically leaped at the opportunity to help Prescious, knowing that she would be indebted to him. Dexter called in every small favor he had and even some added influence from his beloved mother who coddled the young attorney and refused to cut the apron strings of motherhood.

Dexter came to her rescue and even sent Prescious across the continent to New York with forged transcripts, cash, and a new start so that she could enroll into NYU. Having never been stupid, just naive, Prescious tried to put her past behind her and apply herself to her schooling. She worked hard and found that she had a natural aptitude for marketing and public relations. But as time went on, Dexter become more possessive and controlling.

After four years of being Dexter's slave, Prescious had had enough. She felt that she'd done more than enough to repay Dexter for helping her, but Dexter wasn't satisfied. He wanted it all, marriage and the whole nine yards. Prescious had other plans. Though Dexter had paid for her education, paid all her bills, and had taken care of her for the entire four years of college, he charged a price that Prescious couldn't afford.

Prescious' college buddies, Amin and Nina, whom she befriended on campus while listening to spoken word poetry, talked of leaving for Texas. Prescious thought it would be a good idea and had been saving all of her money for her inevitable escape from Dexter. She'd had it set up so that directly after graduation she would leave for Texas with Amin and Nina, who planned on getting married and starting a record company.

Prescious had jumped from the frying pan into the fire, because out of all the years she had been with Dexter, she never once had asked him where he was from. Dexter proved to be more resourceful than Prescious had imagined. By Dexter already being from Texas, he'd found it very easy to relocate once he found out where Prescious had fled to. He hunted her down and showed up on her doorstep one day, unannounced! He threatened to send her to prison for life if she ever tried to run again, thus starting the cycle of abuse all over again.

Prescious hid her pain in her work, helping to make Murder One the multi-million dollar record label that it was.

"I'm ... I'm ... scared, Dexter. Amin and Black Jack are smart. They are going to figure out that somebody is leaking information. It won't take long for them to catch on to me, man. I know they'll have me killed," she rattled nervously.

Dexter laughed haughtily as if Prescious was the dumbest person on God's green earth. He shook his head at her. "You are so stupid, hoe! You belong to me, in mind, body and soul. Nobody is going to harm a hair on that pretty head of yours, especially after I make district attorney. I can't even believe that you would doubt me. Murder One Records and any power that they wield now will be far surpassed once Ruff House acquires that seat. Then you can leave Murder One and work for them, making twice as much as you do now," he told her, cleaning his glasses as if they were steamed by all the hot air he'd been blowing.

This lame-assed nigga is really full of himself, Prescious thought. He is blinded by his own power, and he thinks that he can really protect me. Street power and political power were two different things, she knew. In the street, nobody gives a fuck who you or your momma is. You step over the line, you die. Dexter just didn't understand how these people play. The only law out there was the law of the land. He's been smoking too much of that damn crack, she surmised. His lips were turning black. Amin and Black Jack didn't joke about their livelihood or their loved ones, but trying to get Dexter to understand that was like trying to climb Mount Everest without a rope; it just wasn't happening!

Prescious shook her head. "Dexter, please, I'll do whatever, but not this. I'm not feeling this," she whined, hating herself for it.

"Yeah! I know you will, you'll do whatever the fuck I say, and I want your tramp ass to stay put. I need to know what's going on within that company. I refuse to let my mother's dream be tainted by Murder One. I know they are foul, I just have to find proof. And I know what it is," he snidely remarked. "You've been rubbing elbows with too many rap stars. You've been gappin your legs open for all those Hip-Hop boys and you think you're too good for me now," he figured, his voice getting dangerously soft like it always did before he had a violent outburst.

"But Dexter ..." she started to explain when he reached across the table and slapped her so hard that the entire restaurant stopped what they were doing and looked.

"Shut up! I don't want to hear another word," he shouted standing over her. He snatched his coat to leave. "I'll be by later on tonight for the usual," he informed her, shrugging into his suit coat. Dexter peeled off a hundred dollar bill from his money clip and threw it at her. He spat on her as he walked away.

Embarrassment set in before complete, utter shame overwhelmed her, and she erupted in a flood of tears that stained her very essence.

Chapter 21

The Darrington Unit's small visitation room was unusually crowded for a Sunday morning, Daddy Bo noticed, as he stepped out from the shakedown room and headed to the officers' desk to check in. All eight tables in the inside visitation area were filled, with the exception of one. Clyde was anxious to see his oldest son after ten long years of corresponding through the mail.

He passed by some brothers who he associated with who were visiting their loved ones and spoke to them and their families, wishing them a good visit. His state-issued boots were polished to a mirror shine, and his uniform was as white as a cottontail's ass, with enough pressed creases in all the right places for any four-star general. Daddy Bo scanned the visitation room for his son as he made his way in his nonchalant manner, which bespoke of age and wisdom.

"Hey, old-timer," Correctional Officer Christina Jarvis, his daughter's best friend, spoke, smiling a beautiful, innocent smile. She was a high yellow-skinned version of Felicia. The baggy TDCJ blue and gray uniform didn't do her curvy body any justice. Neither did the hat add any femininity to her facial structure, as her long sandy red hair lay pinned up underneath the black TDCJ cap. Daddy Bo loved the young woman's attitude. She did her eight and hit the gate, refusing to get caught up in the psychological degradation that prison officials insisted their officers practice.

"What's really good, kid?" Daddy Bo replied. "How's it flowing this morning?" he asked, reverting to his street lingo, which made Christina giggle. Daddy Bo had been determined to stay abreast of the happs on the street. It gave him hope in an environment where hope died with the first laid red brick.

"I'm cool, Daddy, but I'd be even better if you gave my phone number to that fine ass son of yours," she asked teasingly, but Daddy Bo saw the small scrap of paper between two of her manicured fingers. Daddy Bo liked Christina's style, so he took the piece of paper on the down low.

"He's outside waiting on you at one of the picnic tables," she told him. "Don't worry about the time limit, I'll fix that for you. Oh, and I talked to Felicia last night, too. She asked me if I would get a package to you. I told her that I would. I'll get it and bring it to you tomorrow."

"Awight, just come holla at me," Daddy advised.

"Have a nice visit, and don't forget to hook ya girl up," she reminded.

Daddy Bo stepped outside the door leading to the outside visitation area and almost got knocked to the ground when he ran into his son's burly chest.

"Pops, what's tha damn deal?" his son shouted, as he grabbed his father to keep him from falling. Kiwan grabbed his father in a bear hug and swooped him off of his feet.

"Nigga, put me down so I can take a good look at you" Daddy Bo chided.

"Man, I was just coming in here to see what the hell was taking you so long," Kiwan said, putting his father back down as they headed toward an empty table to visit. As they walked, Daddy Bo looked his son over from head to toe.

Kiwan looked like a million dollars. He wore a light suede mustard colored shirt by Evisu, black Versace slacks, a black Gucci belt with a chrome buckle, and a pair of mustard colored alligator skinned closed toe sandals. His neck, wrist and earlobes were adorned with plenty of platinum and diamonds. As they found a table somewhat free of bird shit and sat down, Daddy Bo told his son how he felt about his appearance.

"Son, you look like pure 'D' shit!" his father confided.

"What you talking about, Pops?" Kiwan questioned. But he already knew. His father measured a man through his eyes, not by how he looked or what he wore. Daddy Bo had taught him and Amin that a person's eyes told you everything that you needed to know about that individual.

"Boy, you know damn well what I mean," Daddy Bo fussed. "How many hours of sleep have you had since Friday?" he asked. "That's what I mean," he scolded, cutting Kiwan off, who was about to say something on his behalf.

"Listen, son, I understand that you're a grown man and you can handle yourself. All your lives I've let you and your brother pretty much make your own decisions, because as black men you all would have hard lessons to learn as it is. So you might as well learn at a young age. Now my thinking might have been wrong or twisted, but to me the best lessons in life are taught in living, not school. So in the streets is where you and Amin were educated. Hell, I'm proud of you boys no matter what, and I trust your judgements, but now is not the time for mistakes. Now is not the time to slack up. We are on the threshold of being powerful enough to make a difference to our people. Soon, son, we will be powerful enough that when we speak, they listen. They as in the system, our own people, everybody! If power is wielded correctly it could benefit a lot of poor folk. Call me a foolish old man, but I truly believe, and if you don't have something to believe in then you'll fall for anything. Son, you just got home from a ten-year bid. Your mind is fresh, your money is long, and you got that glow. Now is the time for you to step up and take the lead. Your thoughts are new and innovative. If you display your true leadership abilities, there's not a person associated with us who wouldn't follow you."

"But pop, I don't want to lead, I ..."

"Boy, shut up and listen. It's not about what you want any more, hell, you didn't want to do that ten years, did you?" his father asked, leaning toward Kiwan over the table. "So don't tell me what you want, boy, I'll knock ..." Daddy Bo said, shaking his fist at his son. "Don't make me do it to you boy," he joked.

"Seriously, son, you can't keep up with your brother and his idiot friends. Half of them fools are still out there selling dope. That shit is played out. Black Jack and I are depending on you to take this family to the next level. Amin has done the legwork but his discipline has waned. He's lost his vision and drive. The boy is not hungry anymore. He's fell victim to the life. Now it's your turn! And if you get to tripping, believe me we are grooming someone else with the determination and drive. But you have to be your brother's keeper. I won't be around forever, and neither will Black Jack. So you need to step up," his father told him, almost pleading.

"Just look at Nina your sister-in-law, take her for example. The best woman a man could ask for, bar none. She'll do anything, anything for your brother and this family; and she has. But your brother can't appreciate a woman like that, the money has fucked him up. If he was going to do this shit, he should've just kept selling drugs until he wound up getting popped. Money is a tool to be used to elevate your life. If not, then it will destroy you. Your brother wastes money every day on shit he doesn't need. Cars, clothes, jewelry, a bunch of bullshit," his father stressed.

"That shit loses value as soon as you leave the fucking store. But Amin can afford to play, you can't. So I implore you to keep your view from the outside and don't get caught up The industry has enough Idie Amins, Suge Knights, and Puff Daddies. They need more people like Russell Simmons, Spike Lee and John Singleton, and now like Kiwan Rush. Use the business to further your cause, don't let it use you. Your brother has created a monster that he can't even control." Daddy Bo paused and let the information sink in. He knew that his son would definitely take heed.

"Now let me explain this NCAAM thing to you. It's vital to the family and that goes without saying. Although we don't necessarily need the seat, it does speed things up for us. Without the seat it will take about 15 years and twice as many millions to reach our vision and your generation won't see it come to fruition. My grandkids will. But with the clout of the committee and that seat, we can see our family where we want to be in five years."

"Now, I don't expect to make parole on an aggravated life sentence. Therefore, Black Jack will have to represent us on the committee. Now my old friend is as militant as a black man can be, but that keeps the family balanced, because I'm as open minded as they come. To him those people are bourgeoisie and fake, but to me, just because they probably never have been to the streets or lived in the ghetto doesn't make them fake to the cause. I disagree with my friend on that note but we all have a common goal and individuality always brings out the best in a group that strives toward a common vision."

"Now that fucking Romichael and Ruff House Records are a problem, but I have someone working on gathering information on him now. This family will sit on that board. That will probably be the only way that I will make it home, son," Daddy Bo admitted solemnly.

For the next three hours, Daddy Bo outlined and explained everything to his oldest son. What he expected and the instructions concerning the committee were explained in minute detail. The entire visit Kiwan might have said maybe ten words.

The clothing line, production, entertainment, real-estate and various other small investments by the family were Amin's responsibility. The record label would be turned over to Kiwan. The family was playing for keeps. The thing that bothered Kiwan the most was the fact that Ayanna had been married to Romichael. No one had even bothered to tell him about it.

"Damn! Married; no wonder she had fallen off on me, and she didn't even have the decency to tell me," he thought.

Being honest and true to himself, that truth made him want to fuck with Ayanna, just to dog her out, but he had to be bigger than that.

"Did you hear me, fool?" Daddy Bo asked stridently, breaking Kiwan from his reverie.

"Huh; what did you say, Pops? I'm sorry," he apologized.

"I said that the pretty young lady at the desk in there is diggin yo style," his father smiled, passing the small piece of paper to him. Their time had expired an hour ago and it was time for Daddy Bo to go. He didn't want to take advantage of the situation. Before he left, the last thing he told Kiwan was that he loved his granddaughters, but he needed some grandsons. The two men smiled, hugged, shed a few tears and went their separate ways.

It pained Kiwan to go but he knew that he'd be back soon. Already, thoughts of getting his father home were on his mind. Hopefully, his father was right. Once Murder One procured that seat, on influence alone they would be able to get Daddy Bo freed. God willing it would be so.

Chapter 22

Business is slow tonight, Romichael thought, as he sat butt ass naked in his leather executive swivel chair. He was smoking a joint while getting a blowjob and a massage in his office in the back of his gentleman's club. Morris Day and the Time's "Gigolos get lonely too," played on the office entertainment center as he indulged himself. Romichael loved to indulge himself in such carnal pleasures. He chose to bed every woman who worked in his club. He kept at his side those who pleased him in the most special ways. At this moment a new girl who had started working for him Friday night was giving him some of the best head he'd ever had. She wasn't even using her hands, and his sexual release was imminent. Monica, his mistress, was massaging his neck while the new girl was massaging his knob with her tongue and mouth.

Damn! He felt his member swelling in her mouth as she picked up speed, sucking and bobbing her head. He knew that she felt it too, which was why she shifted her point of concentration to the head of his phallus. The explosion and release rocked his entire body, making him lose his grip on the blunt. As it fell, it burned him on his upper thigh. Romichael felt only the heat of passion instead of the burning physical pain. The orgasm that he was having nullified any other feeling as he moaned in joy and pleasure.

Monica noticed, and when he dropped the blunt, she stopped massaging his neck and picked it up from his lap. The girl drained Ro of every drop of cum as his orgasm came to an end. He leaned back and reclined in his chair, speechless. He was in another zone but he didn't want the young lady to know that she'd had that effect on him.

"Damn, love, what is your name?" he asked, his eyes still closed.

"You like?" she asked, as she sat on his desk with her legs spread open, revealing her soaking wet pussy. She began to flex her pussy muscles, making small smacking noises. Romichael smiled as he opened his eyes, thinking that this girl truly had skills. He was looking at her and what she had to offer while the smell of weed and sex permeated the air of his office. Monica, a brown-skinned vixen with the body of a professional volleyball player, sashayed around the desk and immediately bent down to begin lapping between the young girl's legs.

"Felicia," the girl whispered as she threw her head back, closed her eyes and grabbed the back of Monica's braided head in pleasure.

"Well, Felicia ... yes, I like, I like a lot," Romichael whispered in her ear as he stroked her hard nipples. The sound of his office phone ringing broke the mood. He cursed and looked at the caller ID screen.

"Fuck." It was imperative that he answer this call. It could be important. Romichael snatched the phone from his desk.

"This better be muthafuckin important," he growled into the receiver as Felicia pushed him back into the chair. She looked intent on getting off.

"Yeah, I ... I ... uh, I need to, um ... see you?" the voice on the other end asked timidly.

"Say, man! We ain't gonna play no bitch ass games with each other ya know where I'm at!" Romichael snapped.

"But, but, I ... wanted to make sure that it was cool to come by because it's important that we talk. The sooner the better," he said, almost in a whisper.

"Awight," Romichael said. "Come on over. I'll leave word at the front desk with security to let you in," he said, hanging up the phone.

If it's anything that Romichael Turner had learned it is 15 years of selling drugs and dealing in crime, it was to never, ever trust the telephone. He was in no mood for sex now. He wondered what the hell was so important that Dexter Cunningham had to risk coming to see him in person. Probably nothing, he thought, he knew that Dexter was a bitch. He liked to take his anger and aggression out on women and live out his freaky fetishes. Sex and crack - those were the assistant district attorney's vices, and that was why Ro had him by the nuts.

Romichael owned The Parlay Lounge, an exclusive gentlemen's club in the heart of the Montrose area of Houston, and thanks to Monica, the reason behind Dexter's frequent visits to his club, Romichael owned the bitch ass punk. He'd revealed his freaky habits to Monica, wanting her to beat and whip him, and Romichael had pounced. Together he and Monica had set up video tape recorders, wired for sound, and they caught Dexter in the midst of his explicit and devious behavior. When Romichael confronted him with the videotapes, the man broke down and cried like a bitch. Ro didn't threaten him for fear that he would run off or worse, maybe kill himself. If that happened he would gain nothing. Instead he coddled and befriended the man and catered to his freaky fetishes and drug habit. He gave him an all-access pass to all the gentlemen's clubs and industry parties. Ro gave him all of the women he could sleep with and supplied his crack habit. With this inside connection to the NCAAM committee, the seat was surely going to belong to Ruff House Records. With the seat, Romichael Turner's power, net worth and community status would triple. He would far surpass that of Murder One, and that self-righteous muthafucka Amin Rush!

Romichael knew that Amin, Black Jack and Daddy Bo were some powerful enemies to have, but he'd tried to ally himself with them. If he'd only been more patient. It was hard for him to contain the hate that he had for his goody two shoes wife and her handicap made it even worse. He had gotten tired of leading the blind bitch around and playing the good husband role. That was all right, Romichael thought. Now we'll see who's the man of the hour when I procure the committee seat! He was looking for a way out of the dope game and the seat was it.

After fifteen years and a few million, 10 to be exact, it was time for him to retire. He informed Cory, his partner, who handled all of his drug transactions, that he would soon retire from the business. The committee would be his way out and he would have the seat by any means necessary.

"Fuck Daddy Bo and the Rushes, fuck Murder One!" he yelled out loud, startling the naked women and interrupting their sex session. "Ladies, please excuse me," he said good-naturedly. Thinking about fucking over the Rushes always put him in a good mood.

"Monica, why don't you and the lovely Felicia go and do some shopping. I'll call you later. I have some business to take care of." Reaching into his desk, he pulled out two thick stacks of hundred dollar bills. He placed them on Felicia's thigh. When she reached for the money, he placed his hand on hers. Halting her movement, he leaned over and whispered, "stay close to Monica and it will in turn keep you close to me, which can do 'nothing but benefit you. You can be a valuable asset to the Ruff House Family. I like your style," he informed her, then kissed her in the mouth with lust and hard passion.

Chapter 23

Music is the essence of the soul. Music can catapult your emotions, taking them on a natural high or the depths of sorrow. Music tames the savage beast within us all, Kiwan thought, as he bobbed his head, driving down Highway 288, while listening to Scarface's "Mary Jane." He was tired from a hectic weekend with virtually no sleep. The wind rushed through the open windows and sunroof, invigorating Kiwan as the decibels of bass-filled music pounded his nerve endings and filled him with adrenaline. Kiwan had the surround sound system in the Escalade crunk to the max. He didn't think that he would be able to tolerate the breath-stealing wind that emanated from the woofers if the windows were rolled up, but this was his genre of music and he blasted it.

Kiwan grew up in the era when hip-hop and rap was born. Curtis Blow, Grand Masterflash and the Furious Five, Whoodini, just to name a few, were the artists he'd listened to as a youngster. He'd watched rap grow up, from the Crush Groove and Breakin days, to what it was now with 50 Cent and the G-Unit, and everyone in between. Kiwan didn't take anything from the talented artists who were out now, but if you went to a party with individuals from his generation, the way to get the party crunk would be to play some "Cindafella" by Dana Dane, or you'd play some L.L. Cool J, any L.L. Cool J! He didn't even want to mention gangster rap with N.W.A. and Houston's own Ghetto Boyz. It wasn't about the bling bling back then.

Of course, everyone wanted to make a living at what they loved to do, but being an avid fan of Brad Jordan's "a.k.a. Mr. Scarface," Kiwan knew the passion and hard work the man had brought to the rap game. Kiwan felt that after almost twenty years in the business of rap and hip-hop, Jordan's style of flowing and story telling was the best in the business, bar none.

Kiwan knew that Brad was in a category of his own, and was only recently compared with the likes of "the Lox," but he didn't have near the money that he was supposed to have. That was a trend in the rap industry that had afflicted the entire music industry - musicians getting royally fucked. Standard contracts needed to change, industry wide. All artists needed to be paid according to the quality of material they produced. If they deserved it, give it to them, and if a man could make money meanwhile, cool, Kiwan mused. Maybe his father was on to something with this NCAAM thing, he figured. His thoughts started to coalesce, giving him the beginnings of his own vision concerning his family's empire.

His thoughts were interrupted by a ringing throughout the truck, which seemed to be part of the song. But Kiwan had been locked up when 'Mary Jane' had dropped, and he didn't remember hearing a ringing on the song when he'd heard it on the radio. As the ringing continued, he knew that it wasn't a part of the song, but his onboard phone through 'On Star.'

"Damn!" he shouted. Now he wished he'd been paying better attention to Amin when he tried to explain the system the previous night, because Kiwan didn't have the time to pull over and retrieve the manual from the glove compartment.

"Fuck it," he thought, ain't nothing beats a failure but a try. He lowered the volume of the music with the remote, then pressed the blue 'On Star' button with the phone pictured on it above his rearview mirror. "Yo!" he shouted into the truck, snapping to the fact that he needed to roll the damn windows up.

"Hey, killer," a feminine voice cooed through the speakers."

"Cool," Kiwan though, that was easy. Now he could talk hands free. "Yeah, who dis?" Kiwan shouted, realizing that he didn't have to shout anymore since the windows were now up. He'd get the hang of this shit yet, he knew.

"Damn boo, that's how you answer your phone?" the sweet voice asked.

"Check this out, whoever this is, I'm not into playing games, especially now while I'm trying to drive, which is something I haven't done in ten years," he informed the caller. "So if I introduce you to my friend Mr. Click, it's nothing personal."

"Damn, I see your grouchy ass hasn't changed; you are still serious. Boy, this is Ayanna."

"Oh, hey! What's really good, lady?" he greeted. He wondered why he was happy to hear from her. "Girl, how'd you get this number?" he asked.

I'm your brother's personal secretary. I know almost everything Amin has because I'm the one who orders it. I ordered the truck you're driving and everything in it," she informed him.

"Oh," was all he could say. He still didn't know how the inner workings of a corporation as big as Murder One functioned. He made a mental note to educate himself on the subject.

"Well, anyway, boo, I was just hollering at you to find out what you got jumping off for the rest of the day? Oh, and by the way, how was your visit with your father?"

Kiwan couldn't help but beam at the thought of Daddy Bo. It gave him a warm and euphoric sensation all over his body as the love he held for his father emanated through every part of his body, manifesting itself as the huge, shit-eating grin plastered on his face. If Ayanna could see him she would know that he actually blushed at the question.

"Aw, shit, it was cool, ya know," he answered modestly, not wanting to be too emotional with Ayanna. She knew how he loved his father. They had a father/best friend type of relationship. "That old man is still looking good, even for his age. He doesn't have a lick of gray in his head and has a head full of waves, not to mention that he looks like he's been taking care of his body," Kiwan stated proudly.

"That's good, now if we can just get Amin over his phobia of prisons, then both of you can go to see him together. That would be something, wouldn't it?" she asked.

"Yeah, but we all know that ain't about to happen," Kiwan mumbled.

"Well look," Ayanna said, reverting back to the purpose of her call. "If you're not doing anything today, let's go to Sharpstown, like we used to, and I'll treat you to lunch."

Though Amin was tired and really didn't want to be involved with Ayanna so as to not open any wounds on his heart, Kiwan couldn't find it in himself to turn her down. He was also curious to find out what was going on in her life. Besides, he had a few odds and ends to pick up. He was basically starting his life anew. "Awight, where you at, I'll swing by and scoop you."

"I'm in the Trey at the studio. Murder One has a studio in the Trey off of Dowling Street, right next to Black Jack's detail shop," she told him.

"Damn, Black Jack still got that detail shop?" Kiwan marveled. Talk about longevity. He still remembered that detail shop from the days of his misspent youth.

"You damn straight, the studio is the brick building right before you get to the shop. You'll see his silver 745 out front and there's about a hundred motorcycles and cars out front. Your brother's Bentley is next door at the shop."

"Damn, A, who's all up there?"

"The people from Source are here doing an article on 'Idie Amin,'" she said. "Oh excuse me; the 'infamous Idie Amin,'" she corrected.

"Awight, I'm on my way, I should be there in about 15 minutes." Kiwan cranked the music back up full blast and let the windows back down. Scarface's "Fuckfaces" was on. The chorus played and Kiwan was immediately reminded of his father's message. He smiled a knowing smile as the chorus rang through the Escalade ..."You must be used to all the finer things/infatuated by what money brings/it seems to me you ain't gon never change/so all that's left is for us to exchange." The words played in his head as he floated down the freeway.

Chapter 24

It felt good to be riding through his old stomping grounds again. Kiwan did not go directly to the studio. Instead, he drove up Southmore Street and cruised around. He turned his music down a bit because, if he remembered correctly, the police were strict on noise pollution coming from vehicles with expensive sound systems. Especially if they thought that you were a drug dealer...racial profiling at its best.

The heart of Third Ward hadn't changed much, he thought, as he cruised by TSU, Jack Yates High, and Wheeler Avenue Baptist Church. The outer areas were what surprised Kiwan. McGregor Estates and Almeda Road had changed drastically. He had heard that those areas were going through the gentrification process. What disturbed Kiwan most was that the older, poor people had no idea what gentrification meant. The white folks came in and offered them a few thousand dollars for their property while they made a mint. To the locals, a couple of thousand was a lot of money when in reality it wasn't shit. For those who didn't sell out, they would be assed out anyway, because property taxes would soon be so high hat they wouldn't be able to afford them and would lose the property anyway. That is FUCKED UP!!! Kiwan thought. White folks were moving back in and driving black folks out.

He drove up Scott Street and came back to Elgin toward Dowling and passed Emancipation Park. It was a beautiful Sunday afternoon and his neighborhood was out in full effect, enjoyed the day. Sistas with cutoff shorts, sandals and sundresses grouped up watching the brothers play basketball, showing off their skills. It reminded Kiwan of the saying, "the more things change, the more they stay the same." He could remember a time when he used to rule those same courts. Those were happy and carefree times. Kiwan loved his neighborhood and the strong black roots they represented. Despite the crime, drugs and trash it was his heritage, his roots. In reality, there is no place like home.

Kiwan pulled into Black Jack's detail shop. He'd changed the name and theme but the layout was the same. It had been called, "Suds," but now it was named, "On the Block Detailing." Black Jack used young men who fit a certain criteria. Now he employed anyone in the neighborhood who was serious about a job. He donated half of his profits to his and Daddy Bo's youth organization. The detail shop was always busy, and it wasn't unusual to see celebrities, rappers, city officials, teachers; people from all walks of life pull into the shop to have their cars cleaned. On the weekends, Black Jack had "dope fiend Chester," on the barbeque pit, grilling burgers, hot dogs, beef, chicken and ribs. He provided sandwiches for his patrons, but if anyone walked off the streets and wanted something to eat he wouldn't turn them away. It was not about money anymore with Black Jack. It was about his community and his people. The time had come to give back.

Kiwan parked next to his brother's midnight blue Bentley as two young boys polished its chrome rims. Kiwan hopped out of the Escalade, turning off his ignition and music. The sound system at the detail shop was blasting Jay Z's "The Black Album" CD. The youngsters at the detail shop, male and female, were grooving to the music. Kiwan marveled at how a little music could do wonders. Everyone reacted to music in some way.

The two youngsters who were working on Amin's car approached Kiwan. The youths looked no older than eleven or twelve. "Say baby! What ... what cha' gettin done to this bad boy'?" the older of the two said, the younger one standing behind him bobbing his head to the music.

"I don't know, youngster, y'all gon do a good job? Ya know, hook me

up?" Kiwan asked.

"Do cows shit? Ya damn straight we gon shine and grind, baby!" the youngster answered.

"Awight, how much fo da works?" Kiwan asked, mocking the youngster.

"Wax or no wax?" the boy questioned.

"No wax," Kiwan said.

"I think, $75?" he said, scratching his and looking at his younger brother as though he was unsure of his answer. The younger brother nodded his head in agreement.

Kiwan pulled a knot of hundreds out of his pocket. The two boys' eyes bulged at the sight of so much cash on one person. "Urn ... mmm - mister, ya in the Trey. You don't need to be walkin round here with that kind of ched'ar," the youngest finally said.

Kiwan smiled and peeled off two C notes. "I know, baby," Kiwan said, mocking them still "I'm from the Trey. I don't worry about getting jacked," he winked, reassuring them. They both nodded their heads in unison. What's understood need not be explained, even to the youngest who was born and raised in the Trey. Everyone from the Trey was like family. Kiwan gave the youngsters the two bills.

"Now pay for two washes with details and both of you can keep $25 each. That means you will owe me one the next time I drive up," he told them. They pocketed the cash, thanked him, and returned to finish up the Bentley, eager to get started on the Escalade. They were about their issue and wanted to please the new customer they had just gotten, a high roller for sure.

Kiwan walked next door to the studio. It was surrounded by a chain link fence with razor wire around the top of the fence. There were security cameras posted all around the building. It reminded Kiwan of the prison he had just left. He was surprised that there were no attack dogs around. He walked to the gate within the fence that faced the parking lot, a camera recording all his activities. As he approached the gate he heard a buzzer. The gate to the compound swung open. He walked up the walkway and passed a row of tricked out motorcycles. He approached another door adorned with burglar bars. Damn, he thought, it must be a million dollars worth of shit in here. The burglar bars also had an automatic locking mechanism because as he tried the door, thinking it would be locked, the door opened with ease. He immediately walked up on two red nosed pit bulls that started barking as soon as he opened the door. They were beautiful animals. One was cocaine white and the other was a sandy red. Kiwan did not like dogs.

"Brutus, Barron, come here!" a female voice called out, as the dogs tried to get at the unfamiliar intruder coming through the door. The dogs obeyed the command and the barking subsided. Kiwan opened the door fully to see where they had gone. They were behind a desk that was in a reception area, and a short young lady held both animals by their collars.

"You can come in," she invited. He hesitated.

"Why are you holding them if I can come in?" he asked.

"They don't bite, they just bark and scare people. I'm holding them because they run outside the door and they'll knock the motorcycles over, because they like to play around them," the girl answered.

"Oh," was all he could say, not believing it. Never in the history of the Trey had anyone kept pits that didn't bite. But he stepped into the office and closed the door. He noticed for the first time that the young girl, a woman, actually, had the most beautiful hazel eyes that he'd seen in his life. they were eyes that bespoke a watchful awareness, and at the present they showed the influence of some good bud!

"Hi, my name is Sheba," she said, offering her hand as the two dogs walked to Kiwan and started sniffing and panting. "Go. Sit!" she ordered, taking note of Kiwan's hesitation. "You must be Amin's older brother," she said.

Kiwan could hardly answer. Not only was he captivated by the girl's eyes, but she had on a see-through mesh and lycra shirt with no bra. Sheba noticed that Kiwan had noticed and she smiled a seductive smile.

"Yeah, that's my brother baby ... I mean baby brother," he corrected himself, shaking his head. He finally looked up at Sheba and saw that the girl had a mouthful of platinum and diamond baguettes. "Damn," he thought. "She could almost pass the bill."

"They are in the back, in the middle of an interview with the people from Source Magazine," she told him, moving closer and jutting out her chest.

"Ahem," came a voice from the doorway leading to the back offices. "I see you made it and have met Sheba already," Ayanna said from the doorway, with her hand on the frame of the door and a snide smirk upon her face. Kiwan blushed, knowing that he'd been, caught in the act, but not knowing how the fuck she did it. She was fuckin blind!

"C'mon back here, Negro, before you get yourself in some trouble," Ayanna told him. Kiwan followed Ayanna to the back where the studio was. She walked directly back without being led.

"She must spend a lot of time here," Kiwan thought although it wouldn't have been hard for him to find his way himself, if he'd been blind, because all he had to do was follow the noise and the weed smoke that hung in the air like early morning fog.

The other area of the studio was a giant living room. It was complete with a huge crescent shaped sectional sofa that covered half of the room, two big screen televisions, coffee and end tables, several loungers, and play station connected to both televisions. The place was packed. Most of the people present were with the artist that were signed to the label. Kiwan could see the engineer's booth and 2min, Tiffany Reed, the reporter for Source and his photographer were sitting in there talking. From where Kiwan was standing, Amin looked very nervous. Amin verified his suspicions when she said that this was Amin's most important article in a major magazine. She told Kiwan that there were so many people in the studio because they were trying to finish a major project. She also said their artist Mister "is having a barbeque today. He is trying to promote his album's release, which is Friday, and he's throwing a party. So after the interview everyone is headed to his crib," she said, "Come on, let me get my purse, then we can go. That is unless you want to hang out with them and go to the barbeque?" Ayanna asked.

"Naw, let's bail. It's too damn crowded in here for me," he replied. Ayanna entered the engineer's booth to get her purse. Kiwan stood in the doorway and smiled at his brother. As always, Amin was decked out. He had on an old fashioned black and white pinstriped Pierre Cardin three piece suit and a black fedora with a gold tipped cane. Kiwan assumed that he was dressed to take pictures for the article.

"Sorry, Amin," Ayanna said, interrupting the reporter in mid-sentence. "I need my purse. I'm heading out to take Kiwan to lunch."

Amin was so enthralled with the interview that he hadn't even noticed Kiwan in the doorway. "Hey, big bro, you just in time. This cluck ass youngster is asking me about the feud between Murder One and Ruff House and if the feud is affecting our ability to make music!" Amin yelled. "I'm trying to tell the young brother that Murder One is still on track and will have another multi-platinum hit shortly."

"Do you care to comment about the allegations of the feud between the two Houston-based powerhouses, Mr. Rush?" the young reporter asked. Kiwan was new to the business and to politics. He did not want to say anything that would hurt Murder One or start any additional shit between the two companies. Besides, the way everyone was looking at him, he figured that they expected him to comment.

"Houston is big enough for everybody to make a living. There is no cause for Murder One and Ruff House to clash, especially since we are both a part of the same music scene. I have no doubt about Idie Amin being able to give the South another multi-platinum album. He's very talented and a musical genius!" Kiwan boasted proudly.

"Well, can you explain why he refused to join forces with Ruff House?" the reporter shot back, with a knowing smile.

Amin was about to speak when Kiwan stopped him.

"C'mon, man, be for real, playa," Kiwan said, chuckling. "That's like Source and Vibe combining forces! Do you think Quincy Jones would let that go down if he couldn't completely buy out Source? Hell, no!" Kiwan said, not giving the reporter the opportunity to respond.

"So can you see Idie Amin working with a noose around his neck and one arm tied behind his back? That's like pairing him with Suge Knight, or Lyor Cohen. It just ain't happening, homes. We got our own thang, our own family," he gestured to the crowded area outside the engineer's booth, where most of the Murder One family was congregated. "So now YOU tell me why he didn't merge?" Kiwan said as he looked at the reporter, smiling, pleased with himself. The reporter got the point and moved back to Amin.

Amin moved on to talk about a card he had up his sleeve that he was going to play in the near future. He just needed Tiffany to work out a few more details. Kiwan and Ayanna left as Amin finished up the interview. As Kiwan and Ayanna passed Sheba in the reception area, Kiwan tried hard not to stare. "It was nice meeting you, Kiwan," Sheba giggled as they were leaving.

Ayanna couldn't help but laugh at the big man's bashfulness. "Girl, you crazy!" Ayanna laughed.

"And we all know this ... OKAY!" Sheba said haughtily. They all laughed.

Chapter 25

Romichael sat with his legs crossed in one of the booths in the back of his club. His view permitted him every angle of the club, including the stage. He sat smoking some hydro, sipping on a glass of Remi Martin, while reflecting on what Dexter had just shared with him. Romichael leaned back to let the silence between them make the weaker man uncomfortable. Knowing that it would not last long, Romichael enjoyed Dexter's silence and uneasiness. Sade's "Cherish the Day" blared through the club's speakers as one of Dexter's favorite dancers worked the stage to the sultry sounds. But he could not get into his favorite dancers because of his present worries.

Romichael let a few more moments pass before speaking, as he watched - Dexter fidget in his seat. "Let me get this straight," he said, breaking the silence. "You mean to tell me that this bitch is getting cold feet on you? I thought you had her under control?" Romichael asked, gritting his teeth.

"I did ... um, I mean, I do, but she's more frightened of them than she is of me. I think that she is going to expose me," he said worriedly.

"Listen, motherfucka!" Romichael shouted. "You told me one thang and now it's something else. We cannot afford to lose our advantage over Murder One. They are well connected EVERYWHERE! By the time your mother starts to investigate, their tracks will be covered! They have the talent and resources to secure their independence from

Syon Music. We cannot afford to let this opportunity slip. They will capitalize on our mishaps. Trust this; if they win this seat, I will expose yo ass for what you are and it will ruin not only your career but your mom's as well. Now you make the call!" Romichael finished.

Dexter held his head down as if he were defeated already. Romichael was disgusted with Dexter. He'd have to take matters into his own hands. "Fuck it," he said. "I'll take care of it," he told Dexter in a dismissive tone as he got up to leave. He left Dexter sitting in the booth as he headed to his office. He did not want to embarrass the man, in the club, especially if they hoped for Dexter to become the next district attorney. "He is like a time bomb and if I push him he might fuck that up, too," he thought as he entered his office.

His right hand man, Cory, was already seated and waiting on him as Romichael stormed into his office. "What ya think?" Romichael asked.

Cory had been watching and listening from the office. Cory held the reins of Romichael's drug empire so that Romichael could be free to handle Ruff House and his other legitimate businesses. His opinion was always important and necessary in Romichael's eyes.

"Man, I think the fool is telling the truth. I really think that he can't handle the bitch. I know that ho and I don't think anybody can keep her in check. She's too well known in the business. She feels like she's above the laws of the streets," Cory confided.

"Yeah, but the nigga say he got dirt on the ho," Romichael countered. "If that's true, then why can't he control her?"

Cory hunched his shoulders. "You know how bitches are, man. She knows his secrets as well and she knows that he cannot afford for his dirty laundry to be aired. Bitches are very emotional and. devious," Cory responded.

Romichael faced Cory in anger, his face contorted with fury and said, "Man, we ain't got time for emotions. We ain't got time to play games! Fuck that bitch; she either roll or-gets rolled on. We ain't chasing cash no more, we chasing history. History that I intend to be a part of, Cory. If this bitch breaks not only will Dexter be exposed but the NCAAN seat will be in jeopardy. I can't let that go down!"

"Well, you know what time it is, then. Let's load up and make that trip to the Nickel," Cory said with his menacing smile.

Chapter 26

The crowd at Sharpstown Mall was heavy for a Sunday afternoon. There were mostly couples out browsing, as young, rambunctious teens hovered around the mall in different groups. It was that time of year, Kiwan reflected, that people were out shopping for shorts and summer clothes. Kiwan marveled at how little the mall had changed in the ten years that he'd been gone. Sharpstown Mall used to be one of his spots as a youth growing up in H-town. Other than a few new stores, some paint, some name changes of other stores he could recall, the place looked the same.

Kiwan held Ayanna's hand, guiding her through the mall, just like old times. Walking through the mall was much different than running through it with Precious. Ayanna was a different breed of woman than Precious. Kiwan couldn't put his finger on it, maybe because he hadn't thought too hard about it, but something wasn't right about Precious.

"Hey, does Precious have a boyfriend that you know of?" Kiwan asked Ayanna.

"Why?" Ayanna blurted, obviously offended. "Don't ask me about no other woman, Kiwan."

"Damn, I was just asking because she had a few bruises, and I thought maybe ..."

"Bruises, what, did you give her a cavity search too?" Ayanna sarcastically shouted. She was about to go off on Kiwan's ass because he was acting weird. He hadn't really talked to her since he picked her up, and that wasn't like Kiwan. After all, they had been almost married until he went to prison. So far she was giving him the benefit of the doubt after ten years away from her, but he was kind of pushing it.

Kiwan chuckled at Ayanna's apparent jealousy. She must've known that he'd slept with Precious. Good, he wanted her to be jealous.

"Look, Ayanna, you trippin fo real! We ain't together no more," he started, as they got on the escalator headed to the upstairs food court. People were starting to stare but Kiwan really didn't give a fuck at this point. He wanted to get this off his chest and he didn't care who heard. "You forfeited the strings you had on me when you left me and married that bitch ass nigga Romichael Turner."

"Is that what you think, Kiwan? You think that I left you?" Ayanna asked, her mouth set and her tone hard.

"Well, what the fuck do you call it, A? You stopped writing and stopped coming to see me. It was like you fell off the face of the earth," he said.

She crossed her arms over her chest and stood on the back of her legs, clearly agitated. "Take me to the truck. We need to talk and this is not the place," she announced.

Chapter 27

The Houston Arboretum was located off of 610 and Memorial Drive. Kiwan had never been there and wondered how Ayanna knew. He was tempted to ask but thought better of it. He didn't want to open a new can of worms. As it was, he hadn't spoken since they had stopped at Quizno's to buy their lunch.

The Arboretum was tucked behind a forest of trees as soon as you exited the 610 freeway. As soon as you made the right on to Memorial Drive, another quick right and you would be in the drive of the Arboretum's entrance. As many times as Kiwan had passed by the place on his way to Memorial Park, he'd never noticed it, that's how discreet it was.

Kiwan pulled the Escalade into the long drive of the Arboretum, which curved through a densely wooded area. The killing part of the matter was that if Kiwan looked to the right, he could see glimpses of the 610 freeway through the trees.

"You can park by the building on either side," Ayanna let him know.

What building, Kiwan was about to ask until he rounded the bend in the drive and a small, nondescript wood and glass building appeared.

"It's where they grow all different kind of plants for the benefit of science. I used to come here with A-dray and study. She used to get pamphlets and we'd walk the trails while she explained all of the exotic flowers. We did this when I was in law school, but I haven't been here in a while. Sometimes we'd bring a lunch and we'd picnic at one of the tables. It's a special place to me and I thought that I would bring you here and share it with you, not to mention that it's a good place to talk," she confided.

Kiwan was moved, but he had to play his hardcore role to the tee. He refused to be suckered again. His modesty would be guarded by the armor of God from this day forward.

"Oh," was all he said as he got out of the truck to help Ayanna.

Chapter 28

"This is ya boy, the infamous Deejay J-Delay out in the place to play, coming at you live out here in Tom Bass Park, where Murder One records is hosting a pre-album release bar-b-que for the boy Mister's upcoming sophomore album, "A New Breed Down South." Fellas, it's going down out here! We got the ladies out here looking fly, and little caramel motels running around, hold up ... let me stop a couple: these around-the-way cluck mavens ... hold on, lil mama, come on up here and give your shout out ... Just say your name and where you're from."

"What's up, H-Town, my name is Candy, representing that Greenspoint, and I want to give a shout out to my baby Gavin, my homegirls Tanish, Danetta, Crystal, Re-Re, Jaquanette ..."

"Girl, give me my damn mic back ... trying to shout out to the whole daggone H-Town! Look out, what's your name, ma?"

"Heeyy, what's up Houston, this is ya girl Kim, shouting out to that Mo City. Willowridge in tha house!"

"Are ya'll enjoying the festivities?"

"Yeeesss!"

"You see, that's love, that's love, so you know it's all good out here at Tom Bass today. The sun is shining, the wind is blowing, and so are some of the, you know, fellas! Anyway, ladies, we got the ballers all out here on slabs, the bikes rolling, it's going down! So come on out and get your bar-b-que on. No cover charge, no admission, it's free! That's right, I said free. There's going to be live performances by Big Moe, lil Flip, Mister, Quan, Devin the Dude, and Tela, as well as a $500 wet t-shirt contest. So make your way and show some of the H-Town love as these boyz wreck tha stage. Wait a minute ... Hold up ... Oh oh! I see Slim Thug and his crew rolling up in them cars that don't speak no English, baby; that's right. They got the 20s and rolling in them foreigns. I see a 600 Benz and a couple of Jags in the line, as well as them Southwest Gorrilla's pulling up behind them with that red line on display. Man, Tom Bass is off tha heezy fo sheezy, so come get your play on while you still can, cause I'm about to put some serious parking lot pimping in effect. Once again out here at Tom Bass Park it's ya boy J-Delay live and in full flavor. Matter of fact, the next 50 cars to pull up are going to get free t-shirts, bumper stickers and CD packs, courtesy of the station that will play what you say, KMJQ, Magic 102, Houston/Galveston, Jamz!"

"Yo, kinfolk, did you hear that?" the young man asked his best friend.

"Yeah, nigga, I heard it. I'm sitting right here next to you, fool! Pass that mothafuckin blunt," his friend demanded.

"Here," the young man said, passing him the oversized joint. The youngster reached into the pocket of his Pelle Pelle jeans to retrieve his cellular phone. "Call Mike," he said into his automated voice programmed phone, while fingering his $65,000 diamond encrusted Ruff House Records pendant.

The phone rang twice before it was answered. "Yo, let me holler at Mike," the youngster demanded. After a short pause, Romichael Turner was on the other end of the line.

"What's up, youngster?" Romichael barked into the phone, chewing.

"Say, I just heard on the radio that Murder One is out at Tom Bass Park today."

"Oh, yeah!" Romichael replied, the remnants of a slice of pizza in his mouth. He finished chewing before he spoke. "Listen to me very carefully," he said, in a slow, methodical tone so youngster would understand. "You and the boys out the bottom need to get together and roll on through there and liven up the festivities. Let em know that

Fifth Ward can roll, too. Make em dance, just take care that y'all don't get rolled on," he instructed.

"Cool, I'm on top of it now. I'll let Duck know so he can give us some dancing shoes," the youngster told him.

"Awight, and come by the house later on. Duck should know where," Romichael said, smiling from ear to ear, stretching his cherubic face.

"Yeah, bet! Peace out," the youngster signed off.

"Come on fool, we got a party to liven up," Youngster told his friend, who raised up from the couch in Youngster's living room, and adjusted his shoulder holster, two H and K MP-5 automatic pistols hanging menacingly.

Chapter 29

As Kiwan led Ayanna down the marked and wooded trails of the Arboretum, his mind relived the pain and heartache of his many sleepless nights and lonely mornings without his high school sweetheart. The pain of betrayal swirled in and around his heart and mind as he held her hand.

"Kiwan, why do you hate me so much?" Ayanna asked warily.

"What? I don't hate you, A. Why you ask me some bullshit like that?" he wanted to know.

"I can feel it, K. You're squeezing my hand and you're walking too fast," she let him know.

"Oh, I'm sorry, A. Man, I just spaced out for a second ... It is pretty out here," he noticed, searching the skies as if they held the answers to life.

"Come one, Ki, let's not kid one another, let's get this out in the open and off our chests. Because beating around the bush won't solve shit. Should I go first?" she asked, stopping in the middle of the trail, looking in the direction of Kiwan's face.

"Come on over here and let me tell you," he said, as he spotted a bird-watching stand with a bench underneath.

Kiwan set the Quizno's bag down and they sat on a sanded, pinewood bench next to one another. "No holds barred, Kiwan, I'm a big girl, I can take it," Ayanna said, her voice breaking up with unchecked emotion. She demurely placed both of her hands in her lap. Kiwan knew this to be a for-sure sign that she was nervous.

"Man, A!" Kiwan exhaled, running his hands across the back of his wavy black hair. He didn't want to hurt her, then again, he wanted her to feel a little of what he felt. He cleared his throat before he started.

"You just don't know how it feels," he began, "to have to try and struggle and fight for what you love, what you believe in and every fuckin thing that you stand on with both hands tied behind your back. Nobody believed that I was innocent, A. Everyone just assumed that it was my dope. Even Daddy Bo thought that I had fucked up. He never said so, but in my heart I felt that he did. Do you know how that makes me feel? Even though I was moving weight at the time, everyone just assumed, everyone but you, A. When you told me at the hospital that you knew the dope wasn't mine and that I was innocent, that meant the world to me. I wanted to marry you right then, Ayanna, I swear I did. But then I thought, what the fuck could I offer her. There I was, a washed-up jock who's only source of income was drugs. No college degree to fall back on, nothing. So how could a nigga like me take care of a blind wife? Then when you promised me that you'd be down with me for the entire ride, no matter what, I laid in that hospital bed and swore on my mother's grave that I would suffer any indignity, any indecency, anything, just as long as I had a wife like you to come home to. I made up my mind that day that I would finish my degree, no matter how long it took. There wasn't a day that passed that I didn't think of you, my dad, my brother, Black Jack, my hood. I would stare at the bare walls after you left me and try not to hate my life, my brother, ... you," he solemnly told her, dropping his head.

"I wanted to scream myself into delirium some days. I could do nothing but workout and write poems. I was focused on pain and thought that this was God's funny way of punishing me for shit that I'd done in the past. I questioned the reasons of why you left me. Since you didn't say why you left, I just made up a few of my own. I told myself that you left to move on with your life. You had been oh so crazy and in love with me that if you would've stayed you would've been stagnated and I would've scarred you emotionally. I told myself that you didn't want to see me suffer, that was the bitch ass excuse Amin used to not come and visit. I wanted to know who you were with, why no one would discuss except to tell me that you had graduated law school, or that Amin had hired you."

"Man, Ayanna, so many what ifs and could've beens had run through my mind plenty of times in the course of those years. What if we had married before it happened, would you have stayed? What if we had kids together? What would they look like," he chuckled. "Who would they favor the most, their mother or their father?"

"It was killing me, Kiwan," Ayanna blurted out. "I was so hurt and confused and devastated, I almost dropped out of school. I went into a shell," she attempted to explain. "I wondered what other hardships I'd have to face. I was weak, Kiwan. I just wasn't strong enough at the time. Do you realize that you were my first love, my first steady boyfriend, my first kiss, my first fuck," she giggled, tears streaming down her face behind her glasses.

"All I knew was you, Ki, and when someone else showed interest in me, I flipped. I felt renewed, I felt free, Ki. I don't know how to explain it. You weren't a burden, but you weighed on me physically, mentally and emotionally, and I didn't know what to say or how to say it," she cried.

"I'm a man, A. In a sense I've been one since the death of my mother. I don't take too kindly to having my heart, my love and my trust violated. A black man goes through enough in this world without having to deal with humiliation and betrayal from the ones he loves. I was dedicated to you. I would've laid down my life for you, Ayanna. I don't think there's a greater love than that. You could've talked to me, I would've understood. Understanding beats the world, Ayanna, and my world was flipped upside down because I didn't have any. We didn't have to stay in a committed relationship. We were friends before we were anything else. I just needed your support. I would've been content just to see you happy. Every woman needs a man in her life who she can depend on without any strings attached. If it can't be her father or brothers, then a good friend, at least."

"I felt that I was that man, A. sisters are always crying about a good black man, but they always fuck over the good ones and wonder why we go bad.

Don't get me wrong because I know that I have my doggish side, too, but for the most part it was all about Ayanna Vincent. In a million years I never would've thought that you would fall off. First you were there, then poof, you adopted a Chinese name, Wan Gon," he expressed, revealing the true ills of his heart.

"I know, Kiwan, I know baby, and I'm sorry, I apologize," Ayanna sullenly spoke, raising her hands, trying to feel for Kiwan's face. She started to sob uncontrollably as she placed her hands to Kiwan's face and felt a single tear on his cheek.

"I was young and inexperienced. I just didn't know, Ki," she sobbed.

"You know what, A? I don't harbor any hard feelings or a grudge, but we could never be together again because I know what you'll do when the storms of life hit ..."

"Don't say that, Kiwan," she blurted through her tears, with her hands still on his face.

"Maan, A; I ain't tha nigga with a million dollars handed to him on a silver platter, I'm not accepting mine like that. I'm that nigga capable of making his own million his own way, baby girl. The only thing is, is that you didn't stay long enough to find out. What is a woman really willing to sacrifice to find and keep the good man that she searches for?" Kiwan added, really piling it on. He'd fantasized many a night about pouring his heart out, and now that he had the chance, he didn't want anything left when he finished. "You knew I wasn't going to be gone forever. I never wanted you to be locked up with me, I just wanted you to be with me while I was locked up. Once was enough, Boo! I have joined the fraternity of the good niggas gone bad," he whispered.

Kiwan's heart literally hurt as he watched Ayanna cry. He didn't want to hurt her, but he was a scorned man and needed to get that extra baggage off his shoulders so that he could heal and move forward. He was about to reach and hold Ayanna to let her know that his friendship with her was everlasting and unconditional, when her cell phone rang.

She jumped, startled at the loud tone of the phone in such an intimate setting. She wiped her eyes and nose, sniffled a bit and retrieved the phone, reluctantly, from her purse. "Hello," her voice cracked.

Ayanna listened a moment, as Kiwan stood up to stretch the tension from his body. As he yawned and stretched his legs, he heard a loud thump. When he turned around Ayanna had passed out, the cell phone open in her lap.

BOOK II: 'INDUSTRY SEX'

Chapter 30

Hermann Hospital, which was located in the heart of Houston's Medical Center, is world renowned for its trauma center. The normally overcrowded emergency room, which was usually packed with gunshot, stab wound and burn victims, was in total chaos as victims from the Tom Bass Park shooting were ushered in.

This time, Kiwan really was dragging Ayanna along through the crowded corridors of the emergency room, and she didn't complain one bit.

Upon finding that her baby sister had been shot, Ayanna truly feared the worst. "Anybody but A-dray," Ayanna had cried the entire way to the hospital.

On the way to the hospital, Kiwan had violated every major and minor traffic law, knowing that it was by the grace of God that they had made it there safely. Jogging through the corridors of ailing and dying people, with intercoms screeching code blue's, smelling acrid blood and antiseptic, Kiwan said a short prayer that the young woman would be okay.

"Nurse, can you tell me how I can find my, uh ... sister-in-law? Her name is Andrea Vincent, and she was just brought in," he asked, on the borderline of becoming frantic. He willed himself to calm down. The short, chubby nurse, a grim expression on her face, had been looking down at a chart when Kiwan stopped her in the hallway.

"I don't know, sir, if she was just brought in, then you might want to check with some of the paramedics because it's likely that she hasn't been registered yet."

Just as the nurse was speaking, a gurney was being rushed past them by two paramedics, with two nurses hot on its ass. Kiwan spotted A-dray's angelic face upon it. Had it not been for the blood all over her neck and torso, Kiwan would've sworn that she was sleeping. After not having seen the child since she last visited him with Black Jack two years prior, Kiwan could spot the girl a mile away. That's how much love he had for her. A-dray had that effect on everyone who knew her.

Nina and Black Jack, who had ridden in the ambulance with A-dray, spotted Kiwan and called to him, Nina's voice piercing through the noise. "Kiwan! How in the hell did you guys beat us up here?" Nina asked. Holding out her arms for an embrace, Kiwan saw that Nina had also been crying. He had to let go of Ayanna's hand to hug his sister-in-law. When Nina had buried herself in Kiwan's loving and supporting embrace, she broke down in a sobbing heap. Kiwan had to pick her up and carry her to a seat in the hospital's emergency waiting room. Black Jack and Ayanna went ahead to A-dray's bedside, both eagerly anticipating some positive word.

Kiwan sat Nina down and let her cry on his shoulder for a minute before he rose to get her some tissue to compose herself. When he returned he handed her the tissue to wipe her eyes.

"Talk to me, sis, what happened out there?" Kiwan demanded. Nina wiped her eyes and blew her nose.

"Well," she started, fidgeting with her tissue. "Everything was going well. Lil Flip and Slim Thug was free-styling with Mister, and A-dray was sitting on one of the stage speakers. I was at the booth we had set up counting some money. All of us were there; me, Black Jack, Amin, Moochie, Tony, all of us. Security was tight," she blubbered. "I don't know exactly, but I heard an engine rev, then gunshots rang out, I don't know who they were shooting at. You know lil Flip got shot before, that's who they could've been after, but a lot of people in the crowd was shot. Somebody said that a blue Expedition was where the shots came from, but I just don't know."

As she tried to explain, the already frantic atmosphere of the emergency room went into over load as the entire Murder One family mobbed into the emergency room's waiting area, with grim and dire expressions carved on their faces. Amin led the charge.

It was as if the brothers were reliving their reunion of the ten-year separation as they embraced without shame. It wasn't spoken aloud, but both men were glad that the other was unharmed. They lived for the day that they got to reunite their small family unit, despite all of the obstacles they faced. After Amin hugged his brother, he embraced his wife, making sure that she was emotionally all right, taking her off to the side. Moochie stepped forward to till Kiwan in on what they knew.

"What's up, Mooch, holla at me, man. This whole scene is fucking me up. I don't know what tha hell is going down around here. All I know is that me and Ayanna was at the Arboretum chillin, and Nina calls. Ayanna had passed the fuck out so I picked up the phone and Nina said that A-dray had been shot and that they were on their way to Herman. I got up here so fast that we beat the ambulance," he said.

"Maan, we don't know shit, all we know that it was a blue Expedition that did the shooting. We don't know why or who, the only thing we can do is wait. Whoever did it, if it was a hit, then they'll strike again," Moochie said. "Meanwhile, we gon get geared and ready for they ass. We just got to be careful, cause the po-pos is sniffing around. That's what took us a second to get up here. They tried to block the park off and we had to answer a few questions before we left."

At that moment, Black Jack came in and announced that the doctor said that Andrea was stable and had pulled through the worst. It was up to her now.

The whole crew cheered and clapped, sending the entire waiting room into an uproar. Even people who didn't know A-dray clapped and cheered her on, hoping for a successful recovery.

Andrea's shooting had been the result of a stray bullet fired too high from an automatic weapon. The shooter had actually fired too high into the crowd, and his bad aim had resulted in many people either shot or grazed in the head. A-dray had actually been lucky. Had she not been sitting on the speaker she could possibly be among the few souls that had been shot in the head or face. Many people were injured, not only in the shooting, but in the aftermath, when they were trampled and stomped by the hysterical crowd.

Andrea had been hit by two bullets. One had gone through her upper left shoulder, and one had embedded itself in her abdomen, below her left lung. She also had suffered a concussion and bruised ribs from flipping backwards onto the stage from the impact of the bullets, which had knocked her off the speaker.

Silence had spread through the crowded waiting area when a slew of uniformed and plain-clothed police officers entered, with none other than Congresswoman Cunningham and her entourage in tow. She walked directly to Black Jack in her serious no-nonsense, brisk manner. Black Jack could see the concern etched into the lines of the Congresswoman's forehead. He immediately spotted the blue-eyed sister among the Congresswoman's aides and assistants.

"Mr. Vincent, I was on my way to Washington when I heard the news. Can you please fill me in on what happened? I am deeply concerned for the young lady," she asked.

"Oh, so now you know who I am," said a deeply angry and upset Black Jack. "That's nice. May I ask how you found out that my child was shot? We told the police not to release that information." Black Jack didn't like the way she approached him in her accusing and bourgeoisie manner.

"That's neither here nor there, Mr. Vincent. The important thing is that we apprehend the party or parties responsible for this unfortunate incident. The police do not have much to go on. We would like to know if you or anyone here knows anything that would help further the investigation and assist in catching the culprits.

Black Jack was almost speechless. Almost. "Nobody in here knows shit, Congresswoman. And if we did, you'd read about it," he snapped.

She read the message implied in his words. "I would think that vigilante justice would be a part of your past, not something a man of your age and position would stoop to now, especially since you and your company are trying to elevate everyone concerned with Murder One to a higher plateau. Now is not the time for thugs to take to the streets, spraying bullets in a misguided attempt to redeem honor and save face. If you don't care enough to ..."

"Say, man, fuck that old bitch, Black Jack," yelled out Jamarcus, A-dray's youngest brother, who had to be restrained by his other brothers. He had tried to run at the Congresswoman, who was clearly insulting the entire family.

"No! Chill out, Jamarcus," Black Jack warned. I got this," he addressed the irate young man.

He turned to face the Congresswoman with tears in his eyes. He nodded his head a few times before he spoke, stroking his salt and pepper goatee.

"Charlette, you seriously have me fucked up!" Black Jack stated with icy calm, so much so that it gave everyone in the room chills. "I don't know what rules you live by or what reality you live in, but where I'm from, there are certain morals and principles that we live by until death do us part. So I'm sorry if what we live by conflicts with your high and mighty rules of the way life is supposed to be, but I will not compromise what I believe in, what I live by and what I die by for you or nobody else in this room, not even my own child, because if you don't have anything that you'll die for or anything that you believe in, then you'll fall for anything. And I did not get where I am in life by falling for whatever is fashionable. So if that type of attitude is not prudent or acceptable for you and your committee, then you and the rest of your sheltered, pompous, brown-nosing Negroes can suck my shriveled up old dick, he stressed, walking off to get some fresh air, leaving the Congresswoman looking super stupid. Everyone affiliated with Murder One walked off with him.

Black Jack thought that he had just blown the seat when in all actuality he gained the Congresswoman's respect.

In the parking lot of the emergency room's exit, Ayanna walked up to Kiwan and asked if he would take her home. As they left, hidden behind a waiting ambulance, Prescious watched them leave, envy and regret evident on her beautiful but strained features.

Chapter 31

"Where you living at now A?" Kiwan asked Ayanna as they headed down Main Street toward the 610 freeway.

"Oh, when me and Rom separated I bought a house in Katy and moved A-dray and Jamarcus in with me," she said softly, wiping tears from her eyes. "Do you know that that silly ass child drives an hour to school and back every day? She refuses to attend any other high school but. Jack Yates. That girl is so headstrong and I love her to death," Ayanna said.

"Man, she'll pull through, "Kiwan stated, really and truly believing the words he spoke.

"I know, Ki, but it's hard, knowing that she's laid up in a hospital. I can just imagine how she looks. I'm glad I can't see my sister like that."

Kiwan started to laugh to himself.

"What's funny?" Ayanna questioned.

"Now, I just remember that when I used to come by the house when we first started college, she was only five years old, but that girl was bad!"

"She sure in the hell was," Ayanna giggled. "Do you remember the time she locked your ass out of the house in Third Ward when you were baby sitting her for me?"

"Yeah! Maan, I was so embarrassed when all of y'all got home. That girl was something else. And she was smart as hell, even back then."

"And you couldn't keep a diaper on her little pissy tail. She would always take them off and shit behind the damn sofa," Ayanna remembered.

"Damn sure did," Kiwan blurted as they both roared with laughter, strolling down memory lane. When the laughter subsided there was an awkward moment of silence in the Escalade.

"You know, for what it's worth, Kiwan, I do love you. Always have, always will," Ayanna softly said.

Her words confused Kiwan. Though they were words that he'd been longing to hear for ten years, they went against his resolve to get Ayanna out of his system. In prison he'd sworn not to get involved with her anymore, no matter what, but when you're faced with the actual situation, what's in your heart is what manifests itself, and it was confusing him. He did the best thing he could think of in his present situation, one that he'd dreamed of and had played out in his mind on many, lonely nights. He ignored her, not trusting himself to speak, and pressed the button activating his CD changer. The surroundsound system in Kiwan's truck came to life with the sounds of R Kelly's "T.P.Z. Dot Com," the song "Three Knocks" flowing through the Escalade.

R Kelly's music didn't do anything to make Kiwan's situation better. But it did relax and clear up his thoughts for the time being, as the rest of the 30-minute drive to Katy was ridden to R Kelly's music.

Ayanna didn't know what to do concerning Kiwan. Maybe she should just let him go, she thought. But they'd been through a lot together, and other than Romichael, she'd never really struggled with any other man. She was vexed by a restless desire for a change between the two of them, and cry was the only thing that she could think to do. She thought maybe that fighting for what she believed in would be a solution to her problem, because if there was anybody Ayanna truly believed in, it was Kiwan Jovan Rush. Enough tears for one day, she thought. Tonight she was all cried out. She'd get some rest and go to see about A-dray first thing in the morning.

Kiwan exited off of Fry Road in Katy. Ayanna gave him explicit instructions to the gated community she lived in, called the Lakes of Kelliwood. The neighborhood reminded Kiwan of his newly acquired

Clear Lake estate. The homes were all done with a touch of neo-gothic flavor, he noticed. Ayanna directed him to a huge stucco and terra cotta style manor with a round drive in front. In the center of the round drive was a picturesque fountain of an African maiden carrying a water vessel atop her head, spouting illuminated sea green water.

When Kiwan pulled up to the huge double doors of Ayanna's home the doors flew open. A huge golden retriever bounded to the passenger side of the truck where Ayanna sat and stood there, placing his paws on the window of Kiwan's brand new truck.

An oddly familiar face stood at the entrance to the house with his hands on his hips and whistled. "Get down, Duke, bring your yellow ass back over here," he yelled.

Ayanna opened her door with minimal difficulty and Duke immediately jumped into the truck, right in Ayanna's lap. His tail wagged frantically as he tried to lick, her face.

"Duke, stop! You act as if I've been gone for years," she giggled, pushing Duke away. The dog was Ayanna's seeing-eye dog in training, along with being her friend and her companion. She'd never had a dog until she and Romichael split up. It had been A-dray's idea.

"Is that you, Miss Ayanna?" the man in the foyer asked.

"Yeah, Chester, it's me," she replied as Duke finally climbed off her and out of the truck, padding reluctantly toward the house, looking behind him to reassure himself that Ayanna was following. Convinced that she wasn't moving fast enough, Duke sat on the steps leading to the door and waited for her.

"No wonder Duke was acting so crazy, I just thought he wanted to go outside," Chester commented. At the mention of his name, Duke's ears perked up, but his focus remained intently on Ayanna. He whined, then yawned.

"Well, I'll be damned," Kiwan exclaimed, finally recognizing the wispy figure at the foyer. "Dopefiend Chester!" he shouted, getting out of the Escalade and greeting the most notorious shit starter that Third Ward had ever known.

Dopefiend Chester had done everything on God's green Earth to supply his habit of smoking crack, short of, Murder. But Chester was so well-known throughout the Trey for his antics and schemes designed to get him crack that, by the mid-80s, most drug dealers would just give him crack to avoid the havoc the addict was apt to foster. Kiwan remembered one stunt in particular, which had taken its spot in Third Ward lore as an example of Chester's slyness. The man had been on the prowl for crack in the wee hours of a fog-filled morning. Someone had made the mistake of asking Chester of watching out for the police. In return, Chester would receive a 10-dollar rock at the end of the night's run. But Chester had argued for the dope up front, swearing that he would come back and keep his end of the bargain.

Well, of course nobody believed him and they refused to give him his pay up front. To this day, no one knew where the fuck Chester had gotten the bullhorn, which had a built-in siren, but that's what he used to get over. When the corner stared hopping with the activities and dope started flying out of bags and into the hands of waiting customers, Chester had eased off to the corner of a building and let loose with the bullhorn's siren. He came bolting around the corner shouting, "Police, Police!" Not hip to Chester's ruse, every drug dealer on the corner took off running, throwing down crack left and right. Chester just eased up behind the fooled dealers and picked up at least $1,800 worth of rocks.

Stunts like that were more of a joke to the dealers and earned Chester respect instead of a bullet in the head. It was funny as shit and you had to respect it.

Daddy Bo had seen the essential goodness in the addict and had given the ex-con a chance by giving him a job in the after-hours club that he and Black Jack ran. Chester had appreciated the measure of faith so much that he returned that same faith tenfold.

"Who dat?" Chester asked, squinting his eyes, trying to get a good look at the strange man coming toward him. Kiwan stood face-to-face with one of his teachers in the game of life. Through Dopefiend Chester, Kiwan truly understood the meaning behind the phrase, "conversation rules the nation."

"Young Bo?" Chester eyed Kiwan in a questioning stare. "Is that you, boy?" he asked, giving Kiwan a hug. "Boy when did you get out? It's sho good to see you. I was jes thinking about Big Bo," he told the young man he had watched grow up, referring to Daddy Bo as Big Bo. Chester had always called he and Amin Young Bo and Lil Bo, because he'd seen so many attributes of their father in both young men.

"Kiwan, you didn't know that Chester was my guardian angel, did you?" Ayanna asked. "He keeps the house running smoothly when I'm not here, which is often. Keeping up with Amin is hell. I'm barely home six months out of the year."

"Yeah, and I don't smoke that shit no mo either," he stated proudly. Duke barked as if to call him a lying muthafucka. "You shut up," Chester scolded the spry dog.

Kiwan bent down and scratched Duke between the ears. Duke sidled up to Kiwan, sniffed twice, approved, then placed his head on Kiwan's knee. "Ayanna, I didn't know you had a seeing eye dog. Why don't you use him?"

"Well, he's sort of still in obedience school. He gets a little too excited at times. I've had him since he was a few weeks old." She smiled, looking at Duke, who was enjoying the attention. "He's still young. Right now I'm a bit jealous. Come here, Duke, come to momma," Ayanna called. Duke looked at Ayanna with one eye cocked as if to say, woman, are you crazy, then thought better of it and went to her, whining, tail wagging and tongue out. "I thought so," she chided her furry friend. "I was going to make your ass sleep in the garage tonight, wasn't I," she cooed at Duke.

"Well, come on y'all let's get inside befo baby girl catch a cold," Chester prompted.

As soon as they entered the house, a maid appeared to cater to the lady of the house. To Kiwan, the elderly maid sparked a memory of his mother. He wondered if his mother would've resembled the maid in her graceful manner, had she lived to be the maid's age. When the maid passed in front of Chester, he patted her on her ass. She spun on her heels, but was to embarrassed to speak. She huffed at Chester and went to retrieve Ayanna's purse.

"Stop it, Chester, I heard that. Leave Francis alone," Ayanna fussed. "You are perverted. That's why I can't keep no help around here."

Kiwan laughed. Now he-saw where Ayanna had gotten it from. Chester was influential like that with those who stayed around him long enough. Dopefiend Chester was still a character.

Chapter 32

Amin was sitting in the living room of his Clear Lake home, deep in thought. It was a strange coincidence that violence would just all of a sudden erupt at a crucial time such as this for his company and family. 'Idie Amin' was a realist; he didn't believe in coincidences. He remembered the conversation that he'd. had with Romichael early Saturday morning and his heart filled with rage. He knew in the depths of his soul that Romichael had been behind the senseless shooting. And the Congresswoman, just popping up the way she had? There was some strange shit going on and he was determined to get to the bottom of it if it took his last breath. A-dray didn't do anything to deserve getting shot.

Amin typed two messages on his personal two-way pager. His first message went to Prescious. Amin instructed her to make sure that she got Duck some VIP passes and courtesy limo service to Mister's album release party. He wanted to make damn sure that Duck was there. If anybody knew anything about the shooting, Duck did. Amin would ask him in away that he couldn't refuse. He thought about the possible consequences and repercussions for the actions he was about to take. He could see no way around the situation. Romichael had just upped the stakes in the game. But what if he was wrong? The thought was fleeting, because even if Romichael had nothing to do with the shooting, which was highly unlikely, he should've. Amin sent the message and there was no turning back.

Amin's A&R director, Tiffany Reed, had informed him that morning during the interview that she'd spoken with platinum recording rap artist, K-Flex, and he'd said that Arista was playing hardball and didn't want to release him from his contract. Tiffany had known K-Flex through his mother ever since he'd been born. K-flex's mother, who'd been Tiffany's classmate in high school, knew that she worked for Murder One and she informed Tiffany of the raw deal that her son was getting despite his platinum success. K-flex wanted out, but he'd fucked up royally and relied upon Arista for everything, from a manager to his accountant, all of whom were really looking out for the best interest of the company. This often happened to young, aspiring rappers with little patience. Tiffany had mentioned the situation to Amin once and Amin thought nothing of it until just the other day. Now his second message went to a subsidiary of Murder One called Rock Hard Records. It's C.E.O, Rueben Valiz, Nina's well-connected cousin from Spanish Harlem, came on the line. Amin asked for his assistance involving Arista Records. He explained that measures needed to be taken to expedite the contractual release of Broderick Nelson, aka K-flex, by any means necessary!

Rueben and Amin went back a long way, since Amin's first days in New York. Rueben had been instrumental in orchestrating Amin's pre-record label wealth through the sale of the drugs that were shipped to Texas through Nina. Amin rewarded Rueben's loyalty with a record label of his own under the Murder One umbrella that specialized in salsa, merengue and barrio rap. Both men capitalized on the influx of cash brought on by the drugs, but where Amin had given up the game, Rueben continued.

Amin's daughter Kya startled the bejeezus out of him just as he was finished typing. He didn't know how long she'd been standing nearby, looking at him, but his baby girl gave him a disapproving look, as if she'd caught her father doing a very bad thing.

"Hey, baby girl, you scared daddy. What's wrong?" he asked in a loving father's way.

"I can't sweep, daddy," she mumbled, rubbing her eyes.

"Oh, yeah," he whispered, picking up his most delicate possession, cradling her in his arms. It was early for Kya to be going- to bed, so he assumed that she'd just awakened from a nap. He actually had forgotten that he was in his home, so many things were running through his mind. The speed in which the industry moved disoriented his perception of location more often than not. To him every one of his offices looked alike, every one of his homes, all of his possessions and even certain cities minus-the landmarks all seemed to meld together at times when his thoughts were thoroughly occupied. Often he had to keep reminding himself of where he was, which city he was in, and sometimes which woman he was with. He knew he needed a vacation. No, what he needed was to start spending more time at home.

"What are, you to up to?" Nina wondered aloud, as she entered the spacious living room. Amin looked up at his wife, who stood in the light cast by the setting sun as it lazily spread through the room from the west-facing windows. He realized that his wife's beauty was not jut physical. In her face, Amin could see her wisdom, her love, and her resolve, which radiated through her courage and compassion. This other beauty, her spiritual, beauty, is what had really sustained Amin throughout the years, and for that he was grateful beyond words. At times like these, when the little things in his life, in his marriage, carried the weight of an aircraft carrier, Amin knew they had to be seized.

"Nina, take the girls and get them dressed. As a matter of fact, pack them a bag for a couple of days. You too, but make sure it's just for a couple of days, not a year," he joked.

"Why baby? Where are we going?" she asked her husband.

"I'm calling the hangar in Oklahoma to get the jet to meet us at Hobby Airport. We're going to leave for Orlando tonight and do Disney World for a couple of days and be back by Wednesday. I'm going to call Kiwan and let him know. He and Black Jack can handle everything for a day or so. I'm going to buy my girl A-dray the biggest stuffed Mickey Mouse that Disney World has to offer," he smiled.

Maybe there was hope for her marriage, Nina thought. Maybe all hope was not lost. Maybe.

Chapter 33

The sparkling platinum and blue H2-Hummer coasted through the evening traffic with ease despite its cumbersome size. The shiny chrome rims reflected the burnt orange light of the setting sun off the windows of the glass buildings that seemed to be floating by.

Felicia sat in the back seat between Monica and Romichael, watching-a porno flick on the 14-inch screen that dropped from the roof. Her mind remained focused on what she planned to do. Different outcomes danced a jig in her mind as she marveled again at how a little pussy could go a long way.

She had just met Romichael on Friday and already she was in his inner circle of friends and business associates. A lot of niggas are stupid, she thought, peacocks. They show off and strut around, looking for attention instead of being gamecocks. That attitude was the downfall of many powerful men.

Money and power were like double-edged swords. They could make you a target, just as they could make you untouchable.

Her father and his seemingly omniscient wisdom proved to be true once again. He'd told Felicia on many occasions that most men were tender dick tricks, and that the more you held out, the more you got from them. He warned her of who and when to give it up to. "Suckers are as plentiful as taxes," he was fond of saying. "God bless a sucker's heart, because without it a real nigga couldn't keep his head above water," he had told her. Felicia hoped that these truths held for Romichael Turner, because his ass was going down.

Romichael was too smug of a muthafucka. Like a lot of rich men, Romichael felt untouchable behind his money, Felicia knew. This prompted him to be too flamboyant concerning his false security, leaving him vulnerable to someone as determined as Felicia to breach those defenses. She knew that in this day and age, information was power, and that power could translate into, her father's freedom, which she'd longed for since his incarceration. Felicia kept telling herself that what she was doing was strictly to benefit her father; but in the deep recesses of her heart she knew that she also had an underlying notice that would benefit not only her father, but her mother.

Growing up, she watched her mother run the gauntlet of emotions concerning her father, and she had always dreamed that her dysfunctional family would become one functioning unit once again. That fantasy included Kiwan and Amin, who to this day did not know that she existed. Felicia's mother, Doris, had been quietly reconciling her relationship with Clyde through visits and correspondence. Felicia watched her mother rebound from a deep, life-threatening depression, and become rejuvenated, a vibrant woman of fifty who looked forward to each and every day, now that Clyde Rush had returned to her life. Felicia didn't care that her mother felt that her self worth demanded the love of her father, she just wanted to see her family happy and together, and she was willing to go to extremes to make that happen. At the age of 22 she knew that she had plenty of time to start her own family.

For these reasons, she subjected herself to the sexual degradations and humiliations of Romichael Turner, who thought that he was pimping Don Juan or some shit! Felicia thought about where they were headed because she didn't know and didn't want to risk asking. It didn't matter. Her only purpose was to relay any vital information in which she came across to her only link to her brothers, Nina. Ever since Felicia had met Nina, the two women had been discussing ways and options to get her father released. Felicia had conveyed her wants and dreams to Nina, and the two had been scheming. When the two women learned of the seat, their hopes shot up, and their minds went into hyper drive. When Romichael entered the picture, casting a dark, ominous cloud over their best hope since Daddy Bo's last appeal, Felicia decided to take measures into her own hands.

Not for the first time, Felicia second guessed her methods, for she knew that sleeping with a man to get next to him was the oldest trick in the book. Just look at R Kelly, Mystikal, Mike Tyson and Tupac. The shit was just plain tired. Where many men fell victim was when they failed to study their history, making them more liable to repeat it. That and the ignorant thinking of "that could never happen to me." One thing that lulled a man's defenses against the devious intentions of women, Felicia knew, was when the man thought that the woman was independent, self sufficient, and didn't need him as a crutch.

At the last possible minute, Nina managed to arrange for Felicia to move into one of the Rush Properties homes in Champion Forest, and. had provided her with a late model Lexus in Nina's name from Amin's car collection. Nina knew that Amin wouldn't miss the car, and if he did, she would just tell him that she loaned it out to one of the many people who worked for them.

Truth be told, Felicia was working for them toward a common goal, which would be written in the annals family history.

Felicia's sudden appearance in Romichael's world was not without suspicion and she knew it. Flip had his doubts about Felicia and had let it be known to her yesterday when she refused his advances. She had to be careful, because she knew that her cover was shaky and wouldn't stand up to any thorough scrutiny. Flip had been coming on strong ever since Friday, but in a very subtle an feminine way, she made it understood that she didn't get down like that unless ... She didn't want to be a toss-up in nobody's crew! If she gave in to such indecencies, then all respect for her would be tossed out of the window. Especially if she did it for free! So she hit on Flip for $700, if he really wanted some pussy, because her house note alone was $3,000 a month.

After Flip cursed her ass out, Felicia could see in his eyes that he was actually thinking about paying for it. Either way she figured that he got the hint that she was about her paper and wasn't going for any bullshit. But she knew that there had to be a purpose, something believable and shallow so as to draw suspicion away from her real purpose, something that would not cast her as a peon. Felicia figured that in order to get close enough to learn all of the dirt or any vital information, she had to earn trust, and that would be the only way to learn what she needed.

Felicia could see Flip watching her in the rearview mirror, as he drove, behind her flash tinted Fendi glasses. She ignored him and inched closer to Romichael.

The Hummer exited the Cavalcade exit off of U.S. 59, southbound. Felicia pretended to be deeply interested in the porno, rocking and fluttering her legs with her hands between her lap, when she actually was paying acute attention to her surroundings and to where they were headed.

They passed the Cavalcade Blvd. and proceeded to the next street, which as Collingsworth. Felicia knew by the neglected, roughshod Collingsworth Apartments that they were in the Fifth Ward. When Flip made a right on Collingsworth instead of a left under the freeway, Felicia became more attentive. She'd never been on this side of town before. They were leaving the residential area, heading into the downtown district if they continued in the direction they were headed. They crossed a set of railroad tracks that dissected a shipping yard that claimed both sides of Collingsworth.

The street curved into another, smaller residential area, with small shotgun row houses that had seen better days. They were approaching a signal light intersecting, a one-way street coming directly from downtown, she knew. The only one-way streets that Felicia knew of were in downtown. Before Felicia could make out the name of the one-way street, Flip made a left into the residential neighborhood. These homes were so old that they didn't even have driveways. Each property was fronted by a drainage ditch with a concrete cylinder covered with gravel, which provided a dusty bridge entering each property. Felicia could imagine the hell the residents caught when it rained. The name of the street was Rosedale, she noted. Felicia saw two huge, nondescript warehouses next to one another to her left, as the Hummer slowed to a crawl. The tin buildings, with weather-beaten faded blue paint jobs, boasted a sign that read, Paint and Body. Flip turned into the yard.

Flip navigated the truck through the graveled yard of cars and trucks to the huge cargo doors, which were closed. The place appeared deserted, despite the vehicles in the paint and body shop's yard. Little did Felicia know, but Saturdays and Sundays were their busiest days of the week.

Flip blew the horn in five rapid successions and waited. The one-minute wait seemed to Felicia like ten minutes as her keen eyes took in every facet of the buildings, including the surveillance cameras that were mounted to each corner of the cargo bay doors. The doors rose mechanically to reveal what Felicia guessed was a chop shop... The way that technology was today, Felicia would've guessed that this sort of enterprise would be extinct, though she was looking at a real life example of how wrong she was.

The question of why they would be at a chop shop nagged at her but she would run it by Nina to see if she could make sense of it.

Flip parked next to a late model, peach colored Silver Spur Rolls Royce. The garage was a flurry of activity, with torches ablaze, machinery humming and all of it lit by garish, bright fluorescent lights, giving it all a clandestine quality that added to Felicia's apprehension.

"You girls behave while I'm gone," Romichael quipped as he .got out of the Hummer. "I'll be back shortly." He and Flip weaved their way through the throng of activity, heading to a set of old, rickety wooden stairs that led to an upstairs loft with glass-enclosed offices. "Shit," Felicia sighed. What she wouldn't give to be privy to what was going on upstairs. But if it was one thing she had, that was patience. There was nothing she could do but wait. Her opportunity would come.

Chapter 34

Ayanna gently nudged Kiwan awake. Disoriented, Kiwan looked around, dazed and confused, wondering how the interior of a federal prison could have changed so drastically, until Ayanna's face swam into view. Now he was embarrassed because he'd been drooling out the side of his mouth. He wiped the corners of his mouth with his hand and sat up on the sofa. "What's up, A?" he groggily asked hoarsely.

Ayanna smiled apologetically and handed Kiwan the phone. "Amin wants to speak with you," she told him.

"'Lo," Kiwan said, his voice a whisper.

"Man, get yo ass up and take yo mothafuckin ass to yo house!" Amin yelled.

Kiwan jerked the phone away from his ear. When he replaced the phone to his ear, Amin was laughing. He wondered what time it was and looked around for a clock. "You play too much," Kiwan managed to say as realization hit him and he looked at his watch, which read 11:45 p.m.

"Aw, man, chill out," Amin told his brother. "You do need to go home, you got to see your probation officer in the morning, don't you?" Amin reminded him.

That was Kiwan thought. He'd been so tired that he'd fallen asleep on Ayanna's sofa. He'd been so busy living his life in the past three days, that he'd forgotten about his responsibilities. He did not want to get a fresh start on his life on the wrong foot, something that his father had warned him not to do.

"Yeah, you're right," he assured Amin. "I'm on my way home now."

"Yeah, man, because I was going to take you but I'm on my way to Florida now. I'll be there a couple of days with the family. I'll be back Wednesday. Moochie and Tony are with us. So I'll get Prescious to show you where the parole office is. She'll be by the house to pick you up in the morning, then she's going to take you shopping to put some furniture in your house. You've got to start over, big bra, and get your shit together, man."

"I know," Kiwan agreed. "I've had enough fun to last me," he said, thinking about all of the things he needed to do, such as get his license, a new birth certificate, Social Security card and a myriad of other small necessities that most people took for granted.

"You haven't seen fun yet," Amin boasted. "But when I get back we're going to meet with my lawyers and get you straight on the money issue. This company is just as much yours as it is mine," Amin stated with true love for his brother as he thought of the sacrifice Kiwan had made for him.

Kiwan wanted to tell his brother to keep his money and that he didn't owe him shit, but he knew that Amin wouldn't be trying to hear it, that and the fact that he wasn't a fool. He talked Big Six Shit, but there were things in life that he wanted to accomplish, and this money would be his means to achieve his dreams.

"We'll see," is all Kiwan said.

"Maan, don't start that shit, don't play that hard role with me, this is the family, man. This is what we have and what we do, everybody functions in some capacity or another and shoulders some type of responsibility. You ain't no fucking Lone Wolf McQuaid, muthafucka," Amin ranted.

"I said okay, sucka, I'll still kick your ass. Your boxing game ain't tight enough for you to be trying to handle me," Kiwan warned his baby brother.

"Don't be surprised," Amin told him. "Because if you're looking for 'It,' then 'It's' definitely looking for you."

"Oh, so you're tough now. We'll see. I'm sure Reverend Martin will let us use the gym," Kiwan said.

"Ha, the easy part's done. You done talked about it, now comes the hard part," Amin teased. "Your mouth has written a check that your ass is going to have to cash."

"We'll see," Kiwan said, as they both laughed. Although they would really fight, it would be with gloves on and in friendly competition. Bragging rights went to the victor.

"Well, I'll holla at you tomorrow," Amin said. "I'll call to make sure you're taken care of."

"You don't have to baby me," Kiwan said, making sure Amin understood. "I'm a struggler, man, you know I've been one all my life. If you want to make sure I'm all right you can't do it with a phone call. Quality time is how you do it. Just like you're spending it with your family, man. We have plenty of time to make sure that we both are all right and to be each other's keeper. Everything'll be awight," Kiwan wanted him to know. He knew that the guilt of Amin's actions were weighing on him and he really wanted Amin to know that he loved him no matter what and if he had to do it all over again, he would do it again for Amin.

"Yeah, you're right," Amin said somberly. "Love you, man. When I get back we're going to kick it and I'm going to show you the business myself."

"One," Amin signed off.

"One," Kiwan replied.

Kiwan handed the phone to Ayanna.

"I'm sorry for waking you, Kiwan. You looked so tired, and I didn't want to wake you," Ayanna told him softly.

"Don't sweat it," he said, rising from the couch, stretching his fatigued body.

"Kiwan, don't take this the wrong way or anything, but I would appreciate it if you stayed here with me tonight, please. I enjoy your company and with A-dray in the hospital, I really don't want to be alone right now," she pleaded.

Here we go, Kiwan thought. He knew exactly what would end up happening if he stayed. Then again, maybe not. He didn't have to have sex with Ayanna, but who was he fooling. He wanted to, then again he didn't want to, or knew he didn't need to cross that line with her. Confusion reigned in his mind.

Ayanna could sense his reluctance in his silence. "Never mind," she whispered. "I wonder how many times did Prescious have to ask you to fuck her," she mumbled.

Kiwan laughed, and remembered that he had intended to fuck Ayanna anyway and play with her emotions out of retribution for what she'd done to him. Her pouting and spiteful attitude made it possible for him to do it without any remorse.

"Look, Ayanna, we're not going to play those games," he started. "We're both grown up and we both know what we're doing. I just didn't want to feel as though I was taking advantage of the situation or taking advantage of you right now because of the circumstances. I was trying to keep it real."

"But Kiwan," she started crying. "I want you to take advantage of me. I love you. I want you back in my life … I … I need you," she sobbed.

Kiwan bent down and scooped Ayanna up in his arms. She put her arms around his neck and buried her head in his chest as she cried. "Where's your room, pretty lady?" Kiwan asked her softly.

Ayanna raised one of her dangling legs and pointed her toes straight out. "Upstairs," she whispered in between sobs. "Last room on the left."

Kiwan didn't know his way around the huge and spacious home, but managed to find his way to the elongated spiral staircase that led to Ayanna's bedroom.

When he reached her bedroom, he had to set her down to open the double mahogany doors that provided access. Ayanna leaned on his shoulder as he opened the sliding doors to the dark cavernous bedroom. Dim lighting from the hallway spilled into the room, not even penetrating a quarter of the way. Ayanna, who knew every inch of her home, walked into the bedroom and dialed up a dim setting of light from the rheostat on the wall. When the light penetrated the gloom, Kiwan's jaw dropped at the sheer size of Ayanna's bedroom, which could rival any five-star hotel's largest suite.

What he liked most was her custom made bed, which sat in the middle of the room on a raised platform hidden behind a plethora of multicolored silk sashes hanging from the vaulted ceiling.

"Damn," Kiwan commented. He'd only seen shit like this in magazines.

"Do you like it?" Ayanna asked, grabbing Kiwan's hand and pulling him into the room as she closed the door behind him.

"This is beautiful, A. If my room looked like this I'd never leave," he told her.

"That's the point," she said. "We stay gone so much that I need to indulge my personal space. Ayanna had a full living room set, complete with an entertainment center, a plush sofa, love seat and chaise lounge, all done in soft golds, tans, browns and reddish browns, in the bedroom. Huge throw pillows were everywhere. It reminded Kiwan of a chamber suited for an African queen, which was the theme of the decor. African statues, masks, with a huge, semi-nude portrait of Ayanna in a Nefertiti hat and sash hung on the back wall behind the bed. To the right was the entrance to the equally large bathroom, which matched the decor of the room. Scented candles were strategically placed throughout. Ayanna tipped around the room and lit each one of them, including the ones in the bathroom.

The scent of jasmine, cinnamon and sandalwood mingled in the room and helped set a relaxing mood. Ayanna was an avid jazz fan and turned on the stereo, playing soft jazz music from David Sanborn's latest CD. Kiwan had an urge to pinch, himself just to make sure that he wasn't dreaming. Ayanna moved to the bathroom and called for Kiwan to follow, but he was still trying to get over his initial shock at the entire scene.

Kiwan wondered about the woman he loved. He knew that a woman's heart was a deep ocean of secrets; how many secrets did the love of his life hold, he wondered, as he entered the bathroom behind her.

The huge marble tiled bathroom boasted a large whirlpool bathtub, a walk-in glass enclosed shower, his and her vanities, gold fixtured, recessed lighting and a built-in cedar steam room, next to the his and her walk-in closets, which in themselves were the size of a high school locker, room. Kiwan estimated that 'Ayanna's bedroom took up at least a quarter of the second story, if not more. All in all it seemed too much for such a petite woman, but then he knew how much she loved her space because of her handicap.

Kiwan watched Ayanna intently as she punched a sequence of buttons on a Braille inlaid-electronic control panel outside of the shower. The shower cut on automatically as a small steam of steam started to rise. Kiwan watched Ayanna disrobe, removing her glasses last. She closed her eyes because she had always believed the milky white iris of her eyes were crude and ugly, memories from a childhood of being teased.

He marveled at how such a small woman could be so voluptuous as he gazed silently at her flawless almond colored skin. Her eyes fluttered.

She knew he was watching. She grabbed a tube of something as she fumbled around her vanity table for a second. Everything on the vanity was labeled with small braille stickers, identifying the item. She found what she was looking for with relative ease.

"Are you coming in or are you content to watch?" she asked, breaking Kiwan out of his slack-jawed reverie. He hurriedly disrobed, seemingly in synch to Sandborn's jazz, as the music poured softly from hidden speakers. He placed his jewelry on the off white marble sink and stepped into the steaming shower with Ayanna.

To say that the entire scene was relaxing to Kiwan would be an understatement. Euphoric disembodiment would better describe the situation as Ayanna removed the oval showerhead with built-in massager and circulated it on different parts of his body.

"Damn baby, that shit feels sooo good," he whispered as he closed his eyes and drowned himself in the different sensations that he was experiencing in his mind, body and heart. It was too good to be true. When he and Ayanna were teenagers playing grown up, they had planned a future together. Here they were now, nothing between them but past feelings and opportunity.

Ayanna slowly raised on her tiptoes and planted a moist and sensuous kiss on his mouth. Kiwan's erection was instantaneous, as the flood of sensations overwhelmed him all at once. Kiwan had a glimpse of the world in which Ayanna' lived, as he kept his eyes closed. In doing so, it enhanced the sensitivity to his other five senses.

The shower had a built-in bench and Kiwan sat down. He pulled Ayanna to him and slowly explored her body. With each touch of her most sensitive spots, Kiwan could hear her barely breath catching despite the sound of the stream of water and jazz.

Ayanna placed the nozzle back into its holder and grabbed her bath sponge, squeezing a liberal amount onto it before applying it to her body. When she had worked up a generous amount of lather, she placed the sponge into Kiwan's hand. She guided his hand in rhythmic circles in a figure eight pattern that went from her breasts to her pubic mound and back again.

The hot water cascading from the shower head, which rotated automatically, provided different degrees of flow intensity due to the oscillating nozzles.

"I missed you so much," Ayanna whispered.

"I missed you too." Kiwan heard himself say. Ayanna pulled Kiwan up to a standing position and began lathering him up. She didn't miss a spot. She soaped his entire body, including his erection, which she took personal care to show a little extra attention to.

When all of the soap rinsed away from his body, Ayanna reached for the tube that she'd been fumbling around for on her vanity. Kiwan, whose eyes had been closed up until this point, heard a click that prompted him to peek. He knew that she wouldn't try any super kinky shit, but he had to check to make sure. He sighed with relief when he realized what it was. Ayanna turned him so that his back partially obscured the flow of the water as she inched closer to him, pressing her breasts firmly into his back. He closed his eyes again, relatively that he was safe from any super kinky shit. Ayanna positioned her arms around Kiwan's waist and squeezed the clear gel into her hand. She closed the tube and dropped it onto the floor. She rubbed the gel into both palms, then applied it to Kiwan's phallus, grabbing it from the shaft first. This surprised Kiwan for a second as she stroked his member in smooth strokes with both hands. This was kind of kinky, he thought as she rubbed the foreign substance on him.

On first contact, the gel was cool, then as the friction increased, so did the heat. His eyes popped open. The gel's warmth gradually increased. "What the fuck!" Kiwan thought. This was some new shit to him.

He found the sensation, though intensifying, to be not a hot as in heat, but hot as in electrifying. He could actually feel his dick throbbing in Ayanna's hand. The flow of blood rushing to the head threatened to burst it wide open as she continued to stroke him.

Kiwan didn't want to but he felt the beginnings of an intense orgasm underlying in the base of his scrotum, working its way to the surface. Ayanna started using just one hand as his body went rigid with the impending release. She squeezed, pulled, stroked and fondled, all the while placing gentle kisses up and down his back.

"Don't lose it baby," Ayanna called out as his breath quickened. "Not. yet."

Shit, Kiwan thought. You've got the wrong brother. This shit is feeling too good. You grow a dick and go without pussy for ten years, then let me do this to you so you can see how it feels, he wanted to tell her. But he couldn't even utter his name, and couldn't have if his life had depended on it.

Suddenly Ayanna stopped, spun Kiwan around, propped one leg on the marble bench, bent over and inserted him inside of her. Too late! The moment Kiwan broke the folds of her vagina he began to come. He squirted boiling hot semen up into Ayanna, who moaned in anticipation, then from the sweet pleasure of the pain, then from frustration, as Kiwan started to go limp.

"Damn, I'm sorry, A, but I couldn't help it. That shit was intense," Kiwan apologized.

"That's all right," she assured him. "We got all night," she said, hitting a button under the shower head that cut the shower off. "But for future reference, that's not a good thing."

They toweled off together and. Kiwan carried Ayanna into the candlelit room as the change in air temperature from the bathroom into the bedroom gave them goose bumps.

They jumped under the covers together, running from the cool of the air conditioner. Kiwan got comfortable and propped his back against a pile of Ayanna's pillow. She crawled between his legs and leaned her back onto his stomach and chest.

Kiwan gently traced circles around her nipples and her inner thigh as they both let the mood return with the help of the jazz and the candles. For Ayanna, this was heaven. In the arms of the man she loved, she felt secure and protected, like everything had to come through Kiwan before it reached her. She listened to the jazz as she relaxed to the rise and fall of Kiwan's chest. She thought about what they had been talking about earlier, and she wondered if Kiwan meant what he had said that .they could never be together again. Despite his words, Ayanna felt that he was mistaken, or confused. Why else would he be there?

Trust would be the key to her winning his heart again, she understood now. His trust in her had been betrayed. If she stood any chance of claiming what was truly hers, she'd have to start making him believe in her now.

She hesitated, but decided that he should know everything, even before they made love.

"Kiwan, there's something I have to tell you," she said warily. She was scared but she forged on anyway. No matter what, he deserved to know the truth.

In the midst of her thoughts, Kiwan stopped touching her. Maybe he already knew and was mad at her because of that and was just waiting to see how long it took for her to tell him.

"Kiwan, did you hear me?" she said a bit louder, startling him.

"Huh, what?" he replied, disoriented.

Ayanna realized that he'd been sleeping. Poor baby, she thought. "Never mind," she told him. She would tell him tomorrow.

Chapter 35

Prescious heard the key hit the lock on the front door downstairs as she lay in wait in the coal black darkness of her three-storied town house. Her heart raced. Not in fear, but in anticipation of the worst. A wave of revulsion swept over her as she quietly turned her back to her bedroom door. She learned long ago that in order to make the big money in the prostitution game, she had to fulfill the fantasies of the men she 'dated.' With her dates it wasn't always about the pussy. Most of them sought refuge from their unbearable realities through her, so acting became an added appendage to her psyche. Some wanted a mother figure, some wanted an ear, but most wanted things that she'd never heard of taking place in the bedroom. The favorite was the role of the 'victim.' They wanted to dominate.

Fulfilling fantasies had become so commonplace with Prescious that it became hard at times, such as now, to distinguish reality from fantasy, she thought as she listened to footsteps lightly creak up her staircase. No matter how many fantasies she indulged in, she would not allow herself to become accustomed, to become satiated or satisfied. She fought the urge to release with every fiber of her being leaving her empty and desolate after every session, all 725 at her last count. She knew the hearts of many men and had developed a loathing for them and their sadistic needs. More often than not Prescious had to finish what they started with her plethora of toys and gadgets.

The majority of the fantasies were so sick in nature that they haunted her dreams. She could recall every one of them, every fantasy, every man! From the molester that was her stepfather when she was just twelve, to Kiwan Rush. Most, in between the two men, had not stimulated her enough to give her an orgasm, despite her reluctance, she remembered as she listened to the footsteps stop at the threshold of her bedroom. Those few and far between instances had occurred over the span of years, Kiwan having been the last one. It was perplexing to her how he could be different from everyone else. There was something about him that made her want to let go. His aura demanded that she submit to his will even though he didn't assert it in words. It was a natural instinct that she vibed with, even moistening her cat and stirring her juices just thinking of him as a tremen's force pounced on her, not unexpectedly, and she went with the flow.

Her eyes widened in rehearsed fright as a gloved hand was clasped tight over her mouth.

The game had changed a bit, Prescious noticed. He wore a mask now, and was a bit rougher as she struggled to get loose. She bucked, kicked and tried to knee her assailant, abruptly stopping when the figure clad in black slugged her in the jaw, hard. For a moment things got fuzzy and hazy, swimming in and out of view. Starbursts invaded her peripheral as the dull shine of a knife became the point of her focus. Things were definitely different, and the fright in her eyes became genuine. He'd never done this before, she thought.

"Are you surprised, bitch?" came the question from an unfamiliar voice.

She went rigid with fear because she knew that the man who had her was Dexter Cunningham. Many thoughts raced through her mind as she began to relive the very first time that she was raped. The same helpless and gut wrenching emotions began to sweep over her again. Who could this be? What did I do wrong? Is he going to hurt me? Am I going to die? I wish Kiwan were here!

The last thought caught her by surprise, just before the blow to her ribs did. Tears flooded her eyes, not only in agony, but from actual fear for her life. Two more shots to her ribs followed, accompanied by a harsh slap to her face. Prescious doubled up in pain as her assailant pressed the tip of the serrated blade under her eye.

"Aren't you gonna scream?" he asked in a growl, thoroughly enjoying himself. She could tell by his growing erection. Precious could do nothing but cry as her flimsy nightgown was cut away from her body.

"Are you scared?" he teased, pulling off his gloves. "Yeah, you're scared, I can feel it."

The backwash of moonlight revealed a silhouette in the doorway. Precious knew instantly that it was Dexter Cunningham who stood in the doorway. Her unknown assailant unbuckled his pants and pulled them down with one hand while the other remained firmly locked on her throat, squeezing her windpipe. She couldn't scream even if she wanted to. The knife, she thought, as her eyes scanned the bed for the weapon. Dexter crossed the room to her bedside.

"You see. I own you bitch. There is no leaving me," he hissed. "You should fear me more than you do," he said, menace in his tone.

Oh, how she hated Dexter. Maybe she could get to the knife before the other man noticed. Maybe hell was paradise in disguise.

Dexter stood over Precious and urinated in her face and hair as the masked assailant pried open her thighs and began raping her, forcing his penis into her now dried-up vagina. She squeezed her eyes closed as the pain intensified. The masked man became more excited because of her terror and his grip tightened around her throat. Even in her panic, she knew better than to try to wrench-away from his grasp and deliberately inched her hands toward his, trying to lessen his grasp. Dexter positioned himself at the bottom of the bed with a flashlight and masturbated at the sordid scene.

Precious passed out for what seemed like forever but must have been only a few seconds, because when she came to, the assailant had begun raping her anus. She reached for the blackness of unconsciousness as the man pumped. She could tell that he was about to come because of the swelling she felt through the walls of her rectum. Was it a good thing that he was about to finish, she wondered? What would happen to her when he was through?

She could hear Dexter laugh as her assailant pulled his spent and moist phallus out of her ass. Somehow, the knife reappeared, nicking the corner of her right eye. She could feel the small pinprick leak blood down the side of her face.

"Lest you forget bitch, who you belong to," Dexter laughed.

As they left the way they'd come, Prescious couldn't move. She couldn't think. She couldn't act. It was as if she was comatose. How could he, she wondered? But she knew the hearts of some men and some men she knew that she would love to remove their hearts, and Dexter Cunningham would pay if it took her very life: he would pay! Sweet sleep crept upon her, thankfully, as her last thoughts were on how sweet it would be to kill Dexter.

Chapter 36

The skylight above the bed permitted the morning sun to penetrate through Kiwan's sleep as if a tender lover had awakened him with a morning blow job. The sweet smell of his favorite honey buttered cinnamon and raisin biscuits wafted throughout the massive bedroom.

Kiwan sat up and shook off the heavy veil of sleep that threatened to keep him laid up for a couple of days. Never one to be labeled as lazy, though still tired, Kiwan rose from the bed and stretched. Yawning, he realized that Ayanna wasn't in the bed, nor the room. Naked as the day he came into the world, Kiwan happily walked into the bathroom to brush his teeth and wash his face. It still amazed him that he was finally home. After a little bit of searching he finally found an unopened toothbrush. He looked around the bathroom for his clothes and couldn't find them. He assumed that Ayanna had moved them somewhere as he finished his morning hygienic ritual.

When he finished he walked to the shower and attempted to turn it on.

The keypad was in Braille, and attempting to operate it without knowing Braille was out of the question, he thought, as he stood there looking like, a functional retard.

"Would you like me to turn it on for you?" Ayanna asked from behind him, making him jump.

"Damn girl, you scared the fuck outta me. Don't do that anymore," he joked. "I'm a stiff nigga, and sneaking up on a stiff nigga might get you beat up, especially when I'm ass naked. I fight harder than a pit on gunpowder ... How did you know I was trying to take a shower anyway?" he asked.

"I heard you when you started punching the buttons, fool. Move," she told him, sauntering over to him, wearing an oriental silk robe opened to her navel.

Kiwan slapped himself.

Ayanna jumped. "What the hell you doing, fool? Did you just slap yourself?" she asked, laughing.

"Nah, I was scratching an itch I had," he lied.

She shook her head, turning on the shower for him. "I left the instruction panel in Braille because when it was just manual, A-dray would have her ass in here all the time," Ayanna commented, thinking of her baby sister.

"It'll be all right, lady, she'll pull through, "Kiwan assured her, taking her into his arms and squeezing some heartfelt love into her. "When I come back from seeing my P.O., I'mma go up there and sit with her for a while."

"You want me to ride with you, then we can go see her together?" Ayanna asked.

Kiwan thought about it for a second and knew that she was testing him. Did she know that Prescious was supposed to be taking him? "Shit, come on, but you got to put some clothes on," he kidded.

Francis, Ayanna's housekeeper, interrupted Ayanna's reply as she entered the bathroom with Kiwan's clothes, ironed and draped over her outstretched arm. "Oh, I'm sorry, I was just going to hang these up for him," she said to Ayanna, referring to Kiwan.

Kiwan noticed two things about her that he hadn't noticed the night before. One, she had a trace of a Caribbean accent, and two, her eyes were locked on his dangling penis the entire time she was speaking to Ayanna.

"Okay, just lay them across the bed," Ayanna instructed.

"Oh, okay, and breakfast is ready whenever you guys are," she replied, still ogling Kiwan's phallus.

What a mothafuckin freak, Kiwan thought, and an old freak, too! No wonder Chester was on her row so hard. Kiwan laughed to himself, neglecting to mention it to Ayanna. He hopped into the shower, hurrying because his stomach was speaking to him in rapid fire flips which, if translated into a language, would undoubtedly be Spanish.

After his shower, Kiwan quickly dressed, donned his jewelry and ran downstairs in search of the kitchen. The dominating aroma of biscuits led him straight to the breakfast table, where Ayanna sat with Duke at her feet.

Two places were set at the oval glass table, which sat in a sunlit breakfast nook. Ayanna had her phone to her ear as Kiwan sat down and noisily gulped his glass of orange juice. "Okay, well, what did the doctor say?" Ayanna questioned whomever was on the other end of the line. "Okay, well, I'll be up there after a while, tell her I said that I'll bring her some stuff from home. Her nightgowns, underclothes, a couple of comforters and I'll do her hair, too," Ayanna sighed.

"And you bring your ass home, Jamarcus, I know you wasn't at the hospital all night," she fussed "Umm hmm," she said, twisting her lips, showing her disbelief at whatever excuse, he'd given her. "Well, you don't live with Black Jack, you stay with me, don't have me worried like that. You need to call me. Especially at times like these, all this shit going on around here. What? Nigga, I don't give a damn how old you are, as long as you stay here and your ass points toward the ground you betta call me ... What, boy don't you ... Whatever, boy, Love you too, bye" she said in a clipped manner, hanging up the phone.

"That damn Jamarcus," she whined, to no one in particular. "That boy reminds me of you, Kiwan, always into something, never satisfied." She realized that didn't sound right. "I don't mean satisfied as in never satisfied with what, oh shit, never mind, it doesn't matter," she rambled. The whole time Kiwan just watched and waited for the food. He was hungrier than an Ethiopian hostage in Siberia.

"I'm ready to eat," he stated.

"Oh, I'm sorry ... Francis!" she shouted. "I was waiting on you to get out of the shower." As Francis entered the kitchen to fix the plates of food, the phone rang. "Shit!" Ayanna said. "I should not answer this," she hissed.

"Hello?" she answered anyway.

"Ayanna, what's up, what do you have planned for today?" Amin asked on the other end of the phone.

"Nothing, I was just going to spend some time at the hospital with A-dray. Make a few calls and answer some of your e-mails," she told him.

"Well, dig this. Something's come up in New York that needs our attention and I would like you with me, so if you could, I need for you to catch the first thing smoking to NY. I would send the jet for you, but I'm on it now and it wouldn't get to you in time for you to be here today."

"Damn, Amin, we just left New York Friday. I'm sick of New York. I love tha city and all, but it's too cold up there for me, makes my nipples hurt," she complained.

"Shit, they should be sore now because I know that my brother didn't go home like he said he was last night," Amin capped.

"Shut up, Amin, you need to be ... "Ooops, she almost went there with him about her friend Nina, but thought better of it. "Fuck that, I'm on it, before I leave I'm going to take A-dray some stuff."

"That's cool, A. You really don't have to come, but you know it's hard for me to function properly without you," he told her, stroking her ego. "Oh yeah, and before I forget, tell Kiwan to swing by Precious' crib. Make sure he knows the directions. Tell him that there's a key taped to the bottom of her potted palm tree. I've been trying to call the girl all night and I haven't gotten an answer. That's not like her. I would ask Black Jack to send somebody but everybody is at the hospital with A-dray. Black Jack told me that he had to get her moved to another hospital on a private floor because of so many people coming to see her."

"Yeah, I know," Ayanna agreed. "I just got off the phone with Jamarcus and he told me."

"Well, you know that ordinarily I wouldn't trip, but this shit with Romichael is heating up and we still don't know who shot A-dray or why."

"I agree," Ayanna said. "I'll tell him, but let him finish eating first," she giggled. She could hear him attacking his food like a mad Russian. "I'll call you when I get to the airport, alright? Bye.

"What's up?" Kiwan asked, his mouth stuffed with food.

"Trouble in paradise," Ayanna retorted, shaking her head.

"Francis, could you pack me a bag for a couple of days? I'm headed back to New York," she sighed, her mood immediately becoming dour. Not just because she had to go to New York again, but the mention of Prescious' name seemed to unnerve her. For a second, she thought about not telling Kiwan shit, but then again, she didn't want childish jealousies to hinder the growth of what she knew could be the start of a beautiful beginning between her and Kiwan.

Chapter 37

It didn't seem as if only three days had passed since his release from prison, but here Kiwan was on Monday morning, on his way to see his probation officer. It didn't make any sense to him at all, he thought, as he stood in front of Prescious' beveled glass doors. He'd served his entire one hundred and twenty-two month sentence, minus six months for good behavior, which would've been more had he not squandered a few months of good time on a few fights. Despite all of that, he felt he shouldn't have to report to a probation officer for three damn years. That shit didn't make any sense, he thought, as he turned to leave. Evidently Prescious wasn't here, and he wasn't about to go into the girl's house just because Amin was a little nervous. She'll turn up, he figured. He needed to go; he had things to do and a probation officer to see. He could just call and get directions, he surmised, as he PO turned to walk down the stairs leading to the driveway.

Two miniscule spots of dried blood stopped him in his track. The only reason he noticed them was because of the bleached concrete porch, which was virtually spotless otherwise and the tiny spots of blood stood out. He wondered how he had missed them coming up the stairs.

Kiwan backtracked to the door. Damn, he wished he had a pistol. Then again, he didn't. He really didn't know what to do. Maybe he should call the cops, he thought, but found himself looking under the potted palm tree for her extra key. Coward had never been a word used to describe Kiwan Rush, he boasted to himself, as he built his nerve to go ahead and walk into the unknown. He decided that he just wouldn't touch anything.

To his surprise, there was no key! What now, he thought? He went back to the door to peer inside. He beat on the door for a solid thirty seconds.

When there was no answer, he lifted his shirttail out of his pants, and covering his hand, he twisted the knob. Unlocked! His intuition screamed at him to leave. Go, stupid, get tha fuck out you dumb muthafucka! Fuck it, he thought. He was worried about what he'd find, and the implications for him and the woman who lived inside. He'd never be able to live with himself if Precious were hurt and he'd walked away. Again, he screwed-up his resolve.

"Look out, Precious!" he yelled as he entered the townhouse. It was deathly quiet inside her home. He stood inside the foyer listening for any signs of life – ticking clocks, the hum of machinery, anything. But nothing reached him. Damn! Why did Amin have to send him to play Captain-save-a-hoe? Shit just didn't seem right. He tentatively walked throughout the first floor, his senses on full alert.

When he came to her kitchen, he felt silly, because the need to arm himself crossed his mind, and he passed the knife rack with more than a few looks of contemplation. "You're really tripping," he said aloud, breaking the eerie silence. He felt the need to do that, not only to keep ahold of his sanity, but so. anyone stalking would know he was a fearless man. After all, he had come in alone and unarmed, hadn't he?

The ringing of the phone damn near sent him sprinting out of the house. It scared him so much that he almost broke his hip against the counter.

"Fuck!" He screamed. He laughed at himself for hollering like a bitch. The phone continued to ring as he leaned against the counter, willing his heart rate to return to normal. Maybe he really was tripping. Maybe that wasn't even blood. Then again, with as many fights, stabbings and riots he'd seen the last ten years, he knew what dried up blood looked like. Fuck it, he'd look upstairs, then get the hell on about his business.

Kiwan quickened his pace and trotted up the stairs, confident that the place was empty. Noticing that there were only two doors to look into, he quickly went to the first door, which was ajar, and pushed it wide open. All caution was gone now; he just wanted to get it over with, lock the door behind him and call Amin to let him know that Prescious wasn't here. As for the blood, well, that could be attributed to any number of things.

When the bedroom opened all the way, Kiwan got the shock of his life! He went into slackjawed delirium. On first sight, Prescious appeared to be dead. Damn, he'd known this was a bad idea. Now look; he could see the bars and gray suits of the TDCJ guards. Who was going to believe that he had just walked up on her already dead if she'd been murdered? And he had just got out of prison. Shit!

The slow, rhythmic rise and fall of her chest caught his attention as he finally realized that breathing meant life, which meant that she wasn't dead. He wanted to jump for joy.

Kiwan damn near broke his neck to get to her side, as the sight of blood terrified him. When he moved to roll her over, the smell of urine assaulted his nostrils, threatening to make him heave up his favorite biscuits.

Kiwan didn't understand. He couldn't see any visible signs of brutality other than the bruises around her neck and ribs, yet there was a smattering of blood and ... and what? He took a closer look. Shit, which was what it was, blood and shit! Damn; she had been bleeding from her rectum he realized. The smell hit him when he spread her legs to make sure. Tears welled up in his eyes. It was sad; who tha fuck would do some bitch ass shit like this? He shook her hard, attempting to wake her, not realizing his own strength. But it was more raw emotions that controlled his actions as tears broke through his stiff nigga barrier.

"Prescious, wake up!" he cried. She stirred but didn't open her eyes. Kiwan scooped her naked and fragile body up from the bed, turning his head away lest he empty the contents of his stomach all over her.

He carried her into the bathroom and gently placed her into the tub. He then turned on the water to the shower, making sure that it was ice cold. When the cold water hit her naked body, she still didn't open her eyes. Kiwan watched her intently. What to do, what to do? he thought. Tears still flowed freely from his eyes. He then positioned the showerhead to hit her face instead of her body. For a second Kiwan had thought to just go call 911, then her eyes opened abruptly. Her eyelids started fluttering as the water hit her full in the face. She coughed one good time and, very slowly, but deliberately, lifted her arms to cover her face and block the water.

Kiwan rushed to cut off the water. Prescious uncovered her face and Kiwan breathed an audible sigh of relief. "Damn, girl, you scared me. I thought that I was going to lose you," Kiwan whispered, not realizing that he'd been clenching his teeth together until he'd spoken.

When Prescious realized that it was Kiwan who was staring her in the face, the rush of emotions that went through her face and body as she grabbed Kiwan, hugging him fiercely to her chest, sobbing, was enough to break him down to a bawling mess. It tugged at his heart to have to be the one to comfort Prescious, someone whom he'd just met, at a time like this. He wondered if she had any family, anybody who cared, that could comfort her. Then it dawned on him that he cared, and he would be enough for the time being.

"It's all right, it's okay. I'm here for you," he whispered, as they both cried until it physically hurt.

Chapter 38

He couldn't blame his erratic behavior on weed smoking, liquor or any conventional drugs known to man, he thought, as he raced his maroon and gold Suzuki GSXR 1000 at a steady 120 miles per hour on Beltway 8. Monster Pat was addicted to something commonly overlooked by the average person that, in his opinion, far surpassed any high that he'd ever experienced. Adrenaline! Monster Pat was an adrenaline junkie and acted out his fetish, daring many life-threatening feats when he rode his bike. Before he started touring and performing he had ridden everyday. Lately, he had to take the time that was given to him to indulge in his pleasure. Usually, Monday mornings were reserved for sleeping off hangovers induced from weekends of nonstop partying. Even when the party ended, it never really ended when you could afford to partake in whatever your heart desired. "Platinum success allowed for such indulgences," he gloated, as he weaved through vehicles as if they were standing still. Damn, it felt good! Pat downshifted the bike, goosed the throttle to increase the rpms and popped the clutch, bringing the bike up on one wheel. He upshifted in midair, increased speed and continued to weave through traffic, on one wheel. He wished that his homie Sleepy was riding with him. Together they were scary.

Some of the stunts they pulled produced so much adrenaline in Pat that he'd almost passed out from sheer adrenaline overdose on more than one occasion.

Though it might seem as if he was in a rush, Monster Pat was actually taking his time and enjoying the ride. He concentrated on what he was doing, but this particular morning his excitement surpassed the ride. His heart raced with the thought of an anticipated conquest of some new pussy he'd met by happenstance the previous week. Blue eyes were a rarity in women of color and upon first sight he'd assumed that they were contacts. But in the midst of the conversation, she allowed him a closer look when he asked about them to determine if they were real or fake. Talk about a body! The girl had the shape of a 400 dollar coke bottle. His nature rose while he was on the crotch rocket, proving to be a major discomfort, as he undressed her mentally.

Pat slowed his speed from a meager 95 mph to a sedate 80 as he approached the toll booth just past the 1-10 freeway. Without stopping to pay a toll, Pat zoomed through the E-Z tag lane, picking his speed back up to 120 just as he cleared the booth. The mental picture that he summoned changed his agenda from enjoying the ride to trying to get there. The broad Nya had called him this morning, asking if they could spend the day together because she was from Cali and wanted Pat to take her to Sixflags-Astroworld and WaterWorld, which sounded good to Pat, especially the part about WaterWorld. Being from Dallas originally, Pat had never been to the theme park in Houston but had frequented the one in Arlington all of his life. He was curious to see what the one in Houston had to offer, curious about many things really!

Monster Pat rounded the 59 exit heading back into downtown, then exited 59 On Bissonnet, making a right. These were the instructions that Nya had given him to her condo in the Atrium at Braeswood, instructions that he'd committed to memory in less than ten minutes once Nya had given them to him. Normally he wouldn't have left his bed for anyone, but when he realized that it was Nya calling he changed his tune. And hell Yeah! He planned to go to Astroworld . . . tonight, but today he planned on getting acquainted with her bed and body. He'd left some for sho pussy at his house for some more pussy, playing the game of cat and mouse. If she answered the door in her bed clothes then he already knew what it would be, he thought, as he saw her building on the left and turned in. He parked his bike in the spot for visitors and headed into the building.

When he got to the door, he entered the vestibule, noticing how nice and chic the stucco building was. It was well-maintained and cared for, he could tell, by the smudge-free glass, brass fixtures and new paint. Sleepy had told him about when he and his mother had been in the entertainment business, they'd run a promotion and entertainment company called World Wide Entertainment. Sleepy had told him about kicking it with the rapper Scarface at his place in the Atrium on the Southwest side. Pat wondered if this was the same building where Scarface had lived. Ironic. Pat marveled at how this thought just came to his mind. Prison did that to him. He could recall just about every story one of his patnas told him and remember most of the details, especially if the story dealt with sex or music.

The vestibule held a directory and phone that allowed you to call on the residence so that you could be buzzed into the interior of the building. His thoughts gravitated back to how fine Nya was as he picked up the phone and dialed the numbers that she had instructed him to.

"What's up?" Nya answered with that early morning seductiveness that women exuded at just the right moments.

"What's up, lil momma, it's Pat, buzzya boy in," he told her.

"Alright, but you got here quick!" she observed. The mechanical lock on the door clicked as Pat hung the phone up. He walked into the lobby and entered the glass elevators that were awaiting.

This is a nice building, he observed, looking out at the cedarwood gazebos in the middle of the building. The two gazebos flanked a huge bubbling hot tub and were surrounded by large-leafed plants. A skylight allowed the sun to enhance the beauty of the place as it penetrated through the glass in all of its magnificent glory. A rock path wove a figure eight through the atrium amidst a multitude of different color flowers. Pat wondered how much one of the units ran per month. He needed a place closer to the city, anyway. As it stood now he had to drive thirty minutes from his Jersey Village home just to get to the city, he thought as he exited the elevator on the fourth floor. The floor design was a complete square of apartment units that fronted a rail that opened up to the atrium below. So when Pat exited the elevator his options were to go either left or right. The first unit past the elevators was 402 and he was in search of unit 425. Instead of making a right and following from 402 to 425. Pat made a left and went from 430 down five doors, simple. Pat noticed that Nya's door was slightly ajar as he walked up. He could hear Indie Arie softly crooning in the background, singing about how she was ready for love when Nya came to the door to peep out.

"Ooh!" she screamed, startled. "I thought you had gotten lost in here," she confessed to Pat. The rapper was dumbfounded again by Nya's raw black beauty. He really hadn't gotten a decent look at her in the strobe lights of the club where they'd met. He really had been too busy with her blue eyes and other noticeable features when they bumped into one another at "The Sky Bar" in the village, downtown. Pat frequented the classy jazz club, not only for anonymity, but also for a change of pace from the average young gold-digging, around-the-way, car boppers, to your more sophisticated, job having, gold-digging, around-the-way, corporate type car boppers. Pussy was pussy to Pat, but sometimes the packaging that the pussy came in determined if the pussy made the A-team list of pussy that he could kick it with or the B-team list of pussy that got dogged. Nya seemed like she was definitely A-list material, Pat surmised, so far. She actually posed a picture of the settling down kind as he couldn't help but notice how good she looked in her emerald green baby doll pajamas.

"You look cute, young lady," Pat flattered. "Now I know why I rushed over here I would've gotten here sooner if I'd have known that you were going to look extra special for me."

"Paleese," Nya blushed, as she moved aside to let Pat in. "I look rough, don't start lying, boy. We're not going to start that with each other," she added.

"Girl, I'm serious," Pat admitted. "You do look good to have just gotten up. You look like something I could wake up to every morning," he told her as he took off his leather riding jacket.

Nya took his jacket and hung it up in the hall closet. She was flattered but to her this was nothing personal; this was business.

"You're crazy, boy," she laughed. "Have you eaten yet? Because if not, then I'll treat you to breakfast since we are going to be kicking it today."

"Nah, I haven't eaten yet, but if you can cook, I'd rather that than some fast food. Lord knows I'm tired of eating out," he told her. I get enough of that shit when I'm on the road."

"That sounds good, but as you can see," she said, gesturing with a wave of her arm that covered her sparsely decorated abode. "I haven't quite gotten settled in yet and I've been working so much that grocery shopping hasn't been on the top of my list of priorities."

"Yeah, I know the feeling," Pat sympathized. "The music business is so demanding, even on a small scale, that I forget to do the small things in my life that's needed. That's why I need me a good girl to take care of me," he hinted at Nya.

"Boy, please, I'm not one to be a part of a tribe. I know how you niggas are," she said, sitting on the couch next to Pat. "You probably got women lined up in seven states," she kidded, tucking her legs under her.

Nya was cool, Pat thought. He just didn't have the urge to fuck now, she piqued his curiosity. Now he wanted to really get better acquainted with her. "So do you want to go to the grocery store?" he asked. "Then we can decide how we're going to tackle the rest of the day."

"All right, let me go put on some clothes," she agreed. Nya hopped up from the sofa and sashayed to her room to change. Pat couldn't resist the temptation to look at her ass as it shook in the loose fitting pajamas, for a tall and slim chick, the girl had a nice round caboose back there, he noted. Looked like two pound puppies fighting in the back of her pants, he thought as his cell phone rang. Damn! He thought that he'd turned the daggone thing off for fear ... of one of his tribe calling while he was getting to know his new recruit better. He was getting ready to turn it off completely until he looked at the caller I.D. screen. Pat recognized the number. It was Romichael. And Romichael calling him this early on a Monday meant that it was important.

"What's up, Ro?" Pat answered.

"Man, we got problems. Have you spoken with your lawyer yet?" Romichael asked, already knowing the answer.

"Naw, why?" Pat wanted to know.

"You remember them funky bitches we put off the tour bus? Well, those stupid hoes had the nerve to file suit against me and you. Your lawyer should be calling you. They did it first thing this morning as soon as the courts opened. Can you believe that shit?"

"You bullshittin!" Pat screamed.

"Actually, I'm not. We need to meet up this morning and discuss our strategy on how to handle this shit before it gets blown out of proportion," Romichael advised.

Romichael only wanted to meet for the sake of meeting. He already knew how he was going to handle the problem. He couldn't afford any mishaps right now. He didn't need any image problems and had to act on the situation quickly before the Congresswoman and the committee found out.

"Awight, man, where you wanna meet?" Pat asked dejectedly. He wasn't even officially platinum yet and already the lawsuits were starting.

"Meet me at the office," Romichael told him. "I'm headed that way now."

"Yeah, all right, I'm on my way," Pat conceded. He knew that this business needed to be addressed. "Fuck!" he muttered to himself as he hung up the phone.

"What's wrong?" Nya asked, having stood there unknowingly by Pat, listening to the entire one-sided conversation. Pat took notice that she still had her pajamas on.

"Aw, nothing, I got to take a rain check on that breakfast thing. There's something I have to take care of," he told her.

Nya automatically went into pout mode. Her acting skills far surpassed her beauty, only Pat didn't know it. "Well, are we still going to Astroworld and WaterWorld?" she wanted, to know.

"Fo sho; I'm going to call you when I get through taking care of my business," he told her as he stood, signaling that he was on his way out. Nya got his jacket for him.

"Make sure you do that because I have a bikini that I've been dying to wear," she teased as she walked him to the door. She wondered what he had to do and thought about where he could be going this time of the morning. Maybe it was a drug deal, she thought.

"Bet yo ass I'll be back as soon as I'm finished," he boasted.

"I'll be waiting," Nya seductively cooed before closing the door. Now what, she thought. She really didn't want to sit up doing nothing. She had information to gather. Maybe she could call Nina back to see what she was doing, she asked herself.

Chapter 39

Broderick Nelson, aka K-Flex, sat in the booking and processing tank of a Manhattan precinct, feeling dejected and alone. The 18-year-old platinum selling artist had lost all hope in the rap game. He was not happy. Although he'd realized his dreams of becoming a rap star he had no idea at all of what the title had entailed. No one warned him of the cheaters, snakes and the backstabbers in the game. Now he understood why Jay-Z had said the industry was shady and needed to be taken over.

The entire experience started out like a dream come true. The money, the cars, the clothes, the jewelry, even the women. But hell! K-Flex had all of those things when he sold dope on the corners of the Southside of Houston. He just wasn't nationally known. Now look at him. In a cramped smelly ass jail cell and not one person to come to his aid. The rap game was serving him a low blow.

His banking account was frozen, a lien placed on his house, his Bentley Arnage was not in his name, but in the name of his record company, and his other vehicles were leased. All of his rights to his music had been signed away with the help of the company's in-house lawyer, so suing was out of the question. K-Flex had gotten ripped off on payment for his tour and all hope for his future looked to be lost. He felt like a straight ho. He had been pimped, he thought, as the strong smell of stale urine and bile started to make him feel nauseated.

"Fuck!" He knew where he'd gone wrong. When the record company executive from Arista had come to Houston to court him, he'd flown K-Flex around the country introducing him to the big names in the business and impressed him with the connections that he had. K-Flex had record deal offers from most of the local companies in Houston. Companies like Suave House, Rap-A-Lot, Ruff House, and Swisha House to name a few. Even the late DJ Screw wanted him to be down with the screwed up clique because Screw recognized K-Flex's talent. After all, K-Flex started his career rapping Screw's mixed tapes. Since his friend "Fat Pat" was murdered over a money dispute, K-Flex longed to leave Texas. He never, wanted it to be mistaken that he was not a Southsider for life, as he stressed to the magazine and industry news media. He just wanted to broaden his horizons, wanted to be different from all of his comrades. After all, there were only three major rap groups to come out of Houston's rap scene that had ever gone platinum, and no solo artist from Houston had ever accomplished this feat. Compared to Arista, who boasted a slew of platinum selling solo artists, there was no contest. K-Flex was broke, disgusted and couldn't be trusted. If he ever got out of this mess he would lobby to change some things in the industry. For now he just concentrated on getting up out of this fuckin hell hole. He was no stranger to jail but he had never been under such a serious charge.

Attempted Murder. Give me a break, he thought! This shit was so outrageous. He figured the record company was just applying pressure to scare him. But he knew better. Or did he? Okay, maybe he shouldn't have barged into Arista's offices demanding an audience with the CEO, and maybe he shouldn't have went ballistic and trashed the outer office. Okay! Maybe he went a little too far when his cheating ass manager showed up fresh out of a meeting and K-Flex began to choke the life out of the scrawny little weasel.

But attempted murder! Nah, he didn't deserve that one.

"Nelson!" one of the jailers called out, his keys jangling, breaking K-flex out of his trance. He rose and walked back to the bars of the holding tank. "You made bail, bama," the black-haired, Hispanic-sounding jailer informed him. K-Flex was too shocked to speak. He couldn't believe it. He wondered who had bailed him out. He gladly went through the releasing process, slow as it was. He was too happy to notice the vehement stares that the guards bestowed upon him. Haters were everywhere and K-Flex had learned early oh in the game that you couldn't run from them. A lot of people held envy and hatred in their hearts because they felt as if stars in the industry led glamorous and unique lives. To whom much is given, much is required.

K-Flex was escorted out of the booking and receiving area and into the discharge area of the precinct, where a distinguished looking brother in a Brooks Brother suit and gold-rimmed Versace glasses awaited him. "Mr. Nelson, I presume?" the brother asked, his arm extended.

"Yeah, uh, what's up? Who is you?" he asked as he took the brother's hand and gave him the once over.

"I'm acting liaison in the interest of Murder One Records. My name is Tyrick Blackmon, attorney at law," he informed K-Flex.

Murder One! Damn, Tiffany must've pulled through for him, K-Flex thought. As a friend of his mothers', he'd confided in her about his situation. She'd told him that she would see what could be done about it on her end. That was a week ago. "Damn! She took care of the biz pretty fast," he said.

"Pardon me?" Tyrick asked, confused.

"Never mind," Flex told him. The lawyer would not divulge any more information, despite the third degree given by K-Flex. He remained cool and vague in his conversation, which pissed the young rapper off. "Just chill out," the lawyer told him. "Your questions will be answered in a few short moments. Now I must warn you that there are press hounds from the industry media right outside the precinct. My client asks that you decline any comments until your initial meeting with the company is over. There is a car awaiting you out front. Just head straight for the car and it will take you to the meeting. Are you ready?" K-Flex nodded his head. He adjusted his platinum "Flex" pendant with its gaudy diamonds, repositioned his Cartier diamond beveled watch and tried to straighten his appearance as best as he could, considering what he'd just gone through, and headed for the double doors leading to the streets.

As the double doors opened, the sunlight hit K-Flex and the lawyer in the eyes, temporarily blinding them. K-Flex squinted and tried to shield his eyes as the reporters rushed the young rapper. The long line of reporters barked for a comment, showing no mercy. Things were

Koto

happening so fast that by the time K-Flex could see more than a yard beyond the, microphones that were thrust in his face, he ran directly into the chest of Tony, Amin's personal bodyguard. Maybe he should've worn shades, like the lawyer.

Tony looked down at K-Flex and grunted at the young man. He then stepped aside and opened the door to the midnight blue Rolls Royce limo that had been awaiting K-Flex's arrival, Tony held off the hungry reporters as K-Flex climbed into the limo.

The first thing he noticed as he stepped in the car were Ayanna's sexy thighs, demurely crossed under a red skirt that was trying its damndest to squeeze the life out of 'them. He was so enthused with the view that he failed to notice Tiffany and Amin seated across from her.

"You can come in all the way so Tony can close the door," Amin stated, startling K-Flex. "We need to go before one of those nosy ass reporters climbs in here with us. And quit gawking at my personal assistant. Get one good look, then pick up your face," he said, as Tiffany and Ayanna giggled.

K-Flex entered the car and sat next to Ayanna as Tony closed the door behind him. Tiffany did the honors of making the introductions since K-Flex was still rudely ogling Ayanna.

"Broderick, this is Amin Rush, CEO of Murder One Records," Tiffany introduced K-Flex was impressed, shaking Amin's hand in the normal street fashion instead of being formal. He'd only met the CEO of his former record company once and that was after his album went platinum.

"Glad to meet ya," Amin said.

"And this is Ayanna, as you know, Amin's personal assistant," Tiffany pointed out as K-Flex gladly turned to Ayanna with a smile. He took in her appearance in one full swoop. He prided himself on being a smooth teenage lady killer. Ayanna sported a French roll hairstyle that accentuated her graceful neck, a red Liz Claiborne jacket with a matching skirt and a cream colored blouse with matching red pumps. She smiled, holding out her fist for some dap, surprising the young star.

"Nigga, don't leave me hanging," she told him, flattered at the attention. K-Flex reluctantly gave her some dap., He would've rather had a hug.

"Don't mind her," Amin said. "She's been acting strange since last night."

"Don't start, Amin!" Ayanna warned. Ayanna then did something that surprised them all. She gently felt Broderick's face with both of her hands. Everyone was shocked speechless, because Ayanna would normally ask if it were OK to feel someone's face before doing it. This had never happened to him before, K-Flex thought, as the shockingly intimate feel of Ayanna's warm hands caressing his face left him, far once in his young life, unable to respond to a woman's touch.

"You are cute!" Ayanna proclaimed as she and Tiffany burst out laughing." I know that you must have plenty of women on your team," she added teasingly. "I see why all these young girls be hollering about K-Flex this and K-Flex that."

"Enough flirting," Amin announced, as the Rolls Royce crept through the downtown traffic. "I wanted to be the first one to tell you that I have acquired your release from your Arista contract" Amin explained. "It seems that your little stunt put them on edge and it was all the push that was needed to get you released. So, technically, you are on my roster and an official member of the Murder One family. That is, if that's not a problem with you?" he asked. "Tiffany has made me a believer in your talents and your platinum success on your freshman album has. backed that belief." Amin paused, waiting for K-Flex's reaction.

Although Broderick was excited to hear that he was no longer a part of Arista, he did not want to rush into another contract. "Well, uh … I'm really down with who's down with me, but I just don't want to be indebted to somebody for the rest of my life," he confided. "I need my creative space and peace of mind so that I can have a repeat or a project better than the first."

"Check this out, youngster. I feel where you're coming from," Amin said. "Believe me, I do. This situation is only for one album. We're not trying to trap you. The only thing we will bind you for is just that one. If you decide after that to stay with the family, then cool. But so far, here is where we stand. First of all, I've paid off all outstanding expenses you wed Arista. That came to a total of $3 million. Then I bought the lien that was on your house and I paid off your former manager for the remainder of his contract. I also negotiated more points for you off the back end of your last album and the next one for us. The only problem is that you forgo your rights on the next album to us. That album will be due before the end of the third quarter so you have to work pretty quick, but you have our support and resources at no charge, including the services of your label mates and anyone under the Syon umbrella. This way you can release your album and tour by the end of the fiscal year, because that is the only money you'll be making. After this album you're free to shop around for the label of your choice even if I don't recoup my money. In addition I will release the lien to your house." Amin stressed. "I like you, kid. You just got a shitty deal and we don't roll like that at Murder One," he assured K-Flex.

"Damn, that's a hell of a deal," K-Flex said. Of course, he was in a bad situation and he needed the help, but this was too good to be true. He'd have to start going to church on Sunday because God was smiling on him. "How can I say no to that?" he questioned.

"You don't!" Tiffany said. "Murder One is looking out for your best interests.

"Sounds good, but you know that I produced my own music, right? Do I get points for that from my next album," he asked.

"Yeah, I forgot about that. You do get a piece of that," Amin assured him.

K-Flex shook his head as the interior of the limo quieted. "It's cool, man. I'm down, but this business is a muthafucka!" K-Flex said ruefully. "After this album, I get my own lawyers and manager," he added, causing everyone to burst out laughing.

"You should've done that from jump," Tiffany told him. "Your young ass wouldn't be in this fix now if you had done that from the beginning. Hell! Let me call your mother and give her the good news, because she has been worrying me about you."

"Oh! One more thing," Amin said. "Your mother gets to stay in the house, but you stay with me until the album is finished. I don't want any distractions, OK?"

"Deal," Broderick told him, happy to be invited to 'Idie' Amin's crib. Maybe if he paid attention he could learn a bit more about the biz. Hell, maybe he'd even get to hang out with Ayanna, he thought, placing his hand on her exposed knee. It tickled Ayanna and she laughed and shook her head.

"Ooh, you freaky! I've got to introduce him to Sheba, she'll love him," she laughed, taking his hand off her knee.

Chapter 40

"Girl, I'm not going to tell you again. Let me take you to the hospital, even if you don't want to go to the police at least you can let me take you to the emergency room," Kiwan insisted for what seemed to Prescious as the hundredth time.

"Nooooo," she drug out so that maybe Kiwan would get a complete understanding this time. There was no doubt that she was hurting, but she'd taken a Valium and Kiwan had her drinking some concoction that his father used to make him when he was ailing from a sports injury. It was tea with lemon, honey, peppermint and a splash of Jack Daniels. Since Prescious didn't have any Jack Daniels lying around the house, Kiwan had to use vodka. Same difference, he thought.

"Well, fuck you then Prescious, I'm gon blaze if you don't need me anymore since you got everything under control," he stated, clearly agitated. "Wit yo silly ass," he added, as he stood up getting ready to leave. Prescious hurriedly set her drink down and painfully stretched to pull Kiwan back down on the bed.

"Wait up," she told him. Prescious had been bathed, dressed and had her wounds attended to by Kiwan. He had changed her sheets, aired out her room and fixed her that damned drink. Though she wasn't clear about her feelings for Kiwan, the least she could do was reciprocate the concern that he obviously had for her. She smiled a smile that didn't reach her eyes as she contemplated letting her guard down. Lord knew she needed a shoulder to lean on. All of her past relations with people were on such a superficial level, especially where her feelings were involved. It had been her defense mechanism ever since her first traumatic experience.

"Let's not regress, Kiwan."

"What?" he asked, puzzled.

"You know, I'm saying that first of all, I apologize. It's just that I've never had anybody show me any genuine concern. Niggas always want something, they don't give a fuck about how I feel, so I've been really fucked up," she confessed as tears welled up in the corners of her eyes. "I hate my life," she cried.

Kiwan couldn't really understand. How could this flawlessly beautiful woman who seemingly had a boss ass job, nice cash flow, and could have just about any man she wanted, hate her life? That didn't make a bit of sense. Then again, in life, Kiwan knew that everything wasn't always as it seemed.

"I guess I can relate, Man, Lord knows how tired of niggas I am. Especially after doing that ten year bid, if I don't kick it with a nigga for another 50 years it'll still be too soon. I can sympathize with you on that one," he shared, holding her as she cried again.

"You couldn't possibly know," Precious sniffled.

"I never said that I knew, boo, I said that I sympathized wit cha. But I do know one thing. . . I do know that you can talk to me," he assured her.

Precious wasn't so sure about that. They had just met, but her gut feeling agreed with Kiwan, so she decided to try something first, the vodka in the drink combined with the Valium creeping up on her and lowering her defenses.

"Truth or dare?" Precious asked, drying her eyes. She was tired of crying. Crying never really did her any good. She'd always had to be strong for herself.

"Excuse me?" Kiwan asked, in mock pretentiousness.

"You heard me; you scared?" Precious dared the big man.

"Hell naw!" he yelled. "Bring that bullshit on, I'll bat that punk shit back to Hawaii."

"Awight, I go first," she insisted.

"Bet! Come on."

"Okay, truth or dare?" she wanted to know again.

"Truth," he said, calling her bluff.

"Are you in love with Ayanna?"

Damn! Why did she have to go there, Kiwan thought. Precious sat up because she felt Kiwan tense up. She wanted to look into his eyes. The truth always lived there no matter how much you tried to hide it.

Me and my big mouth, Kiwan told himself. "If you can't handle it, you can always take the dare," Precious capped. Although she said it in a joking manner, Kiwan knew that this was a pivotal point in their relationship, and how he answered was vital to more than just Precious' knowledge. He had to really ask himself, was it worth it to be honest with her? What would it benefit him? Frankly, to be honest, he didn't know the answer to the question himself; did he really love Ayanna?

"What's the matter, Kiwan?" Precious asked him mockingly. Her tight-eyed anticipation spoke of a more serious nature than her manner revealed. Kiwan could smell the peppermint on her breath, she was so close.

"Yeah, man, I love her, but I'm not in love with her," he answered truthfully. "I love what we had, I love the Ayanna I knew ten years ago. But honestly, P, the way she did me while I was on lock really fucked with me. I'm bitter and I can't get over it no matter how hard I try, but I feel that I owe it to myself to at least put forth the effort to put the past behind me and try. The love I had has to still be in me, if not, then why would I still hold a grudge?" he questioned. Kiwan couldn't believe that he was divulging the contents of his heart to a virtual stranger, but actually if kind of felt liberating.

"It's simple, you still love her," Precious said, solemnly, speaking what she felt.

Kiwan thought, about that for a second. He began to shake his head. "Nah, I would trade all of that love for loyalty. Now that I think about how I felt on all of those days without the support of my woman, I have to say that really, love don't have shit to do with nothing. It's loyalty, support, then love that a nigga like me needs."

Precious couldn't believe her ears. That's exactly how she felt. What else did she and Kiwan have in common, she wondered?

"You mean that all a woman has to do is be loyal, support you through whatever and she's won your love and loyalty in return?" she wanted to know as Kiwan now had her undivided attention.

"Yeah, I guess you could put it that way. But we not gon elaborate on that right now. Right now it's my turn. Truth or dare?"

"Dare," she blurted. Prescious had been so used to taking the dare, being deathly afraid of the truth on any level for fear of exposure, her answer came without thought.

"Oh, hell, naw!" Kiwan protested. Then he thought about it a second.

"What, you can't get mad about me choosing the dare. You're the one who chose the truth, nobody twisted your arm. That was that manly pride," she told him.

Kiwan cocked a crooked grin. "You're right," he said, smiling. "You sure that you want the dare?" he asked, trying to exude a little seductivity to throw her off.

She nodded her head solemnly, just knowing that his dare would be sexual in some way, shape, fashion, or form. Thought it really didn't faze her one or another, she was disappointed in Kiwan, expecting him to be more sympathetic to her condition. Whatever he asked, she knew that she could dig deep, put aside her wants and perform, just as she always had in the past.

"You sure?" he reiterated, still smiling.

"Nigga, I said yeah, didn't I?" she snapped. He was starting to get on her nerves. Let's just get it over with, she thought.

For a second, Kiwan wanted to let the thug loose on her ass to let her know that, Bitch, you yell at your kids, don't yell at him, but he thought better of it. He knew that this dare would fix her ass.

"Awight, I dare you to let that tough Bitch role go and tell me the truth about your most darkest secret. That shit doesn't impress me, and I'm not the least bit intimidated by your looks. I want the real Prescious," he demanded.

Damn, she thought. He'd thrown her for a complete loop with that one. "Why?" she whispered. "What do you care?"

"A little something you need to know about Kiwan," he warned her. "If I didn't give a damn I wouldn't be here."

And that was how it started. Prescious shared one thing and then ended up releasing thirty years of pent up anger, frustration, abuse, unrequited love, and heartache, not mention the story of Dexter and how he was using her as a mole inside of Murder One. Not once did Kiwan interrupt her. He just let her talk. He sensed that this moment had been a long time coming. he listened, Kiwan came to the realization that Prescious was just a victim in the whole sordid mess. He understood now why she was the way she was. She was alone, she'd always been alone. "Okay, okay," Kiwan said, finally speaking. "Let me get this shit straight. This punk ass dude Dexter is the Congresswoman's son, and he's also an assistant D.A., correct?"

Prescious slowly nodded her head. Now she was a bit skeptical of Kiwan. She didn't know how he would treat her knowing her past, or what he would do to her knowing that she'd betrayed his brother.

"Plus; he was one of the two men who raped you last night because you told him that basically you didn't want to spy for him anymore, right?" Kiwan clarified.

Prescious could tell he was in a rage. He was pacing the floor, jaw muscles twitching, and he pounded one fist into the other palm. She hoped that he wasn't directing that fury at her. She sat on her bed, knees pulled to her chest, and questioned herself. She felt as if she needed his approval. Why? Was she falling in love with him? Prescious realized that she'd never been in love before. Did she really want love? No, she concluded. Love was expected, love wasn't enough to keep a man true and by her side. Prescious wanted what Kiwan wanted loyalty!

"Put some clothes on," Kiwan demanded. "We gotta jet. There's a few more questions I want to ask you, but we can do it on the way."

To her surprise, Prescious found herself hopping to it. "Where are we going?" she asked.

"I just remembered that I gotta go see my P.O.," he reminded her. "I just hope he or she don't trip out on me for being late."

Chapter 41

"Would you look at this shit?" Tiffany commented, referring to the throng of press vans that cluttered the front of the Plaza Hotel in midtown Manhattan. The Rolls Royce limo pulled into the drive that fronted the hotel. Reporters busied themselves for the cameras as their lead story for the midday news had just arrived.

"I figured as much," Amin stated, spying the reporters through his Gucci shades. "Everybody stick to the script, that means no comment, Flex. Damon should be inside the door waiting on us. Just shoot straight for the lobby. The reporters can't enter the hotel," Amin assured them.

The sharply dressed doorman maneuvered his way through the reporters trying to clear a path to the limo. When Tony exited the passenger side of the Rolls, he quickly covered the back door. K-Flex was the first to exit. He tried his damndest to make a mad dash to the reporter-free zone, the hotel's lobby, where Damon awaited.

The zealous reporters swarmed the young man like a hive of angry Yellow Jackets on meth, shoving microphones and screaming questions.

"K-Flex, is it true that you tried to kill your manager in cold blood?"

"Mr. Nelson, why has Arista dropped all charges against you? Is it true that Murder One is your new label?"

"K-Flex, how do you respond to the rumors of your affair with Beyonce Knowles? The two of you are both from Houston," one reporter stated.

Where did that bullshit come from, K-flex wondered. Despite the ridiculous nature of the question, K-flex was tempted to stop and answer the stupid shit.

"Are you really broke? One meal away from the soup kitchen, and Murder One was actually your savior?" came the next antagonizing question from behind K-flex just as he made it to the lobby door. Damon stood there, beckoning for him to enter. K-flex abruptly stopped and turned to face a brazen, no-nonsense looking female reporter. Flex could tell that she was a mulatto because of her mixed features. He was getting ready to give the bitch a piece of news that she'd never forget. Luckily, Tiffany rushed to him, almost having to drag his ass into the lobby.

"Boy," Tiffany called out as they made it inside the lobby. "We're going to have to do something about that temper," she scolded. "Save that shit for the music," she suggested.

'Idie' Amin stepped form the limo gator hoes first. When Amin stood, he smoothed his suit coat, a stern look upon his face. As Ayanna held out her hand for Amin to take, he gracefully helped her out of the car. The reporters pounced.

"Mr. Rush, is it true that K-flex is on your roster, and did you have anything to do with his attack on Arista executives?"

"Why did you bail him out of jail?" "Is this some sort of publicity stunt?"

"Yes and no," he answered smoothly, with his back to the crowd as if he didn't have a care in the world, still helping Ayanna out of the limo. Giving a comment, any type of comment, was an open invitation for a reporter to invade your personal space, Amin knew. But through his media experience, he also found it best to at least be cordial. At this point, camera lights blazed and microphones were pushed close enough for him to kiss as the hounds jockeyed for position. Ayanna waved her hand in front of her face blindly as a deterrent for anyone coming too close to her. Tony began to get downright rude, and physically shoved reporters, cameras, and microphones out of the way in an attempt to clear a path. It was almost like the second parting of the Red Sea as the big red giant moved the New York media aside. Amin and Ayanna slowly followed.

"Mr. Rush, does adding K-flex to your label have anything to do with your reluctance to accept Syon's proposal to merge your company?" Damn! Amin wondered how that bit of information had leaked to the press. He paused to adjust his $2,000 Hermes tie. He might as well give a statement. This had to be good, though, because the streets would both be watching, especially Syon.

"Listen," he began in a business-like tone. "I'm in the business of making music, good music at that. The entire industry knows this," he campaigned. "K-flex is an artist whom I felt could add to the foundation of this record company as we endeavor to take it to the next level. He brings new flavor and raw talent, not to mention an undoubtedly strong rivalry amongst his labelmates that will push everyone to excel. As far as Murder One merging, I don't see that happening anytime in the near future. Our infrastructure remains stable, and we fear that any unnecessary shift could disrupt our current as well as future agendas. Murder One is solely focused on progression, not regression." Amin signaled Tony to finish bowling his way through because he was finished commenting.

Once they were all grouped together in the lobby safe from the media, they all breathed a sigh of relief and headed to the bank of elevators.

"Damn people are relentless," Tony said.

Shocked by his bodyguard's unscheduled and unexpected words - more words than he'd spoken in weeks - Amin replied, "You got that right!"

"Un oh," Damon sighed. "More company," he said, referring to a group of women heading their way, calling K-Flex's name.

In the industry, there were two type of fans. There were the groupies, which fell in two categories, and regular fans, who just supported their favorite artists. Where groupies were concerned there were regular groupies, then there were your professional groupies. The group of women that were headed toward the small Murder One entourage were, in K-flex's opinion, professional groupies. During his tour promoting his recent platinum-selling album, K-flex had seen this particular group of women on numerous occasions. Knowing two of them intimately from a past ménage a trois encounter that had resulted from too much Hennessy and chronic, K-flex couldn't just blow these women off.

"Hold up, y'all, I know 'em," he bragged to the two bodyguards as he stepped forward. K-flex didn't even want to know how they just happened to be in the same hotel as he at this particular time.

"Hey, Flex!" one of the woman cooed in an obvious sexual tone, as they all walked up to him.

"What's tha damn deal?" K-flex spoke. He couldn't help but shake his head at the 'already' clothes that the women seemed to wear like a second skin. They were so scantily dressed he knew that none of them could be wearing undergarments. Tattoos and body piercings dominated and covered their bodies, strategically placed to draw attention to certain body parts. His definition of the 'already' clothes were clothes that were so easy to remove, that you were always ready for sex, anytime, anywhere.

"What tha fuck y'all doing up here in New York?" he wanted to know, fingering his platinum chain.

"Actually we came up here to bond you out of jail, but we found that somebody beat us to the punch," the leader of the quartet spoke.

"Oh yeah, well, that was sweet, ma. Who are your friends?"

"Oh, these my girls, Tish and Q. We figured, you know, that since we came down here we might as well hang. And since we found you, how about blessing me and my girls with some of that dick?"

K-flex flinched at her boldness. He wanted to go with the girls bad as shit, but he knew that now was not a good time. He looked back at the Murder One executives, who seemed to not be listening, but he knew better.

"Nah, ma, I'm going to have to take a raincheck," he said.

"Ahhh, are you sure, boo?" the honey-colored female asked as she sidled up to K-Flex, her semi-exposed breast under the barely fitting halter top touching his arm. "Because we had a special treat for you this time. Real special," she emphasized.

"Nah, I'm good," he said with more certainty than he felt. "Why don't you hit me off when I get back to the H?"

Koto

"Unh unh, we got invited to Springfest with the G-Unit. You just missed out," she popped off with major attitude, stalking off with her friends in tow.

"I'm proud of you, kid," Amin commented, coming up to stand. next to K-flex. "I thought that I was going to have to burst your bubble. There's hope for you yet, junior," Amin kidded. "Come on, Moochie should be waiting on us."

Damon and Tony led the way. The small crew bypassed the regular elevators and hitched a ride on the service elevator to the basement of the hotel. K-flex was a bit confused by the out-of-the-ordinary route they were taking, as some staff members of the hotel peeked in curiosity. Flex knew that there was a purpose to the circuitous route but he didn't know what, although he did know enough not to ask. They walked through the laundry room, past steam pipes, ironing tables and commercial washers and dryers. They finally came to a set of stairs that led to an exit. Tony took the stairs three steps at a time, reaching the top before everyone else. He opened the door as he hit the top of the stairs, letting the sun stream down. Damon stood between Tony and the crew as he came to a complete halt before reaching the top. Tony stuck his head outside and looked both ways. He must have approved of the view because he motioned for the rest of them to come out like the coast was clear.

As they exited the door, K-flex realized that they were in the service alley, where all of the hotel deliveries were made. A black Yukon Denali with tinted windows sat facing the exit with its rear doors open. As everyone got into the truck and the driver finally pulled away, K-flex's curiosity got the best of him.

"If you don't mind me asking," Flex addressed Amin, "can you tell me exactly where we're headed?"

"And you were doing so good," Amin kidded. He knew the kid didn't know what the hell was going on. "We're going to Harlem."

"Oh," was all K-flex could think to say. Fuck it, he thought. Anything was better than jail.

Chapter 42

Justin's is a favorite spot for record executives and industry types during the lunch hour, was owned by hip-hop mogul. Sean 'P-Diddy' Combs. The eclectic atmosphere lent credence to the massive egos of the money makers, movers and shakers of the industry. Massive high definition plasma screen televisions dominated the bar area so that those unlucky souls absent-minded enough to show up without reservations, or those who just wanted to drink and mingle could be provided with sports, the latest news, or the hottest videos.

Chad Stevens sat at the bar enjoying his drink and the plethora of beautiful, business-oriented black women when he happened to glance up at the screen to see 'Idie' Amin and his assistant on the midday news. "Um, turn that up a second!" Chad yelled to the bartender, as he momentarily forgot where he was.

"Who you yelling at, white boy?" the husky bartender replied surlily, which was ironic because he just so happened to be white, also "You ain't on Wall Street, playa," the hip bartender retorted. "You don't bark orders at me and expect me to hop."

"All right, all right," Chad conceded. He didn't want to argue right now, he just wanted to hear what Amin was saying, and most importantly find out what he was doing in New York. "Would you please turn it up?"

Reluctantly, the bartender picked up the remote and raised the volume on the television, just in time to catch the gist of the story. As Chad watched Amin, he couldn't help but admire the moves that the young entrepreneur was trying to make. In numerous ways, Amin reminded Chad of himself in his early years in the industry, the fact remained that Amin too often bit the hand that fed him. Despite Chad's admiration, Amin had to be punished, Chad decided and he picked up his cell phone and began dialing.

He was so engrossed in his vindictive actions that he completely missed his lunch date, who stood at the hostess station surveying the crowd. The sharply dressed female executive at B.M.G.'s headquarters in New York looked around in disgust, the high cheekboned coffee-colored sister in the cream-colored pantsuit tapped her leg impatiently. If it was one thing she hated, it was being lied to. When she phoned Chad thirty minutes ago, he'd said that he'd be waiting on her at the hostess' station when she arrived.

Fuck it, she thought. If he didn't want to consummate the deal, which would further his career, then that was on him. Why she fucked with over-ambitious white men was beyond her, she thought as she left the restaurant. That was one thing that she could control, she surmised.

Chapter 43

Felicia knew that Romichael was testing her. She'd just gotten off the phone with him. He'd asked if she would drive Corey and his homie to New Orleans for some business. This was just the thing that Felicia needed to prove herself. They were probably going to make a drug run, she figured. It didn't matter because it wouldn't be anything that she hadn't done before. Felicia could remember a time when she'd made a pretty penny running drugs from Texas to Louisiana and back for her friend, Blue, from Missouri City. It was something she did when she was younger, not because she had to, but because she wanted to. In a lot of ways, Daddy Bo had said that she reminded him of Amin, and her "I don't need nobody, I can do fine on my own" attitude was one of the characteristics that the siblings shared.

She pondered on her father and wondered what he was doing as she prepared for her short trip. "I wonder what my father would say if he knew what I was doing," she thought as her doorbell rang, surprising her.

Who could that be, she thought? The only other person who knew that she was there was Nina and she knew Nina was in New York. She had just spoken with Nina that morning. Felicia grabbed her .380 Berretta from under her mattress before she went to answer the door. Better safe than sorry, she figured. Felicia was a few inches shorter than the peephole in the door of the home, and had to stand on her tip toes to peek out.

Four well-dressed men stood on her doorstep. "Now who the fuck is this?" she wondered aloud. Felicia checked the safety on her pistol to make certain that it was off, just in case. "Who is it?" she called out, a bit agitated.

"Felicia, Nina sent us over here to check on you to make sure you were all right," came the reply.

Damn! Felicia thought. Nina should know better; they had a pact. She wasn't supposed to tell anybody. Maybe something was wrong.

Felicia slung the door open disgustedly. "What's up?" Dominick greeted as he nodded his head. He didn't fail to see the pistol, either. "What's with the gun, you don't need that," he attempted at reassuring her. "Shit, that remains to be seen. Who are you?" she asked without inviting them in.

"I said you can trust us, put the damn gun up," Dominick demanded.

Jamarcus emerged from the middle of the pack and tried to snatch the gun from Felicia. She pulled her right hand back and landed a left hook flush on Jamarcus' jaw. She stepped back and drew down on the four men.

"Wait a minute," Black Jack said, stepping to the front with his hands up. He should've taken the initiative from the beginning and done the talking. He should've known that dealing with one of Clyde Rush's children wasn't going to be as simple as it looked. "Girl, we are friends of your father's; Nina sent us to check on you because she was worried about you. She said that you didn't sound too cool on the phone. Now if you don't believe me I can get her on the phone for you, she's in New York with your half-brother Amin. Am I correct?" Black Jack revealed in an attempt to convince her to put the pistol away.

Felicia slowly lowered the pistol. Only Nina and Daddy Bo, outside of herself, her mother and Christy knew that Amin and Kiwan were her brothers.

"Can we come in now? You know how these white folks are. They see too many niggas grouped up in one area for too long they gon call the laws. And we out here in Champion Forest, girl, if they call the police you know that they ain't gonna do no talking; we all going to be explaining in the back of the squad car with the handcuffs on," Black Jack said.

Felicia didn't speak, but reluctantly let the four men in as she moved aside. She was still a bit confused and kept a tight grip on her pistol. Jamarcus gave her a look that would have fried an egg as he worked the muscles in his jaws slowly.

"Okay, so you know me and my family, but who are you guys?" Felicia wanted to know.

"Oh, I apologize, where are my manners? My name is Keith Vincent, but you probably know me as Black Jack. And these are my sons Dominick, Jamarcus and Willie."

Jamarcus was still eyeing her viciously. "You got a good one," he said, referring to his jaw. "But revenge is best served cold, so keep your coat on," he advised Felicia, who smirked.

"Aw, shut up, nobody told your silly ass to grab for her gun. You lucky your tough ass didn't get shot," his older brother, Dominick told him. Willie just laughed.

"Man, she full of shit, she ain't gon shoot nobody," Jamarcus yelled.

"Yeah, well I betcha I ain't gonna find out without being armed myself," Willie told him.

I apologize for my son," Black Jack said. "He's just a baby, so you must excuse him."

"Black Jack, I've heard of you. My father speaks highly of you. I'm sorry, I didn't know it was you," Felicia told the elderly man with respect and a hint of awe in her voice.

"Shiiit, as much money as me and that Negro has made together, he needs to have my name tattooed on his ass," Black Jack joked. Everyone laughed as Felicia showed them to her living room so they could sit and talk before she left to pick up Corey.

"I'm sorry that I can't offer you all something to drink as far as alcohol, but I do have water and juice," she commented. "I know that you big ballers are used to kingly service, but I don't have it like that," she said, cutting her eyes at Jamarcus. She could tell that Jamarcus' little manhood pride was hurt over the earlier incident and she couldn't help but rub it in.

"That's all right," Black Jack said as he leaned back into her plush Mexican-leather sofa and jacked his slacks, crossing his legs as a finale to his smooth move. Felicia couldn't help but think this was one smooth, cool, old muthafucka!

"Look, we're not going to stay that long because we understand the ramifications and the importance of us not being seen here. I would've called and spoken to you on the phone, but you have to understand that your father is like family to me and I've raised his kids as my own in his absence. And when I got the call about you, another of his children whom I had to learn about from someone else. I just had to come and see for myself because of the love that I have for your father," Black Jack told her with a sincere heart. "And Felicia, your father doesn't know what you're doing, but I do and I'm begging you to pull out. Don't get too close to this cat. You don't have to do what you're doing because we're going to take care of Romichael, and baby when we drop that bomb on his ass you don't want to be nowhere around.

"That's the point," Felicia said, cutting Black Jack off. "I'll sacrifice my life for my father and his cause. Because I believe in Murder One attaining that seat. That seat could mean my father's freedom. I would die to see him home. I need him, my mother needs him, and there's nothing I wouldn't do to make that happen," she ranted.

Black Jack nodded his head. He understood as he sat there looking at his best friend's daughter. "Listen, baby girl, I have a daughter, two of them. One is blind and one is shot, laying up in some hospital. I'm sure that losing you to Romichael would not be worth the committee seat to your father, especially if he kept you a secret from me all these years. I'm begging you to pull out. And believe me when I tell you that Black Jack doesn't beg."

Felicia smiled the most beautiful and innocent smile that Black Jack had seen in a long while. "I'm already in. It doesn't make sense to pull out now. I can tell that you are a man who's used to having it his way, but I'll make a deal with you. If I can't find anything that you guys can use against Romichael within the next month to take that seat away then I'll pull out." Black Jack didn't want to acquiesce, but he saw the determination in her eyes and could hear it in her voice. She had a fierce love for her mother and father. Who was he to stand in the way of it? She was a grown woman. Black Jack reflected on all of the bad decisions he'd made concerning the kids and he knew that one day somebody was eventually going to get killed. All of his mistakes would come back to haunt him. Luckily A-dray was not the one to die and hopefully Felicia wouldn't be killed either. He knew the hearts of men who sought power for selfish reasons; they played for keeps.

Black Jack just shook his head. "All right, Felicia, we'll play it your way, baby girl. But you got one month. After that, we're coming in to get you with guns blazing, if need be," he said as he stood to leave.

Felicia held out her hand demurely for them to shake on it. Black Jack couldn't help but embrace the young woman who reminded him so much of her brothers.

Dominick gave her a cell phone. "All of our numbers are programmed in here already without names. You can program it for voice recognition. If you need anyone of us don't hesitate to call, no matter what," he told her as everyone hugged her, even Jamarcus.

"When this is all over, you're going to get a proper induction into the clique, I mean family," Jamarcus told her.

Felicia was touched and couldn't help but shed a few tears at the love they offered. "Wait til Amin and Kiwan find out that they got a fine ass sister," Jamarcus blurted.

Willie slapped him upside his head, causing his huge diamond and platinum Murder One pendant to hit him on the forehead. "Shut up, you talk too much. You best not say a fucking word," his older brother warned. "This goes no farther than us until she sees fit to tell them. You know it ain't your business.

Felicia closed the door and broke down crying. Now she longed to join up with the people who loved her. She would be glad when it was over. Now she knew that she had to find something concrete on Romichael. Ruff House was going down.

Chapter 44

'Idle' Amin tried to gather his thoughts amidst the chorus of laughter, jokes and boisterous talking. The mood inside of Sylvia's Soulfood restaurant in Harlem was festive. The Murder One entourage as well as Nina's family were there en masse to celebrate. Rueben and his crew had enough: stroke with the manager of Sylvia's to pull off this last minute get together to welcome K-flex into the family. The smiles, drinks, and family love flowed freely around the six tables that were pulled together to accommodate the large party.

Not that it mattered. The entire place was closed in the middle of the day for the gathering, and they partied like they owned it. The down-home smell of the soul food: that the waiters .kept bringing to the table made Amin's stomach growl as he sat back in a booth off to the side with his two-way pager out.

Ever since Friday and his episode with the gonorrhea, Amin was seriously thinking about his lifestyle and the many women he flaunted when he was away from Houston. There were Candice and Tameka there in New York, Tawanna in North Carolina, Regina and DeeDee in Atlanta, Cassidy and her homegirls in Cali. Cassidy was cool; she let Amin and his crew fuck all of her home girls. There's a real house of sin. And last was Yvette in Miami, who he happened to be conversing with via two-way pager at this very moment. Amin knew that out of all his women, Yvette was the one that he definitely didn't need to be fucking around with. Every woman he messed around with was a career-wise professional. Each woman had her own, and her priorities as far as taking care of themselves were in order. They ranged from doctors to models, all with the exception of Yvette. All Yvette wanted to do was spend money and look cute doing it. She was convinced beyond a shadow of a doubt that her pussy and her good looks would be able to secure a future of wealth, which would last the rest of her life. Wrong! She had no ambition or drive, and if Amin had to guess, she was the most likely candidate to have given him the disease. She would be the first to go, he thought as he sipped his cognac, slouched in the booth.

- Why haven't you called?

- Busy! Amin typed.

- I miss u. when are u coming down 2 pay strawberry a visit, she misses U.

Amin cringed a bit as he glanced over at his wife, who was doting over their two girls. A smile creeped upon his face because he knew that Strawberry was Yvette's pussy and she probably didn't know that Strawberry was sick! Amin glanced at Nina again. She probably figured that he was handling business. Though he was playing with fire, he went ahead and typed. Fuck it, he thought; it had to be done.

- R u there? don't b stingy with the dick. Me and strawberry need 2 c u.

- I just left u 2 weeks ago, u know I be busy. Plus I been 2 the doctor.

- Doctor!? 4 what?

- listen, we'll talk in person. I'll b down next week, until then don't call me anymore.

- What's wrong wit u, what did I do? Why the doctor visit? r u sick?

- Not now, I'm busy, Amin typed as he watched one of Rueben's friends, whom Nina used to date, whisper in her ear. Amin knew that the young Puerto Rican had major bread from the sale of drugs he ran. He was the reason Nina knew the game so well; he'd taught her all he knew.

As he watched, envy and jealousy started to surface. His wife's body language gave the impression that she didn't want to be bothered as she cut her eyes at her husband. Amin wanted her to go off on the faggot, but she gave him a look as if to say, "Don't trip, you know. It's still all about you, let me handle this." Her glowing green-eyed look said it all to Amin, so he let it be as he read his lcd screen. Yvette's message read: We're both grown. I respect u and your decisions, but don't play me, Amin. B real, don't front on me. I know that u love your wife, but 'I know that you're in luv wit this pussy. U'll b back.

Amin's message was simple in response and summed up the seriousness of his decision. It read: Not this time!! We'll talk later. One! As he signed off his cell phone rang. He thought that it might be Yvette calling, but he remembered that she only had the number to the penthouse. He looked at the caller ID and saw that it was Kiwan.

"What's tha damn deal?" Amin asked as he answered his phone.

"Sup, fool?" Kiwan asked. "What you got crackin?"

"Ain't too much. We took care of that biz with that youngster outta South Park, K-flex. Now we in Harlem at Sylvia's. Nina and her peeps up in here spoiling his young ass," Amin told his brother. . .

"Hell, they spose to the young nigga can rap tha stank ... outta shit. I'm surprised nobody scooped him before you did. He got too much talent."

Kiwan stressed. He didn't want to jump into what he had to tell Amin about the developing situation with Precious. He was trying to figure out a way to tactfully break the news to his younger brother.

"Shiit, nobody had time. We had the inside track, thanks to Tiffany. It just so happened that his mother called Tiffany right after he called her from jail," Amin revealed. "Yo, what did your. P.O. say? Did they give you an asshole?" he asked as he turned his gaze back on his wife, who had just pushed her ex out of her face. As bad as he wanted to jump up, he let it ride. Rueben came over and pulled his friend aside. Lucky him, Amin thought.

"Hell yeah! They gave me this ole crab tree lookin bitch, who gave me this ole long-winded ass speech. I just wanted to slap the shit outta her," Kiwan fussed. "I really don't blame her because I was a few hours late," Kiwan admitted.

"For what?" Amin yelled. "What happened to Precious? Did you ever get in touch with her? Her funky ass was supposed to show you how to get there. Damn! She really been bullshittin' lately. This ain't like . . ."

"Hold up, Amin," Kiwan broke in. "I found her, but maaan," he said solemnly. Amin did not like the sound of his brother's voice. Especially the part about him finding her. He immediately knew that something was wrong.

"What happened?" Amin asked, sitting up in the booth. He dreaded more bad news.

"Check this out. Do you remember Rameka Jefferson, that fine ass girl you went to school with who ran track? She stayed off of Truvilla and Delano. You remember what happened?" Kiwan asked. He spoke softly and seriously, trying to jog his brother's memory without giving away too much. He never was comfortable talking about real personal or business issues over the phone.

Amin took a second to reflect. Rameka Jefferson. . . Yeah, yeah! He remembered now. Rameka was one of the most popular girls at Yates at the time Amin was there. She'd been a senior when Amin was just a sophomore. She was also the smartest and the sexiest in her class. Her and Serena Williams could pass for twins. Especially as far as their bodies were concerned, Amin thought. Despite her other attributes, the most important thing that stood out to everyone at school was that she was humble. Her personality was the most memorable feature about her and everyone respected that about her. Considering the hardships and trials, that the kids in their hood faced, Rameka's personality made her exceptional.

If Amin remembered correctly, one day on her way home from school someone had dragged her into an abandoned house and brutally beat as well as repeatedly raped her. Two crackheads found her comatose body a couple of days later in an empty house, naked and battered. To this day the girl walked around the "Trey" doped up on thioridazine, smoking crack and sucking dicks by the dozen, just to get a bump. And she was still as fine as a Hollywood hooker, just crazy. The thought of Prescious in that kind of state infuriated Amin. The entire room glowed red as his blood pressure shot up and his heartbeat accelerated. He knew that Romichael was behind whatever happened.

"Amin," Kiwan called out. "It goes deeper than that, baby boy. Prescious is cool for the time being, but maan, we most definitely need to talk NOW! I've been with Black Jack since I've been back from the P.O.'s office, and you have some serious problems. You need to get here on the first thing smoking and keep the reasons to yourself. Right now you don't know who to trust, just get here as fast as you can," Kiwan warned. Amin knew that the stakes in the game has just gone up.

"I'm on my way," he said, hopping out of the booth, before he could even finish speaking.

Just as he got up, Amin saw the manager of Sylvia's leading a swarm of blue and gold-jacketed men into the restaurant with a dour look upon her face. The stern-faced had guns drawn and A.T.F. printed across the breast of their raid jackets. Amin knew that he wouldn't make it to H-town tonight because an entirely new set of obstacles lay right before him.

Chapter 45

The more Felicia thought about it, the more she came to believe that they weren't in town for a drug deal. Corey and his crony from the Fifth, whose name she didn't know and didn't care to know, were acting strange.

When she'd picked up the two men from a motel room, the first thing she noticed was that neither man carried any big, bulky bags or packages that would constitute a large amount of drugs or money. They only carried backpacks. Now that wasn't to say that the backpacks. couldn't be filled with drugs or money, but after she'd rented a Yukon and picked them up, they neither stashed anything in the truck and they didn't use any special vehicle already outfitted with drop spots for such covert activities. More importantly, they rode with their luggage, so that ruled out anything illegal being on their persons, Felicia thought, as she sat up contemplating. Once they'd arrived in New Orleans, they'd checked into a motel close to the French Quarter right off the freeway. After checking into the room, they all left again. Corey had Felicia drive to the airport and rent yet another vehicle, a dark blue late model Impala. Things just weren't adding up and Felicia was curious.

Why were they in New Orleans? After renting the second vehicle, they drove across town and had Felicia rent two suites in the Hyatt Regency. The suites were next door to one another and Felicia took one suite, and the two men went into the other. After about twenty minutes Felicia got restless and her curiosity was getting the best of her. She left the room to speak with Corey next door when she overheard them talking right by the door. At first all she could make out were their voices until she put her ear to the door. Though the voices weren't clear, through the door she could make out bits and pieces of the conversation.

"Michael . . . that . . . stayed in Ninth Ward . . . got the address . . . they supposed . . . at the club tonight." Felicia overheard. "Let me go get her settled," she cold hear Corey say a bit more clearly. That meant that he was closer to the door. Felicia scurried back to her room, trying to make as little noise as possible as she closed her door. The moment her door closed, she could hear Corey's room door open. She could hear him step out and close his door. She tried to time him getting ready to knock on her door before she opened it.

"Damn! What's up, man? You scared the living shit out of me," she told Corey in mock surprise.

"Come over here and let me holla at you," Corey instructed, brushing past Felicia.

"Listen, me and my patna getting ready to go handle up on some business. It's important that you don't leave the room until we get back. We shouldn't be gone long," he told her. He reached into his jacket pocket and handed her a cell phone. "Take this 'burner.' It's for an emergency. Don't use it otherwise. If I need you, I'ma call you, so you need to stay packed just in case," he told her.

One thing Felicia knew about men is that they loved women who they could trust and who could follow instructions. Felicia just nodded and took everything. Besides, Corey wasn't really leaving any room for her to question him.

"You got it?" he asked. "Oh," he remembered, before he left. "Romichael said to call him."

"Cool," she replied, stern-faced. That had been four hours ago. Now, here it was, two in the morning and she'd already been to sleep and lain awake in bed and still no Corey. Felicia couldn't make any sense of the bits of conversation she'd overheard and had decided to occupy herself with a bit of television.

She cut the TV on and then decided to call her sister-in-law to see what was up.

Nina's cell phone rang three times before she answered. Felicia heard a raspy Nina on the other end. "Hello?" she said, clearing her throat. Felicia knew that it was three a.m. in New York but Nina and Amin were night owls, and for Nina to be sleeping at this hour was uncharacteristic.

"What's up, sis?" Felicia quipped.

"Giiirl, hold on a second," Nina told her. Felicia could hear rattling and movement on the other end. There was a constant noise, a hum, that Felicia kept hearing and just couldn't place. Then she distinctly heard a door close. "Hello. I'm back," Nina said. "What's going on witcha?"

"Nothing, where are you?" Felicia wanted to know.

"Girl, we are on the jet headed back to Houston. We were going to leave earlier but can you believe that the fucking hip-hop task force raided a party that we were throwing at Sylvia's and took everybody that had a gun with no license to jail?" Nina said.

"Hip-hop task force? What the fuck is that?"

"It's a long story," Nina told her. "But I was wondering the very same thing."

"Well, damn, who went to jail?"

"Shit, if we'd have been in Houston, everybody would've been in jail. Luckily, when we're out of town and we fly on the company jet, Amin makes everybody leave their guns on the plane. The only people who were arrested were my cousin and most of his crew, not to mention my ex. Girl, we've been downtown all morning trying to get everybody's bail posted. The judge won't be in until later so we left instructions with a lawyer. The only person who is fucked is my ex, and a few of them who were on parole. Amin said that they don't give bonds to people already on parole."

"Hmph," Felicia huffed. "And I thought we had a deal; I thought that we were going to keep what I was doing between us," Felicia said, a little anger in her voice.

"I'm sorry Felicia. I got worried and I trust Black Jack. If anything happened to you and your brother found out that I could've prevented it, he'd never forgive me," Nina pleaded.

"Speaking of Amin, where is he?"

"He's out there sleeping. I'm in the bathroom."

"Oh, you really love that nigga, don't you?". Felicia commented.

"Maaan, me and this nigga done been through hell and back. And you best believe that it's straight up death do us part, with his narcisstic ass," Nina added.

"Narsi-what?"

"Selfish," Nina explained, "but it's a little deeper than that. What are you doing anyway? What's going on with Romichael? Have you found out anything yet?"

"No, see, that's why I called you because I'm down here in New Orleans with his flunky and some ole ruffle bait ass nigga. At first I thought that they were down here to take care of some business on the illegal tip, but they're not. I overheard them talking about some funky ass club and. I'm stuck in this bitch ass room by myself until they get back," Felicia complained.

"Aw, you want me to come and keep you company," Nina teased.

"Shut up, shit!" Felicia laughed. "Girl, I'm getting sick of this and I've only been around these trifling ass, show off, wanna-be-balling, wanksta bustas since Friday."

"Felicia, I'm sure that your father loves and appreciates you. Let these boys handle that fool Romichael. Come home to your family and get to know your brothers," Nina pleaded.

"I am," Felicia whined as tears threatened to break free from the grip that the brim of her eyes held. "I just have to do everything I can, don't you understand?"

A moment of uncomfortable silence pervaded their conversation before Nina spoke. "I might understand more than you think, but you do what you gotta do, just be careful because I love you. We love you."

"I love y'all too," Felicia sniffled.

"Call me when you get back to Houston and keep your eyes open because you never know. You just may catch them niggas slipping," Nina said seriously.

"All right, I will. I'll catch you later, sis," Felicia said.

"Later," Nina signed off before hanging up. Felicia felt a bit better after she hung up with her sister, and she watched movie until the movie watched her. It seemed as the moment she closed her eyes someone rapidly knocked on the door, startling her.

"Felicia," Corey called. Felicia had been sleeping like a damn fireman, with all her clothes on as she got up to answer the door, funky breath and all. When she opened the door Corey stepped back a little and snickered. Her hair was all over her head.

"Um, go ahead and get yourself together, baby and, uh, get ready cause we're heading out," Corey explained.

Felicia didn't even respond, she was so pissed off and frustrated. She just slammed the door in Corey's face. She really didn't have to pack shit, but she decided that she would make them hoe ass niggas wait. She was going to take her a long bath and pamper herself. She looked at the clock and noticed that it was 6:30 a.m. Now where the fuck were them two at all night, she wondered as she turned the TV to the morning news.

Felicia sauntered into the bathroom and started drawing her bath water. She pulled her hair back into a ponytail and went to retrieve her make-up bag. This was her little bag that she kept all of her "womanly" things in, because other than lipstick, lip gloss and eye liner, Felicia didn't wear any make-up. As she got her bag from a lounge chaise next to the bed, Felicia stopped short as the picture on the TV caught her attention.

An anchorman was standing outside of a popular New Orleans club called Voodoo Daddy's, with yellow crime scene tape across the front door. The tape read, "Murder Scene: Police Line - Do Not Cross." She cut the volume up to listen.

"... What police have described as an accidental shooting. They have witnesses who say two men were arguing in the club and one of the men pulled out a gun and started shooting. Two women were killed in the ensuing gunfire. Police say the two women were regulars at the club. Details are sketchy, but witnesses say one of the men stood out because he wore blue alligator shoes. They say the altercation began over someone stepping on those shoes," the anchorman said.

The picture changed to an eyewitness being interviewed. The witness, a young woman with a mouth full of gold fronts who still had glitter on her face, was grinning. This is some country shit, Felicia thought as she watched the girl.

"Um, see, I really don't know what happened. See me and my girls wuz jus chillin, see, and then we see this fine dark-skinned dude, arguing by tha bar. They was fussin and cussin about the guy steppin on the dark skin guy's gator shoes. Then all a sudden, we see dis guy pull his strap, but what was strange was that he pointed at the guy wit da shoes but swung the gun in our direction by tha bar and shot dose two girls," the gold-toothed woman explained excitedly. "He was actin all drunk., but when everybody started runnin he was the first nigg. . . oh, I mean, the first mothafu. . . I mean person, outta the door."

That's a shame, Felicia thought, as she went to the bathroom to brush her teeth, bathe and freshen up. "I wonder if them two fools went there . . ." she thought aloud, then stopped in mid-sentence. Couldn't be, she thought, as she tried to remember exactly what Corey had been wearing last night, if he or that other trifling ass nigga had been wearing blue alligator shoes. This could be the break she needed. This could be what would bring Romichael down. "Fuck!" she yelled. She put a little pep in her step. She crossed her fingers, hoping she could find out something, anything!

Chapter 46

Kiwan's brand new 2004 coal black Chevy C-6 Corvette was one of the first of its kind. The car had not been released to the general public yet and the attention it received would have made its designers proud. But Kiwan didn't know if the attention was directed at the car or the car's driver, as he and Precious moved through the traffic with the agility and speed of a professional soccer player who single-handedly breaks down defenses.

Precious handled the Vette with a reckless abandon and a touch of defensiveness that Kiwan admired. She drove the Vette like it was supposed to be driven. After her rape of the night before, Kiwan had not left her side. She'd packed a few belongings and temporarily moved in with Kiwan for the time being. He didn't mind; hell, his house was so big that he'd never be able to fill all of the rooms, of which he'd made a mental note to get an accurate count. Though his relationship with Precious and Ayanna wasn't clearly defined, Kiwan justified insisting that Precious stay with him through her need to be protected from any further assaults. Ayanna would just have to understand that it was business and not pleasure when it came to Precious staying at his house. He tried to stand on his reasoning with himself but knew the ground to be quite shaky.

He was thankful that the Vette had a top-of-the-line audio system and didn't mind the fact that Precious was jamming R Kelly's "Etcetera,

Etcetera," even though he wasn't in the mood to listen to no bitch ass love songs.

At least he didn't have to talk to her; he already felt vulnerable around her. He found that the more he talked to her, the more he knew that he was falling for her, so much that he didn't even fuck her last night despite the fact that she begged him to sleep with her.

After ten years in prison, Kiwan didn't want anymore chains around his neck, no matter what form they came in, but he didn't want to be caught up in any drama by leading either woman on, he stressed. Prescious was cool, but choosing her would leave Kiwan drained eventually, he knew, due to her emotional and mental scars. Ayanna had few hang-ups, but the nagging thought of her leaving when times got rough would always be in the back of Kiwan's mind, if he chose her. Fuck it; he would just deal with it as it came. Let the cards fall where they may, he concluded.

Right now he had bigger issues. And one of them was the Desert Eagle 357 that he'd gotten from Black Jack. That had been like pulling teeth from a hungry lion, getting the older man to give him the gun. Black Jack had preached to him the consequences of getting caught with the pistol while on parole. He told Kiwan that he'd had the same problem out of Moochie after he'd gotten home. Black Jack had then explained that there were plenty of young hired guns Kiwan could hire from the hood, if he just really felt that he had to have protection. "Even one of these boys can hold you down," Black Jack had insisted, meaning his sons. But Kiwan was not the type to have a bodyguard or a few niggas toting heat behind him when. He could carry his own weight. Kiwan had told Black Jack that if he didn't give him the gun he would find it somewhere else, and that had ended the debate.

Kiwan chuckled at himself as he looked at Prescious. She shifted the car with precision and perfect taming with her graceful hands, which seemed made for the car. The more he got to know her and spend time with her, the firmer his belief became that he had to separate himself from her before he fell too hard for her.

Prescious peeked over at Kiwan from behind her pink-tinted Chanel shades. When she saw the smile on his face, she grinned and blew him a kiss. Kiwan laughed. Even her demeanor, when dealing with him, had changed in the last 24 hours, he thought. Nothing brings people together like tragedy.

Fifteen minutes later they were pulling into the parking garage of the Arena Towers, where the Rush family had its conglomerate headquarters. The complex was located off Fondren and the 59 freeway on the Southwest side of Houston. The famed Sharpstown Mall sat behind the complex, providing a frequented business district that generated a lot of capital, which likely was the reason that Amin chose the site over the new and rejuvenated downtown area. Not only was the complex fronted with parking for customers and visitors, it had its own three-story parking garage for staff and employees. It also contained a theatre, which was generally used for small concerts and comedy shows.

When Murder One started out, they had occupied Suite 200 on the second floor of Tower Two. As the company grew, it moved upstairs and its hold on the Tower space expanded. They moved from the second floor to the more spacious eighth, then to the bigger suites of the fifteenth floor and finally ended up occupying the entire twenty-sixth floor, which was now the Mecca of the Rush family business.

Precious pulled the Vette into the parking garage. As she cutoff the engine, Kiwan could see a slight tremor in her hands that he hadn't noticed while she was driving. He leaned closer to the door and took a good look at her as she took a deep breath and fumbled around for her purse. She checked her appearance in the rearview mirror and fumbled with the clasp on the purse. It took her a second, but she noticed that Kiwan was staring at her.

Kiwan smile at her and stroked his chin. He couldn't help but smile, because the stern, no-nonsense, emotionally detached woman that he'd met on Friday was gone.

"What?" she asked, a bit agitated. She found in her purse and refreshed the sensuous lips that Kiwan was becoming attached to. He watched as she applied the glossy lip covering. His stare must've bothered her because she stopped what she was doing and turned completely to face him, removing her shades. Her hazel eyes reflected the depths of sorrow that Kiwan wanted so desperately to erase. He guessed that's why her hold was becoming so strong on him. Kiwan wanted to fulfill the loneliness of not having a love of his own for the last 10 years. He'd learned long ago that the support from a significant other far surpassed any amount of money, pictures, magazines, his family could provide. He was no stranger to the loneliness of lost, unrequited or misguided love. He and Precious were two kindred spirits in this whole mess known as life.

"What's up, Kiwan. Don't just look through me; what's up? Say what's on your mind. I thought that we were past all of the bullshit," she said candidly.

Kiwan reflected a second as his eyelids dropped and hooded his deep brown eyes in a thoughtful expression. "Before we go in there," he finally said, "I want you to know that I got your back no matter what. I understand and for what it's worth, you didn't do anything that anybody else wouldn't do."

Precious leaned over with tears in her eyes and, for the first time, kissed Kiwan without lust. Her stomach did flips as the kiss escalated into something deeper. Her tongue ring-danced inside of Kiwan's mouth like a hummingbird in search of nectar. As a rule Precious didn't kiss men, but Kiwan had broken that stigma on their first night of crazy sex, and now he was breaking another rule that she'd set for her life: never allow a man close to your heart.

Kiwan was the first to pull away. "No strings, no regrets," he quoted to her from their first night in the hotel in New Orleans. He exited the Vette, preparing himself mentally to face his brother and defend a woman who he knew that he wasn't supposed to care about.

Staying true to the unwritten rule that the Rush family lived by, which Kiwan had unflinchingly adhered to for the past ten years – family first - was the crimp in his play.

Chapter 47

Okay! Two plus two has always equalled four, Felicia thought happily as she held the clothes in her hand.

She had just returned the rented Yukon to the rental place after dropping off Corey and his nasty friend back at their motel room. Monica had followed in her Lexus after meeting Felicia at a Shell station close to Monica's townhome. While at the Shell station filling up the Yukon and cleaning it out before returning it to avoid any extra fees, Felicia found an ominous-looking plastic trash bag in the back of the truck. Monica was bent over in the front, cleaning out the ash tray of weed square butts when Felica ran across the bag. For some reason, Felicia hesitated before she grabbed the bag. It was stuffed in the corner behind the third row seat, half hidden. The way it was scrunched up and folded, Felicia could tell it contained clothing. A dark premonition of death enveloped her as she reached for the bag – it seemed as if the bag represented a dark, ugly future, and she had to force herself to reach for it. Her heart kicked into overdrive just staring at the bag. Fuck it, she thought, ignoring her intuition, which was screaming obscenities at her.

As she opened the bag her heart dropped in her chest as if she were on a steep roller coaster ride, dropping into a freefall from its highest point. As she fingered the blood—stained fabric, her first feelings of foreboding switched to elation because she knew that in her hands was proof that Corey and his accomplice had been the two men in the New Orleans club responsible for the deaths of those two women.

"Did you hear me?" Monica repeated from the front of the truck.

"Huh? What's up?" Felicia asked, quickly closing the bag and stuffing it in her luggage bag.

"I asked, are you going to the club tonight to work or are you going to chill, since it's such a slow night?" Monica asked her.

"Oh, I ain't tripping. I'll work until about twelve and then I'll bail to the crib to get me some rest," Felicia answered.

"All right, that's cool. Do you mind if we kick it tonight?" Monica asked, her sexual innuendo apparent. "I have a girlfriend I want you to meet," Monica cooed.

Chapter 48

The elegant diamond cut Waterford crystal pitcher shattered into a million tiny fragments against the hurricane-proof windows that ran floor to ceiling in the twenty-sixth floor conference room.

"You have got to be bullshitting me! I can't believe that bitch," Amin bellowed. Kiwan had just finished explaining the situation that developed while Amin was in New York. Amin didn't know what prompted the tears to drip from his eyes. Was it the weight of being a CEO of a multimillion dollar record label? Was it the fact that he had the burden of so many people who depended on him for their livelihood? Was it that things were escalating beyond his control, or was it just everything? One of those times where a man just has to cry.

Black Jack had warned Kiwan that Amin might get overly emotional. He instructed him to just let Amin vent. Black Jack, who understood explicitly the things that Amin was going through, told Kiwan to follow his lead. He knew that between men, what's already understood need not be said. In no particular rush Black Jack ambled over to the window and inspected it for any cracks before he gingerly bent down in his Versace suit to pick up the biggest pieces of crystal.

"That bitch has got to go," Amin continued in his tirade, tears still flowing freely "I've been too good to that bitch for her to do me like that; I opened my heart, my home and my family to her when I knew she didn't have anyone else. Fuck that ungrateful hoe! If it wasn't for me, she'd be just like these other dick suckin bitches runnin round here givin up tha pussy for rent money . . . They should've cut tha bitch's throat after they raped her," Amin ranted, as he wiped the unwanted tears from his face.

Kiwan couldn't believe the silly shit that Amin was saying. He was caught up in his feelings and being ruled by his emotions instead of his relentless sense of business, which had propelled him and the family to the level they were at now. Their father had always said that a man ruled by his emotions was destined for destruction, along with everything he touched. Kiwan hated to see his brother like that and wanted to slap some sense into him. It was a hard pill to swallow, but he took a deep breath and looked to Black Jack, who slowly stood and walked back to his chair. Amin was still pacing and cursing as Black Jack jacked his slacks and sort of melted into the polished leather chair. He pulled his sleeves down from under his suit jacket by his $4,000 diamond cuff links.

Amin banged his fist on the cherrywood conference table for effect. Kiwan understood that Amin was upset, but he was being a bit too dramatic. Who was he trying to impress with his show. 'Idie' Amin, hmph, Kiwan huffed, he was acting more like Benny Hill.

"Are you finished bitching and complaining, young blood? Let me know when you're finished so I can tell you about yourself," Black Jack said icily, void of all emotion. His tone reflected his demeanor, which surprised the shit out of Amin. He was stunned into gaped jaw silence. In all of the years he'd known Keith Vincent, the man had never spoken to Amin in that tone. Not even when Amin had made the mistake costing his brother and father God knows how many years of their lives behind bars. The tone in Black Jack's voice was reserved for outsiders and strangers, of which Amin was neither.

"Young blood," Black Jack started reflectively, "I've known you since you were knee high to a duck's ass. I've watched you grow up to be a man, and I'm proud to say that I've even had a hand in influencing your life. I've watched you do the right thing and I've also watched you do the wrong thing, all without a motherfuckin peep out of my mouth," Black Jack said, almost in a whisper. "You are my partner, my brother, my friend, my son, and at times my motivation. But as long as your ass points toward God's green earth, I will not sit back and let you single handedly ruin what WE ALL have struggled, sacrificed, and have shed blood for. You need to check your emotions at the door, because you need to get up, walk outside and let's try this shit again," Back Jack scorned him, his small black eyes boring through Amin's skull, penetrating his shallow veneer and bringing him back to his senses.

Amin couldn't help but feel like a scorned child. Kiwan looked at his younger brother for the first time with a dispassionate sorrow. He did not envy what and who his brother had become, and in a way he knew that all of the paternal figures in Amin's life were to blame, himself included.

Black Jack was about to continue his sermon to Amin when the conference room opened and Nina eased in, closing the door behind her. "Sorry I'm late, I just finished talking to Prescious," she spoke rapidly, trying not to be too much of a distraction.

"Late, late for what? You trippin," Amin scolded his wife, freezing her in her tracks. "We're busy, man," he told her.

Nina could not believe her ears, so much so that she even looked behind her to see who the hell this fool was really talking to. Her green eyes hooded over as she realized, he was actually talking to her. Hell, she thought that maybe somebody walked in behind her or that he'd mistaken her for somebody else. But, no! He was talking to her. In seconds her facial expression changed in intensity ashen eyes revealed a hatred that even she never thought could exist toward the man who she whole heartedly and unconditionally devoted her life to. Kiwan and Black Jack subconsciously cringed in their seats under her gaze. Nina then did the strangest thing: she cracked a beautiful smile that never quite reached her green eyes. There was a sinister look in her smile that said, "If we were alone there might be some blood shed between the two of us."

"Would you like me to leave, honey?" she asked with malice and sarcasm. "Because I just want to sit here and be nosy like I always do, with nothing to contribute and nothing to do. You know how I am at all the trey sixty meetings. I just like to watch, or maybe I could go do your laundry. Or no! Better yet, you must need momma to fix your lunch for you and the boys, and I could get the kids from the nursery and they could help. Whatever domestic shit you would have me do since you don't want me in here, boo," she remarked snidely, venom dripping off every syllable.

Kiwan just shook his head. He knew that his brother had hurt her, but he also knew that if anyone truly understood the pressures Amin was going through and the way it was affecting his better sense and judgement, it was Nina. She knew him better than he did himself. He recalled on one of her visits after he'd gotten transferred back to Texas from El Reno, Oklahoma, she'd confided in him that "Amin is not Amin anymore. He's like an actor in a stage play who's ignored the fact that the lights have gone off and the curtain is drawn. I wish that we could go back to the days when we used to move that shit across the country, when all we could do was think about you and Daddy Bo. He was so focused and determined back then, Kiwan. He used to always say that we have to save money and go on a budget to have something for you and Daddy Bo to come home to. Those were the days," she'd shared with her brother-in-law.

Amin felt stupid now. He saw for a moment through his wife's eyes how he was slowly losing his grip. He knew that he was tripping. What tha fuck was he thinking; Nina was as much Murder One as the name itself. "I apologize," he said sincerely and simply as he reached into his Burrberry pant suit pocket and pulled out a Black & Vanilla cigar. He lit it with a gold and platinum Zippo lighter with Murder One's logo engraved on it, which Nina had made especially for him when they first opened for business.

Nina didn't even respond. She sat disgustedly in one of the chairs, crossing her legs demurely, still trying to maintain her composure. "Like I was saying," she continued as if she had never been interrupted. "I just finished talking with Prescious." She paused, trying to gather her thoughts and verbalize them in a tactful way. Men of power were fickle about how they took advice, especially from a woman, Nina knew. She found herself in the same position that Kiwan had faced earlier. She didn't want to be seen as betraying the family when she tried explaining reason concerning a traitor to their cause.

An awkward silence hung in the air between the family members as each realized that they were at a crossroad. The events of the last week had shown them to be vulnerable in a way they had never thought possible. Their climb to the top, while not complete, had not been without problems, but due to a combination of luck, hard work and good taming, Murder One had scaled the heights of the industry in an astonishingly short time. But their pursuit of the committee seat, along with the current contract dispute with Syon and Chad Stevens, had introduced an element of uncertainty and had brought along with it an ominous cloud of danger in the person of Romichael Turner. His hand threatened to be the instrument of their undoing, if not by his person, by the way he had set them to fighting among themselves. They all knew that their ambition to expand, to become the force they knew they could become — a force to unify the black community nationwide, to give them something to aspire to and rally around – was threatened. Yet they also knew that they could not lose sight of their number one goal of what above all else they had to maintain focus on — the release of Daddy Bo.

"At first I really didn't understand her betrayal," Nina said, breaking the heavy silence. "I didn't see what harm she could cause with the little information that she said she passed. I listened carefully, I listened to everything she said. I heard everything about Dexter and their relationship and started putting things together. But before I go on, I have to first tell you about the meeting I had the other day with Nya Phillips, an old friend of Amin and I." Nina looked her husband in his eyes with heartfelt sincerity. "I'm sorry, Amin, I should've told you about it sooner, but the incident with the gon. . . you know," she said, looking around sheepishly. She looked back at her husband. He knew and he didn't want her to have to relive his faults and shortcomings as her husband, as a man. Amin nodded behind a cloud of vanilla-smelling smoke, tight-eyed, hoping like hell a tear wouldn't fall again.

"I was fucked up emotionally, and I didn't really know if we would get back together, so I didn't register what she was trying to tell me because it didn't make a lot of sense at the time and I put it in the back of my mind, but Saturday ..."

"Hold up," Black Jack said, cutting her off. "This wouldn't happen to be the same blue-eyed dark-skinned chick that I asked you about Saturday night at the meeting, would it, Amin?" Black Jack wanted to know.

"Yeah, but I didn't know that she had been in contact with Nina or even met up with her. What did she tell you?" Amin asked Nina.

"Well, she said that she worked for a lawyer who serviced the Congresswoman's committee and that Dexter was the intermediary. She said that one night she saw Dexter meet up with two people from Ruff House. But she also told me that she overheard Dexter talking about how he was going to make sure that Ruff House got the committee seat," Nina revealed.

"Okay, wait a minute," Black Jack said, holding up his hand. "First of all, that would explain why they were so unprepared at the meeting that me and A—dray went to, but my question is, if Romichael has Dexter and he feels confident about getting the seat, why be worried about what we're doing? So I have to tell myself that he must be uncertain of Dexter's influence with his mother. From the way she spoke Saturday night, I don't think that just because her son suggests something that she's going to automatically jump on it. Especially something as important as the committee seat, and Romichael must've sensed that on Saturday night. That's why this chain of events started happening to us," Black Jack pieced together. He began to get exited as the puzzle became clearer, and he rose to his feet and began pacing.

"First, A—dray gets shot at the park. Then Prescious is threatened and raped, then the ATF mysteriously shows up at a private party. This Nya bitch pops up out of the blue," Black Jack continued. "I don't believe in coincidences."

"Well, when we met her at the mall she explained where she'd been. and..."

"Wait," Amin told her. "You said we, who is we?"

"Well, it was me and Ayanna," Nina answered.

"Ayanna, why tha fuck didn't she say shit?" Amin wanted to know.

Nina shrugged her shoulders. "She probably thought that you knew already," Nina suggested. "But let me finish what I was saying." All kinds of questions popped up in Amin's mind, but he let his wife continue. Some strange shit was going on and everything needed to come out into the open so they could figure out their next move. "My point," Nina continued, "is that Prescious is not in a position to harm us as much as she is in a position to harm them. What could she have told Dexter that he couldn't have gotten from his mother? Plus, Prescious is in public relations. She didn't know about the committee seat until I told her. But she knows all of Dexter's private business, that ugly shit he likes, and that makes him vulnerable, especially to us," Nina emphasized. Amin started – he hadn't even thought about using what Precious had said were Dexter's sexual perversions against him. Man, his wife was devious.

"Didn't you say that Romichael called you Saturday bragging about the seat?" Black Jack asked, referring to the conversation that they'd had in the penthouse office.

"So if Precious didn't tell him, who did?" Amin wondered out loud. Everyone looked around the room at one another, silently pointing fingers. Not so much at each other, but at everybody.

Kiwan spoke for the first time; "It doesn't matter."

Everyone looked at him, confused at his statement. "It really doesn't matter," he repeated. "We are missing the point. To my understanding, all of this didn't start Saturday after the meeting with the Congresswoman, or after the call Amin got from Romichael. It all started Friday, after Amin got into it with, one of the most powerful men in the music business, who just so happens to work for a billion-dollar record company. "Stop me if I'm wrong," Kiwan insisted, "but not only did you turn down a billion-dollar business deal, but you insulted the man, a white boy who's just as arrogant as you," he said, pointing at Amin. "To me it looks like Romichael is being used by someone bigger. Maybe Syon, maybe the Congresswoman, but I would "bet on Syon. This business is shady, man. Personally, I think we've got problems bigger than Romichael. The question is: who stands to lose the most by our gain? Syon or Romichael?" Kiwan asked as his eyebrows shot up for dramatic effect, lightening the mood. "Answer that, then that's who needs to be taken out. Amin, you told me yourself that these people didn't play fair."

Kiwan made sense. Amin had not figured Syon and Chad Stevens into his equations, but none of that changed the fact that Romichael was the more immediate threat, if only because Romichael worked with violence, as seen by what had happened with A—dray and Precious.

Amin took a deep breath and put his palms flat on the table. Before he stood, he exhaled with an audible sigh. "All right. Questions. Number one: How did Romichael find out about the committee seat? Dexter, maybe. Number two: what happened at the park when

A—dray got shot? Who was behind that? Number three: who told the feds that we were at Sylvia's, or did somebody with me call somebody else and tell them where we were and that someone else called the feds? That was the ATF and some hip-hop task force that investigates beefs between artists and record labels of the industry, not to mention the background of the record companies concerning being started with laundered drug money. I have to ask myself a million questions. But the main thing is that all of this starts with two people. Dexter Cunningham and Prescious! If we get Dexter we get Romichael. If we get Romichael, we find out who's really behind all of this, and I'll be a lying switching bitch if I don't go broke to destroy whoever is behind all of this," Amin screamed.

"And that's by whatever means we deem necessary," he emphasized. It had come down to that, if need be and everyone knew that there was no way around it. The stakes were too, too much. Kiwan had once heard Daddy Bo say that "We have done so much, for so long, with so little, that we can now do anything with nothing," but now the family had something and somebody was in trouble, he knew. This time, instead of Amin's outburst infuriating him, it motivated him. They all knew what had to be done.

"Don't worry," Kiwan told them. "I have a plan. It'll work, trust me."

After the three-hour trey sixty of planning, replanning and planning again, everybody knew that it was time for a lunch break. They stepped out of the conference room, winded and tired. Kiwan knew that his plan would work, but he also knew that everything depended on Prescious. He needed to coach her, but most importantly he needed to make sure she'd be willing to go through with it.

"Say, I'm treating everyone to lunch at the Aquarium," Amin told Kiwan. "You riding with us?" he asked holding Nina's hand.

"Naw, I gotta do something. Where's Prescious?"

"Probably in her office," Nina suggested.

"Where is that?" Kiwan wondered.

"Oh, I'm sorry. Come on, I'll show you," Nina volunteered.

"I'll pick you up in front," Amin told Nina, who agreed. She walked with long strides, leading Kiwan to Prescious' office. As they approached the elevators, Ayanna stepped off with her baby brother Jamarcus on her arm.

Damn, Kiwan thought. His heartbeat quickened when he saw her. He wondered if it was possible to be in love with two women at once. "What's up, A?" Kiwan said, kissing her on her forehead, an endearing kiss that made her temporarily forget why, she'd left her sister's bedside at Southwest Memorial Hospital. Almost.

"Nigga, don't kiss me," she jerked back, telling him after the fact. "Come over here and let me talk to you," she said angrily, her voice quivering with emotion. They stepped around the corner into the women's restroom. "I've been trying to call you since I left Monday morning. Why didn't you return my call?" she fussed before the bathroom door closed good.

"Ayanna, I know you heard what's been going on." I've been busy. Quit tripping," he told her.

"Yeah, I heard, and I heard that the bitch moved in with you. What type of shit is that, Kiwan? You've only known that devious bitch for four days. Fucking her is one thing, but living with' her is completely different," she yelled, her long hair flying in front of her face as if in response to her anger, covering one side of her glasses like Aaliyah used to wear it. She brushed it back with her fingers and Kiwan could see the tears flow from under her shades. He shook his head.

"Look, you trippin, A. What I'm doing with Prescious is my personal business. I got, a 6,500-square-foot house with Lord knows how many bedrooms. She and the band could stay there and it wouldn't make a difference in my personal space. She's there for business reasons, not pleasure. And by the way, when did I start reporting to you? You forfeited that right about ten years ago," he told her defiantly. He dared her to challenge his reasoning. He dared her to define their relationship right then and there.

Ayanna couldn't do anything but drop down to the floor and sob. There were things he needed to know, things he had to know, but now was not the time. She wanted to tell him but not now. She sobbed uncontrollably, shoulders shaking, snot dripping, the whole nine yards. Her demons and skeletons beat on the closet door to come out.

As cold and uncaring as Kiwan made himself out to be, he was a sucker for tears from a helpless woman, especially a woman he still cared for. "Come on, Ayanna, getup," he said softly as she cried harder.

"I never thought you'd handle me like that, Kiwan. Never. Where ... did we go ... wrong?" she sobbed. Kiwan just held her. "Kiwan, if it's business and not personal, come to the house and be with me tonight. I need to talk to you. There's something I have to tell you," Ayanna spoke, trying to compose herself. Kiwan felt compelled to say yes. Not that he owed Ayanna anything, but he had to make certain where his heart and loyalties really lay.

"Yeah, I'll be there, A."

Chapter 49

Felicia slithered onto the stage to Juvenile and Soljah Slim's unreleased "Slow Motion," and the DJ introduced her with a whispered announcement that rose to a crescendo, "Put your hands together for Cherokeeee!"

The black light cast an eerie glow throughout the club that illuminated everything fabricated with white material. Glow sticks from the many exotic drinks punctuated her peripheral as she strutted onto the stage to perform her act. Strobe light flashes captured her movements, as if in still life, with each step she took.

The club requirements for every girl's act were the same. Each act was composed of two parts, topless and completely nude. Two songs for each girl, and she determined what two songs she would dance to. Felicia had come to the conclusion that the music was as important, if not more so, than the performance itself. When she heard Romichael listening to an unreleased promotional CD by Juvenile that he'd gotten from the last hip-hop and rap convention he'd attended, she had to have it.

Dressed in her buckskin leather Indian outfit set off by leg and headbands accentuated by turquoise jewelry, Felicia strode to the edge of the stage and discreetly surveyed the crowd. She flipped one of her long plaits over her shoulder, using the movement to search some more. When the bass line to the song kicked in, Felicia did a runway model turn, making her way to the pole in the middle of the stage. She used the turn to scan more of the crowd, still searching for Romichael. Normally he'd be the back in one of the booths, watching her performance. He'd just sent word backstage that he needed to holla at her when her set was over. Felicia knew what it pertained to, especially when she suddenly, spotted Romichael in a corner booth with Corey, watching her. She was neither nervous nor afraid as she focused on her performance. Since Friday, she'd gained a new respect for strippers and how hard they worked for their money.

Felicia's skin glowed from the glitter-based lotion that Monica had rubbed all over her body before her set. With her hair parted down the center in two long plaits, and her face streaked with stripes of red and yellow paint, Felicia looked like a real Indian. When Soljah Slim kicked in with his verse, Felicia was at the pole holding on with one arm slowly spinning, into a split, which had been choreographed earlier with Monica. Monica's help and advice had been pivotal in helping Felicia get acclimated to stripping, something she'd never done in public. Felicia knew that after this was over with and her life returned to normal, she'd be the first in line enrolling into Texas Southern University.

"Just make like you're doing a private dance for the man of your dreams and that each dollar is a rose that he's showering you with," Monica had told her. That belief and the thought of destroying Romichael, were what allowed her to gyrate on the stage. The evidence she held took her one step closer to her goal, Felicia thought, removing the headband and flinging it into the crowd. Although Felicia lacked experience, she made it up in raw talent and passion, which most girls lacked despite how pretty or sexy they were. After exhibiting her dexterity, Felicia sauntered purposefully toward a group of white men in business, suits. She swayed seductively with her arms wrapped around herself.

Felicia found herself freed by the atmosphere and feeling brazen, wanting to make the white patrons uncomfortable. With a move, unseen by the men in front of her, she untied the buckskin halter from around her neck, letting it fall to the floor, exposing her breasts, and she felt her nipples hardening. She made eye contact with one geeky looking man in particular and bent over, putting her chest in his face. He turned beet red and his glasses fogged up. The captivated fool slipped a twenty between her breasts, where the lotion and sweat held it. One of his friends punched him in the arm, holding up and pointing to a stack of one-dollar bills he held in his hands. Felicia smiled, still holding eye contact with the geek. "Eye contact is important," Monica had told her. "It makes: the tricks feel special, and if they feel special they spend more money." Monica had been correct, but Felicia didn't give a fat rat's ass about the money. She just listened and obeyed Monica, who seemed to be keeping a close eye on her, in order to pacify her. Monica had confided that Felicia's take-it-or-leave-it attitude was what partially had hooked Romichael, that and the monster blow job that she'd given him. Maybe she was jealous. Felicia made her way around, the stage as she danced, her breasts jiggling and glistening. She got to the very end of the stage, shimmied out of her skirt with her back to the crowd and bent all the way over to the floor, pulling her skirt with her. Men fought for position to get a better look at what her momma gave her, or to cop a feel. Dollar bills surrounded her along with the catcalls and groping touches that always seemed to follow, but neither penetrated her thoughts, which were now gravitating toward a way that she could tie Romichael into the murder of those two women in New Orleans. As it stood, if she went to the police with what she had now, her only accomplishment would be getting rid of Corey, which was cool, but she needed Romichael out of the way for Daddy Bo and her family.

Felicia stepped out of her skirt gapped her legs open while resting her hands on her knees for balance. She then squatted low with a deep arch in her back that pronounced the heart shape of her ass cheeks. She started to bounce her ass, flexing her glute muscles in synchronized harmony with the beat. The men were getting more into her act as the music, alcohol and half-naked women running through the club provided well-sought relief from whatever life had dished out that day, Felicia guessed. She could feel fingers pull her red lace g-string to the side and slide into her vagina. She looked over her shoulder and pouted at the man, giving him a look of scorn, as the bouncer snatched the man's arm back. Touching was allowed in the club, but not penetration, at least not in the open. Besides, Monica had warned her that that was the easiest way to get a yeast infection, from unclean or too many hands touching her private area. Despite the minor interruption, Felicia didn't miss a beat. She worked the stage like a pro. She popped her coochie, worked the pole, and danced masterfully all in time with the rhythm of he first song. It was just a preliminary to the main event about to take place. Her first song began to fade out as she ended up in a split barely bouncing off the floor, her ass jiggling.

With the exception of the candlelit tables, every light in the club momentarily went out as the intro to Felicia's next song began. It was a slow, smooth, love ballad by Morris Day and the Time, called, "Don't Wait For Me." When the chorus kicked in after the intro, the light of the club came back on, casting a purple tint throughout. Only the, red and blue lights were illuminated as part of Felicia's act. When the men were able to see again, Felicia's naked purple body was up against the pole with part of the pole in between the crack of her ass. Her back was arched and her arms were outstretched above her head, handcuffed to the pole. By this time, she had everyone's attention. Even the women on the floor working the crowd with lap dances and VIP room visits stopped to watch. The entire stage the whole way around was now jam packed with whooping, barking, rambunctious money-throwing men. Even a few women were waving bills of their hard-earned money. It was the music! Shrill whistles and yelling threatened to drown out the music for a few seconds. Even more so when Monica, dressed in nothing but a cowboy hat and leather riding chaps, strutted onto the stage as Morris Day began to sing. "You think that you're in love, with meee ... think you're beautiful and should be free."

Monica's strides were sultry and purposeful as she approached the naked and bound figure of Felicia. Monica, into her role, eyed Felicia suspiciously, circling her prone and vulnerable body. Monica took her finger and lightly traced the outline of Felicia's ample breast. She then slowly moved down her body, past her pierced navel, to the hairline of her pubis, before stopping.

Monica bent over, fully exposing her shaved vagina, and pretended to sniff Felicia's body, crotch first. She slowly, methodically, moved up, then back down, letting her tongue flicker over Felicia's body. When she approached Felicia's crotch again, she sniffed it repeatedly, as if it interested her. The crowd urged her on with cheers and money. Monica then stepped back and pulled out a plastic water pistol from the inside of her chaps. She shot Felicia with a stream of dark red liquid that could've been blood, but in fact was concentrated Hawaiian punch. Felicia slid down the pole to the floor, slowly settling onto the floor with her legs splayed open. Monica then stepped between Felicia's outstretched legs and nudged her with her foot, making sure the prisoner was dead. Monica then got down on all fours, booting her ass in the air and putting her face into Felicia's crotch. She took her thumbs, and spread Felicia open and slowly licked. The act had so many men heated, and the crowd was loving it so much, that two black men had actually climbed up onto the stage. They were quickly yanked back down and warned by the team of bouncers were always standing at the ready.

Suddenly, Felicia's legs locked around Monica's neck and Monica's eyes opened wide in mock surprise. The lights were extinguished again, the taming coinciding with the instrumental guitar solo at the song's end. When the lights returned to their original, strobing pattern, Monica was handcuffed to the pole, bent over with Felicia straddling her. Felicia held a hand full of Monica's braided hair, her arm outstretched and holding a long black dildo pretending to jab it into Monica's ass, causing Monica to scream in mock ecstasy.

As she screamed, the song ended and the women received a standing ovation amid a chorus of "Encores!" Monica scooped up all of the money on the stage as Felicity stepped off. Felicity declined the many invitations to the VIP lounge, along with numerous requests for lap dances as she made her way to Romichael's table. She plopped, her ass right in is lap to see if he would push her off of his expensive clothes. She knew and could feel that Romichael wasn't thinking about her sticky and sweaty body ruining his clothes after the performance she'd just put on.

"What's up, daddy? You wanted to holla at me," she asked, kissing his cheek. She cut her eyes at Corey, who was looking at her menacingly.

"I cut for that," Romichael told her. "When did you and Monica come up with that?" he asked.

"We rehearsed it a couple of times today after I got back from New Orleans," she told him, cutting her eyes at Corey again.

"Yeah?" Romichael inquired, nodding his head. "That was nice, I dug that ... Oh, speaking of New Orleans, did everything go OK?" he slipped in.

"Hmmph," Felicia shrugged, rolling her eyes. "I don't know, I stayed in the room all fucking night," she pouted.

"Yeah, I'm sorry about that, but I appreciate you taking care of that business for me. Next time it's just gonna be me and you. We'll probably hit Jamaica or Cancun, somewhere," Romichael stated. "But I do appreciate you," he told her, rubbing on her ass. "By the way, when you dropped the rental truck off did you clean it out and stuff?"

"Yeah, me and Monica cleaned it out and filled it up before we took it back," she assured him. She'd made up her mind to play dumb. She was already prepared for his questions.

"Did anybody leave anything, anything like a suitcase, a bag, some clothes maybe?"

Felicia pretended to reflect on his question as she shook her head. "Um um, no. I didn't find anything but some trash and I threw that shit away. Did you ask Monica?"

"Naw, not yet. What you doing tonight?" Romichael quizzed, still rubbing on her body.

"Nothing, I was gonna leave about twelve and catch up on my sleep," she told him, wondering where he was heading.

"Well, look, I want you to ride with me tonight. I got something to take care of, then I'll treat you to a late or early morning breakfast" Romichael suggested.

"That's cool, Felicia told him.

"Now go holla at Monica for me and tell her that I said come here," he instructed Felicia, palming a handful of her ass.

Felicia got up and sashayed off in search of Monica. "Man, that bitch is a bald-faced liar. I told you we should've had Monica drive us. I don't trust that hoe," Corey told Romichael.

"Shut tha fuck up, nigga," Romichael snapped. "Nobody told you to leave the fucking evidence in the damn truck, fool. She might not have it."

"Well, if she doesn't have it, Monica's got it because I know I put it in the back of the truck. I know I left it in there," Corey whined.

"Look, I'm tired of having to think for you niggas. You should've burned those damn clothes before you left New Orleans. That shit could put you and Key-lo on death row. It don't make sense for her to have the bag because if she had it, why not give it back unless she knew that you niggas killed somebody?" Romichael spat angrily. "I don't see no reason for her to lie. But just to make sure, I'm taking her and Monica out with me tonight. While we're out, round up some niggas and break into their shit. Search the place and take a few things to make it look good." Romichael told him, exasperated. "We don't need no fucking slip ups now, Corey. This seat is important to me. I ain't gonna let you and nobody else fuck it up." He raised his voice, expressing his displeasure.

Corey started to speak until Romichael cut him off. "Ain't shit else to say, muthafucka. Go handle up. Find what you need to find and if not, you better pray that it don't come back to you because, Corey," Romichael looked directly into the man's eyes so that he would know how serious the situation was, "because if it does come back on you, you won't make it to court. I swear. And I won't make the same mistakes as you did," he hissed, rising from the table and storming off to his office.

Chapter 50

"Are you sure?" Amin questioned the man sitting across the desk from him.

"Yeah, black, you know I wouldn't fuck around, baby. You're my best turd and I'll never shit you," the rapper from the now-defunct group Underground Kings assured him. The other half of the group, Pimp C, was serving time in the Texas Department of Criminal Justice. Normally, Ayanna would be handling preliminary discussions concerning business on the level they were discussing, but Bun—B was a longtime friend of Amin's. Bun and Amin had been close since Murder One occupied space on the eighth floor of the Arena towers with UKG's original record label, "Big Tyme Records."

Those had been the days, when Amin and Nina were busting their ass promoting concerts, their artists, their label and practically selling CDs out of the trunk of their car. The days of constant struggle: struggles with the radio stations, with Southwest Distribution, a wholesale distributor who had Houston on lock, and the struggle of trying to account for their illicit money funding their operation.

Yep, those were the days, Amin reflected. Back then Bun—B and UKG had made it first, signing a deal with Jive records. Amin had been there to celebrate and vice versa with Amin's deal with Syon. But since then rap had scratched itself out of the underground and into the mainstream, decreasing the demand for the brand of music that UKG was pushing.

Bun was hardcore. Knowing that underground rap had hit an unbreakable ceiling, and deciding to stay true to their roots, fans and image, UKG had decided to bypass the mainstream route that had intersected their path to stardom. The closest they had come to going mainstream in their music had been on a collaborated track with the Jigga man himself entitled, "Big Pimpin." Like most underground rappers, to Bun it was more about the music than the money. Rapping how you live and about the places you come from was a reward in itself for most underground artists, who were content with street fame and the familiarity that the hometown crowd provided. Bun had often said that the price of fame that some of his other industry mates paid was one that he couldn't afford. "I'd rather be an underground legend than mainstream mediocre," he'd shared with Kiwan.

Bun—B had opted to hold down an executive vice—president position at DefJam down south when Brad Jordan, aka Mr. Scarface, had offered it to him. Amin was still pissed about that move! Had he known that Bun was available he'd have swooped him up, and would have spared no expense to do it. Murder One could have benefited greatly from Bun's vast experience and influence in the industry.

"That's truly fucked up," Amin said, with his head down. He began shaking it from side to side as if the news that Bun—B had shared were a shock to him.

"Yeah, I know, man," Bun said sympathetically. "Me and Face asked around about major distribution for y'all, G, and everybody said the same shit. They wouldn't fuck that donkey with my dick, let alone theirs," Bun stressed, leaning his 240—pound frame back into the stainless steel and leather chair in Amin's office at Club Flip Mode, trying his damndest to get comfortable. The sofa looked good to Bun, who thought of moving. He was wrinkling his suit. "Damn, Amin, these bitch ass chairs are uncomfortable like a muthafucka," Bun complained.

"I know, man, I'm. sorry. They were designed for that. I don't want my employees to feel comfortable when they come in here. Here, you can sit in my chair," Amin laughed, standing up.

"Naw, that's cool. If you don't mind, I'm about to head to that boss ass VIP room. That boy Big Moe in there clowning." Bun-B smiled.

"Awight, and tell that nigga Moe not to start no riot up in my club. Last time lil Flip was up in there, that nigga damn near caused a stampede," Amin chided. Club Flip Mode had one of the most coveted VIP rooms in the Houston area. The club maintained three exclusive VIP sections, but the one that every star and celebrity frequented was the glass-enclosed room on the second floor. Part of the VIP room was suspended over the dance floor enabling VIP goers to take advantage of the view that the glass floor provided, but the contrast in lighting and the fog machine that emitted a light mist across the floor of the VIP room didn't allow those dancing on the floor to see the goings-on in the VIP room. They could only see shoes, the occasional bare feet, or in lil Flip's case, the bare asses and breasts of two women eating each other out, as their bodies pressed up against the glass floor. A lot of the people who frequented the VIP room took advantage of its dark recessed lighting, glass walls, ceilings, and floors, light fog, and relaxed atmosphere to blaze a joint, pop ecstasy pills or sip syrup. Getting high enhanced the feeling, and atmosphere of the room, making it seem as though you were having a private party on your own cloud. Amin and Black Jack had thought of the idea themselves and the room proved to be one of the main attractions.

Bun's smile grew even bigger as he rose to leave. "By the way," he stopped to say, "that was a smooth move you put down when you signed K—flex. Him and lil Flip putting H—town on the map. I'll still ask around for y'all about that distribution, but from the way things look, nobody wants to fuck with y'all until your biz is straight with Syon. Just make sure you keep in touch wit ya boy," Bun said, slapping palms with Amin and pulling him in close for a hug.

"Bet that, playa, hopefully I can get you to lay down some tracks for that boy Flex on his next album," Amin said.

"Shiit, you got that, baby. Shoot ya boy a few g's and I'll wreck any track you put in front of me," Bun told him with the confidence of a veteran as he pulled a fat ass blunt from his pocket and stuck in into his mouth.

"You got that nigga! I'mma holla when we hit the studio, just make sure you ready," Amin told him as he walked him out of his office. He had to laugh because business never stopped, and he loved it. As Bun was leaving the office, Amin saw a dreaded situation approaching him with the speed of a locomotive and it actually seemed as though steam was coming from her ears. Tony and Damon were escorting a stalking, furious Yvette straight to his office. "Where tha fuck did she come from?" Amin wondered.

"Amin, we need to talk, seriously," she stated with a stern—faced look that left no room to doubt that she was short a patience and ready to go off.

"She was about to cause a scene. So we brought her back so you could calm her down," Damon said. "She was running off at the mouth about y'all's business all loud and shit."

Amin grabbed Yvette by her arm and slung her into his office so hard she stumbled and almost fell over one of the chairs. "Nigga, get yo mothafuckin hands offa me," she yelled, trying to maintain her balance.

"Say, y'all stay outside this door and if I start killing this bitch make sure y'all stop me despite what I might be saying at the time," Amin instructed. He was pissed, but he was more upset at himself for fucking with this trifling bitch. This hoe had some nerve, though it was a relief to know that he could end this relationship and be done with Yvette. He still wanted to do it on his terms and conditions, not when it suited her. Now, with everything else he had to deal with, here she came, popping up out of the blue, adding more fuel to the fire. "Don't talk! Listen and shut up! What tha fuck you doing here? I told yo ignorant ass that I'd holla at you when I made my way to Miami," he fumed. Yvette brushed her shoulders off as if brushing off Amin's statement.

"You got me fucked up, Amin. I'm tired of you treating me like shit," Yvette stressed.

"You mean to tell me that you flew all the way down here from Miami to tell me that?" he asked in frustration.

"No," Yvette pouted, her lips glossy with expertly applied amber colored lipstick. Amin took in Yvette's flawless appearance. Her hair was parted down the middle and left to hang down past her, shoulders with not a single strand out of place, looking like she just stepped off a dark and lovely box. She wore a velour long-sleeved shirt that flared out at the sleeves and around the waist. The shirt had one big button, which buttoned across her inviting B-cup breasts. She also sported a pair of skintight velour shorts in the same dookey brown color as the shirt with a silver chain ring belt around her waist. Her knee high stiletto heeled boots were beige. Amin knew that she didn't wear jewelry, with the exception of a watch, but she had on the chain and diamond solitaire that he'd gotten her on Valentine's Day of this year. It was a subtle statement that almost made him want to reconcile; almost. Amin looked down at her thick butterscotch colored thighs and remembered what lay at the end of that yellow brick road.

Yvette could sense his hunger for her, and his resolve weakening. "Look, boo," she cooed, sauntering up to Amin. "It doesn't have to be this way, why you tripping?" she asked, rubbing his chest seductively. "This is your pussy," she told him, putting his hand between her thighs, slowly moving it up to her crotch. "You know this pussy is tha bomb, feel how warm it's getting, how could you trip on this?"

Yvette had Amin backed up against his desk. He wanted to fuck Yvette but then again, he didn't. He was confused and experiencing a rare moment of weakness. She began kissing his neck. He knew that he couldn't have sex for six weeks due to his treatment for the gonorrhea, but he'd already broken that rule with Nina as soon as he'd left the doctor's office that Saturday. To make matters worse, he still wasn't sure who burned him, and being as though he didn't have any rubbers handy, he would have to settle for a head job. He scooted back onto the desk as Yvette unbuttoned his shirt, still kissing and licking. Damn, this girl had a touch that made his dick harder than Korean calculus. He shrugged out of his shirt, letting it fail onto the desk. In doing so, he knocked over something behind him. Amin looked to see what had fallen and picked up the picture frame holding pictures of his two daughters. He snapped back to his senses.

"Yvette, we can't do this," he sternly told her with more conviction than his heart felt.

"There you go tripping again," she said agitatedly as she rolled her neck and smacked her lips. "Why can't you just chill and we go back to doing what we do?"

"Because I don't love you, I love my wife and it's about time I start appreciating her for sticking by me," he said.

"Well, what tha fuck am I supposed to do? What about my feelings? How can you just walk away?" she yelled. Yvette was getting worked up again as she bucked up to Amin.

"Bitch, you better sit yo punk ass down somewhere," Amin stressed.

"Oh, so now I'm a bitch, huh? I'm not a bitch when you jumping up and down in, this pussy," she screamed at him, grabbing her crotch. Amin could see that this was going to get out of hand. Yvette was just too damn ghetto despite the beautiful package she came in. It was one thing to be who you are, but she portrayed the image of something that she wasn't, making her personality conflict with her mannerisms. It was another reason she had to go; he didn't have room in his life for fake people.

"Fuck that shit, Yvette, you act like you ain't got no understanding. Get it through your head, I don't want to fuck wit your trifling ass no mo. It's about me and my wife, like it should've been all along."

"Fuck you, Amin. Yo hoe ass momma is trifling," she yelled before she knew what she was saying.

Uh oh! Amin thought. I know she didn't say what I thought she just said. Yvette didn't make it any better because she stood there defiantly as if to say, Yeah, nigga, I said it, now what? Before he knew it, Amin drew back to knock the shit out of her but something held his arm back. He looked up to see Tony holding his arm from behind the desk as Moochie and Damon stood to his left. His wife stood in the doorway, leaning against the door jamb.

"Bitch, I heard everything y'all been saying and I've heard enough. If you're campaigning for an ass whipping you are about to get elected," Nina hissed, her green eyes as dark as Colombian emeralds. She started taking off her earrings and her shoes. "I'm about to open this Puerto Rican can of whup ass on you," Nina announced, dead serious.

"Uh uh, bitch, I ain't the one you need to check. It's not gonna happen; I'm not gonna fight you over what's supposed to be yours. You need to check your man," Yvette told Nina, backing down.

"Naw, bitch, I'm gon check you, hija de puta," Nina spoke, reverting to her native tongue. Oh damn, there's fixing to be some shit now, Amin thought. The only time Nina spoke her language around him was either when they were making love or she was fighting mad. She knew he didn't understand Spanish. But what came next was a surprise to everyone in the room.

"Mira," Yvette said. "Es tu hombre. No vamos a tener dificultades por un cabron que no puede dejar su pinga en sus pantalones. 'Ta bien. Cuidalo." Yvette told Nina in Spanish, in essence, that she did not want to fight Nina over her husband. The two women, looked at each other in a new light, realizing who was really to blame for this entire mess: Amin.

Nina looked at her husband disappointedly as she saw that his shirt was off and traces of lipstick were on his neck, lipstick that was not hers. She moved aside and let Yvette walk out the door.

"What tha fuck?" Amin said.' He was still in shock from Yvette speaking Spanish to his wife.

As Yvette was walking out of the room, she turned to Nina and told her, "En Miami, no peleamos sobre los machos. Ellos se pelean sobre nosotros." In Miami, we don't fight for the men. They fight for us.

Nina could do nothing but nod her head in agreement as Yvette left.

"What tha fuck did she tell you?" Amin asked, dumfounded.

Nina turned and spoke to the bodyguards. "Can you all excuse us? I need to speak to ya boy a second. It won't take long."

The men left the couple to their business, closing the door behind them. This time, they didn't wait outside the door.

Chapter 51

Kiwan entered the parking lot with the top down on his Vette, jammin Big Moe's new song, "Just a dog." Big Moe himself had given the CD to K—Flex to listen to. As the syrupy voiced baritone spun a story of an average day in the hood, K—flex bobbed his head to the infectious beat, sipping on a pint of syrup in a 2—quart Gatorade container. Kiwan had frowned when K—flex was mixing the drink up. By the way K-flex had expertly fixed the mixture, Kiwan knew that he'd been doing it awhile. So there probably wouldn't be any use for a lecture. Kiwan had read about how most artists got high before studio sessions in order to get better into their music, and after they got their hair cuts Kiwan was supposed to drop K-flex off at Track & Designs Studios to listen to some tracks for his upcoming album on the Murder One label. Kiwan couldn't knock it; to each was his own. If syrup was what K—flex needed to produce another multi-platinum album, then who was Kiwan to complain.

The strip center complex that Swift's Fades Barber Shop was housed in was located between Third Ward and South Pack in the McGregor area. The complex was situated off Martin Luther King Boulevard and Old Spanish Trail. As both men exited the Vette in front of the barber shop, the ever-popular Spreewell rims still spun from inertia. "That boy Big Moe got a bad muthafucka, don't he?" K—flex asked. Kiwan had to agree that if the song was pushed right, Moe could go platinum just on the Third Coast alone.

"Yeah, he definitely wrecked that bitch," Kiwan told the young man. Kiwan didn't fail to notice how amped K—flex was after hearing Big Moe's song. They'd listened to it repeatedly the whole ride to the Shop. K—flex paced next to the Vette as he spoke, letting Kiwan know that the codeine hadn't hit him yet.

"Man, I got to wreak dem boys on my next album," K-flex said, pounding his fist into the palm of his hand, his brand new platinum Murder One pendant filled with diamond baguettes swinging from his neck on the 32-inch platinum chain. "I got to put that H—town on the map," K—flex said.

Kiwan laughed. "Somebody's already done that," he told him.

"Yeah, well, I'm gon put H—town and Murder One on the map and be the first artist on the label to sell 10 million copies. Fuck platinum and gold, I want to go diamond! A lot of these niggas in the industry don't even know what diamond is," Flex dared.

Kiwan liked the youngster. He liked his determination and the way he felt that he had to still prove himself, even after reaching platinum status. That attitude could carry him far, or farther even, than he already was. But Kiwan also saw that the fire K—flex possessed, if not channeled into the right direction, could also consume him. K—flex had the same dreamy eyed look that Amin used to have when Kiwan would come home with gym bags full of money. K—flex was still hungry for success.

"Well, I'm pretty sur? that Amin will give you all of the creative space to do your thizzle, babyboy," Kiwan assured him.

"Yeah, I know man. I'm feelin that boy Amin," flex confided. "Your brother is keepin it real with me and showin me nuthin but love. What can I do but do my thang the best I can. Quiet as it's kept, I haven't even released' my best material. I was saving it for when I 'got' my own label deal, but now, I'm gon bless you boys wit it," K-flex smiled a platinum filled smile, $365,000 to be exact. The boy had 'to be wearing most of his, money between the gaudy watch, ostentatious bracelet and dazzling teeth, Kiwan thought.

Kiwan just smiled back, nodded his head and looked out across the parking lot. "Shit has changed in the ten years I've been gone', man," Kiwan marveled.

"Man, ten years is a long time," K—flex agreed.

"To tell you the truth, man, it doesn't even seem like I've been gone that long. In the five days I've been home, I have all but forgotten about the bullshit I've had to put up with in the last ten years."

"Shit, you was lucky, man. You got to do time in the fed, and your peeps had paper. I got kinfolk in TDC and them boys say they catching hell down there. Especially them boys in West Texas and in the Panhandle. That's Klan country a nigga ain't got no win wit them white folks down there," flex surmised.

"I agree, fool, you ain't never lied about that. That's why we got my old man shipped down South it makes for doing better "time" Kiwan stressed", still looking out across the lot, reminiscing in his mind.

K—flex lit a joint of Acapulco Gold that he'd gotten from Prescious earlier that day. He damn near coughed up his lung when he pulled too hard inhaling the pungent smoke. "This some boss ass shit," he wheezed. "That girl Prescious is playa, I dig her style," flex told Kiwan, tears rolling down his cheeks from the stinging smoke. Kiwan didn't respond, still lost in thought.

"Man, Houston's changing, times are different now," Kiwan reflected. "They are rebuilding shit, making the hoods look nice again, especially on the South Side. But the other day I rolled through the hood and some of the same niggas was on the corners when I left were still there, doing the same shit. I guess the more things change, the more they stay the same. That shit don't make any sense to me," Kiwan chuckled. "Hell, I remember a time when this whole street used to be jam packed with niggas on Sunday night. Traffic was bumper to bumper from that Exxon station over there," he pointed out, "all the way back to the 610 freeway. McGregor Park used to be the shit. All the car boppers would out in full effect and niggas would be walking the strip getting they mack on, showing out in they cars, and with they dogs and shit," Kiwan laughed at the memory of it all.

"I even remember one fool brought a pet tiger up here and cleared the park." Suddenly Kiwan's smile vanished. Then, like always, the laws busted it up. Boy, I tell you, we can't have shit for ourselves."

Kiwan turned to face the strip center that they were standing in front of, his mind still in flashback mode as K—flex smoked and watched him intently. "This whole complex," Kiwan said, turning around, "was fucked off. Potholes all up in the. Lot the size of ditches, graffiti all over the walls, forty bottles, crack pipes, broken glass and empty food containers everywhere you stepped. Yeah, shit is changing and sometimes that change is good," Kiwan told the youngster. K-flex didn't know if it was the weed or what, but he got the feeling that the big man was referring to something deeper than the eye could see.

"You wanna hit this?" K—flex offered him what was left of his joint. Kiwan declined. K—fl ex looked around and could imagine, how it used to be, but Kiwan was referring to a time long before, to a time when little fl ex, then known only as Broderick Nelson, had to be in the house by the time the street lights came on. "Come on, man," K-flex said as he noticed a new Ford Expedition pulling up to the shop, sitting on 22s. "Let's go get faded up before we be up in this bitch til 7 o'clock tomorrow morning." Kiwan was still perplexed, because getting a haircut at 11 o'clock at night was some new shit to him.

"What kind of barbershop services people 24 hours a day?" Kiwan voiced what he was thinking.

"K—flex looked at him as if he were the lamest muthafucka on the planet Earth "While you bullshittin, that boy Swift is a beast on them clippers. The fool got mad clientele. He be so packed on the weekday and on the weekends that he had to start shutting down the shop for the regulars at 9 o'clock and had to open for the VIPs at 10. No tellin who up in this bitch now," flex informed Kiwan. Kiwan figured that's why there were so many luxury cars and SUVs sitting on 20s or better in the lot as he activated his alarm. He also noticed a closed circuit camera mounted above the door as he and K—flex were buzzed into the shop's interior.

Swift's was unlike any barber shop Kiwan had ever seen. Customers were greeted by a receptionist, eyeballed by an armed guard, then buzzed into the back, which was split into three areas. On the right was a traditionally styled barber section, with six barber stations and a shoe shine stand, complete with black and white checkered floor tiles. On the left was the waiting area, which shocked many first time patrons with its luxury. It was decorated like a conventional living room, if

Koto

your living room had huge plasma screen televisions, burgundy leather sofas with brass and glass coffee and end tables and pictures on the wall of local celebrities. Swift was in all of the photos, along with some of his most popular customers, such as Dee Jay Screw, lil Flip, Steve Francis, Houston's top radio personalities and Kiwan recognized Gary Walker of the Texans. His eye was caught by the pool table and fully stocked bar directly in the back of the section. The club atmosphere was enhanced by After 7s hit, "Ready or not," which played softly in the background.'

Swift, a few of the other barbers and many of the customers greeted K—flex enthusiastically. The kid was a celebrity, and his troubles with his prior label in New York had made him the talk of his neighborhood. Kiwan smiled as he watched Flex accept the high fives and slaps on the back. Suddenly, someone called Kiwan's name. He looked around, not recognizing anyone, and wondered if his hearing was playing tricks on him. "Young nigga, what it be like?" Kiwan heard. This time he looked to the patrons in the chair and saw a vaguely familiar face. "How's it going, youngster?" the familiar face asked. "How's Daddy Bo holding up?" the man asked. He finally recognized the confused look on Kiwan's face, and realized that Kiwan couldn't place him. "Man, it's me. Denny!"

"Denzel Avery!" Kiwan shouted, as he made his way over to the man, who was one of his father's and Black Jack's oldest friends. "Damn, it's been a long time," Kiwan said.

"No shit," Denny said, raising out of the chair to give the younger man a hug.

"Nigga, give me some dap, I don't want that hair all over me," Kiwan laughed, pointing to the hair all over the apron protecting Denny's clothes.

"That's Daddy Bo's son?" Swift asked.

"Yeah, his oldest boy," Denny offered.

"Cool, what's up?" Swift said, offering his hand to Kiwan. "I know your brother, man. Him and your father helped me out with this shop," Swift confided. "Here, sit down, man. Denny, move, you finished." Swift urged the man out of the chair. Everyone who knew Denny knew that he was a shit-talking muthafucka and that Swift was going to get an earful.

"Muthafucka, don't rush me," Denny told Swift, with the comedic flair that he was known for. It wasn't so much what he said, but how he said it and the faces and gestures that accompanied his statements. Everyone laughed.

"Don't start no shit, Denny man. Get your old decrepit ass up," Swift said.

"I bet my money ain't old, nigga," Denny told him.

"Nigga, I bet you still got Confederate money in your pocket wit yo tight ass," Swift capped. The entire shop erupted in laughter.

"Yo Kiwan, when did you get home?" another voice called out from the smoke-filled bar area by the pool table. Kiwan looked to see who the voice belonged to. "Who dat?" he asked, peering through the haze, trying to put a face with the voice. The dark figure stepped into the light. It was another friend of his from the neighborhood, who everyone knew as Robot.

"Damn, everybody up in this bitch," Kiwan exclaimed. "What's up, Bot?" Kiwan called to the youngster. Robot was one of the boys from the Trey who grew up with Amin, but Robot had been a young hustler, selling drugs while the rest of the crew was in school.

"Look at your boy Soc," Robot told Kiwan, pointing with the cue stick to a prone figure on the sofa with his head back, mouth open, and a DVD player in his lap.

"Damn," Kiwan said. "What's wrong wit my boy?"

"He syruped out," Bot said. Soc was another Third-Ward regular. All of them had come up under Kiwan and had at one time or another moved major weight for Black Jack. Though Kiwan didn't know what they were into now, from the looks of them, they were still hustling. "I know it must feel good to be home," Bot said, as Kiwan took a seat in Swift's chair. "I heard about your coming-home party the other night, man. I heard you boys wrecked shop out there in Clear Lake. We would've come, but we had to flip through Alabama and Soc was driving so slow we couldn't get back in time," Robot told him.

"That's alright," K-flex told him. "Friday is the jump off at Flip Mode for Mister's album release party. I'm a put you boys on the VIP list, cause I want y'all to be there when I wreck set," K—flex stated boldly.

"Make sure I'm on the list, too," Denny blurted.

"That's a bet," Kiwan said. "We gon make sure all of y'all get in." Kiwan had to admit that it felt good being home and around familiar faces. The men talked about old times as Swift expertly faded Kiwan's and K—flex's head. They talked about how the original Timmy Chans on MLK used to be so crowded that you couldn't even park. Now Timmy Chans had franchised with four other restaurants on the South Side. They discussed everything from politics to 84 elbows and Vogues, how the rims and tires would never go out of style despite the infusion of the fancy spinning wheels upon the H-town scene. Kiwan was so enthralled with the conversation that he hadn't noticed Precious standing in front of him until he heard Denny say, "Look at the ass on that filly."

Kiwan looked up to see a worried and troubled expression upon her face. His heart skipped a beat and he could sense immediately that something was wrong.

"Where's your phone? I've been trying to call you for the last thirty minutes. I think somebody's following me," she told him, trying to be strong and not show how frightened she really was.

"Where?" Kiwan asked, springing to his feet. He was out the door as fast as the receptionist could buzz the locks, even before Precious finished speaking. He stalked to his Vette, disengaged the alarm popped his trunk and reached under the convertible top to grab his pistol. When he finally turned to look for Precious, she wasn't alone. Robot, Soc, and even Denny were behind him with pistols in their hands.

"Man, what's up?" Robot asked, eager for trouble. Precious stepped through the crowd of adrenaline-pumped, gun-toting men and pointed to a non-descript sedan on the other side of the lot.

"I'm getting too old for this shit," Denny commented. Kiwan tried to look into the car to see how many heads were in there, but his efforts were in vain. The car was facing them, and it had the advantage because the group of men stood under the lights of the complex's walkway. Just as Kiwan was getting ready to head over to the car, despite Precious protests the sedan's lights popped on and the car sped off. Kiwan found himself pointing the pistol at the fleeing car and wondered, what the hell was he doing? Was he really ready to kill behind this intriguing woman he barely knew? Yes, he was, he had to admit. He wasn't a gangster or a killer, but something about this woman brought out the worst in him, or maybe it was his best. Either way he was grateful that the driver of the car had caught pussy.

"Robot," Kiwan called out.

"Yeah, what's up, baby boy?" Bot answered.

"What you got planned tonight?" Kiwan asked.

"Nuthin really. I was gonna meet up wit these hoes that came down here from Alabama later on, but I can freeze that shit. What's on your mind, what you need me to do?"

"Hold on," Kiwan told him. He pulled Precious to the side as the men put their guns up. "Come here," he told her. "You and Flex take my car. Take Flex to the studio, then go straight to the house. I'mma take your car and see if they follow me. Robot and Soc gonna follow you to make sure you're OK. I'll keep the phone on in case you need me, all right?" he asked, looking into Precious' hazel eyes. She surprised him when she grabbed him and pulled him into her arms, embracing him with surprising strength. Kiwan squeezed her back hard, reassuring her that it would be all right. When he looked back into her eyes he could see the tears welling up.

"I've never really needed anyone in my life, Kiwan Rush, but it feels good to know that if I needed you, that you would be there," she whispered.

They kissed each other softly at first, but the kiss escalated into a full-blown experience.

"Ahem," K—flex interrupted, looking at his watch.

"Go ahead," Kiwan told her, breaking the kiss as he walked over to Robot. "Call me when you get to the house," he instructed her.

Chapter 52

Kiwan enjoyed the smooth ride that the money green X-type Jaguar provided. It wasn't a Lincoln or a Caddy, but it was nice. Anita Baker sung about "Joy" as if the song was especially recorded for and dedicated to him. Or maybe it was just the mood he was in. Periodically he checked his rearview, trying to spot a tail as his thoughts succumbed to the mellow music and easy ride.

"Change was good," he remembered telling K—flex not too long ago. Maybe it was time for him to change, to let go. So what if he loved Ayanna? He needed to get over her and move on, and that's not to say that he would settle down with Prescious, either. They didn't have the history that he and Ayanna had, but then again when he really needed to depend on that history, Ayanna had shown him that it didn't mean as much to her as it did to him. All machismo and pride to the side, when you got right down to it, Kiwan knew that he was afraid of being hurt again. Enhanced by his untimely incarceration, the unbearable pains and heartaches were things he vowed that he would never go through again, not if he could help it. But Prescious was now his Prescious, he realized, because the two of them had set something in motion that was spinning out of their control. It could be love, but Kiwan knew that it went deeper than that. More like loyalty, the same loyalty he wished he could've gotten from Ayanna. He didn't care about Prescious' past, although she did. Hell, his mother had been a prostitute. Prescious was a boss bitch for the boss type nigga that he was and he wouldn't have it any other way. So what was holding him beck? What's stopping him from just letting go with her? It had to be Ayanna, he figured. After tonight, he'd tell Ayanna that it definitely could be nothing but friendship between the two of them. He knew that he'd been totally confused before, but now it all seemed wonderfully clear in his heart, he felt that it was the right thing to do, and the sooner the better, he thought as he sped up in eager anticipation.

He exited off the Fry Road exit in Katy and made a left, crossing the overpass. He thought about it and remembered to turn his cell phone on. He needed to call Ayanna anyway so that she could guide him to the house from the entrance of her gated community. As soon as he turned the phone on, it chirped, letting him know that he had messages. He scrolled down the lists of numbers of the people who'd left the messages and only recognized Amin's and Ayanna's numbers. Ayanna had been calling from her house, probably figuring out if Kiwan was actually coming because it was so late, he guessed. He selected the number, pushed the send button and the phone asked him if he wanted to call the number back or save the number in his file. He chose to call it back. Kiwan chuckled, marveling at the high tech toy. Before he left, all they had were sky pagers, and cell phones that were too cumbersome to carry around.

The phone rang six times before anyone answered. Kiwan felt that maybe everyone was asleep, after all, it was 1:30 in the morning. But I thought these industry execs were people of the night, he wondered when finally some one answered the phone.

"Yeelloo," a male voice answered. At first Kiwan was about to hang up, thinking he had the wrong number until he realized that it was Chester. Kiwan had just pulled up to the gate that provided access to Ayanna's neighborhood.

"Chester, what's up man? I didn't wake anyone up, did I?"

"Naw," Chester said. "I was out back, and I thought dat somebody would pick it up, but when nobody answered it, I just came on in and picked it up my ownself," he told Kiwan. "Who dis is anyway?"

"This young Bo, where Ayanna at?" he asked, the Jag idling at the gate.

"She was just in da garage, let me sees. If I can fetch her fo ya," Chester told him, putting him on hold.

Just as Chester put Kiwan on hold, the massive entrance gate started to swing open as a car approached from within the community. The glare of the headlights from the approaching car blinded Kiwan for a second, making him shield his eyes. When he uncovered his eyes again he recognized Francis, Ayanna's maid, and Ayanna in her topaz blue Escalade. Francis was driving, but where were they going? Kiwan hung up the cell phone and whipped around them to follow. Something about this just didn't feel right.

Chapter 53

"I think that Corey is jealous of you," Felicia said, planting a seed within Romichael's head. Romichael eyed Felicia out of the corner of his eye as he drove down the freeway. He didn't comment right away and Felicia hadn't intended him to. It was a comment tossed from out of the blue, from a female who didn't know what the fuck she was talking about; at least that's what she wanted Romichael to think.

Divide and conquer, throughout history, had always been an effective tactic against one's adversaries, Felicia thought. And she knew from her father that women were the best tool used when implementing this tactic. "If men only knew how many wars have been instigated at the behest of a woman," Daddy Bo had schooled Felicia.

Felicia wondered where the hell they were headed as they traveled down 1-10 heading west toward San Antonio. Monica was in the back seat of the Hummer asleep. She'd dozed off as soon as they'd left the club. Felicia had everything mapped out, but things were moving a bit fast. Before they'd left the club, she'd contacted Nina and told her of her plans. Nina agreed with Felicia and told her that she would relay the message to Black Jack, so Felicia had to work quick. After Romichael had spoken to her in the club about the bag of clothes, which she'd kept with her in her car, she had figured out the perfect way to link Romichael to the killings.

After a few moments of silence, curiosity got the best of Romichael. "Let me ask you something. What would make you say some silly shit like that? You ain't been around us a good week to know what tha fuck you talking about. I don't know what type of games you're into, bitch, but you playing Russian Roulette with your life," he told her. Felicia read into Romichael's statement. It was more of a probe than a threat. He was digging. He was worried, and Felicia smiled inwardly.

Romichael was a typical flashy, arrogant and power-hungry man, a control freak, Felicia knew. And his Achilles heel was the same as most men – his pride. "He could never outthink me," Felicia told herself. "As long as I stay calm and focused, I got this."

Felicia laughed at Romichael's last statement. She brushed her hair behind her ear with her fingers and turned to look at Romichael. She leaned closer to the door a bit before she spoke. Her body relaxed, motions unhurried as she shook her head. "You right, Ro, I haven't been around you long enough to know. That's my bad for even saying some shit like that. I'm not a messy bitch and I don't start shit. It might be just me, something I see, feel, or heard. I'm tripping. It's just that I cut for you because you're a player type nigga," she said, stroking his ego. "Just forget what I said. I apologize."

Felicia leaned over and patted Romichael's leg as she increased the volume on the radio. Aaliyah's "Can I talk to you?" oozed from the speakers easing some of the tension. But Romichael was having none of that. He brushed Felicia's hand off his leg and turned the music back down to a whisper. He was hooked, Felicia could tell, and again she smiled to herself.

"Naw, that's bullshit! Tell me what's up," he demanded.

"Well, I see that you're not gonna drop it, so I'mma tell you, but as my man I really don't expect you to repeat it. This is just between us."

"Bitch, I don't wanna hear all that, talk!" he yelled. Felicia glanced back at Monica, who only stirred. That Visine in your drink shit really works, she saw.

"Don't yell at me, nigga," she told him, still playing with fire, taking it to the edge.

"Talk, gotdammit!" he yelled again, hitting the steering wheel with his palms. "Before I pull this muthafucka over."

Felicia looked frightened, but she really wasn't. Her pistol was her comforter, her equalizer. "Look, Romichael, when we were in New Orleans, I overheard him and that dude talking about some committee seat," she said, looking at him, gauging his reaction. She knew if the seat was all-important to her father then it definitely should stir up some emotion in Romichael. He visibly flinched. "Corey said that you didn't look right in the top spot, he said that he should be the one in control of that aspect of Ruff House."

Silence followed and Felicia could actually see Romichael's mind at work. His face went through many subtle changes. The seed was growing, and doubt was setting in 2-Pac's "Hail Mary" came on the radio. Romichael reached over and jabbed the control button to increase the volume. He jabbed it until the digital display of the volume read 'Max.' Even after it maxed out he hit it a couple of more times, just in case. Felicia could just imagine, what he was thinking and what he would do to Corey if he got his hand on him. Felicia could see the rage building inside of Romichael, but what he didn't realize was that her rage toward him was just as intense, if not more. Fuck this sucka, she thought as she watched him. 2—Pac's lyrics were penetrating his thoughts, stirring up some gangsta type shit inside a nigga who didn't have it naturally, Felicia knew. She became enraged at the audacity of this bitch ass nigga who wasn't even fit to wash her daddy's silk boxers. This punk muthafucka who hid behind his money and his neighborhood. This hoe ass nigga who exploited the talents of incarcerated black males instead of uplifting them. Felicia had to suppress the notion to just end it all right then, and there. Simple — just shoot the bitch, and the problem would be solved. Her hand inched toward her purse, toward the pistol there, as her mind churned with the hate she felt toward Romichael and the possibility of killing him.

Romichael's antic motions relieved her of such thoughts as he turned the Pac down and dug in his pocket for his cell phone. It must've been turned on vibrate because Felicia hadn't heard it ring. "Yeah," he answered as Felicia watched him. When the caller spoke, a grin spread across his face. His manner changed, his features softened, and Felicia knew that it was a woman calling.

"Aight, I'm almost there," he told his caller. "What you in? Who wit you?" he asked. "Better be," he responded to her answer. He laughed. "Yeah, whatever, I'm pulling off the freeway now."

They were in Katy, Felicia noticed. She knew that Katy Mills Mall was a couple of exits up ahead. They were going to meet someone, whoever it was he'd been talking to on the phone, she guessed.

Romichael whipped the Hummer into the parking lot of a strip shopping center right off of Fry Road. He pulled the truck in front of a blue Escalade that was backed into a parking space in front of a Kinko's. Felicia could see that it was two women in the front seat of the Escalade as Romichael parked the Hummer.

2-Pac's and Scarface's collaboration, "Smile," pumped through the speakers, bass flowing, giving Felicia dark thoughts. Something didn't seem right to her about this scene. Romichael jumped out of the Hummer, but the women in the Escalade didn't budge. The one on the passenger side just let her window down. Felicia could see the lips of the two women moving in the truck. The one on the passenger side wore expensive sunglasses even though it was night. She must be high, Felicia thought.

Romichael walked up to the window and began an animated conversation with the passenger of the Escalade with that nerve-wracking shit-eating grin on his face. Felicia looked back at Monica and jumped. A figure was walking up with a pistol. in his hand. Couldn't be, she thought. But her instincts told her that her eyes didn't deceive her even though it had been over ten years since she'd last seen him. It had been at one of his basketball games, when she'd gone to cheer him on even though he didn't know she existed. She'd gone to Rice to see Kiwan, to anonymously cheer on her brother. The look on his face as he neared the Escalade said it all. He was intent and focused, ready to kill.

"Muthafucka," Felicia mumbled. Kiwan was about to fuck the whole thing up. She couldn't let him do it! They were too close, she thought, as she watched the scene unfold before her. She had to do something, but what?

Chapter 54

Kiwan was furious. A tinge of red dominated his vision, he was so mad. The blood rushed to his head, making him dizzy. This bitch didn't think that she could play him again, did she? It just wasn't gonna happen. It wasn't going down like that. How could she stoop so low, he thought? And with that bitch Romichael Turner? What kind of hold did this nigga have on Ayanna?

Kiwan walked right up behind Romichael with the gun pointed at his head. Francis gasped when she caught sight of Kiwan, alerting Romichael, who turned to face the pistol. Gazing down the dark ominous barrel of death, Romichael almost fainted. He steadied himself by grabbing ahold of the Escalade door.

"Nigga, what you trippin on?" Romichael asked, shooting his hands above his head.

"Shut yo ho ass up, nigga," Kiwan stated calmly. "Ayanna, what it do? What's wit this shit?"

Ayanna gasped. "Kiwan, wait a minute, it's not what it looks like," she said hurriedly, trying to open the door. "I can explain," she assured him.

"Stay in the damn truck. Don't you open that got-damned door," he told her in a matter-of-fact tone. The toneless quality of his voice unnerved her. He didn't even sound like Kiwan, the Kiwan she loved and dreamt about and had grown up with. She could sense that this was a different man in front of her.

"Why you trippin, Kiwan, let me explain," she whined, tears already flowing.

Kiwan ignored her "Move over there fat boy," he directed at Romichael, waving the pistol in front of the Hummer. Romichael obliged. "You got a gun on you?" Kiwan asked the terrified man. "Because that would be perfect for me when I put a couple of holes in your chubby ass." At the mention of holes and guns, Romichael's eyes got bigger. Kiwan could feel the fear in the man. He could visibly see it, as it dripped down his face despite the cool night breeze.

"He doesn't have a gun, but I do," a voice called from behind him. Kiwan could feel the pressure of cold steel against the back of his neck. Now why didn't this surprise him?

"Just put it down and we can all "walk up out of this mess," the voice assured Kiwan.

"Romichael, who is that? What's going on?" Ayanna asked.

"Shut up," Felicia ordered. "This shit is behind your trifling ass, I'm sure," she told Ayanna, pointing a second gun she'd found under Romichael's seat at Ayanna.

"Why don't I just kill this hoe ass nigga, I'm sick of this busta," Kiwan spat. "You've been fucking wit my family for too long. GET NAKED, HOE ASS NIGGA!" Kiwan demanded, wanting to degrade the coward. Romichael moved to do as he was told.

"You bet not take off a stitch of clothing," Felicia told him. "Just get in the truck," she said. He began to move, almost tripping over his loafers, which he'd taken off and now had to put back on.

"If you flinch, nigga, I'mma shoot and draw chocolate milk from yo fat ass!" Kiwan yelled. Romichael froze, one loafer dangling from a foot, not knowing which way to move.

Felicia almost burst out laughing at the situation. But it wasn't funny. As much as she wanted Romichael to die, she just wasn't willing to risk another family member to do it. She loved her brothers, even though they didn't even know she existed. She had to stop Kiwan from making a terrible mistake. There was a better way and he, of all people, should know that.

"Look, Kiwan, ain't that your name? Don't do nothin. Just listen to this." Felicia leaned a bit with her left arm extended and pushed Ayanna's nose in with the barrel of Romichael's gun.

Ayanna gasped audibly, recoiling from the cold steel. "OK, bitch, tell him what that was you, just felt." Felicia had known about Kiwan and Ayanna years ago when they first started dating. She'd even sat next to her at one of Kiwan's games. She knew that Ayanna was blind, and she knew how much Kiwan loved her.

"Kiwan, she's got a gun in my face. Please, baby, let them go so I can explain. I only met up with Romichael."

"Shut tha fuck up, Ayanna," Kiwan snapped. He was beyond explaining. "Whoever you are behind me, I don't give a damn; shoot the bitch. She don't mean shit to me no way, but I'm finna kill this nigga," Kiwan stressed. He tensed a bit. Felicia could tell from the muscles in his neck, that he was getting ready to shoot Romichael. This was getting out of hand and she had to do something quick. Ayanna was bawling now and the lady in the driver's seat was pleading for her life.

Just as Felicia was about to tell Kiwan that she was his sister, his flesh and blood, red lights flashed and people started screaming," Police! Don't move! Drop the fucking guns!"

Thank God, she sighed. Nina to the rescue!

Chapter 55

Dexter Cunningham pulled his recently painted 600 Benz into the downtown parking garage at 7 a.m. sharp. His parking was validated through the city, which had reserved the third and fourth levels of the garage for the prosecutors' office. Dexter was a creature of habit – he parked in his usual spot, a spot he considered 'HIS' spot by the stairwell by virtue of his being always one of the first to arrive other than a few of the clerical staff members who parked on the third floor.

He sat in his car a moment before exiting, thinking of Prescious' rape. He hadn't known it would go that far, and was worried about the ramifications it could have on his career, if any of it got out. Romichael had told him that someone would be going with him to scare her, and the whole incident had gotten out of control. But he'd enjoyed it, and had to fight down an erection. The bitch deserved it for scratching his car.

Prescious hadn't been answering any of his calls since her rape, nor had she been home. That was the reason he'd followed her home from work last night. She'd left work late and stopped at her place for only an hour or so, then left right back out, and had gone to that barber shop. That's when those hoodlums had come out of the barber shop. Dexter wondered who they had been, since Prescious didn't have any family. He closed the door and looked at the paint job a bit closer. Fucking slut, had probably paid some of her hoodlum ex-convict friends to wave their guns around. He thought he saw a small flaw in the paint job, but maybe it was just the bad lighting. The whole gang was just lucky he hadn't called some of his friends in the Houston Police Department. He gave one last glance at the gleaming Benz, admiring its line, then retrieved his suit jacket, briefcase and cup of latte from Starbucks from the front seat. He slipped into his jacket, grabbed his briefcase and coffee and headed to the stairs.

He entered the stairwell and noticed two men on the landing. One was gigantic, stretching his suit at its seams, with an imposing scowl upon his face. Even the man's red freckles looked upset to Dexter. The other gentleman wore a nice linen outfit made by Boscelli. Dexter recognized the cut and make because he had the same outfit.

The two men were blocking the way down so Dexter said, "Excuse me," expecting them to move. When neither man did, Dexter tried to nudge his way past without spilling his coffee.

"My main man Sexy Dex," the linen suit said. Dexter was perplexed and looked at the man, trying to place him.

"I'm sorry, I don't believe I've had the pleasure," Dexter said, looking the man in his eye

Moochie couldn't help but laugh, He believed that if the man's hands weren't full he would've tried to shake hands. He mocked Dexter; he couldn't help it. "I'm sorry, I don't think I've had the pleasure." Moochie laughed again. Dexter frowned not finding the blatant insult to his vernacular funny. This muthafucka was too stupid and too arrogant to know that he was in trouble. Ain't this some shit, Moochie thought.

"I don't have time for these silly children's games. Now if you'll excuse me," Dexter said, trying to shoulder past the two men.

"Yo Dexter, don't you want to know how I know your name and how you'd be here?" Moochie asked, stepping into Dexter.

"Look, I'm an assistant district ..."

"Precious told me" Moochie hissed, all his humor gone.

When Dexter looked up, Tony hit him so hard and so swiftly that he knocked the man out of one of his Bally loafers. Dexter hadn't seen the blow coming and was knocked out before he hit the ground. The briefcase and coffee fell at his side.

"Damn, Tony, you was supposed to hit him in the chin, not the mouth. Look at you," Moochie pointed out. Tony had two of Dexter's teeth stuck to his knuckles. Tony just grunted, shrugged and pulled the teeth loose. He placed them in his pocket.

"Come on, man, you somethin else, with yo big dumb ass. That's why you don't talk much, cause you don't want people to know how dumb you really are," Moochie teased. Moochie always teased Tony, who was actually scared of Moochie. Then again, anybody with any sense who knew Moochie would be scared of him. Killing was like changing his clothes to him, Tony thought. Just that bit of knowledge in itself made Tony feel a hell of a lot smarter than Moochie gave him credit for.

Both men worked quickly, duct taping Dexter up and cleaning the stairwell. They stuffed Dexter into the trunk of his car Moochie hopped in as Tony went back to their vehicle. That was fun, Moochie thought. He hoped that he would be the one to kill this asshole. He'd have to ask Prescious for that favor, he thought as he exited the parking garage, Tony following behind.

Chapter 56

Corey sauntered into the Sprint store ten minutes after it opened. A cute button-nosed sales clerk with a small waist, voluptuous hips and a fat ass asked if she could be of some assistance to Corey.

"Yes, you may," Corey responded to her cheery attitude. "Is Valerie in yet?" he wanted to know. After last night's escapade, Corey needed to handle up on this matter as soon as possible. Val was the only person he knew who could get the information he needed quickly, so he'd come straight to the store as soon as it opened without even bothering to call first.

"Yeah, I'll go get her for you. Who should I say is asking for her?" the cutie pie asked.

"Tell her that Dirty is out here; she'll know who I am," Corey told the young woman, referring back to his junior high nickname. The young woman strolled to the back, and Corey admired her feminine walk. The way she twisted and especially the way her ass bounced were immediate turn-ons for Corey. But he could not see himself even remotely intimate with a broad who worked in a Sprint store. It was bad enough that he had to come ask Val for a favor.

Valerie Dickson came from the back offices of the store with a smile so big on her face you could see all 32 teeth in her mouth and could tell that she had one filling in the back. Ten of those were gold capped. By Corey's standards she wasn't fit to keep his house, but he knew that the average cat would consider her fly, despite the fact that she was rail thin. In his early hustling days, before Corey had boosted his standards for women, Valerie had been one of Corey's late night creeps.

"What's tha damn deal, Dirty? What it do, baby boy?" Val greeted Corey, giving him a hug. "You looking throwed," she told' Corey after giving him the once over, admiring his outfit. He was in one of his rare, casual moods today with a Coogi grey and black button down sweater, red Geoffrey Beene tailored slacks and a pair of fold down grey Timberland boots.

"Boy, you stay G'd up everyday, don't you?" she spoke in reference to his manner of dress.

"Is there any other way to be?" he asked her in a half serious tone. He could see the other young woman who'd first offered Corey some help cutting her eyes at them as she pretended to be busy.

"Step over here and let me holla at you," Corey told Val. They stepped to the front of the store by the door, out of earshot.

"What brings a big baller like you to holla at lil ole me?" Val asked Corey with a curious glare. "What's up, you need a hookup or something on the phone blast?"

"Nah, nah, nothing like that. Well, yeah, something like that, but not quite."

Val looked at Corey through squinted eyes as she folded her arms across her tiny breasts. "Just listen," Corey stammered, pulling the cell phone out of his pocket, handing it to Valerie. She took the phone, flipped it over in her hand before turning it on.

"Uh, ok, ... It's a Sprint phone. What's up? What you need me to do?"

"Yo, look, I need for you to run a check on this phone. I need to know who it belongs to, the last twenty-five or thirty numbers called on it and if those numbers are Sprint numbers, who do they belong to."

Valerie thought about it for a second before she answered. She slowly nodded her head. "Yeah, yeah, I can do it, but what's, in it for me, Dirty? You don't come by and holla at a bitch or nothin. I gave you my number at the club three months ago, nigga, you been knowing I worked here," she fussed.

Valerie saw a flush of anger cross Corey's face for a hot second. She batted her eye lashes and bit her bottom lip, the only signs of her nervousness.

"What you want?" Corey asked, reaching in his pocket.

"I don't want yo money, nigga, we better than that," she assured him.

"Well, what's up, what exactly do you want?" he asked skeptically.

"I want two things," she told him. "Cause I can lose my job if my manager finds out about this."

"Okay, talk, what?" he asked, a bit irritated.

"Well, Friday is the album release party for Mister at Club Flip Mode downtown and I have two VIP passes that I won on the radio. You know that bitch gon be crunk and I want you to take me," she told him, biting her bottom lip again. She squirmed a bit as she waited for his answer.

That was a hard pill for Corey to swallow. What tha fuck would he look like with this hood rat on his arm? Hell, she done probably let every nigga from Brewster Park run up in her and here he was contemplating on being seen with her. But damn, he needed that phone information. He needed to find out who that bitch Felicia really was. She had Romichael pussy whipped already and deep down Corey knew that she had that fucking bag with those clothes in it, even though he hadn't found them in her house last night. But when he ran across the phone in her bedroom, he found it strange. Strange because she didn't have any paperwork lying around. No bills, no furniture invoices, even though she didn't have any furniture; she had nothing in her room, just the cell phone. It had been the only tangible thing Corey had to find out who she really was. If it was an old phone registered in her name, at least he could get a Social Security number. He'd even called a few of the numbers back, thinking that maybe some type of police headquarters would answer. He was stumped and had to hang up when a man answered. When the man called back, Corey had to turn the phone off and hadn't cut it back on until now. He desperately wanted that information.

"All right, I'll take you," he decided. Before he could even get it out good, Valerie squealed, jumping up and down and hugged the shit out of him with surprising strength. Damn! He hadn't known it was gonna make tha bitch that happy, though it kind of felt good for him to do so. After all, he and Val had some good memories and fun times. She had been a hustler like him and he'd respected her for that. "Holdup, hold up, hold tha fuck up," he said, separating himself from her unyielding grip.

"What?" she asked, looking at him sideways.

"Let's get a few things straight. Dig this, first of all we ain't no couple. I'm just taking you, I really got a bitch out of Cali who was flying down here to chill with me this weekend. I was going to take her, but I can put her on freeze and do this with you. Second of all, you can throw those little VIP passes in the trash. I'm as VIP as you can get, and lastly, I'mma scoop you up tomorrow to go pop some tags in tha mall, get your wig whipped and your hands and feet gotta be on blast because you can't roll with me no any ole kinda way. If you ain't a dime piece you at least gon look and act like one wit me. I roll wit celebs, baby girl," Corey made clear.

"Shiit, cool wit me," Valerie shrugged her shoulders. She wasn't the least bit offended by Corey's superior attitude and blatant putdown. of her- looks. Valerie didn't give a damn; she was just happy to be roiling.

"Oh, and you said two things," Corey remembered. "What else could you possibly want?"

"Yeah, well," she started sheepishly, she started sheepishly, uncharacteristic of her, she knew. "You know that it'll take me a couple of hours to get what you need. I can have it to you by the time I go on my lunch break," she said.

"Okay, and ..." Corey sighed.

"Well, um ... Why don't you come back and pick me up at 11 and we can shoot to a motel and I'll let you bang me up or I can tighten you up with some head," she cooed.

Corey laughed, but he saw that she was serious. "Awight, Val, but you sure are a demanding bitch. You betta be glad I cut for you," he told her as he walked out the door, shaking his head.

Valerie watched as Corey jumped into his Aston Martin and drove off. "Who would've thought that lil Dirty would be balling out of control the way he is?" Valerie wondered.

"Is that your man, Val?" the cutie pie asked Valerie over her shoulder.

Valerie turned around with a cold stare in her eyes. "You betta stay outta my bidness, bitch, fo I drop these Fifth Ward b's on your lil preppy ass," Val snapped, strutting to the back.

Chapter 57

"You bull shittin, tell me that you're bullshittin, please," Nina addressed her old fiend Nya in the confines of Murder One's conference room. "What am I supposed to tell Amin?" she asked.

"Listen, Nina trust me. I'm trying to help you guys," Nya pleaded.

"Trust you? Trust?" Nina repeated. She was frustrated, hurt, and most of all she felt betrayed. "Be for real with me, Nya. We go too damn far back for this shit. Run this by me one more time." Tears were brimming in her eyes.

"Don't do me like that!" Nya yelled, pain etched in every feature of her face. "I'm doing right by you! I don't have to be here!"

"Just tell me, dammit! I deserve that from you. I stopped them niggas from raping you in college because I am your friend. All I want is the truth, Nya, that's all," Nina cried.

"Can't you see, that's why I'm here, Nina? That's why I don't take you and Amin in. I have done my damndest to misdirect this investigation of Murder One. You are my sister; I love you and Amin like my own blood," Nya wanted her to know, fears of her own surfacing.

"Just tell me one more time, please?" Nina asked. "You don't really work for a lawyer tied in with the Congresswoman, you are really an FBI agent?" Nina didn't want it to be true. Nya slowly nodded her head, sitting down at the head of the table. She propped her elbows upon the table and gently rubbed her blue eyes.

"You don't know how I've felt since my assignment was issued to me. I've known Nina, I've always known. I was there before Amin, when your family and your ex—boyfriend were pushing that shit. I turned the other cheek, I mean it wasn't my thing but you were my girl and in New York, in Harlem, that was your peoples' thing. I accepted that, you respected me and never flaunted it in my face. Then when Amin came into the picture and you two started dating, I knew that you were going to turn him on, huh," Nya shrugged. "But little did I know, little did we know, that the young boy from Texas was already on. His family was already deep in the game. And you know something," Nya added as an afterthought. "I believe that when the two of you met before, in the spring before our first semester, that you guys had already had it all planned out. I believe you went through the motions of dating and playing hard-to-get-for our benefit, for show," Nya reflected. Nina was about to protest, but Nya waved her hand in a dismissive gesture. "Forget about it," she seemed to say. "It doesn't matter now. You got your cowboy, Nina, and the two of you are living the great American dream."

"Boy, if you only knew," Nina wanted to say, remembering last night and Yvette. Amin was still wearing her anger from the picture frame she'd thrown at him. It took three butterfly stitches to close the gash on the back of his hand. "He'd ducked and covered his head just in time," Nina thought.

"That's why they gave me the assignment," Nya went on. "When they found out by digging into your background that we were classmates at NYU, they came to me and asked if I knew you. They didn't,couldn't have possibly known, how close the two of us were and how far back we went. I swear, Nina, when they asked me about you I already knew what it was about and I almost passed up the assignment. Then when I saw how they were targeting all of the minority-owned labels, it pissed me off. You should see the money and manpower they are spending on trying to take these labels down. Not just the small timers, either. The big boys are getting hit just as hard. Agents are infiltrating them all. Bad Boy, Rap—A—Lot, Death Row, Cash Money, Slip—n-Slide, Murder Inc. Everybody that's black-owned has been targeted. Fuck that Enron just sent the entire economy in a slump. Fuck that MCI fucked over a lot of people with the layoffs and downsizing. Fuck the fact that a lot of people's money, pensions, stocks and faith that they put into those companies went down the drain with their stocks. It ain't right and I know it. But I took the assignment just to help you all. I saw what' you do with your company's money. I drove through Third Ward, Fifth Ward and Allen Parkway. Did you know that every minority-owned record company, no matter how big or how small, puts money and manpower back into the community? It doesn't make it right, especially considering where most of the money is coming from, but it's more than the cities do, more than any Fortune 500 company does," she stressed. Nya inhaled deeply and when she exhaled her shoulders slumped over and a sob escaped her throat. Nina sat next to her friend and consoled her as she cried.

"I'm just torn," Nya stressed. "I got into this to do the right thing, to put the bad guys away. I joined the Bureau to make a difference. But every day I wake up, I think to myself that I've joined the wrong team," she sniffed.

"They don't have any concrete proof on you and Amin," Nya continued. "They're trying to build a case on you and Ruff House, build a file and see what turns up. After last night's incident I had to tell you. Somebody tipped police off and they followed Romichael from his club out to Katy to a rendezvous, and they stumbled upon a bad situation."

Nina already knew. After all, she was the one who'd had the detectives following Romichael after Felicia's phone call. She'd had to work quick and use some of her father—in—law's connections within the Houston Police Department, especially without her husband finding out, and that was almost like pulling teeth from a sleeping lion.

"They found some clothes in reference to a murder in New Orleans," Nya continued, "in Romichael's Hummer. The D.A.'s office will likely try to go to the grand jury with this evidence and look for an indictment. Apparently, the D.A. remembers a call about a lawsuit being filed on Ruff House by the two women who were murdered, so he's got evidence and a motive. The problem is that Romichael has an iron-clad alibi proving he couldn't have been in New Orleans the night of the murders, so he'll probably get out real soon. You know he's got connections and money, and that means a lot. But they've got enough to make him sweat. Romichael had two women with him. One, Felicia Brown, is being held on a misdemeanor possession charge for a firearm. The other, Monica Baptiste, is being held on drug possession charges. She was out of it when they found her. She couldn't even walk straight."

Nya had held Kiwan back for a purpose. She had a solution, one to which they would surely agree, or at least she hoped. She sighed heavily. "Now, to Kiwan;. Kiwan's a different story."

Nina knew what was coming next. "The laws in Texas concerning ex-felons with firearms are stiff," Nya started. "Right now, he's looking at no bond, a probation violation and a minimum of five years. Here's what I can do, Nina. I can go to a federal judge and get him released on bond under the ruse that he's an informant and I need him on the street so I can put him to work. Then I can go to the U.S. Attorney's office and get him a 5kl — that is a time cut for cooperating with the government. Depending on how high his criminal points are on the scale, resulting from his pre-sentencing investigation, I can probably get him down to a year or less." Nya paused before going on so that the information could sink in. "Now, I know how your family feels about cooperating with the law, but Nina, somebody has to have some common sense. That is unless Kiwan is willing to sacrifice another five to ten years of his life? You have to make them listen to reason. Now I wouldn't actually use Kiwan in that fashion, but if I go to bat for him and don't produce, then it's my ass."

Nina already knew that getting Kiwan, Amin, and especially Black Jack to cooperate with the US government was completely, totally, and unequivocally out of the question.

But she did have an idea.

"Okay, let me get this straight. Not only are we under investigation, but so is Ruff House?" Nina looked to Nya for confirmation. Nya nodded her head. "And you need a bust, or something concrete to justify your involvement for helping Kiwan, correct?" Nina didn't need confirmation now; she just kept going. "Well, what if Kiwan was the instrument in turning a snitch or informant in Romichael's camp to cooperate with you on setting up a sting operation for a drug bust?" Nina wanted to know.

"That would work," Nya said, staring at her friend. "But how are you going to get him to do that."

"Nina smiled, her green eyes dancing with mischief. "Giirrl, these machos may run their heads but that's all they are, heads! I am the neck that's attached to the body of this company and I turn the head in any direction I please," Nina boasted with the confidence of a veteran quarterback about to lead her team on a fourth-quarter drive to win the Super Bowl. "I have a plan. Don't worry, ojos azules, you just get my brother-in-law out and I need him out before Friday. He'll cooperate, but he won't know it, neither will Amin. I'll go get him a lawyer and lace him up. Kiwan doesn't need to see or sign any paperwork until I'm ready. How much will the bond be?"

"Well, a cooperating bond is free, just your word, but I can ask the judge for one to make it look good. How does a million sound?"

Both women looked at one another and, in unison, said, "Half a million!" and burst out in laughter.

They hugged one another fiercely before separating. Nina knew she had to get to work, and she knew she had to work quickly. Especially before Amin killed Dexter. She needed him alive, at least until Friday. That was the day of the album release party, when everything would either fall into place or collapse. She regretted having to do what she was about to do, but life had taught her to do or die. In the game it was either you or the next man, she thought as she quickly dialed Moochie up.

"I have to go, Nina. We have to also set up surveillance on Dexter Cunningham. We need to see how deep he is involved. We know that Romichael will contact him," Nya said before leaving.

"Oh, all right. Make sure you call me and let me know when I can pick up Kiwan," Nina said, trying to control her reaction to what Nya had just said.

"Hurry up and answer the phone, pinch Moochie, please, Nina thought, tapping her feet as if that would make him answer faster.

Chapter 58

Romichael was furious. Corey was as good as dead, he thought, as he sat in the downtown Houston city jail. Romichael was not a stupid man. This whole thing had been a setup from the start and all the pieces fit. Corey had put those clothes in his truck and had called the police on him to get him out of the way. How else could there have been a two-man HPD homicide detective unit on his tail last night? He should've seen it coming! And Dexter; Corey must have gotten to Dexter on the night that Romichael had him meet up with Dexter in the club, because he hadn't been able to reach him all day. His office said that he'd called in and went on some type of emergency leave. Dexter would die too, if he skipped town. Romichael picked up the phone again and dialed his lawyer's office. His collect call was put through.

"Law offices of Paul Kimbrough, who's calling, please?" the cheery-voiced secretary answered.

"Hey, Jennifer, it's me, Romichael Turner again. Can you put me through to Paul, please?"

"Oh, sure, Ro. I figured it was you. Paul just got in from lunch. Let me put you through."

Romichael fumed while Jennifer put him on hold. He didn't even want to think about how embarrassed he had been after what Kiwan had done. But the Lord knew how dearly they would all pay, the Lord only knew. His thoughts were homicidal because his pride was wounded now. The game had flipped on him last night. He knew that he wasn't supposed to ride anywhere without Flip by his side. He had gotten too lax. "You can bet your ass that won't happen again," he thought.

"Hey, Ro, what's up, my man? I've got good news for you." His lawyer, Paul Kimbrough, one of Houston's top criminal attorneys, was his usual optimistic, loud self and his words blasted in Romichael's ear, oddly comforting. Kimbrough was one of the good ole boys in the Texas legal system and that counted for, a hell of a lot in a state where friendship and kinship tipped the scales of justice, Romichael knew.

"Spit it out then, Paul, you already don burst my ear drum," Romichael winced.

"Dammit, boy, your goat—smellin ass cracks me up, Ro. You're sumthin else, you know that?" Kimbrough loudly delivered in his East Texas drawl. "But I got news, good news, and expensive news to you," Paul slid in.

One thing about Paul that Romichael respected was that he did not bullshit you around like most attorneys. He had a sense of humor that was uncanny in that it was never personal, and it was always based on business.

"Talk to me. How much?"

"Well, I did like you asked and bonded those two fillies out of the clinker for you, and they should be out as we speak. I also relayed your message to em, so you should be able to call em here in about, say, a couple of hours. I also went by the D.A.'s and Mr. Cunningham is nowhere around. Then, I spoke to a detective in Nawleans and tha bronco buster ran your spread by tha eye witnesses and they couldn't pick you out. So they can't put you at tha scene of the crime. Though they aren't ruling, out that you could've had them killed! They know that you most certainly have the means to do that. But if they do indict you, I'll hire counsel down there for you to push for dismissal on circumstantial evidence. So, so far you are just being held on questioning cause that little filly Felicia said that the two firearms were hers. She has a permit for the .380. All in all, you should be one happy pig in shit cause I'll see that you be released on your own recognizance later on tonight and it won't cost you a thing. But," the lawyer chuckled, "there's always a but, boy did you know that? But, my fee is twelve thousand buckaroonies," Paul said, in all seriousness now.

"Awight, Paul, no sweat, I'll bring the cash by as soon as I get out. No problem. What about Kiwan Rush?" Romichael wanted to know.

"Well," Paul said. "Now that is federal and sort of complicated. Without you filing charges on him, that hombre is still in a heap adung," Paul said. "These boys are strict down here about those ex-felons with pistols. But with his money, or his family's money and influence, he might skip through the loop somehow. Hell, I wouldn't be surprised if ole Keith Vincent didn't ring my phone today. Lord knows it would take a grand professional like me to get him out of that jam," Paul boasted. For a second Romichael entertained the idea of getting Paul to spring Kiwan just to kill him, but the thought was only fleeting. he had a better idea. He would hit them where it hurt the most.

"Ok, Paul, I'll call you back in a couple of hours to see if the girls made it there yet," he said.

"Okey dokey, Ro, we'll hollar," Paul yelled before hanging up.

Chapter 59

Amin felt comfortable. in his penthouses office above Club Flip Mode. The atmosphere provided him solace, which was the reason he chose to gather everyone there for such an important meeting.

Black Jack sat comfortably in the corner of the office by the bookcase as Ayanna sat on Amin's sofa, crying and blubbering. She'd repeated over and over about how she didn't mean to cause any harm, she just wanted out of the marriage and Kiwan had overreacted.

Amin was immune to the shock of the betrayals that had been taking place since Friday. But he didn't blame anyone but himself, he thought, as he fingered the wound on the back of his hand. As always, he would shoulder the blame for this chain of events. Had he been more involved with his people and family, none of this would have taken place. He just prayed that tie ramifications of his neglect could be slowed to a trickle of damage that he could somehow control.

"Man, I love you, Ayanna. You could never know how much you mean to me as a person and as a friend. Outside of Nina, you are one of the strongest women I know," Amin confided. "I just wish you would've come to me about the matter. I could've made sure that your divorce went through whether he signed the papers or not. We could've had that taken care of."

"I know, Amin, but you do so much for so many already, I thought that I could handle it," Ayanna cried.

"So let me ask you something. You were the one who told Romichael about the seat?" Amin was almost afraid of the answer.

"No, no," Ayanna attempted to compose herself. "He already knew. He just asked me if it was true. He was using me as a source to verify what Dexter had already told him when Dexter learned it from his mother."

Amin just nodded his head. He didn't know if he believed her or not, but in the grand scheme of things, he knew that it really didn't matter. His primary concern now was his brother.

Black Jack's cell phone rang, disrupting the flow of the conversation. "Yeah, speak on it," he answered in his usual suave manner. "Yeah, all right," he responded after listening a minute, showing no emotion before hanging up. "Young blood, I got somebody you should meet," Black Jack mentioned off-handedly. "I'll be back," he said, exiting the office.

"Amin, I'm sorry about all this," Ayanna apologized for the millionth time. "But Kiwan just snapped, I don't know where he even came from, he must've followed me. He was supposed to meet me at the house after he got his hair cut and dropped flex off at the studio, but he took so long, I didn't think he was coming. Romichael promised to sign those papers and I wanted it to be done, so we'd agreed to meet. I was planning on telling Kiwan that I was still married but every time the opportunity came up, I couldn't do it, Amin, I just couldn't. I love that nigga, despite what it may look like and I just couldn't tell him. I couldn't hurt him anymore than I already had. I thought that we could reconcile and be together, I just needed those papers signed. So I called Romichael and demanded that he sign since I know he thought that he had the seat in the bag. I knew that he was cocksure since he had Dexter, even after the bungled meeting they'd had at the Congresswomen's house. I wanted to see if he was behind the shooting at the park. I know Romichael, Amin, and I knew that the only way that he'd let me loose was if he knew that he didn't need me as a source any longer. So when he agreed to meet me and sign the divorce papers, I knew then," Ayanna said, her voice trailing off as she wound down.

Black Jack then walked back into the office with his sons in tow. Dominick, Eric, Tray, and a cute papersack brown complected sister, who Amin had never met before, all filed into the office.

"Amin," Black Jack said, grabbing the young lady by the hand," I would like you to meet Ms. Felicia Brown, your blood sister by way of your father, Clyde Rush," Black Jack introduced.

A thud resonated throughout the room. All eyes focused on Ayanna, who'd passed out, again.

Chapter 60

Truth be told, Prescious was more afraid of Nina Rush than she was of Amin or Kiwan. Prescious couldn't put her finger on what it was about the sassy Puerto Rican, but she knew that it was best to tread lightly when it came to dealing with her, especially concerning her family.

"Roll with me around the corner a sec," Nina instructed Prescious as she stood in the spacious marbled foyer of Kiwan's Clear Lake home. She didn't leave any room for refusal.

"Okay, let me go put on some clothes," Prescious said, observing Nina's dress. Nina had an olive green pant suit on with matching heels, and a mustard colored blouse that highlighted her green eyes. Prescious put on a Gucci sweat suit and house shoes. She'd been on the phone finalizing all of the details for Friday's album release party when Nina stopped by unexpectedly.

"Girrl, you're cool like that. I've got something I want you to see," Nina told her. "It won't take but a minute."

Prescious' stomach began to flip as she tried to imagine what this could be about. Maybe Amin had sent Nina to lure Prescious out so they could kill her. A hundred things went through her mind as she ambled to Nina's platinum Navigator. She didn't even bother to lock the front door of the house. Her feet felt like 300-pound lead weights the closer she got to the truck. Tony jumped out of the Gator, scaring the shit out of Precious, to open the door for the two of them. Damn! Her nerves were so bad, she almost pissed on herself. She was being ridiculous, wasn't she? If they wanted to do something, they would have done it already, she figured, as she climbed into the truck. Precious found herself missing Kiwan. She really wanted to be by the phone in case he called and needed someone to talk to.

Moochie drove the Navigator out of the gated community to the Clear Lake Yacht club, which was literally around the corner. It was elegant and formal, to say the least, making Precious feel awkward and out of place despite the fact that the small entourage went straight to the docks.

Murder One's yacht, the Queen Donetta, was one of the larger yachts there, requiring one of the largest slips to accommodate it. The Queen was docked at the very end of the pier.

Precious' mind still played tricks on her as she resigned herself to her death, if that is what this had come down to. "Fuck it," she thought, stepping aboard the yacht with Tony's help.

They walked from the aft deck down into the hallway that led to the saloon, passing a few closed doors that Precious figured to be bedrooms. Although she'd never been aboard the company's yacht before, Precious knew that she wasn't here to sightsee. They stopped at the last room on the starboard side of the hallway, and Tony peered inside before they all stepped in. Precious was the last to enter but was not prepared for the spectacle before her eyes.

She smiled so wide she thought she might hurt herself as she saw none other than Dexter Cunningham, the damn devil himself, tethered to the bed in the room. His eyes bucked wildly when he saw Precious, and he strained against the duct tape that held him securely.

Moochie and Tony flanked the bed as Nina offered a chance to Precious to do what she wished, Nina's hand gesturing toward the bed and the bound Dexter. His cruelty over the years had branded itself into Precious' memories and came rushing back with the speed of a flash flood.

"I thought that you might've wanted a little heart—to—heart with Dexter before we kill him in a couple of days," Nina said, her comments only partially explaining her reasons. If Precious had of reacted with dismay, or if she had shown sympathy for Dexter and rushed to his side, Nina was determined to kill Precious. There was room for loyalty to only one family now, and it had better be to the Rushes.

Moochie handed Precious a long, double-edged blade that was serrated on one side. "You can't kill him yet," Nina told her, "but you can hurt him like he did you for so many years. It's okay, I know you want, to . . . I would," Nina said with a devious grin and shrug of her shoulders.

Precious was surprised. After all the years of knowing Nina, Precious had suspected the Puerto Rican possessed what was needed to have someone killed, if not to kill him, or her, herself. Nina came from a hard world, and she had thrived. But to hear it said so matter-of-factly somewhat shocked Precious. But then another thought exploded in her mind, and it brought her a flood of such immense satisfaction that she knew she would do almost anything for Nina - that by telling Precious Dexter was going to die, Nina was telling her that she trusted her, with the most damning secret of all.

That trust shocked Nina, and it made her rethink, what she wanted to do to Dexter. She fingered the blade of the knife. If she could have, she knew she would have done it years ago. But there was a caution in Nina's eyes, and in her tone, that made Precious feel awkward, like this was a test. True, Dexter had hurt her, stalked her, beat her, humiliated her, and degraded her in more ways than she could remember, but by him being helpless it didn't make it fun. Fun! That was it, Precious thought! She would toy with Dexter, after all, Nina was giving her the opportunity to do with him as she wished, with the exception of killing him.

"Untie him" Precious told them. Both Moochie and Tony looked at Nina quizzically. Nina just shrugged her shoulders and nodded her head.

"Can you guys wait outside while I talk to him?" Precious asked the men as they untied Dexter.

Nina laughed, she just couldn't help it. "Oooh, Dexter, you in trouble," Nina teased, wagging her finger. "Have fun, girlfriend," Nina said before leaving. She stopped short of the door. "Tony," she said over her shoulder, "soften his ass up a bit," she instructed before leaving. Tony grunted in response.

Prescious sat down in a sofa chair in the corner of the room as Tony and Moochie stood Dexter by the bed. The' grey duct tape that covered Dexter's mouth and wrist were kept in place. Dexter still had on his clothes from that morning minus his suit jacket. Blood had stained his shirt from the wound to his mouth, which had bled despite the tape.

Moochie tried to hold Dexter up as Tony did the dirty work. Prescious could see the distress written across Dexter's face even before they began. He locked eyes with Prescious in an attempt to plead for his life. She returned his look with a look of sympathy that she hoped gave him some false hope.

After two monstrous blows to Dexter's belly from Tony, which staggered both Dexter and Moochie, Moochie let Dexter fall to the bed, unconscious. Both men looked to Prescious, who smiled with glee.

"Now remember, P, don't kill him," Moochie reminded her.

"I won't," she told Moochie in a sweet voice, which sent chills down his spine.

Both men stepped out of the room as Prescious started to pull her pants off. She needed to wake ole Dexter up; she wanted him conscious. What better way to do it than relieve herself of the urine that had been pressing against the walls of her bladder since she'd left the house? And that was just for starters.

Chapter 61

Amin couldn't believe it as he looked at his sister and hugged her again, for the fifth time. Felicia loved it. She basked in the attention that her brother was giving her. The mood turned from the somberness of Ayanna's tears and pleadings for forgiveness to min's joyful bliss.

"I still can't believe I got a damn sister, after all of these years," Amin stressed. "So that means that I'm not the baby of the family anymore," he said as he playfully nudged his baby sister. Ayanna could tell that Amin was truly happy. She hadn't heard him this happy since he was a child. She could actually feel the love for his sister emanating from the man.

"I always wanted a sister! Hell, I used to wish that Kiwan was a girl sometimes." Everyone laughed. "I'm serious" Amin joked. Amin had a million questions to ask Felicia and he didn't know where to start.

"Why did Daddy Bo keep you a secret from all of us?" Amin wondered aloud.

"That was my decision," Felicia told Amin. "When I first learned who you were after asking my mother a million times why my father never stayed home with us, and she explained that. Clyde Rush chose to remain true to his roots and his sons, well, I hated you and Kiwan. Every time daddy came to see my mother and I, I would refuse to speak with him. I was young, I wanted my father and my mother to be a family, to be as one. I thought that you two were preventing that, so I chose not to even associate myself with y'all or daddy. But as I got older, I got curious. I started keeping tabs on Kiwan's basketball career, and your band playing days. I went to every game I could. I even went to New Orleans one year when Yates played in the Mardi Gras parade, when you were on percussion. I saw you drop that stick boy," Felicia laughed.

"Aw, shit, Amin," Dominick spoke. "Nigga, I remember that shit." Mr. Johnson got on both our asses cause he saw us playing, that's what made you drop that stick." Amin blushed at the memory. He turned serious all of a sudden. "Maan, this shit got a nigga throwed out tha game," he said animatedly. "Daddy Bo still could've told me, man," his voice cracked with emotion. "Our lives could've been ..." he left the rest unsaid.

Black Jack picked up on it and commented. "When have you ever known your father to force his wishes upon you or Kiwan? When has he just ever made you or your brother do anything that y'all didn't want to do? Me and Clyde agree about that aspect of child raising. We teach y'all right from wrong, but we give y'all the freedom to make your own choices. Even when y'all were kids, all of y'all did damn well what you pleased. Every one of you in this room," Black Jack spoke, surveying the room. "So you can't blame him for respecting her wishes."

"I know," Amin said, hanging his head down.

"Oh, Ayanna, about last night," Felicia said, "I wasn't really going to shoot you. I knew who you were and I know how much my brother loves you. I was trying to keep him from killing Romichael."

"That was you?" Amin yelled, startling everyone in the room. "What tha fuck you rollin with Romichael for?"

"All right nigga, don't start with me. My daddy is on the Darrington Unit in Rosharon Texas," Felicia snapped.

"Young blood," Black Jack sternly spoke. "Let your sister talk and tell her story. She has a reason to do what she's been doing and personally I admire her, because she's been flirting with death on her own accord. She's got bigger nuts than half them clowns, Poo—Poo and them you run with," Black Jack scolded.

"All right, well, come on baby girl, let's hear it," Amin said, dropping into the seat next to Ayanna.

Chapter 62

Amin could do nothing but respect his sister after hearing her story. The risks she'd taken so unnecessarily were to be admired. But there were a million and one questions that flowed through his mind. Questions like, where is your mother? What does she look like? Why haven't we met before now? And why now? Most importantly, how could Daddy Bo let all of it happen and not even say anything about it? Amin realized that he really didn't know all the layers of his father. He probably hadn't even scratched the surface of the enigma that the man, Clyde Rush, represented to him. All of his life, his father had been more legend, more street credible than he was father. And he realized how he must be setting the same view of himself up to his kids and the younger generations of kids growing up hearing the name 'Idie Amin' ring like an ice cream truck bell throughout the neighborhood.

"So Nina knew about all of this?" Amin questioned, the hurt evident in his voice. His wife was becoming another enigma to him. Just when he thought he knew her, her strengths, her weaknesses, she surprised him with her versatility and ability to adapt to and overcome almost anything that life threw her way. Nina!

Felicia slowly nodded her head. "Don't trip, that's why I brought her here, youngblood. I knew about her too, so I'm just as much to blame," Black Jack interjected. Felicia had been careful not to reveal

Koto

each and every scrupulous detail of her story. Some things she kept to herself.

"But don't worry. I'm pulling her out as of now. I don't give a damn what kind of' position she's in to help. She's out," Black Jack stated in a matter of fact tone. Felicia looked confused.

"But why? The dangerous part is past. Romichael trusts me now," Felicia pleaded. "I'm in a perfect position to wreck shop."

Black Jack leaned forward and spoke very slowly and deliberately so that everyone would catch his drift. "So he trusts you, does he?" Felicia nodded cautiously, not knowing where he was going with this. Ah! The naiveté of youth, Black Jack thought. "Well, let me ask you something. Where is that phone that we gave you with all of our numbers pre-programmed into it in case you needed us?" he asked.

"It's at home. I don't keep it on me. I'm not stupid," Felicia remarked.

"You see, Dominick, this is why I told you that it was a bad idea to give her that phone. On your person," he pointed at Felicia, "is where you should have kept it. Sometimes when you put something in someone's face, those be the best places to hide things. Last night, somebody called my cell phone from that number, and by you just getting out of jail and coming from Romichael's lawyer's office, I assume that it wasn't you. And when I tried to call the number back, whoever it was had cut the phone off. Now, if you can tell me who used that phone then you can go back. Otherwise your position has been compromised and this discussion we're having is redundant. Pack yo shit and get out of that house. The boys can go with you," he stated as a final conclusion to his argument.

"No, that's all right," Felicia snapped. "I'll do it by myself. I have other womanly things to tend to. I don't need no baby sitters rushing me." Felicia also wanted to bathe and make a few calls and she didn't want anyone looking over her shoulder. Black Jack didn't comment on her last statement because there was no need to. He'd given an order, not an ultimatum.

Suddenly Amin spoke. "I need to go see Daddy Bo. I want to see him tomorrow, "he stated. The whole room went as silent as a monastery. Ayanna was the first to break the silence as all eyes had been on Amin. It was just too much for her. "Oooow," she cried and hugged Amin's neck tightly. She buried her head in the crook of his neck and sobbed. Mostly they were tears of joy, but some of those tears were for Amin, who she knew was finally growing up. Money never made you a man, only the lessons you learned from the struggles of life could do that.

Black Jack just smiled. He knew that sooner or later it was bound to happen. He dared to guess that the new addition to the family is what prompted Amin's wanting to see Clyde. Whatever the reason, it was a relief to him and Keith knew that it would be a joy to Clyde. Dominick, Eric, and Trey all joined their sister in a group hug. "Bout dam time," one of them said. "Yeah, man, that's real," Amin heard as they all gathered together.

Felicia didn't understand what the big deal was about, but she remembered that Amin had never been to Darrington since she'd started working there and she understood. This would be his first time seeing his father in probably the entire years of his incarceration. She knew that would touch her father's heart and bring him joy for his baby boy to come and see him. Tears ran down her face at the realization. She longed for her father to be happy, just as well as her mother.

"Where my sister at, y'all? Hold em up, let her in too," Amin yelled. "Come on here, girl." Felicia rushed over and joined the group, her new family. The love she'd always wanted and needed fled through the arms that were wrapped around her shoulders.

"Maan, what it do, y'all? This is a Kodak moment," Dominick said. "Black Jack, grab a camera," he called out as everyone tried to laugh their tears off.

"Whoa, wait a minute, y'all," Ayanna snapped. "Tomorrow is Thursday. You can't go see Daddy Bo tomorrow. You have to wait until Saturday."

"Yes, he can," Felicia countered. "I got a lil stroke with Warden Scott. I'll see if I can get you in under a special visit as a favor."

"The warden knows he's your father?" Ayanna asked.

"Hell, naw! The only person on tha ranch that knows that is my girl Christy, who looks out for him while I'm gone," Felicia answered. "Let me go so I can do what I need to do," she added leaving the office to get on her stick.

"Hold up," Amin called.

Felicia spun on her heels and looked her brother in his eyes. "Yes, master," she joked.

"Ha, ha, funny. You got jokes," he grinned. "But what else do you and my wife have up your blouses that we should know about?

Felicia blushed, smiling demurely. "Nothing, big brah. You know we wouldn't do nothing without asking you or letting you know," she said before strutting out of the office. After she'd closed the front door, in the interior of the penthouse Black Jack turned to Dominick. "Follow her. Make sure she gets back safe. Don't let nothing happen to her, and take Damon with y'all." Without question the men understood and obeyed.

"That girl is too headstrong," Amin commented.

"Yeah, she could be your twin," Black Jack joked.

Chapter 63

As soon as Felicia walked into the house, she dropped her purse on the banister and ran straight upstairs to search for the phone that Dominick had given her. In her sparsely decorated room, she immediately spotted the phone atop her bed lying next to some papers. Confused, she picked up the phone. She knew she hadn't left it on the bed out in the open like this. And what kind of papers were these, she thought? She picked them up and read through them.

The first page read Sprint P.C.S. Data Sheet. The name atop the list was Dominick Vincent. Browsing over the sheet, she realized that it was a list of numbers from the phone and along with those numbers were names. Black Jack's, Kiwan's, Amin's, Nina's, Ayanna's, and a lot of office numbers as well as a couple of studios. Okay, she thought. What part of the game was this? Was Black Jack trying to prove a point? If so, why would he go through these extremes?

A tiny noise caught her attention in the stillness. Breathing, and not hers. She whirled around. Corey stood in her bathroom doorway, his .40 caliber pistol dangling menacingly in front of him. As she saw him, Felicia almost pissed in her Apple bottom jeans. Fuck! She thought, looking at the door, wondering if she could make it by him. Her gun was downstairs in her purse, which was on the banister. Corey read her thoughts. "Naah, I don't think you'd make it," he gloated. He smiled like a Cheshire cat. He knew he had her. Though Felicia was terrified, she was determined to not let him see it. She used all of her will power to stop her legs from trembling. She stood up straight and glowered at Corey. It was this determination in Felicia that Corey liked. It attracted him to her.

This unbreakable resiliency that she possessed turned him on. But Corey knew that undoubtedly everyone had their breaking point, even him. "At first, I thought you were the law," he said, "at least, until I ran your little phone over there through the computer," he snidely remarked. "Boy, dem gotdamn computers are tha shit. It's amazing what a little money and computers can dig up," he laughed. It was a dark laugh, and it pissed Felicia off. His arrogant attitude made her more defiant. "This hoe ass nigga is so f'sho of himself" she thought. "Fuck him," she thought, vowing not to give him any satisfaction.

"Then I saw all those names from the Murder One camp, and I knew that you was fraud," Corey continued. He took a step closer to Felicia. "Who sent you?" Felicia didn't answer. She searched her mind for a way out. She was determined to see her father and mother together. She wanted her sacrifice to be fruitful; she needed that. "Okay, bitch, you throwed in tha game? You bout it?" Corey yelled, raising his gun to her head. Lord, she needed to do something quick. She knew Corey would kill her if she just stood there.

"I ain't worried about you, nigga. We'll see what Ro gotta say about all of this. You just a flunkie ass nigga, always have been, always will be, no matter how you try to use your money to cover it up," she hissed, realizing too late that she was toying with a real live viper. Corey swung the gun and hit her hard and fast, knocking her to the bed, where she bounced from the force of the impact. Her fingers went to her head, and they came away wet with blood. It was pouring down her face. She saw him advancing and ordered herself to move, but the pain was too much. It came over her in waves. She'd never been hit that hard in her life. Do women get hit that hard, she wondered in her delirium? Corey's voice swam into her consciousness until she was able to focus on it.

"I'm a kill you now," she heard him say. "Romichael is pussy whipped" he continued as she struggled to see and think. The pain was a sharp throb, but she welcomed it now. It brought relief that things couldn't get worse; surely a bullet couldn't hurt as bad as his blow had.

"You a hoe ass nigga," Felicia groaned as she squirmed. around in the bed." "That's why Romichael is going to kill yo bitch ass. You on borrowed time yo damn self."

"Man! This girl was amazing," Corey thought. She didn't know when to quit. Corey wanted to break her, hear her scream, beg and cry out as Precious had when he'd sodomized her that night. He looked upon Felicia's squirming, supple body and the swell of her breasts as she heaved for air made kinky thoughts float to the surface of his brain. Just thinking of the contrast between his dark cock thrusting in and out of Precious' ass made him have to adjust his pants. He set the pistol down on the floor and moved closer to Felicia. She lay there looking up at him.

"God, no," she thought as she saw the lust in his eyes. Anything but that. She would rather take a bullet than let this black ass nigga violate her. Felicia made a last ditch effort for the gun, the door, anything. But Corey was waiting.

"Unh, uh, bitch," he said, grabbing her. "Yo bad ass gon get this dick. You can't run from it," he laughed sardonically. Corey punched her in the stomach, leaning into the blow with all his weight as he tussled with her. She cried out and doubled over in pain.

"Yeah, bitch, that's how I like it. I thought you did too," he quipped grabbing Felicia's throat with one hand. She immediately tried to remove his fingers, but he squeezed. With his free hand, Corey unbuttoned her pants and pulled down the zipper.

"No!" Felicia thought. "Think, girl, think!" But nothing came to mind as Corey smacked her face, hard, and flipped her onto her stomach. She was terrified but didn't have the energy to scream as Corey began to yank the skin tight jeans down her ass. All she had the energy to do was . . . piss! The fear and panic had loosened her full bladder. She couldn't believe it, she thought hysterically; "If he's going to take my pussy, at least it will be pissy pussy."

"Aww, that's cold," Corey said when he noticed the urine. "But guess what? I like it like that, too," he laughed, remembering Precious. She'd pissed on herself too. What kind of nigga was this, Felica whimpered to herself?

"Now, now, pussy, it's going to be all right," Corey cooed while unbuttoning his jeans. He didn't even want any lubrication. He wanted it to hurt, he thought as he ripped Felicia's g—string off. He admired her ass for a second, remembering how she'd popped it on stage last night. So confident, so, so, so . . . determined and purposeful, he decided as he smacked her ass and watched it jiggle. He thought of Precious again and wished he had his mask; it was better that way.

Just as he started to pull his pants down a forearm locked around his neck from behind. His oxygen supply was immediately shut off and he became lightheaded. He was spun around with such force that his neck almost snapped.

"Hold up, D, don't kill him yet, baby. I'm gon punish this bitch," Dominick said. Corey didn't know who they were but the Murder One pendants they wore told him enough. He should've just killed tha bitch Felicia and been done with it.

With Damon keeping just enough-pressure on Corey's neck to keep him from resisting too strongly while keeping him conscious, Dominick started on Corey's ribs, breaking them with a flurry of well-placed punches. Corey passed out from-the-pain-momentarily, Damon knew, as Corey went limp.

Eric went to help Felicia as Dominick and Damon handled Corey. "Man, let's just kill that fool and b—out," Eric said.

"Nuh, uh, hell naw. I'm gon hurt this hoe ass nigga. He probably had something to do with A—dray getting shot, and if he didn't, then too bad cause I'mma act like he did," Dominick responded in a fury. He pulled the black leather gloves that he wore on tighter.

The beating that followed was one that no man should have had to endure, Felicia thought, but she couldn't take her eyes off the massacre. Nor could she move. She sat up and watched, blow for blow, as Dominick pummeled Corey. She had to watch, to check her feelings. This was their world and she was now a part of it. She'd seen some gruesome results of such beatings while working in prison, but she'd never actually seen the deed committed. This was, was ... cruel, Yet nobody seemed to think so but her.

Blood was everywhere, so much blood! She hadn't known a body could have that much blood, could lose that much, and still twitch and obviously live like Corey lived. His twitching became more uncontrollable, and his face, oh my God! She rushed to the bathroom to throw up. She didn't make it, throwing up all over herself and the carpet before making it to the toilet. Damn, she thought, this shit was serious. She could shoot someone, and she could, sure have shot Corey, and fo sho to save her life, or her family's, but . . . then she caught herself, remembering Black Jack's warning that she didn't want to be around when things went down. Now she understood.

Dominick, seeing that Felicia couldn't handle it, decided that Corey'd had enough. "Come on, let's put him out of his misery. Tape his ass up, take all of his money, clothes, and jewelry, and burn the house," Dominick ordered. It would take too much time and effort to clean it up. Just burn it up and collect the insurance money to rebuild it. They'd just kill Corey and dump his body in the ship channel somewhere, Dominick thought, feeling a bit relieved after his work out.

Chapter 64

Romichael was highly pissed as he looked at the city he loved through the drops of rain that pelted the passenger side window in the Hummer. "The Bayou City," he thought. He could recall as a kid, how after it would rain he and his cousins would run outside to play in the water-filled ditches. They would catch crawfish and wrestle one another in the mud, and then their grandmother would whip their asses for disobeying. Those were the days, the simple days in the hood before the drugs, before the money; the days where he and Corey had just met. He and Corey went back forever, it seemed, and whether he wanted to admit it or not, it was going to scar his heart to have to kill him.

"He still ain't answering," Flip told him as they maneuvered through 5th Ward. "Maybe it's too early in the morning," Flip told his boss. Romichael just shook his head. It was hard to find good help these days. He had no idea who was going to take Corey's place. Yet, he did have an idea . . . Felicia! Speaking of whom, she should've been with Flip this morning to pick him up from the city jail.

"What's up with Felicia?" Romichael asked. "Have you talked to her?"

"Yeah, she said that her house was burned down when she got home so she had to take care of a few things," Flip said. This bit of news surprised Romichael. He wondered if Corey had anything to do

- 332 -

with it. He had to find that hoe ass nigga. Damn, where in the hell was Corey, Romichael thought as he and Flip pulled into the paint and body shop Duck ran his business from. Flip blew the horn in the secret code that would permit entrance through the huge cargo door. Romichael noticed that it was all business as usual in Duck's shop. The flurry of activity never ceased, not even at 7 the morning. The two men exited the Hummer and trotted up the old rickety wooden staircase to the upstairs offices.

Romichael didn't bother to knock, barging into Duck's office, almost getting shot for his troubles. He came face to face with the Desert Eagle 44 that Duck wielded from behind the desk. "Don't run up in here like that no mothafuckin mo," Duck scolded. "What's wrong wit you? You betta start showing patience. Now, sit down," Duck instructed, putting the pistol away. Romichael sat, but Flip stood by the door after he'd closed it. Although Romichael had called before coming and Duck had surveillance cameras in every nook and cranny on the property, he understood the reprimand. He was getting ahead of himself.

"Now, tell me; what's got your boxers all bunched up that you had to come see me at 7 in the morning?" Duck asked. "I bet you ain't even been home to change clothes and wash that jailhouse funk off you," Duck commented, knowing that Romichael had come there straight from the city jail.

The first question Romichael asked caught Duck by surprise. "Have you seen or heard from Corey?" At first Duck didn't think that he was referring to his patna Corey; maybe it was some other Corey.

"Corey who?" Duck asked. Romichael was already frustrated, exasperated, and pissed to the max, it showed in his response.

"Maan, you know what mothafuckin Corey I'm talking about, are you playing games wit me or what?" Flip's stance became a bit more tense as his hands dropped to his sides, just in case. He knew that if these two got to trippin with each other, he and Ro were going to have to shoot their way out. And chances of them doing that alive were slim and none, but it was better, to stay ready than to keep from getting ready, the beefy bodyguard reflected, eyeing Duck distrustfully.

Duck looked at Romichael like he'd lost his damn mind, and he had damn sure noticed that little move by his bodyguard. But Duck was from the old school and never panicked. He had too much invested in Romichael with the seat, and he knew that something was terribly wrong. He leaned back and put his hands behind his head, giving a look to Romichael.

"Look brother, if I knew what Corey you were talking about, I wouldn't have asked. But since you feel the need to be disrespectful, then I'm just gonna sit here like Howdy Doody and only talk when you say it's cool to talk," Duck said, gently chiding Romichael.

Romichael knew that he was tripping, but his fuse was short. Things were not adding up. "Look, man, I apologize, but I thought that you were trying to play me for a fool," Romichael said, eyeing the older man. Duck just listened. He understood that the game was stressful sometimes, especially when you were used to having things your way like Romichael was.

"Dexter has jumped up and disappeared. I can't seem to find Corey and now I gotta fight a murder case," Romichael said. Duck didn't know all the details concerning Romichael's dilemmas, but at the mention of Dexter he knew that Romichael's problems ran deep, and that they concerned him.

"You 're gonna have to talk to me, youngster, so we can fix this shit. We've gone too far to turn back now. Now is not the time to try and be prideful and take shit into your own hands. We have a common goal and we need to stay united to achieve that goal." Romichael thought over Duck's words a second, then turned to Flip and told him to wait downstairs. When the door had closed behind Flip, Romichael told Duck the extent of his problems, starting with what Felicia had said about Corey after the clothes came up missing. He told him about Prescious' rape and how Dexter had been missing since. He told of the scene with Kiwan after meeting Ayanna and about his feelings on the seat. Romichael tied everything up in a nice and neat bow, summing up his thoughts with the punctuated statement that, "I'm finna start killing muthafuckas!"

Duck listened to it all and processed the information with the ease of a practiced accountant from the years of his experience in the game.

"Practically speaking, if I were you I would pull out of the whole thing. Back all the way out, man," Duck said, rising out of his chair and walking to his bank of video monitors that were mounted into the wall next to his 200-gallon aquarium. "You've been fortunate enough to have made it this far without getting killed or caught up with the law. A lot of people haven't been so lucky," Duck said with his back to Romichael as he watched the monitors. "You are on the right track with the music blast, and Monster Pat is blowing up. Fuck this committee seat. Syon is willing to sign Ruff House even if Murder One doesn't merge, Ro. You won't own your masters once you sign, but eventually you might. You have plenty of live cash to do whatever the fuck you want to, man. It just comes a point where we have to ask ourselves, when is it enough? When will we be satisfied? I look at this shit everyday and I ask myself, what have I accomplished in all these years of hustling? I've been doing this shit for so long, man, that it doesn't even matter to me anymore. Everybody in 5th Ward knows Duck and what he does. But they don't know why. I started out just trying to make a better way for myself and my family and ended up getting caught up in the cycle. I've made mistakes and been to the joint a few times. I finally learned the politics of the game, and eventually planted my feet in a solid foundation, all before you were probably born. It gets old, man."

"You are fighting more than one mind, Ro," he continued. "They are solidified through family ties and unity toward their common goal," Duck said, referring to Murder One. He turned to face Romichael and looked him square in the eyes. "You are just one man trying to run an empire through fear and discipline. When you sleep, one or two of them are always planning, plotting their next move. Though their family is their strength as well as their weakness, they won't be deterred by small setbacks," he said, referring to the pinpricks of dissension that Romichael had been causing. "If you just want to take out Murder One, you have to stop bullshittin with em. These little drive-bys and small encounters only seem to piss them boys off. They are big, connected, resourceful, and have a shitload of money. It's impossible, almost, to get to Amin or Kiwan. you can forget about Black Jack. You cut off the head and the rest dies," Duck said with an evil smile. "I'll help you to do that. But after this, I'm out. I'm 53 years old. I'm retiring. I'm buying me a ranch like lil J. With your money," he added. "You can buy all of this," he said, indicating the shop and by implication all else he owned with a wave of his hand.

Romichael contemplated. Duck's suggestion. Both men knew that Duck had spoken the truth. Duck had been the muscle behind Romichael's regime throughout the years. But Romichael was blinded by his ambitions for power and his quest to be on top. Duck had counted on that as a way to be rid of his burdens. He knew that in the end he had been chasing the wind the entire time. Because no matter how big you got, how much money you made, there was always somebody out there with more. He wanted out, and to enjoy the rest of his life. "Awight, Duck, "Romichael responded. "So what you're saying is that if you help me, then after all of this die down, I buy you out completely?"

"Now you've got it. The dope, the record company, the shop, everything."

Romichael nodded his acceptance. "Okay, bet that. What you got in mind?"

Duck grinned. "We start from the top."

Chapter 65

The visitation room was empty when Clyde Rush stepped through the door. "You said a legal visit?" he asked the officer before he closed the door.

"No, the warden said a special visit," the young male officer told him. "They're bringing them up now. I'm gonna sit back here and take me a nap. Just holla when you through, tap on tha door," he instructed.

Daddy Bo was confused. Who would be coming to see him on a Thursday, he wondered as he picked a table and sat down? The eerie quiet of the room unsettled him. He occupied his time by thinking, of his daughter and how much he missed her. Daddy Bo made a mental note to call her later that night. The only person he'd been keeping in touch with was Nina, who kept him abreast of everything. Speaking of which, he needed to call her, too. It had been a couple of days since they had spoken. The silence of the room was disturbed by the creak of the door opening as the visitors entered. Daddy Bo turned to see who was visiting him.

Officer Jarvis, his daughter's friend, entered the visitation area and stood by the door. "Hey, young lady," Daddy Bo said with a smile. "Can you enlighten, an old man as to what's poppin around this camp? They act like the president of the United States is coming in here to see me with all this secretive shit." Christina Jarvis didn't say a word, just stepped aside so Amin could move around her. Clyde Rush could not believe his eyes and did a double take to make sure it was Amin.

"Yeah, it's me, old man, it's me," Amin reassured him. Daddy Bo could feel himself moving as if propelled toward his son, but he didn't quite know how he was moving because his legs felt like a ton of steel was dragging them down. The next thing he knew, his youngest son was in his arms and all three of them were crying, even Christina. It took a minute for them to gain their composure.

"Boy, I knew you'd come see your old man one day," Daddy Bo said, sniffling.

"You been waiting in here the whole ten years for me?" Amin joked, trying to break free from the grip his emotions had on him.

"Girl, what tha hell you over there crying for?" Daddy Bo asked Christina as she wiped her eyes with the sleeves of the Confederate gray TDCJ uniform.

"Aw, hush," she giggled. "You sit down and enjoy your visit. I'll be back. I gotta go to the bathroom, she said before turning to leave.

Chapter 66

Precious was feeling blessed and refreshed after taking a long, hot shower. She wrapped her hair in a towel and put on one of Kiwan's shirts from his closet. She was enjoying living with Kiwan though he wasn't there very often. She felt loved and protected. Why was that, she wondered? They were kindred souls, two of a kind. They complemented one another and Kiwan made her feel like no other man ever had. He made her feel wanted without being used.

She started painting her toenails in the middle of Kiwan's bed. She had been sleeping in it ever since his arrest. Maybe she was claiming her territory? Precious had never chased a man in her life, but she was ready to break out her track shoes for Kiwan, if need be. That's, how bad her longing for him had become. Lord only knew that he was much more the man that Dexter was. Dexter! Ironically, she no longer felt remorse for his predicament, now that Nina had explained things to her. Dexter would be the sacrificial lamb that would hopefully set Kiwan free, she thought as the phone rang.

"Shit!" she called out. The phone had startled her, and she'd almost wasted the nail polish. She leaned over and picked up the cordless phone, careful not to upset the nail polish bottle onto the bedspread. "Hello," she answered. When the automated, phone system announced that she had a collect call from the Harris County Jail, she became giddy and anxious, like she was a schoolgirl. She accepted the phone call by pressing #1.

"Hello, Kiwan?" she said.

"What's up, miss lady, what you into while I'm in here?" he asked with a hint of jealousy that made Prescious blush.

"Nothing," she giggled. "What took you so long to call? I've been waiting since yesterday, huhn."

"Shiiit, if you want me to keep it one hundred then I gotta let you know that I was aggravated," he told her sharing something with her that he more than likely wouldn't have shared, with anyone else.

"Aggravated? What's wrong, boo?"

"Ain't shit, man. Check it out, we'll talk about it later. Right now I need you to do something for me."

"What?" she cooed seductively. She'd never had 'a man behind' bars, but she'd had girlfriends who did and they'd shared a lot Of their experiences with her. "You wanna know what I'm wearing?" she teased.

"Hell, naw," Kiwan said, laughing. Then he reconsidered. "Yeah, hold up. What do you have on?" He quickly changed his mind before he lost his train of thought. "No, no, scratch that thought." Prescious was tickled.

"Well, what's the deal? What did you call for? You want me to play in it for you?" she joked.

"No! Stop that, girl. Got me standing up here fixing myself. I'll call back later for all that, or better yet, I'm supposed to be home today."

"Yeah, I know." Kiwan could hear the smile in her voice. He could do nothing but chuckle, liking the fact that she was being assertive with him.

"Hold on," he snapped. "How did you know?"

"Nina told me."

"How did Nina know?" he wondered aloud. "Do me a favor and call her on three-way because something is strange here."

"What's the matter? You don't wanna come home?"

"Yeah, I do, but you don't understand and I don't want to spend all day trying to explain it. Just call her for me," he told her.

"Awight, but seriously, let me ask you a question before I call her," Prescious got serious all of a sudden.

"Yeah, go ahead."

"Do you miss me?"

Kiwan was caught off guard by the question. Now why did she have to go and ask that? "One hundred?" he asked, wanting to know if she wanted the truth.

"One hundred!" she replied, letting him know that hell, yeah, nigga, I want the truth.

"Yeah, I miss you," he told her sheepishly. Prescious had a grin on her face big enough to light up Las Vegas. She clicked over to call Nina on the phone. As the phone started ringing, she clicked back over.

"Hey Prescious. What's up?" Nina answered her phone.

"Hey, girl, you brother-in-law is on the phone. He wanted to holla at you," Prescious informed her.

"Heey, Ki, what's up, boy? How you holding up?" Nina asked.

"I'm cool, what's jumping on that end?.."

"Nothing. Our brother went up there to see your Daddy," Nina broke the news to him.

"Whaat!? No shit? What on earth made him. just up and do that? I thought he was allergic to the jail house."

"I think it might've had something to do with your sister," Nina said, bracing herself for his reaction.

Kiwan was confused. "Sister? We don't have no sister."

"Yes you do. You just never knew it," Nina told him.

"Bullshit," he countered.

"No, seriously," Nina said. "You'll see when you get home," she said, bringing him back to the purpose of his phone call.

"Yeah, speaking of coming home, how the hell did I get a bond? What did Amin do? I know these feds, Nina, and they don't give bonds to probation violators unless they puttin them to work, and I ain't working for nobody."

"We got you a good lawyer, cunado," she assured him. Nina didn't need him flipping out on her. It was integral to her plans to have him out, but she knew that he wasn't a dummy. "The lawyer pulled some strings and got you a bond. Boy, you know that Money Moves Mountains. But this is just a bond. We're really buying you some time on the streets because the lawyer already said that it's an open and shut case about the pistol."

"I . . . don't . . . know," Kiwan said slowly. "How much is the bond?" Nina thought about lying to him, then second guessed herself. "Half a mil," she told him. "But that ain't shit. We need you out, Ki. Your brother needs you, I need you," she said in a forceful manner, knowing he would catch her meaning. "Your. sister needs you."

"I need you too, Kiwan," Prescious added.

"All right," he conceded. "I'm glad to get out of this bitch anyway."

"Well, it's settled then," Prescious said. "I'll be waiting out front of the federal building for you."

"Yeah, cause I'm on the way to sign the bond now. The lawyer said that you'd probably be released later on this evening," Nina said.

"I'll be there with bells on," Prescious joked.

"Is that all?" Kiwan said.

"Maybe!"

Chapter 67

"Moochie, we gotta hurry up before Kiwan changes his mind about coming home," Nina said as she hung up the phone.

"Well, what you want me to do, Nina, grow wings and fly you there?" he asked sarcastically as he wheeled the Navigator through the downtown traffic. Nina rolled her eyes at him Moochie had been short with her lately, ever since she'd explained to him that the events taking place the last few days needed to remain between the two of them. He felt that Nina was trying to make him choose between her and Amin. He made it known that his loyalty couldn't be bought, and that although he'd pledged his loyalty and his life to guard her, Amin and Kiwan were still his boys. Then she'd had to explain the program to him. He'd agreed, reluctantly, and been testy with her ever since. But she knew what would cheer him up.

"Moochie," she said.

"What?" he snapped.

"When we get through, we also have to go pick up Goddess from the airport. Her plane from Puerto Rico is due at Intercontinental at 11:45," she told him, smiling. That got his attention.

"Your cousin Goddess?"

"Who else?" she responded flippantly. From the back seat Nina could see both Moochie and Tony grin. She knew that everybody loved Goddess.

"She coming to work or to visit?" Moochie wanted to know.

"I don't know, depends on how you act; I might let her stay after she does what she gotta do," Nina said.

"So that means that you ain't gonna let me rob the bondsman once you give that fool that 75 Gees you got," Moochie said, and he and Nina both laughed. They both knew that he would have tried some shit like that if he was sure he would get away with it.

"Boy, you silly," Nina said, laughing.

Despite the laughter, everybody in the truck knew that the moves they were making were no laughing matter. Lives would be changed and especially with the Goddess coming into town.

Chapter 68

"Why daddy, why didn't you tell us about our sister?" Amin solemnly asked his father. He wanted to ask him more than that, but that was as good a question as any to start with.

Daddy Bo thought for a second before speaking. How could he make his son understand? How could he explain? Just tell him what's in your heart, Clyde, he urged himself as he looked into his son's eyes.

"Son, I've made a lot of mistakes in my life. I'm not perfect. As a matter of fact, I've been rehearsing what I would tell you for years if you ever decided to come and see me, but now that you are actually here, all I can do is tell you what's in my heart," his father said, searching his son's eyes for . . . understanding?

"I used to hold up and portray an image to you and you're your brother that I myself thought was sho nuff about something until I got locked up. You see, when your mother died, I vowed that I would slow up and be there for the two of you and raise you the best I could. And in my blind determination, I overlooked a special woman who I thought would never fit into our world and our scheme of things."

"And that would be Felicia's mom?" Amin asked.

"Yeah," nodded Daddy Bo. "That woman loved my dirty draws. Kind, of like the way Nina loves you," he said, touching the back of Amin's hand where the butterfly stitches were. "But she wasn't down for just anything, and I felt it best to leave her out of our family equation, despite the fact that she'd become pregnant with our child. You see, son, that's just it! It's a cycle that needs to be broken. My dad was a hustler and had a fucked up concept of fatherhood. He passed that on to me, both the hustling and the concept, and I've passed it on to y'all. When does that end?"

Both men let a comfortable silence invade the conversation as they each followed the paths of their thoughts. Daddy Bo wondered the ever-present question that haunts the thoughts of incarcerated men: What if?

But for Amin it was different. Here was a man who could do no wrong in his eyes. Daddy Bo. No, Clyde Rush. Daddy Bo was an image, a product of the streets, a name that Amin associated with street fame. Clyde was his father, a father who he now realized he really didn't know well. As a child, it wasn't acceptable to hang on to your father's coattails. It wasn't manly to ask your father his feelings on matters of the heart. You were just supposed to follow his example and accept the teaching he gave you when he saw fit. Of course, in many ways, his father had set a good example, but it hadn't been enough, and both men knew that. Amin was confused. He didn't want to judge his father or second guess his upbringing. He was afraid to. Where would that leave him?

"I know what you thinking boy, but you can go ahead and blame me. It is my fault. I did fail as a father in not showing you and Kiwan that the way we were living wasn't right. But I rationalized that my boys would be the hunters instead of the hunted. And of course, y'all knew what the rules of the game were and you had good teachers in me and Black Jack. But what you didn't know was that we were all fighting a losing battle. We were climbing uphill, going nowhere fast. But you changed that, son, and I'm proud of you. You took the game to the next level. You made the family legit. You conquered the American dream and changed the game. I will always be beholden to you for that; we all will. But the cycle has to stop, son. Not everybody can be as fortunate as we were, or can have a man as ambitious and resourceful as you on their side. We climbed on the backs of our people to get. here," Daddy Bo told Amin.

"But daddy, we give back to the community. We have programs, Little League teams. We provide jobs. We do a lot," Amin pointed out.

"Bullshit! Hush money is all that is," Daddy Bo spat. Amin was shocked. "Tax write offs," his father added disgustedly.

"Why is it bullshit when we do it but it ain't bullshit when the Kennedys, Rockafellas or the Bushes do it? They didn't get all of their money legal. They do all kinds of illegal shit and give back to clear their consciences."

"Is that why we give back, Amin? To clear our conscience? I don't think so," his father answered for him. "If that's the case, then you'd be better off keeping your money in your pocket. Black people don't need that kind of help. You're no better than them white folks then, tearing us down and our community down without trying to rebuild it better than before," Daddy Bo said. The harsh words stung Amin, especially coming from his father. He dropped his head.

"Pick yo head up, son," his father scolded. "Don't feel bad or sorry, we're all guilty of it. What you do is take action. Son, that's what the seat is for. It's not just to take this company to a higher plateau. We really don't need society's approval of us! We ain't trying to move in bigger circles to be accepted by the Black bourgeoisie just for money or power. There is a method to my madness, son. What we are going to put down will be a legacy to follow, a dynasty," Clyde said. "Nina knows, your brother knows. He and I communicated about it for five years. But the concept would probably be foreign to you," his father picked at Amin, trying to gauge his reaction.

"Try me, daddy! See, that's the problem. Everybody underestimates me," Amin said, blowing up.

"And that's what's kept you pushing forward, son," his father yelled, matching his son' anger. "We don't underestimate you; quite the opposite. We know what you are capable of, but Amin, you aren't ready for the concept. When the time is right, Kiwan will lay it out for you, but you haven't suffered enough to understand," his father told him.

"Maan!" Amin jumped up. "What tha fuck is this shit! I'm out here suffering every day that you're away. I suffer everyday that I can't talk to you! I suffer every time that I see my daughters and they ask about you or their Uncle Kiwan, because I know that I was the reason for that," Amin yelled, tears streaming down his face.

"Son," his father said humbly, "I know. I understand, but in life, like everything else, everything is not for everybody. Know your limitations and know when to step aside for the betterment of someone else. Sacrifice your pride and be content that you've done your best. The burden you carry is one that you've placed on yourself. If I could carry it for you, I would, but nobody can free you from those chains but you. It has nothing to do with being locked up, yet it has everything to do with it." Daddy Bo leaned back and closed his eyes. It was a sign that Amin knew and remembered all too well; the discussion was over, case closed.

Amin was furious. His jaw muscles twitched. He reflected on what his father had just said, saw the wisdom in it and sat down.

"Now, what's my daughter been up to?" Daddy Bo asked. By the look that Amin gave him, Daddy Bo knew that something had happened to his only daughter.

Chapter 69

Kiwan walked out of the federal building as the setting sun cast a burnt orange and purple tinge to Houston's skyline. Smog from the dwindling rush hour traffic threatened to choke him as he surveyed the streets for Prescious. He didn't have to look too hard or wait too long. He actually heard her before he saw her. The bass from the Escalade vibrated the concrete and shook the windows as Prescious turned the corner, pulling the truck right up to Kiwan.

He couldn't conceal his smile as he walked to the driver's side. She lowered the burgundy colored tinted window and turned down the music.

"It's like deja vu, huh?" she asked, smiling.

"Almost," he said, looking, into the truck. "Girl, you got my shirt on."

Prescious just nodded and smiled. "Ain't got no bra or panties on, though."

"I don't care. That's Egyptian cotton, that shirt cost three hundred dollars," Kiwan joked. "Give me my shit now. Take it off."

If he didn't think she would do it, he had another think coming, she decided as she stepped from the Escalade.

Damn, she looked good in his shirt, he thought as he admired her full curves and womanly shape through the fabric. Even her feet were cute, he told himself, noticing her freshly painted toes in her sandals.

Prescious began to unbutton Kiwan's shirt and got down to three before he stopped her. "Awight, awight, he laughed as he embraced her and swung her around. "I get it, I get it."

"You do?" she asked, arching one eyebrow suspiciously.

"Yeah, I get it now," he assured her.

"What do you get?"

"I tell you what. Let's go home and consummate this relationship with some lovemaking," he offered.

Prescious smiled. "We can't. Flex is there sleeping and I don't want to wake him up. But I got us a room," she told, him, pulling out a key card from the shirt's front pocket.

"Deja vu." Kiwan said. "Deja vu." He shook his head.

Chapter 70

FRIDAY NIGHT LIVE

The spotlight illuminating the Batman emblem blazed in the sky over Club Flip Mode. Murder One records had summoned the support of H—Town, Screwston, the City of Syrup, and the city had responded. They were determined to do things Southern-styled and Texas-sized. It was an H-Town ballerfest at its finest. Third—Coast stunting was what some dubbed it, and the limos, Hummers and Escalades were lined up bumper to bumper on the street in front of the club. The immediate half block in front of the club was cordoned off. It was a staging area, a red—carpeted walkway for the peacocks to strut, a platform 'for the players of the industry to flaunt their dazzling wealth and personal style, and they were shining.

Tour buses lined the opposite side of the street occupying the far lane. Teams of valets stood sentinel at the door. directly in front of the club, where orange cones announced a drop-off zone. The traffic flowed one way and the two middle lanes were congested with low-lows, tricked out 'slabs,' and candy painted S.U.V.'s. Mounted police kept the traffic flow moving, and the bicycle units frantically pedaled up and down the street, unsuccessfully trying to strangle the raucous behavior.

Horns and police whistles were drowned out by the bass of high-dollar stereo systems that shook the concrete, sending shock waves of music that set off car alarms a block away. It was a cacophonous, crazy, glittery scene, and the crowd was loving it. The patrons squirming restlessly behind a roped-off line, which circled the block, were kept in check by security guards posted every ten feet. VIPs bypassed the line, and flashes from the disposable and digital cameras captured them strutting by. The laminated passes adorning their necks, along with the gaudy diamond-studded necklaces, bracelets and earrings separated the ballers, movers and shakers from the fakers.

Kiwan Rush and two other road managers led the Murder One entourage and the seven label artists off the tour bus that had pulled up behind the long line of buses already waiting to unload. Company employees and some hangers-on were already waiting for them as they exited the bus, bringing Murder One's entourage to 21. They were one of the hometown favorites and the crowd screamed for autographs and the opportunity to chill with the VIPs.

K—flex didn't waste any time, grabbing two females outfitted in leather and lace for his own personal escorts. By the way he palmed their asses as they marched to the entrance, things were already understood. Scantily dressed women enticed the crew with seductively blown kisses, inviting winks and insinuating touches as they passed. At 9 p.m., the club was almost at full capacity.

Things were getting tight, Valerie thought. She might not get to make it inside. She knew that over half of the people in line, would be sent home. "Bitch!" she cursed Corey under her breath as she prayed to be let in. She'd listened to Corey and had given her VIP passes to her cousin, Shartel, who had already passed her by without so much as a, "Hey bitch!" That was some cold shit, but not as cold as Corey leaving her hanging. "If I ever catch up to his ass," she mumbled, keeping a wary eye out for his snake ass and she'd known better than to fuck with them dog ass niggas from her hood. They'd been sending her through the wringer since grade school. She'd trusted Corey and had given, him what he needed only to get a wet ass for her troubles. Stupid, she thought. Valerie watched as another group of VIPs made their way down the red carpet. It was the Murder One clique, she could tell, as thoughts of ducking under the velvet rope entered her mind. But the scowl and brawn of the hawk-eyed security guard changed her mind. Her eyes skimmed over the flamboyant group as she made eye contact with a familiar face. She turned away hurriedly to avoid the inevitable shame that was sure to follow.

"Valerie?" the voice called out. Valerie turned back, dreading facing her coworker. "Hey, Val, I thought that was you." Kendra said in a pleasant voice. Valerie thought about being nasty with the bitch before she got the chance to dis her first, but Valerie was too embarrassed to do anything but be cordial.

"Hey, Kendra," Valerie muttered." I see you lookin playa," she said, commenting on Kendra's dress.

"Look, I know we don't see eye-to-eye, but we work together. I'mma be bigger than our petty differences that we seem to have and squash the animosity," Kendra said, offering her hand to Valerie. Valerie took her hand and shook it. "Listen, my cousin Sheeba works for Murder One and we're going up to the glass VIP room. You can come if you wanna," Kendra offered. "I have an extra VIP pass, Kendra held the pass out to Valerie, who went wide-eyed with astonishment. She snatched the pass, draped it around her neck and ducked under the rope. Envy shone on the other female faces as the two caught up with the rest of the crew. The Ecstasy pills that Val had taken earlier acted as a euphoriant enhancing each of her five senses as she took in the experience of her life. Even the Kappa beach party the previous two years hadn't been this crunk. The gleam of the flashy rides, sparkling jewelry, shining rims that spun, and exotic colognes and perfumes threatened to overload her already heightened senses. Someone from behind grabbed her ass through her skintight skirt, and a nameless guy from the crowd grabbed her hand. She didn't even acknowledge the gropes, just went with the night's flow. It all felt wonderful to her and she wanted it to never stop. This night might turn out to be alright after all, and fuck Corey, she thought. The hoe ass nigga could drop dead for all she cared.

*   *   *   *   *   *   *   *   *   *   *   *

Romichael was on a mission as he and his Ruff House crew entered the lobby of the club, trailing J. Prince and the Rap-A-Lot family. Being from the bloody nickel, 5th Ward, both CEOs had decided to represent by showing up together. Ruff House wanted to be seen as a major contender in the music game. What better way to do it than to have a young platinum-selling artist such as Monster Pat rubbing elbows and allying his fame with the likes of Willie 'D' and the 5th Ward Boys? They were a part of the label that put H-Town on the world map for Southern-styled rap. But that agenda came secondary to Romichael. His only purpose for attending was to find Corey, who was still missing. Plus, he still hadn't heard from Felicia. He was worried sick about her. Maybe Corey had scared her off, or worse, maybe Corey had killed her? Romichael knew that if Corey was in town he'd show up here, and he was prepared to deal with him tonight. Romichael knew that since they ran in the same circles, he could not contract a hit on Corey through the usual route, because it would be sure to get back to him and scare him off. So Romichael went about everything as normal and planned to catch Corey unawares. He knew that Corey was behind trying to set him up. Why else would he not be returning Romichael's calls?

J. Prince and his Rap-A-Lot crew passed through the metal detectors in the lobby with some minor hassle caused by their jewelry. Those that set off the alarm were expertly patted, down by security for concealed weapons. This was an unexpected turn of events for Romichael, who was strapped. He and half of his crew were carrying, especially a few of the penitentiary hoodlums that he had on his roster. Damn the consequences, Romichael thought people were scheduled to die tonight, as he'd sent the Grim Reaper on a mission by way of Duck and his hit squad. Duck and a few of the boys went through the detectors as their jewelry registered on the lighted meter gauge, setting off the shrill beeps. The beeping drew attention to Romichael and a few others who's tried to sneak past the detectors. A beefy bouncer dressed in all black headed them off. "Hey, man, y'all gotta go through the detectors like everybody else, VIP's or not."

"Look, we don't want no trouble, black, but I ain't walking through no metal detectors like some common hood. You gots me fucked up," Romichael said angrily, furrows of frustration creasing his brow. Flip and a few others doubled back to Romichael's side.

"It's either, that or get patted down," the bouncer said as members of his staff started gathering around.

* * * * * * * * * * * *

Nya Phillips and her partner were watching the scene unfold in the lobby. "You think it's going to get out of hand?" Debra asked.

"Nah, I got faith in the staff. They seem capable of handling the situation," Nya responded, her cold blue eyes professionally assessing the situation.

"What if they don't and things start to get nasty? You know Ruff House got beef with the owners of this club. What are they doing here anyway?" Debra pointed out. Nya knew that Debra was questioning her judgement. Debra was also working on her last nerve. Nya had to put up with her recently assigned partner because the director of the Houston field office had felt she needed help after the incident with Kiwan and Romichael. At least that's what he'd said. But Nya felt that Debra was there as a spy for the director after she'd pulled those strings to get Kiwan released. No matter, she concluded. She was resigning after this case was over with, anyway. They could keep this job and shove it up their hypocritical, bureaucratic asses. She didn't need the hassle.

"It doesn't matter. We let the local police handle it. We will not break cover, you understand?" Nya asked testily. Debra just grunted in response, but eased closer to the action. What the fuck was she doing, Nya wondered? She was going to fuck up Nya's plans of, getting closer, to the Ruff House clique, through Monster Pat. Nya had planned on surprising Monster Pat in the VIP room and playing the jealous role. She wanted to catch him with another woman and scorn him for not returning to her place earlier that week. Then she would seduce him, but it wouldn't work if he saw her now. Nya eased closer, watching as a tall, well-dressed man with two of Murder One's bodyguards, whom Nya recognized, stepped in to defuse the scene. Big Tony and Moochie shadowed the man as they approached the head bouncer. Where had they come from, Nya asked herself? More importantly, why? Nya scanned the lobby and spotted Nina and another beautiful, light—skinned complected sister by the bank of elevators, watching. Interesting, Nya thought.

*   *   *   *   *   *   *   *   *   *   *   *   *

Nina, Tony, Moochie, Precious, and Derrick Hopes, the general manager of Club Flip Mode, had been awaiting the arrival of Romichael and his crew. It had been a part of Nina's plans. What was unexpected was the fact that Romichael would cause a scene. Nina had planned on separating Romichael and Duck at the front door anyway. Now, Romichael was playing right into her plans. Nina dispatched Tony, Moochie and Derrick to handle the situation before it got out of hand. When they left, Nina turned to Prescious and asked, "You understand what you gotta do, right?"

"I got it as good as I'll ever have it," Prescious answered.

"Are you nervous?" Nina wanted to know, more out of concern for her well-being than for the task ahead of her. Prescious pursed her lips and sucked her teeth, looking Nina in the eye.

"Come on, Nina, this is me, Prescious; remember? I stopped being nervous about anything the day I lost my virginity."

As an afterthought, Nina decided to be real with Prescious while it was on her mind. "For what it's worth, I think that you and my brother-in-law complement each other well. I think that you two would make a good couple. But girrrl, if you break his heart or hurt him in anyway," Nina shook her head at the thought, "It's gonna be some shit," she teased.

Prescious just smiled. It felt good to hear those words from Nina, especially after all the years of knowing her and how protective Nina was of her family. Prescious knew that Nina would do anything and by any means to protect what she loved. What surprised Prescious was the fact that she, too, was adopting that concept about what little she had in life. After all the years of being a loner, a soloist, and loving nothing, not even herself at times, Prescious wanted to hold on to the love she knew she had for Kiwan. That was why she participated in Nina's plans, despite the consequences that they could have. It felt good to Prescious to finally long to something worth sacrificing for. Something worth her love, something worth her life.

A cause to live and die for. Loyalty above all else, and death before dishonor, her family! She was now a part of the family and she was determined to carry her weight. "Thanks, Nina," Prescious said, tears brimming at the corners of her eyes.

"Thank me by keeping it one hundred with that boy. Because after all the years being with Amin, I've learned a lot. Despite all of the shit he's taken me through, I've realized one important thing that Daddy

Bo pointed out to me. Wherever you find a good man, the only way that he can be great is with an exceptional woman behind him. And I want my husband to be a great man, Prescious. I just have to work on his ass a little more," Nina smiled. "Kiwan can be great too."

* * * * * * * * * * * * *

"What's the problem?" Derrick asked the head bouncer. 'Dee-Dee,' as his friends and employees called him, was a quiet storm, mild mannered but quick tempered once aroused. Rarely did Dee-Dee allow his temper to flare despite the temptation provided by running a successful club of this magnitude. He prided himself on being able to use his head and outthink his adversary. Violence was always his last resort, but violence was something he knew well, especially growing up on the North side of town off of Homestead Road. Dee—Dee spoke softly but carried a huge stick. He adjusted the Ice-tek watch on his wrist as Romicheal continued to rant.

"Tha mothafuckin problem is that your boy here is disrespecting me," Romichael accused.

"Yo, get off the bullshit," the bouncer said. "The man refused to go through the detectors and a pat search, so I told him that they had to bounce."

"Well, he gotta go then," Moochie said, stepping into Romichael's face aggressively.

"Nigga, you betta give me 50 feet," Romichael hissed.

"Hold on, Mooch," Dee—Dee said. "Here's the deal," he said, adjusting his tinted spectacles and placing his hands behind his back, clearly in charge of the situation and of the violent men around him. "We're responsible for the lives of the patrons as well as the performers in this club. Ever since the incident at Tom Bass Park, we've tightened up security around Murder One events. There seems to be some haters out there who don't want to see the label prosper," Dee—Dee prodded, gauging Romichael's reaction. The look on Romichael's face was a dead give away. "So, everybody is checked. We're all here to have a good time and party. I'm sure you are too. We don't mean any disrespect. It's just concern for the lives in the club."

Romichael almost went into another rage. Duck grabbed him and pulled him aside. "Look," Duck hissed. "Don't push your luck,

Romichael. Now is not the time to get into your feelings. Chill out. Go somewhere and establish an alibi for your whereabouts tonight. Let me work my jelly. If Corey shows, I'll call you and put a tail on him, but don't add fuel to the fire. You are out of your league and your element. You don't need to be packing, anyway. Don't let the turn of events dictate your behavior. Just relax, man," Duck assured. "Now you and Flip can ride out. Grab a couple of bitches and throw your own party. I'll get back to you later on when everything is in order," Duck said. "Oh, and watch the news in the morning. It might make you feel better."

Romichael couldn't help but agree with what Duck was saying. He spun on his heels and left. Everyone who was packing heat followed. That left Duck with one bodyguard and three of Ruff Houses' artists. Mission almost accomplished, Nina thought. She looked at Precious and nodded.

"You're up to bat," she said. Precious went into action.

* * * * * * * * * * * * *

Her long, supple, wavy hair was pinned up with four glossy black Oriental chopsticks. The only makeup she wore other than her fuchsia colored lipstick was eye mascara painted on to give her hazel eyes an Oriental look. She wore a pair of oblong shaped gold, ruby and pink diamond studded earrings. Her gold and black choker boasted 12 octagonal shaped rubies that enhanced her long, graceful neck. The fuchsia body suit she wore hugged every curve of her body for dear life, exposing her back and the new tattoo she'd gotten at Dragon Mike's last night with Kiwan. It was a statement, a proclamation of love. It was a tattoo of a green-eyed black panther with a diamond-studded collar and chain. The collar had a 'P' that dangled from it. The panther was ever-watchful, stretched out atop the letters K.I.W.A.N. "You tamed-me, Kiwan, and no matter where we end up, I want to always remember you," Precious had told him last night after they'd made love and she'd gotten tatted. People stopped and stared at Precious as was usual when she dressed to impress. But tonight she had a different swagger, the confidence of a woman who seemed to have it all. She was the bitch that every woman there wanted to be, she knew as she walked up to Duck and what was left of the clique.

"This has got to be the luckiest night of your lives, "Prescious addresses the group.

"I don't believe in luck," Duck said, "but please tell me, how so?"

"Because you got me, the hostess of this gathering, as your chaperone for the remainder of the night," Prescious said.

*   *   *   *   *   *   *   *   *   *   *   *   *

The concert was already underway when Prescious and the Ruff House crew entered the club. Zero was on the stage blessing the mic with his song "I hate you," and K—flex was scheduled to go up next. The spacious interior of the club was jam packed with celebrities. Prescious had outdone herself. She greeted hometown as well as out—of-town ballers. She mingled with the right amount of grace, style and political correctness as she moved through the crowd. Hometown radio personalities, local drug lords, magazine editors, actors, professional athletes, as well as professional groupies drank, mingled, networked, and enjoyed themselves. The Cash Money Millionaires and their N'awlins clique were at one of the many bars buying it out and doing what they did best, stunting. Prescious walked up to T.Q. and hugged him before moving on. Eric Cooper otherwise known as "Big E," the owner of Ballertician Entertainment, based in Houston, pulled Prescious to him.

"What it do, 'P'? You lookin too playa to pass me by without flickin it up," he yelled above the music.

"Awight, I'm wit it baby, but let me get my guest seated in the glass room first. Then I'll come back and we can take as many pictures as you want," she assured him before moving on.

As they made their way through the crowd, Prescious spotted a friend.

She grabbed Duck's hand and told him that there was someone she wanted him to meet.

*   *   *   *   *   *   *   *   *   *   *   *   *

Kiwan and Amin stood at the glass partition that overlooked the entire first floor of the club. Both men held drinks of NYAC cognac in their hands as they watched Prescious escorting Duck, introducing him to Lyor Cohen. They were standing in Dee-Dee's office in the dark. They could see out, but one had to have the vision of an eagle to spot them.

"Do you love her?" Amin asked, taking a sip of his 8-year aged drink.

"Yeah, I do, man. I can't explain how I know I do, but I do. It seems kind of sudden to me but the more I fight it, the deeper I fall."

"I feel you," Amin said. "But what about Ayanna? That girl still loves you?"

"She'll get over it."

"It's not her who I'm worried about getting over it," Amin told him.

"I'm watching this girl," Kiwan said, changing the subject. It amazes me how versatile she is; when she's around the big shots of the industry her demeanor, speech, and body language changes. But when she's around the fellas, she gets ghetto. I'm surprised she ain't married by now." Kiwan watched as Prescious quickly made the introduction between Lyor and Duck, then slid off to the side, bumping her ass against a surprised Vivica Fox. The two women exchanged pleasantries and hugs before she moved on.

"Believe me," Amin said, "niggas have tried. And I mean niggas with major bread. I know a couple of ballin ass niggas in New York whose pockets are lighter from fucking with that girl. . . But fool, I know you ain't thinking about marrying an ex-prostitute? You really don't even know her."

Now Prescious was on the edge of the dance floor backing her ass up on a lively Fonsworth Bently from Puffy's group, 'Tha Band.' Fonsworth was the life of any event he attended with his crazy antics, unique style of dress and dance moves. Prescious was vibing to Aaliyah's "Back and forth," as Bently did his thing. People were starting to clear space.

Kiwan looked crazy at Amin. "Now you sounding silly, man. Our mother was a prostitute, fool. Who am I to judge a woman's past? My concern is with the woman she is now. I'll bet my money that her story is no different from our mother's or any other woman who does what she feels she has to do," Kiwan scolded. "Man, we ain't no different than they are. How many times have you cheated on Nina?" Amin stayed silent, brooding. "Did you get paid, or did you pay them? Does that make either one of y'all a prostitute, or any less of a person? No, it doesn't. You got a lot of growing to do. We have a lot of growing to do. All of this shit," Kiwan said, pointing to his Murder One emblem, "is really superficial."

"Yo, I didn't mean it like that," Amin protested. "I'm just looking out. I cut for 'P', but Ayanna's my girl. I know for a fact that she loves you."

When Kiwan turned to find Prescious, he saw her on the stage with the mic in her hand addressing the crowd. What Amin paid, to him was idiotic. "Well, if she's that much of your girl, then you fuck her," he told his younger brother. Amin could tell that Kiwan was upset, so he left well enough alone. He had his own problems to think about.

"It's all good, man. I just wanna see you happy. I wouldn't give a damn if you was fucking Scooby Do," Amin laughed.

"You silly," Kiwan chuckled. "Seriously though, man, I'm still tripping on how I got a bond, man. That shit escapes me. It don't sit too well with me, Amin. I didn't know you had that much stroke."

"Man, Nina got that done. That shit was weird, wasn't it?"

"No, what was weird was when the laws rolled up on me out of nowhere. Them muthafuckas was plain clothes detectives," Kiwan said. Their conversation was interrupted by Dee—Dee opening the door to his office.

Hey," Dee-Dee said, sticking his head in the open door. "Ya boy K—flex finna blast off. He say come enjoy the show." The brothers looked at each other, grinned and hurried out of the room.

    *   *   *   *   *   *   *   *   *   *   *   *

Waitresses weaving their way through the crowd carrying neon plastic trays filled with drinks. The 7-foot speakers vibrated with the bass-filled intro of K-Flex's song, "Southside bound." Clubbers venturing too close to the speakers had their breath taken away and lost temporary control of their heartbeat due to the insistent, almost physical weight of the music. K-flex graced the stage wearing a 'Koto' velour warm-up with a spinning Murder One pendant, like the rims, which Amin had custom made for all of his artists. He grabbed the mic and addressed the crowd before going into his song.

"H-town, what's the damn deal?" he screamed. The crowd screamed back in response, showing hometown spirit. They had all been primed and prepped from the opening acts. They were ready to throw down. "Yo, yo, check this out. I'mma blast off with a little sumtin sumtin I wrote especially for tonight. Is that awight wit y'all?" Flex bellowed into the microphone, working his way up and down the stage, his piece and chain swinging wildly. The crowd responded in earnest. Big Moe stepped on the stage as the intro faded. The crowd went berserk as Big Moe began to croon the hook to K-flex's song.

"It's that boy big Moe, Yeah, Yeeahhh!" A bass line sampled from the Soul for Real song, "Candy Coated Raindrops," kicked in with the horns, snares, and strings, signature of an Amin Rush produced track.

"Girrrlfriend/Do you know where I'm goooing/I'm headed for that Hhhh—town/No disrespect but I'm Southside bound," Big Moe sang. K-flex cut in with his 1st verse.

"I'm up early in tha mornin where I'm creased an starched down/ I'm shakin off that purple stuff cause I'm H-town bound/I'm outta pocket can't knock it, tryna ball and parlay/rim outta state, niggas hate, and the feds don't play/I won tha baddest bitch in town/but I gotsta move around, I'm headed back to that "H" where it forever go down/ Don't pistol play no mo, I just dress and fuck hoes, cuz nigga where I'm from that's how this damn thing goes!"

Mister then stepped on the stage into the light and started his verse.

"Murder what, Murder who?/Murder me? or murder you?/ Nigga, paleese, I'd rather jam my screw/," he rapped as the beat slowed down to the screwed up tempo. "Drop my top and parlay/as I flip through the Trey/My damn cup stay full/I swang on fours every day/I keep them hoes on pause/I don't bar no laws/I don't slip, never trip, and they won't jack up my draws/Won't grab my balls/Won't scope my walls/ Bitch, get off my porch with no probable cause/So from a playa to hater it's too much that go down/So I gotsta move around cause I'm Southside bound."

By the time Big Moe kicked in with the chorus, the hometown crowd was off the chain. The part of the show that took the cake was when Bun-B and Brad Jordan 'AKA' Mr. Scarface stepped onto the stage to set off a freestyle battle for the toughest lyricist in the club. It was a sight to behold and a party to remember as Kiwan, Amin, and Black Jack complimented Precious for putting such an outstanding show together.

Chapter 71

The energy of the all-glass enclosed VIP room surged through Nya's body as the hometown crowd showed out for their out—of—town celebrity guests.

Lil Flip and his entourage of bikini—clad females entertained Young Buck of the G—Unit, David Banner and Jermaine Dupree. Slim Thug, Paul Wall, Chameleon, and Mike Jones held council with Jada kiss and a few of the Ruff Ryder clan, as Nya searched through the smoke—filled lounge searching for Monster Pat. Many people looked at these concerts as groupie-filled, drugged-out orgy sessions, but Nya knew better. Underneath the sex, drugs, egos, and animosity, a lot of artists promoted themselves and furthered their careers, establishing connections, shopping producers, acts, and forging alliances within the industry.

Nya spotted Monster Pat at a table with Trick Daddy, Trina, and three other women, one of whom was in his lap. Perfect, she thought, as she approached the table.

"Boo, I wanna go on tour with you the next time you go," Nya heard the girl in Monster Pat's lap suggest.

"Shit, ma, what you do?" Pat asked the female.

"You and your crew if that's what it takes," the bold young lady responded. Trina just shook her head.

"Pat, lemme holla at you?" Nya asked a startled Monster Pat.

"Oh, shit . . . Yeah . . hold up, ma," Pat tapped the girl in his lap on her ass. Pat excused himself from the table and pulled Nya to the side. "What up, lady, how did you get up in here," he asked Nya once they were alone.

"I got my ways," Nya blushed. "But what I wanna know is what type of games you playing? I thought you was gonna get back at me Monday?"

"Maaan, I was meaning to but it be so much shit poppin off. How about if I make it up to you tonight?" he said, taking in her appearance from head to toe. "I gotcha, just let me be me," he told her, but judging from her look, he assumed she wouldn't bite.

"I don't know," Nya cooed, sucking her teeth. "It's almost two in the morning, what we gon do? I did wanna go to the after party."

"Look, don't question a real nigga, just go with the flow, boo," he said, wrapping his arms around her small waist. "I don't bite. But since you're not sure, I thought that we'd roll down to Padre Island and have breakfast."

"Where is Padre Island? I'm not from Texas, so I don't know."

"Maan, let's just go. No questions . . . No hesitation . . . and I promise, no regrets," he smiled.

"All right," she agreed, allowing herself to be persuaded. As they were walking out of the glass room, Nya looked at Prescious in passing. Prescious smiled. Nina was on the money, Prescious thought. Now for round two.

*   *   *   *   *   *   *   *   *   *   *   *   *

Kiwan understood that Prescious was working, but nevertheless, he found himself getting a bit jealous at the lack of attention she was showing him. He could tell her mind was on something else.

"What's up, baby girl?" He asked her, stepping in front of her with a big fat blunt full of Purple Haze between his fingers. Prescious had her head turned looking at someoné and didn't notice Kiwan until the last minute. Kiwan followed her gaze to a couple leaving through the door.

"Oh, hey, baby," she said, hugging and kissing Kiwan on his cheek. She noticed the blunt in his hand and procured it for a couple of quick puffs before giving it back.

"What's up for tonight, hotel or home?" Kiwan asked. In unison, both of them responded, "Hotel!" and burst out laughing. "Cool," Kiwan said. "What time you wanna leave?"

"Well, I gotta take my company to the after party and get them settled. Once they're straight, then I'll be ready to leave," she told him.

"Awight, just keep it warm for me," he told her, squeezing her ample rear end.

"Move your hand to the front and see if you can tell how warm I got it for you now," Precious teased. They kissed deeply. before separating. "Be good," she warned him. Kiwan just winked at her. He knew he had a good thing and had no intentions of fucking that up.

Precious sashayed over to Duck's table. Duck was deep in conversation with a promoter from North Carolina who was affiliated with Peetey Pablo.

"Say, if I can get you boys to come up to Myrtle Beach for Bike Weekend, we can build you a fan base in North and South Carolina," Precious heard the promoter stressing. She excused herself and spoke to Duck.

"I'm sorry to bother you guys, but the after party is in the upstairs penthouse, and it's getting underway. Duck, as your host, I've got something planned for you that you don't wanna miss."

"Well, look, uh . . ."

"Cliff," the promoter reminded him.

"Yeah, Cliff, that's a good idea. Here's my card," Duck offered. The promoter took the card gladly, as Duck and what was left of his entourage rose from the table to leave. "Where's Pat?" Duck asked, looking around the lounge.

"That nigga took off with some fine ass bitch," one of the other artists said.

"Call him and make sure he's safe," Duck ordered.

"That nigga awight," one of them chimed in.

"Just do what tha fuck I said," Duck snapped as they made their way to the private elevators in the hallway that led to the penthouse's vestibule.

*   *   *   *   *   *   *   *   *   *   *   *   *

Kiwan walked over to K—flex's table, where he was chopping it up with Big Moe, Bun-B and the rest of the Murder One family, reveling in the glory of their awesome performance. Females were plentiful around the table as they fawned 'over the stars of the night.

"What's tha damn deal, crew?" Kiwan asked. Nobody answered, just nodded to the sky and smiled their platinum, gold and diamond studded smiles. They were obviously euphoric, and not just because of the show.

This is what most of these artists lived and rapped for, Kiwan thought. The good times. But all play and no work set up most artists to get fucked over. These fools were lucky to have his brother in their corner, Kiwan knew. He shook his head in disgust, remembering a lot of the false smiles, fake handshakes, and fictitious camaraderie among the artists, managers, producers, and label heads that he'd witnessed earlier. After ten years of being surrounded by a cornucopia of personalities, Kiwan felt that he was a good judge of character and those mannerisms attached to those characters. He knew that very few of those smiles were genuine. He hated for K-flex to be involved, having taken a personal as well as a professional interest in him.

"Flex, let me scream at you a hot second," he said. "Check this out," he told the young rapper after separating him from the crowd. "What you got jumping off for tonight?"

"Maan, me and Mister and Qwan was gonna get a suite and knock these bitches off," he smiled, motioning, to the women who would be his latest conquests. "I'm tryna get me a ménage a trois going."

"Oh, yeah, well, peep game. You can take your little threesome to the crib. Me and P stepping out tonight. So enjoy. And here," he told flex, handing him the keys to his Escalade. "roll the truck. But whatever you do, go by yourself. Keep them other niggas outta my house. They ain't got no respect for nobody," he stressed, remembering the incident at his house party, when he and Amin walked up on two of the label's artists receiving fellatio.

"Shiiit, you ain't said nothing, baby. I preciate that. I preciate you and Amin lookin out for ya boy. I'm on my way out now as a matter of fact. I'm gonna stop and get sumthin to eat, then blaze to the lake. Fuck the after party! I'm gonna have my own private bash," K-flex said, eyeing both of the young ladies seductively.

"That's cool," Kiwan told him. "Just be careful."

"No doubt," flex answered, returning to his private harem.

Chapter 72

The after party was an extension of the main event, only on a smaller and more private scale. The crowd was more of an eclectic group of celebrities, Kiwan, as he weaved his way through the gathering. People of the industry mingled and relaxed to the smooth beats and lyrics of Biggie Smalls, as the music wafted throughout Amin's huge three-story penthouse.

Cristal champagne, liquor, and catered food floated freely around the party. 'Free,' from the 106th and Park fame, chatted girl talk in a circle of women with Eve, MC lyte, Lisa Ray, and DJ Portia Surreal. Kiwan noticed that most of the celebrities, were more at ease and comfortable at the after party than at the concert. Even among the street gangsters and ballers, the celebrities enjoyed themselves as if they were at a normal weekend house party. In this light, Kiwan saw them as just regular people.

Someone tugged on his arm as he tried to make his way upstairs to the playroom, the Badaboom Room. He turned to face a chocolate-colored sister with a fish net body suit. She had enough curves to make a circle mad. "Excuse me," she said, taking her lips away from the flute of Cristal she held and licking them sexily. Kiwan couldn't help but notice the matching lace turquoise bra and bloomer set through her black fish net body suit.

"What's up? What it do?" he asked her, still admiring her outfit. The stranger slithered up to Kiwan, wrapped her arms around him and planted a big wet kiss on his lips. What tha fuck! he thought, separating himself from the woman quickly, lest Precious walk up on him. "Damn, what you trippin on, lil momma?" Kiwan blushed, which was uncharacteristic of him.

"Hi, my name's Debra. I've been watching your fine ass all night and I've been dying to do that," she admitted with the most seductive, come-fuck-me look on her face that Kiwan had ever had the pleasure of seeing in his life.

"Uh, excuse you, bitch," a voice called out from behind Debra. Kiwan felt Debra being pulled away from him. When Debra whirled around, Kiwan went wide-eyed and almost choked. Ayanna's baby sister A-dray stood there like she was ready to take on the world. The amazing part was the fact that she didn't look like a young girl who'd just been in the hospital with multiple gunshot wounds. She looked like a tigress who'd just lost a cub.

Debra was getting ready to go off, setting her drink down. Kiwan stepped in. "Jump up, bitch," A-dray said from behind Kiwan. "You should ask niggas if they're with someone before wrapping your dick-sucking lips around them," A-dray blurted out.

Kiwan separated the women by dragging A—dray through the crowd into a secluded corner. The edge that Kiwan saw in A-dray's eyes and mannerisms was a look that he'd seen in numerous of his friends from the hood who'd gotten shot and made a speedy recovery. It was the look of a struggler who's battled death and lived to tell about it, a look that not many street thugs even had. A look that said, "Okay, life, you threw a curve ball at me and I batted that punk shit over the fence, what's next?" Though he didn't care too much to see that look on A—dray, he was overjoyed to see her and wanted to hug the shit out of her. But he knew that she had to have still been recuperating and didn't want to hurt her.

"Girrl, what that hell's wrong with you? You crazy!" he told her, laughing.

"Booy, that bitch ran me hot," she said, fanning herself. "I came over here to talk to you and she got her crusty ass lips all over my sister's man. Fuck that trash," she said, sounding like a grown woman.

"Fuck that shit," Kiwan said. "What yo fast ass doing out of the hospital? Better yet, when did you get out?"

"I discharged this morning. I had to leave, they were trying to put me out anyway. People wouldn't let me get no rest and I had so many gifts that I couldn't even go to the bathroom." -

"Well, what tha hell you doing here? You should be at home, recovering," Kiwan fussed.

"Boy, please, I had to help Prescious and A work tha phones to arrange all of this. I wouldn't have missed this after party for shit! But bump that, Kiwan. I need to holla at you about something. Let's go to the office and talk, then I'll go home because I'm getting tired."

Kiwan looked around. He wanted to head upstairs to the big dice game in the playroom, but he also wanted A-dray to go home. She look taxed. He knew she wanted to talk about Ayanna and what happened between the two of them. "Awight, but make it quick. Then you gon take yo ass home."

"Just give me five minutes," she smiled. Her cute smile that Kiwan had never been able to resist.

*   *   *   *   *   *   *   *   *   *   *   *   *

The rowdier bunch of the guests were hanging out in the Badaboom Room. Amin's playroom boasted a split decor. Half of the room was designed in the style of a glass and brass gentlemen's lounge, complete with a stage, pole, and runway lights. There were lounge chairs, tables and half—naked strippers walking around doing their thing. None of which piqued Duck's interest in the least. He was more concerned with the other half of the room, which was designed like the floor of a Las Vegas casino. This side of the room had two dice tables, two blackjack tables, and one high stakes poker game, which cost a cool twenty thousand dollars to play. The playroom had a surround sound system that was playing a Lil John and the East Side Boyz song that one of the strippers was dancing to.

Ungodly amounts of money was won and lost at the dice tables, especially the one that Duck was standing at. The smaller table was reflective of the Las Vegas styled crap games where the house covered all bets. The second table, where the more thuggish types gambled, was a free—for—all, where the house only cut on eights, taking ten percent of all money placed on the point eight by the shooter or his fader. Whomever won the bet would have to pay the house. This table was cash only; the smaller stake table was played with chips.

Black Jack and Nina watched Duck and Prescious at the dice table from a secluded corner of the room with drinks in their hands. "You're good, Nina, but you ain't slick," Black Jack said, eyeing her over the rim of his glass of Remy. Nina smiled shyly, her green eyes glowing.

"What do you mean?"

"Amin and Kiwan may not have put two and two together yet, but they will. So whatever you got up your sleeve, for your sake, I hope it works." Nina just smiled in response. "Okay," Black Jack continued, "so you gonna play it like, that?" He smiled at the game she was trying to play, a game that he had played with the best of them. "You're covering your tracks pretty well, but you fucked up by using your boy Moochie," Black Jack told her to see if she would give anything away. She didn't budge, just flashed that enigmatic smile. Black Jack took another approach. "You wanna know why I've lasted so long in tha game? Partly due to luck, but mostly because I pay attention to detail. You see, baby girl, your boy is only crazy about one woman in this world. His entire. demeanor changes when he's around her, his rough edges smoothed," Black Jack said. "And there is only one woman he talks about, and that is Goddess. So I ask myself what tha fuck is Goddess doing here unless she's working? She's too much of a hustler to be visiting for any other reason than to put in some work. Now of course you can deny it and say that she's only down here for the party but I'm not buying that. Now, I'm watching Prescious cling to Duck, stroking him, and I start putting two and two together. I'm willing to bet my life that Goddess walks in and takes the mark for all his cash and he doesn't even see it coming," Black Jack said, pointing at Duck.

"You're reaching," Nina allowed. "What's to say that she's not here to break the table?"

"Could be," Black Jack said. "But if that was the case then she'd be working already. It's a good setup. But what I haven't figured out is the purpose. And, I want to see how this plays out. Where does it all tie in? Why are you fucking with a killer? Duck's been in the game for years, and you don't get that kind of longevity by slipping in your game, running your mouth, or falling for every pretty face you see," Black Jack warned in his subtle way.

"Well," Nina said, grooving in her seat to Tanks "Maybe I deserve." "I got a lot riding on Goddess. I'm betting heavy that she pulls it off."

"Well, I hope everything plays out according to your plans. If not, holla at me, like you should've done in the first place," he said, rising to head to the dice table.

* * * * * * * * * * * * *

Kiwan entered Amin's office with A—dray close behind. When he saw who was seated on the sofa he spun around to face A—dray, who pushed him in the chest and scrambled back out the door, slamming it behind her.

"Maan, that's fucked up, Ayanna. How you gon use A—dray to do your dirty work?" Kiwan asked, shaking his head.

"Kiwan, it was her idea, not mine. You know how she is," Ayanna said solemnly. Kiwan didn't know if he believed her. He took a deep breath and sighed heavily.

"Okay! I'm here. Let's get this over with. What's on your mind?"

"Nigga, I just told you this was A-dray's idea. True enough, I love you, but I know that I can't make no nigga love me," Ayanna said. She bent over, put her elbows on her knees and started rubbing her forehead. "Look, Kiwan, how many times, how many ways do I have to say I'm sorry? I'm sorry that I didn't tell you about my divorce. I'm sorry I wasn't there to support you while you were locked up. I'm sorry I can't be pretty enough like Prescious," Ayanna yelled. Kiwan started to get upset.

"Get off tha fuckin gas, Ayanna. None of that has anything to do with us.

It's not what you do, love, it's how you do it. When you love somebody, it's not just physical love that's required to sustain a long-term relationship.

It's about verbal intimacy, physical intimacy, and everything in between.

Talk to me. Tell me how you feel, what's wrong, where does it hurt? Something, Ayanna, anything. We grew up friends before we became lovers," Kiwan stressed. Crying now, she told him, "You could never know what it's like for me, Kiwan. You could never know what I go through being blind."

Kiwan was furious now. He ran over to Ayanna and jerked her to her feet, shaking her. "You and every other black woman in America has a hang-up. That shit is psychological, 'A.' You are beautiful whether you can see or not. It's who you are that drives me to love you, not what you look like. Because if you really loved yourself and were, satisfied with who you were it would manifest to outer beauty, Ayanna. I don't give a damn how you look or if you are blind, fat, or what. I've loved you for being you and the way you supported me, stuck by me, and stayed loyal to me. It was the little things that always meant so much to me," he told her, tears streaming down his face now.

Ayanna reached up and gently touched his tear-stained cheek. "I understand what you had to go through. I may not know exactly, boo, but it's the same for us all. We have the same struggle, just a different fight," Kiwan told her.

Before he could stop it, they were locked in a deep kiss. Her hair, her nails, her perfume, everything about her enticed him. The feel of her backside as he rubbed his hands up and down stirred something in him, brought back long ago memories that had been carved into his brain through countless hours of meditating on her in an 8' by 12' prison cell. And not once, not one time did he remember that he loved Precious Daynette Williams until it was all over.

*   *   *   *   *   *   *   *   *   *   *   *   *

"Shoot 10 Gs!" a young rapper called out, throwing a wad of hundred dollar bills on the table.

"Bet that," a well-known producer with a penchant for the dice responded. Duck watched the action closely. The youngster fingered the dice, inspected them, then whispered to them before he started shaking them.

"Nigga, you gon fuck the damn dice or shoot them muthafuckas?!" one of the old school gangsters shouted. The young rapper rolled the dice to the wall of the green felt table, per house rules, and promptly rolled an eleven.

"Eleven!" the stickman yelled, moving the dice back to the young rapper with his stick.

Money quickly exchanged hands, wads of bills being stuffed into pockets or just stacked on the table. All bets were paid off before the next roll. The youngster duplicated his first bet and various gamblers called side bets and were all faded. The young rapper hit three points in a row before falling off. The dice went to the next shooter and the betting continued, accompanied by a never-ending stream of comments, insults and wisecracks. Duck watched intently. He never jumped head first into the action. He was always one to watch first. He watched for cheating, and to see if the game was fixed. As far as his trained eye could tell the game was wide open. No one particular shooter was pad rolling, or cuffing the dice. Satisfied after an hour of spectating, Duck finally got in on the action at the crowded table. Hundreds of thousands of dollars exchanged hands at every roll of the dice. No one bet under ten thousand despite the fact that the table didn't enforce a minimum or a limit. It was just understood amongst the players that no small change would be covered. This was strictly the table for the ballers. Come correct or don't come at all.

A Def Jam executive made the mistake of calling a small change bet out loud. He was immediately laughed from the table. "Hold on, pimp," Baby, of the Cash Money crew, yelled out. "I'll give you ten grand not to holla that bullshit out no more."

"Naw, I'll give the fool eight grand just to clean my yacht," Denny Avery called out. "Then he can patch that up with his two grand and come on back for one shot." The group of gamblers roared with laughter. The Def Jam exec was so shamed that he left his small wad of money on the table.

"Hold down, nigga, you forget your gas money," a voice cried out, The crowd was in hysterics now. As the young executive left the table and exited the playroom, he experienced a moment that took his mind off his shame, a moment he would never forget for the rest of his life. DMXs "Who we be" reverberated through the room and his mind as he ran into the most beautiful woman that he'd ever seen or heard of. He wondered what she was doing coming into the playroom? If she was a stripper, then he was going to do an about face, retrieve his gas money and spend it all with this gorgeous, grey-eyed lady. Her skin was the golden bronze of Sahara desert sand. Her raven hair was pulled into a pony tail with a part in the middle. The small—framed tortoise shell glasses were props, meant to add age to her deeply dimpled. nineteen—year—old features. Her big hoop earrings dangled as she took in the scene.

"Excuse me," the executive stammered. The Goddess spun to face the man. Her six feet, two inches allowed her to look down on the man. "I don't mean any disrespect, but are you here to dance?" he asked, gazing into her captivating grey eyes.

She shook her head, giggling. "No, she answered, her voice husky as if she'd just awakened from a deep sleep. The executive loved that in a woman. "But I am here to make some money," she added. "So if you would like to get paid, then it would be in your best interest to roll with me."

He could tell by her accent that she was Latina. He didn't spare any wasted time following her back to the crap table. One of the shooters, a heavyset artist manager wearing more than a hundred thousand dollars worth of blinding jewelry, spotted her and froze. His slack-jawed expression quickly got the attention of the rest of the table, and the gamblers looked to see what vision could make such an experienced playa drool.

The table quieted as the Goddess approached. The smooth Puerto Rican princess glided as if her legs were oiled. Her skin glowed in the ambient lighting. The hot pink Baby Phat halter top barely covered her nipples. Her glowing, fluorescent g—string rode over her matching wraparound Baby Phat miniskirt, cut low in front. Her naval ring dangled in the middle of the tribal art tattooed enticingly around her belly button. White Chanel Roman sandals were strapped high up her smooth calves, hugging them as seductively as the Chinese writing that was tattooed on her left leg. A white leather Chanel bag hung loosely from her shoulder, barely swinging with her runway model approach.

Some of the men broke from their lustful trance and began whistling and cat calling. "Damn, mommi, holla at ya boy!" someone called out. "Girl, I'll drink your bath water if you shitted in it!" another man blurted out.

"That shit ain't cute; you just a nasty motherfucka," one of the few women who were shooting said. The table erupted in laughter.

The Goddess ignored them all. She positioned herself right behind Duck with her focus on her business at hand. The stickman finally took control of the game. "Come on fellas, get one good look, and let's get back to the gambling. Whose shot is it?" he asked.

"Mine," Duck announced, still captivated by the woman at his shoulder. The stickman pushed the dice in front of Duck. Goddess scooted closer to Duck and the table, pressing her pert young breasts into his back. She was as tall as Duck, who was 6'2" himself. Lord forbid if she were wearing high heels, Duck thought.

"You don't mind, do you daddy?" she asked Duck, whispering in his ear. Duck chuckled.

"In front of me would be better," he said, to gauge her response. She didn't hesitate, moving directly in front of him, poking her ample ass out.

"Better? "she asked seriously.

"Better," Duck agreed.

"What you betting?" she asked, getting straight to the point.

"You might be out of your league at this table," Duck capped. "You might wanna just watch first, hold on to your little coins," he joked, evoking laughter from a surrounding few.

"If you can sing it, I'll bring it," she challenged, her accent more pronounced.

"Oooh," one instigator egged on, prompting others to cap on Duck. "Nigga, If you don't want none of that money, pass the dice, cause I don't give a damn how pretty she is. I came to get paid," the rapper next to Goddess called out.

Duck smiled. The Goddess could tell he was falling for her. by the hard-on that he was pressing into her ass. "I'm shooting twenty, lil momma," Duck said. "I ain't talking about twenty dollars. That's a lot of manicure and pedicure money," he joked. Goddess smiled inwardly. The mark had taken the bait. Too easy, she thought.

She began pulling stacks and stacks of bills from her purse. Precious, who was still watching, smiled, marveling at the astonished looks on the men's faces. It was evident to her that the fools were asleep to the fact that they were about to be taken. She looked over to where Nina was seated. Precious could see Nina's grin from where she stood. This would work, Precious surmised.

The gamblers quickly recovered and placed bets around the table. The Goddess faded the shooter, placing her twenty Gs on the table in front of Duck. She stacked another twenty thousand in front of Duck on top of the first twenty. "I have another twenty that says you crap out in three rolls.

"I believe that you're just full of ... what's the word ... bullshit?"

"Shit, let's see if you're as lucky as you are pretty," Duck said, pulling the cash from his money belt, matching her bet.

Despite the fact that the fix was in on Duck, Goddess was taking a chance that Duck wouldn't hit a natural in the door, because she knew that the stickman hadn't slid the mercury loaded dice under his ass yet. Normally, Duck wouldn't have let anyone dictate his betting, but his pride and his mouth had gotten the best of him. Fuck it, he thought, he couldn't be shown up by no woman.

Duck threw the dice up against the green felt wall of the table and hit a nine. "Bet they don't five or nine before they crap for another ten," Goddess challenged while the stickman slid the twelves under Duck's nose.

"That's a bet," Duck responded, dropping another stack on the table. He picked up the dice and started shaking them vigorously. He threw the dice in the air, caught them, and threw them backhanded against the wall of the table. The fancy moves looked good to Goddess and the rest of the crowd, but that's as far as it went to help Duck, who shot a twelve.

"Twelve," the stickman called out. And just that fast, Duck had lost fifty thousand dollars. His confidence left as quickly as his money had. "Next shooter," the stickman called out, switching the dice out again. The move was so smooth, with the stick moving so fast, changing the pair for a set from the numerous sets in front of him, that it was impossible to see the play go down unless you were God. The look on Duck's face spoke volumes. He almost didn't want to ask, but he did anyway.

"What you shootin?" he asked Goddess. Normally he didn't chase after his money, but he normally didn't lose fifty grand in one roll. That one hurt, he thought, but he was determined to not let it show.

"For you, I'm shootin it all, poppi," the Goddess cooed.

"Bet that," Duck called, pulling out his last fifty thousand, trying to save face. Normally he tried not to carry more than fifty grand on his person, but he'd brought a hundred specifically to shoot dice. There were always big money dice games at big industry events.

"This is how you do it?" Goddess asked, mimicking Duck's throw expertly.

"Eleven!" the stickman shouted. The crowd went wild, attracting everyone in the room's attention. Duck grimaced at his luck. He wiped the beads of sweat from his face with a silk handkerchief. Goddess drew down fifty thousand, leaving her original fifty on the table Duck shook, his head.

"What you shootin now, bitch?" he asked.

Goddess' neck almost snapped as she turned, her head at the insult. She turned completely around "I'm shooting whatever you got left, jefe," she spat.

"What you got? Whatever it is I can have here in ten minutes with one phone call," Duck said.

Prescious stepped up to intercede as some of the players began giggling at Duck's predicament. They knew he was temporarily tapped. Embarrassment was written 'all over his face and evident in his voice. "He's covered," she said, nodding her head to the stickman, who went into his money vest to cover the bet.

"No, that's alright. It's time for me to go. This is too much baller attitude for me," Goddess capped, grabbing the remainder of her winnings from the table and handing it to the executive she'd met as soon as she'd entered the playroom. She sashayed off, slinging her purse over head, almost hitting Duck's bodyguard.

Damn, Duck thought. He knew that he'd just lost, his tact and demeanor in front of the crowd. He felt small and slighted. "Wait up," Duck called after her, chasing her down before she left the room. He caught her by the door. "Look, that was small of me. I truly apologize. Let me make it up to you by treating you to breakfast or sumthin?"

Goddess narrowed her eyes into slits. "If I'm not mistaken, you're' broke. I might have to treat you," she said, adjusting her weight to the back of her legs and placing her hands on her hips.

Duck laughed. "Sho you right," he said. "I guess I deserved that, but I would like to make it up to you."

Koto

"I really don't want to be rude, but I'm going to be frank with you. I only do two things at night, and that's fuck and make money. However it comes, and in any order," she said.

"Damn," Duck said, shocked. "What will it cost me?"

"I don't sell pussy. I sell fantasies, and you've lost enough to have one of yours fulfilled. I quote prices for tricks," she honestly said.

"Well, I guess the talking is done," he said. "Let me lose my company and we can head out."

* * * * * * * * * * * * *

"I can't believe we just did what we did," Kiwan told Ayanna, putting his shirt back on.

"Why?" she asked, hesitating to put her underwear back on under her skirt. She needed to go to the bathroom first to clean herself up. "Take me to the bathroom, Kiwan, please?" she- asked, holding out her hand to him.

"Man, A, to be honest, I love you, but I'm in love with Prescious," Kiwan admitted to her.

"Kiwan! You could've told me that shit before you put your dick in me!" Ayanna shouted, yanking skirt down disgustedly.

"I didn't ask for your pussy, Ayanna, this shit just happened."

"Nigga, please. You knew you loved the bitch before you came in here. You didn't exactly turn the pussy down, either," she said, smacking her lips and jumping up off the sofa with her panties in her hand. "You make me sick. You're a trifling muthafucka, just like that bitch!" she screamed. She stalked toward the door, stumbling. A—dray burst into the room before Ayanna could make it to the door.

"What's wrong, Ayanna?" A—dray asked worriedly.

"Nothin, nothin," Ayanna cried, feeling the weight of her embarrassment now that her sister was in the room. She knew that A—dray had been outside the door the whole time to make sure that nobody walked in on them. "Just take me to the bathroom," Ayanna told her, trying to staunch the flow of tears.

A-dray gave Kiwan the evil eye before helping her sister. Kiwan just shrugged his shoulders in a helpless gesture. This was bullshit, he thought. He didn't have time for this drama. He left the room to look for Prescious and tell her before she found out second hand.

*   *   *   *   *   *   *   *   *   *   *   *   *

Duck was overwhelmed with anticipation as he and the Goddess awaited the private elevator in the foyer. His hands were all over her body as he envisioned the carnal pleasures that lay in store. He kissed and licked her neck while fingering her rock hard nipples.

"Damn, love, what's your name?" Duck asked.

"Money," she giggled.

"Well, money, they call me Duck."

"Well, Duck," she cooed "where would you like to go? I have a suite at the Sheraton around the corner."

"That's cool," he said as they got into the elevator. They were on the sixth floor of the building when they boarded. Duck thought they were heading to the lobby. Goddess kissed him passionately, distracting him as she maneuvered his back against the button panel. She pushed the button for the fifth floor where Amin's private studio was located.

Duck felt the elevator descending, only to stop after clearing one floor. Just as he turned to see what was going on, the elevator doors opened. Damon, Moochie and Tony stood awaiting an astonished Duck. Before he could utter a word, Goddess immobilized him from behind with a concealed stun gun. Duck crumpled at the Goddess' feet.

She looked up at Moochie, smiled, winked and blew him a kiss.

BOOK IV -— INDUSTRY RESPECT

Chapter 73

Precious sat in the passenger's seat of Kiwan's Vette with tears in her eyes, as, the Isley Brothers' song, "How lucky I am," played softly. She felt betrayed and hurt. She didn't even want to look at Kiwan. The top of the Vette was off and the cool April night breeze slipped through the car. At 4:00 in the morning, the downtown streets were deserted with the exception for the derelicts, the police and the occasional insomniac cruising around.

"I don't know why. I thought that you would be different from any other man," Precious spat at Kiwan, trying desperately to hold back the tears that were determined to fall. "I must've bumped my damn head," she said, her voice cracking up. Kiwan could hear the disappointment in her voice.

Precious wanted to be strong again, turn a cold shoulder on this nigga, but it just wasn't happening. Her shield had been penetrated. He was locked into her heart and there was no way to push him back out. She wasn't that strong, yet!

"How could you fuck her?" she yelled suddenly. And there it was, she knew. The stage of stupidity that she'd seen her girlfriends stuck in, time and time again. It didn't matter what he did, really. He was all that she had and she knew that she would forgive him, whatever he did to her. She knew that she was just putting up a front so he wouldn't know how sprung she was behind him. How the fuck did she end up this far gone, so fast, she wondered? All the years of denying herself love were watching up to her. At least she respected the fact that he told her as soon as happened. Look at him, she thought, cutting her eyes at him. Now he's over there looking like a dumb ass, can't even talk, she thought. She almost burst out laughing. It wasn't funny but what else could she do besides cry, and shedding tears wasn't her forte. To make matters worse her favorite song by the Isleys came on, "Don't say goodnight."

"Maybe I should get my shit out of your house and move back into mine," she pressed.

"Look, if that's what you want to do then it's fine by me. We both can do bad on our own. But I fucked up, what more can I say? I'm sorry; I'm sorry, I'm sorry. I love you, I want to be with you I need you to understand. I mean it's done, it's over with. I needed to get that out of my system so that I could go on with my life, P. You can judge me, say I'm full of shit, whatever. But please don't turn your back on me. I ain't gon lie, I'm at a point in my life where I need you. I feel like nobody understands me but you."

"I hate you, Kiwan," she cried, tears cutting a path through her mascara. "How can I deny you? As long as you keep it real with me, nigga, I'll never leave you. Do you know what you have in me?" she asked seriously.

"Naw, P, that shit working both ways. Do you know what we have in each other?" he countered.

"I'm not enthused with what you say, I wanna see how act you from here on out," she said.

The two were so enthralled in the mood and conversation that they never noticed the blue Ford Expedition that was trailing them.

* * * * * * * * * * * * *

The cold water splashed on his face revived him. The last thing Duck remembered was kissing that beautiful broad in the elevator. He began to analyze his current predicament. Water dripped from his face, but he couldn't move his hands to wipe it off.

"Hey, hey. Sleeping Beauty has awakened." A voice mocked him. That's when Duck realized that he was blindfolded as well as tied up.

Moochie snatched the blindfold from Ducks face. The suddenness of the invading light made Duck squint. Objects swam in and out of focus for a few seconds, but eventually his vision cleared. He could see that he was in a warehouse of some sort.

Nina Rush scooted an old rickety wooden chair in front of Duck, flipped it backwards, and sat gap-legged facing him. Moochie, Tony and Damon flanked him. "What type of games you niggas playin?" Duck yelled, trying his damndest not to reveal the fear he felt creeping in on him.

"That's funny, old man, because I was just about to ask you the same thing," Nina said.

"What that fuck you talkin bout? Cut me loose, what tha fuck you got me tied up for? I ain't done shit!" Duck yelled, his anger overwhelming his rage.

"We don't see it like that, gangster," Moochie called out from the corner of Duck's peripheral vision. "Yo bitch ass is knee deep in this shit, playa," Moochie told him, moving into, view. His pistol hung loosely in his hand.

"What tha fuck you talkin bout?" Before Duck could get the rest out, Moochie swung the pistol around and shot Duck in the shoulder. The report of the gun in the cavernous warehouse was deafening. Duck screamed; the pain was so intense his breath caught in his throat.

"We ain't playin with you, bitch!" Moochie snarled.

"Look," Nina cut in. "Here's the deal. We're not gonna kill you, that's my word."

"Your word, your word," Duck chuckled despite the pain. "Right now your word don't mean jack shit to me, you silly bitch."

Moochie swung the pistol around again, this time aiming for Duck's head. "Nooo!" Nina yelled, and Tony moved like a cobra, shoving Duck's chair out of the way and knocking both to the floor. The shot barely missed, taking Duck's ear off instead of his head. "Moochie!" Nina yelled;

"He was asking for it;" Moochie shrugged.

Duck was too shook up to scream. He was paralyzed with fear and bleeding like a stuck pig. "Pick him up," Nina ordered "Listen, Duck," Nina said after Tony and Damon had sat him back up. "You don't have that many options in play right now. Do you see that Mercedes over there?" Nina pointed behind Duck. Tony spun him around so he could look at it. He could see it clearly and he could also see Dexter Cunningham behind the wheel, a bullet hole in his temple. Now Duck knew that he would never make it out of the warehouse alive.

"Now I said that we wouldn't kill you," Nina said, reading his thoughts. "But the state of Texas will fry your ass when they find what you've done to this poor assistant D.A., the infamous son of Congresswoman Charlette Cunningham. I'm sure she will use every resource and favor due her to make sure you die in prison. Or, we can get rid of this, make it all go away if you give us some information," Nina offered. She still held in her mind what Black Jack had said about Duck not talking. She hoped like hell that the circumstances that he was surrounded by would change his mind.

Duck's mind was working at warp speed. He began to hold onto a sliver of hope that maybe, just maybe, he could live through this mess and buy that ranch he'd always wanted.

"All we want is a little information about Romichael Turner and his drug operation," Nina said. Duck abruptly laughed out loud, a sinister laugh that confused everyone else in the room, especially Nina. It made Moochie want to kill him all the more. His laugh echoed in the warehouse.

"What's, what's so mothafucking funny?" Nina asked. She was beginning to lose patience.

"You brought me in here, set me up, and ended up wasting your time. You're asking me something that only one person can tell you and we've been looking for his ass since Wednesday," Duck laughed.

"Corey," Nina whispered. Why hadn't she thought of that before? The worst thing about it was that she knew from talking with Felicia that Corey was dead. She was becoming dizzy, and the room began to spin. Duck's laughter began to fade into her subconscious, and she was getting more and more lightheaded. What was she going to do now, she wondered? She couldn't possibly just keep having people killed. That would draw too much heat, too much speculation. But she'd promised Nya. What could she do to help her out now?

The gunshot shook her out of her temporary daze. When she looked up, Duck was flipped over, still tied to the chair with his brains all over the driver's side of the Mercedes. Nina dropped her head. Fuck it, she thought. Now she had to rethink her plans.

"Let's clean this up. Burn the, car, and take the bodies to the yacht so we can dump them in the Gulf," she ordered, standing on unsteady legs.

"Are you alright?" Moochie asked.

"Yeah," she said, massaging her temples.

"What's next?" Moochie wanted to know.

"The only thing that we can do, what we should've did in the first place. We find Romichael Turner and kill him. End of story."

Chapter 74

"Where are we going? You passed UP the hotel," Prescious observed.

"I don't know about you, but I'm hungry;. I wanted to roll by this spot that Dominick and them was talking about."

"At 4:30 in the morning?" Prescious asked; confused. "You must be talking about Chachos."

"Yeah, that's it. How'd you know?"

"Cause that's the spot, especially after the clubs close. That bitch stay crunk," Prescious told him. "After tonight's concert, it should be packed, even at this time of the morning. And I didn't know you liked Mexican food."

"Oh! You didn't know that I was a nacho freak."

"No, you didn't tell me."

"Shiiit, pour some queso on your ass and you gon be a nacho freak too, when I get through with you," Kiwan said, trying to lighten her mood. But the sexual innuendo served as a reminder of Kiwan's infidelity.

"Um, I don't think so, you done had enough pussy for one night, don't you think? Maybe for a couple of months," Prescious said, looking at him spitefully.

"You wanna play? You ain't scared to talk to me like that, you must don't know who I am," Kiwan said, still joking.

"Nigga, paleese, you feeling yoself just a lil too much," Precious said, but couldn't help laughing. "I ain't scared of nobody. Especially since I got that gun from your sister Felicia."

"What gun? As a matter of fact, what sister? I go to jail for two days and all of a sudden a nigga got another sibling," Kiwan said, getting serious.

"In essence, you've already met your sister. You just didn't know it. But y'all spose to have a formal get-together this weekend. Amin was going to surprise you."

"Well, if it was supposed to be a surprise, then what you tellin me for?"

"It slipped out."

"Mmm hmm," Kiwan responded. The idea of her carrying a gun around didn't sit well with him, but he let the matter go. The last thing he wanted to do was smother her. But since, he'd gotten out of jail, he'd been thinking seriously of moving on with his life and leaving his brother and the music industry behind. Especially with Precious in his life. Maybe he'd move to North Carolina or South Carolina to carry on his father's dreams. But those had been just fleeting thoughts. It would be hard to leave his family and the city he loved so much.

Just as Precious had predicted, the restaurant was jam packed. The line was out the front door, and the parking lot looked like a los Magnifico car show, Kiwan noticed. From what Kiwan could see, the restaurant was packed inside and out. Even the outside patio area was full to capacity and bustling with activity. Men and women mingled in the parking lot. Many of the same people who had been at the concert earlier were there, showing off again and this time they were going to the extreme. Poppin their high-dollar surround sound trunks with neon lighting, dropping their 14-inch TVs from their roofs with porno flicks showing, cranking up their expensive music systems, and posting up next to their candy painted rides like Jermaine O'Neal in the paint. Kiwan thought of just riding through as he watched only the bravest of souls battle the congested line. Even the drive-through was backed up. One had to really be hungry to put up with this shit, he thought. It was probably a whole lot of nacho freaks in that line.

As he crept through the lot at a sloth's pace, his cell phone vibrated on his hip. He turned down the music in the Vette, without noticing the admiring glances thrown his way by some of the more forward women in the crowd. Precious had noticed, and laid claim to what was hers by reaching over and caressing his neck and face. As he answered his phone, he stopped the car completely.

"What it do?"

"What's the damn deal, nigga?" Jamarcus yelled. "I see you and P shining on dem boys with yo Vette, and them spinners. You out here hurtin these niggas, you betta cut it out for one of these hatin muthafuckas pull that pistol on yo ass," Jamarcus said.

Kiwan couldn't help but smile at the youngster's manner. "What's up, fool? Where you boys at?" Kiwan asked, looking around.

"Nigga, we all the way in the back of the lot boxed in. But we stuntin on them boys, too. We shakin the lot, lettin these boys know how throwed that Trey is. Dominick broke out his new Escalade ESV on em," he said. "Hold on, I'mma tell him to crank it up so you can hear us. We finna shut the rest of this punk shit down!" Jamarcus said excitedly. Kiwan grinned even wider and hung up the phone.

No sooner than Kiwan had hung up the phone that there came a deep, low rumbling that Kiwan actually felt more than heard. It escalated in intensity and the vibrations worked their way from the bottom of Kiwan's feet to his lower back, and the sound quickly drowned out the other systems. People began to stop, look and gravitate toward the beat, which seemed to be a prelude to impending doom for any who would challenge the system's potential.

Slowly, they all got the message and began turning down their music, and the music of the ESV became more distinct. Despite the fact that Kiwan was inching through the congested vehicles toward the source of the music, the louder the music got, the more it seemed to be coming from his own speakers, and he knew that he was still a good forty or fifty yards from the epicenter. Kiwan even recognized the song. It was a song by the late Fat Pat that was never released due to the rapper's untimely death.

"Who tha fuck is that?" Precious asked, trying to look around the parking lot to see if she could see the culprit of illegal noise pollution. "Them fools, they gon shatter somebody's windows."

Kiwan laughed. "That's Dominick and Jamarcus over there acting a ass," he told her.

After another five minutes of crawling through the lot, Kiwan got impatient. "Fuck this shit. I'm finna go see if I can pay somebody for their spot in line, if not then I'm going to Taco Bell," he said, throwing the Vette into neutral and hopping out. "Park over there with Jamarcus and them. I'll be back," he told Precious. - -

"Awight, I'll just follow the music," she said, straddling the console to get into the driver's seat. As she was switching seats, Precious glanced into the rearview mirror out of habit. She had to do a double take to make sure she saw what she thought she saw. The headlights from the vehicle directly behind her were playing tricks with her vision. Had to be. She could've sworn that she saw two men getting out of a vehicle, a couple of cars back with ski masks on and holding pistols. She turned to look again to make sure, and sure enough, she saw two masked gunmen approaching. With everything that had been happening to everyone associated with Murder One lately, it didn't take her long to figure out who they were after.

"Kiwan, baby, look out!" she screamed at the top of her lungs, hoping he would hear her over the music. She bent to reach for her purse on the passenger side floorboard and shots rang out from automatic weapons. One gunman shot at Precious and the other one aimed at Kiwan. Kiwan didn't hesitate, he hit the groundout of sheer instinct. When the shots rang out, all hell flooded the lot. Everyone's first instinct was to hit the ground despite their expensive clothes. People began scrambling to get out of the way, out of the line of fire. In the confusion, a few individuals stumbled between the gunmen and Kiwan and were immediately dropped as the gunmen slowly advanced on their targets, careful in case Kiwan was armed.

Kiwan took a chance and instead of running from the Vette, where Precious was no longer in sight, he struggled to his feet and leaped, stretching out like a black Superman. He landed directly on top of a curled up Precious, who was lying half on the console and half on the passenger seat. The gunmen concentrated their fire on the Vette. Glass showered Kiwan and Precious. Kiwan knew he had to act fast or they were both dead. He saw Precious' purse on the floorboard with the pistol halfway out. He reached for it while simultaneously opening the passenger's door to make their escape. He fingered the safety on the small Beretta .380 with his left hand. He switched the gun to his right to get off a better shot as the bullets inched closer. The urgency to get out of the Vette burned his ass, or was that a bullet, he wondered?

The onslaught of bullets inflicted a brutal punishment on the Vette's fiberglass body, and Kiwan was astonished by the fact that none of the bullets had found their mark yet. Without even looking, he stuck his arm out of the door and began squeezing shots toward the threat on that side of the car. He didn't take the time to aim or find out if he'd hit anything. When the sporadic fire paused a bit, he made his move. He hopped out of the car, crouched by the door, snatched Prescious by the arm out of the death trap and ducked in between two parked vehicles.

The gunman, not expecting any return fire, had ducked when Kiwan started busting back, giving them time to get out of the Vette. But the reprieve from the hail of bullets was short-lived. The gunmen spotted the move and pursued their quarry.

Prescious was hurt. Kiwan could tell by the way she moved and how she stumbled. There was no time to find out how badly she was hurt because the gunmen were on their asses. Prescious was gripping her side and moaning as Kiwan dragged her. She was slowing his progress. He knew that he had to try and make it to the back where Dominick and Jamarcus were. He had to think fast if he wanted to live. He weaved a path through the row of parked vehicles by the grass near the side entrance through the restaurant. He needed to find a spot to try and pick the two shooters off. He knew that he didn't have many more shots left in the Beretta. Kiwan could hear the police sirens in the distance. He thought about making a break for it in the open across the street, but he knew that wouldn't work with him having to drag Prescious. He and Prescious stopped scrambling and crouched low behind a Navigator. The truck provided temporary cover as their pursuers cautiously circled the truck. Kiwan's heart raced and an idea popped into his head.

"Hold down," he told Prescious, setting her down against the bumper of the SUV. Kiwan crawled under the truck and immediately saw the legs of his pursuers at the front bumper of the truck. He could tell that they didn't know where he was. They probably figured that he was just crouched behind the truck, waiting. The shooters then made a fatal mistake. Instead of splitting up, covering both sides of the truck, they started down the same aisle. They must've realized their mistake because they quickly stopped. But it was too late. One of the gunmen made an about face to cover the other side of the vehicle and ran right into a pissed off Kiwan Rush. The last thing he saw was the fury in Kiwan's eyes. His accomplice didn't even get to make a complete 360 before the bullet smashed through his face. The sirens were becoming louder as Dominick, Eric, and Jamarcus finally came running around the truck, AK 47s and pistols at the ready.

"Maaaan, what tha fuck going on?" Dominick yelled at Kiwan.

"I don't know, but Precious is hurt and the po—pos coming, we need to get outta here," Kiwan said, hurrying to the back of the truck.

Precious was breathing through her mouth like she was going into labor when they reached her. "What's wrong, baby, where you hit?" Kiwan asked, noticing the tears in her eyes as she held her side. He bent down to pick her up, looking frantically for blood. Dominick handed his AK to Jamarcus and helped Kiwan.

Precious just shook her head and moaned. "I ain't shot," she managed to get out between breaths. I think you broke my ribs when you jumped on me.

"What? Gotdamn, I thought you was dying!" Kiwan didn't know whether to yell in frustration or laugh in relief.

"Yo, we boxed in fool, and that Vette don't look like it's going nowhere," Erick said as the police converged on the scene.

Jamarcus collected all the guns. "Gimme the heat," he said.

"What you gon do? Dominick asked. Jamarcus didn't respond. He just told Kiwan to follow him.

"Come on, Ki, grab Prescious," Jamarcus said, stepping into the street that ran the side of the lot. Jamarcus walked right up to a car with two young females in it and pointed the pistol at the driver. She stopped the car and threw her hands up as he motioned for her to open the door.

"Lil momma, we need a ride to the Third Ward, how bout it?" he asked. But he was already climbing in behind her before she could get the door opened fully.

"I guess," the petrified driver said as Kiwan and Precious piled in behind Jamarcus.

When they passed by the front of the restaurant's parking lot, the police had the entrance blocked off already. "MAN!" Kiwan shouted.

Chapter 75

In the pre—dawn hours of the morning, Daddy Bo sat quietly on the edge of his bunk, meditating. He relished facing the disheartening monotony of prison life with a clear head. Sometimes a clear head could be the difference between living another day or dying. In prison, Clyde knew, that violence was always a heartbeat away.

On this particular morning he couldn't clear his mind. His thoughts kept gravitating to his children and the fact that he wished he could've been there to introduce them all properly. Maybe the next visit that he got from Belinda, Felicia's mother, he would ask her to intercede for him and try to smooth the transition. Without a doubt he knew that Black Jack was stepping up in his absence. Thank God for Keith Vincent, he thought. If ever there was a friend, a brother, a comrade, Keith Vincent was the epitome.

In his usual routine, Daddy Bo got up and prepared himself for the morning showers that were run for the prison population after the six a.m. shift change. The Darrington Unit was an old, dusty red brick penal farm built in the 1930. Its facilities did not accommodate the convenience of its inmates. The convicts were herded into the showers like chattel. The community shower room could hold up to 120 men at one time, and with TDJ's faulty administrative practices, they always tried to fit in more. Daddy Bo did not particularly like it, but hell, a man had to wash his ass.

"Shower time!" a young male officer yelled as he entered the cell block. After being there for so many years, Clyde could put a face to every voice on the ranch. Although he couldn't always call their names, he knew their faces and their speech patterns. And this particular officer was an asshole, always out to prove something. Daddy Bo knew what type of day this would be, already. "G block, get ready for showers, you hoes are next," he called out.

Right on cue, the inmates responded. "Yo momma's a hoe, bitch ass nigga," one of the younger inmates screamed in reply.

"Bet you won't say it to my face, you coward," the officer yelled back "You know. I'll write yo punk ass a case, and fuckin with me you might not shower."

"Aww, bitch ass hoe, you the one come on the block with that hoe shit, now you wanna hide behind writing a case, then threaten a nigga with not showering. Your momma must didn't give yo country ass no pussy last night, punk. Water is free, nigga, we can wash our ass in the sink," one of the more experienced convicts blurted, reflecting Daddy Bo's thoughts to a T.

And so the day started. Daddy Bo just shook his head. This was the morning ritual of rebellion whenever a dickhead worked the cell block. It was now the duty of the inmates to make his eight hours on shift a living hell. Daddy Bo tried to overlook it all and rise above it. He found that the best way to do his time on a daily basis was twelve hours of minding his business, and twelve of leaving everyone else's alone. It was easier on all parties concerned.

Today Daddy Bo decided to make all of his phone calls, especially to Felicia and Nina. His daughters, he thought. Everything would work out for the best, he knew, once the seat was occupied by Murder One. Maybe then he could concentrate on getting the fuck out of the hell hole he found himself in.

When the doors rolled on three row, the entire population of the run fell out of their cells to shower, with the exception of a few inmates who worked and showered at night, and the odd crusty-ass, goat—smelling muthafuckas who stayed in their cells, which was one of the reasons Daddy Bo was glad he didn't have a cellmate. As usual, Clyde brought up the rear. The men quietly filed down the stairs and into the hallway with soap dishes, face towels, and shower shoes in their hands.

Some officers and inmates greeted Daddy Bo on his way to the shower room. He didn't linger, just spoke and moved on, wanting to get back to his cell as quickly as possible and handle his business.

As they entered the shower area, Daddy Bo immediately sensed that something wasn't right. He tried to put his finger on what was nagging him. He tentatively walked to the officer rostering names off a list as the inmates entered the actual shower. Daddy Bo looked past the officer into the unusual gloom of the showers before giving his name and TDCJ number.

The officer rostering was a maintenance boss named Word. He was one of the old school officers who'd been around for at least 15 years. He was what the inmates referred to as a convict boss. He wasn't as uptight or as strict as the younger officers. Daddy Bo had had the pleasure of working for Word a few years back when he was with the plumbing crew that Word oversaw. When Daddy Bo recited his name and number to Word, he looked up from his clipboard. "Gotdamn, Daddy Bo, Third Ward's 'finest. How's it going this morning, old man?" Word greeted.

"Aw, shit, I can't complain, man. I'm hanging in there," Daddy Bo responded. "How about yourself?"

"Shit, I'm making it," Word told him.

"I see they working you hard. What they got you in here rostering names for? A brother like you should be above the small. They need to delegate that responsibility' to some of these peon muthafuckas," Clyde told him.

"Hell, you know how shorthanded these folks are; I'm just helping out. Odoms is in there fixing on a busted shower head."

"Why is it so dark and gloomy in there?" Daddy Bo asked.

"One of these punk lovin Negroes busted a few of the lights, broke off a shower head or two, and they busted a few of the windows. It's steamy and foggy as hell in there. You can't hardly see shit," Word said.

Clyde didn't know why the situation bothered him, but it did. It wasn't like it had never happened before in the ten years he'd been locked up, and it was exactly for the reason Word spoke of, punk loving niggas! But it was something nagging in the back of Daddy Bo's mind and he just couldn't figure out what it was. He almost turned around to go back to his cell, but thought "Fuck it, I'm already down here. I might as well get it out of the way."

On his way to the showering area, Daddy Bo passed a dark skinned, beady eyed orderly who was posted up against the wall with a push broom in his hand. The way he stood there, eye fucking the inmates coming and going, made Daddy Bo think that the man was in there to either steal or was watching out for the booty bandits. Daddy Bo didn't particularly like the inmate. He'd heard too many bad things about the man. The only things he did know about the man was that he was from the North side of Houston with a life sentence, and that he was a nickel slick hustler who preyed upon the weak. Daddy Bo felt that the man was beneath his association as they made eye contact. Neither man acknowledged the other's presence, which was a form of disrespect on both men's part. Ten years ago, that would have immediately started a fight. Being as though Daddy Bo was walking and staring, he was the first to break eye contact. When he did, the view before him stopped him dead in his tracks. The eerie, desolate gloom of the foggy shower area almost overwhelmed him. Jesus Christ, he muttered. A man could not only get fucked in there, he could get fucked off. He could hear voices coming through the white fog. A creepy feeling came over him, as he felt someone's eyes crawling over the hairy flesh of his back. Daddy BO spun around quickly and noticed that the orderly was no longer there. Strange, he thought. He turned back to face the showers and again, a warning surfaced, a gut feeling gnawing at him. Clyde knew that prison was a place where gut instincts sometimes provided for another day of living and breathing. A modicum of manly pride overrode his gut instincts and propelled him into the showers, dismissing his inner, voices as products of an overactive imagination. He forged ahead and found a spot on the benches to disrobe and put his belongings. Visibility wasn't nil, but it wasn't good either. He heard moans coming from the back of the shower area. Typical, Clyde thought. Fuck it, I'll just hurry up and get the hell out of here. It ain't my business, he told himself. The moaning eased his mind more than he cared to admit and put to rest the foreboding that threatened to swamp him. He chuckled at himself for thinking such foolishness, especially when he spotted a few of the weaker inmates turn around before they entered the fogged up area.

Daddy Bo weaved a path to the nearest shower stand, trying his damndest not to bump into anyone in his nakedness. He found an empty showerhead toward the front and stepped into the warm stream of water. He ignored the mindless chatter, aimless conversation and subtle moans and began to soap, his body down. He excluded his hair and face for obvious reasons. He'd just have to wash his face and hair when he got back to his cell. Daddy Bo didn't waste any time; his motto was, "Get it on and get it on and get it off." Only fags and bisexuals hung around in the showers and bathed like they were at home in the free world. He didn't want to stay too long and give anybody any ideas. After lathering up and scrubbing his private areas, Daddy Bo rinsed off, lathered up again, and rinsed off one more time before stepping out. The common twenty minute shower was cut down to five in prison, two if you didn't wash your hair.

After showering, most inmates dried off by the benches, grabbing towels out of a buggy. Afterward, they grabbed their dirty clothes and stood in one of two lines to receive a fresh set, turning in their dirty clothes. As he dried, two convicts. Who Daddy Bo didn't know entered the shower area. They approached him with their clothes already off and in their arms. They were young and unfamiliar faces with stern, determined looks. Those determined looks, and the fact that they were already undressed and holding their clothes as if they were hiding something sent alarms shrieking through Clyde's brain.

Suddenly, Daddy Bo's mind focused on what it was that had been nagging him since talking with Word. It came to him as clear as spring water. A year after he'd been locked up, a similar incident took place in the shower where it was purposely fogged up. The Mexican Mafia had done it, setting up a hit on an unsuspecting inmate. Daddy Bo didn't see the hit take place, but he saw the enforcers brought out of the showers, in handcuffs and covered with blood, and they had the same looks on their faces that the two determined youngsters displayed.

The realization hit Clyde like a speeding fire truck. Somebody was about to get fucked up. Daddy Bo didn't know who, but he wasn't trying to stick around and find out either. It wasn't his business, he thought, as he hurried to take care of his business and get out of the way.

The two young men bracketed Daddy Bo, shoving other peoples' clothes out of the way. Yep! These fools were looking, for trouble, because that's how you got hurt when you started disrespecting peoples' shit. They must have some mean ass boxing games, he thought. "Here, man, one of y'all can have this spot. I'm finished." Naked, Daddy Bo leaned over to pick up his belongings. When he raised back up, his hands full, one of the men jammed a pillow case over his head. The second man produced a shank and stabbed Daddy Bo in his kidney. The attack erupted so suddenly that other inmates around didn't even know who was being hit. Had they known that it was Daddy Bo, someone surely would've come to his aid. But help or screaming out for it was the farthest thing from Daddy Bo's mind. Survival was all that mattered now, and he swung a vicious elbow behind him. Clyde could feel his elbow connect with bone and he heard a satisfying grunt from one of his attackers. Unfortunately, the elbow connected with the man holding the pillow, not the one with the shank. That convict swung his homemade knife again at Clyde, burying it in Clyde's abdomen, dropping him to his knees. When the knife was yanked free for another strike, blood splattered the faces and necks of Daddy Bo's assailants. The inmate behind Clyde regained his grip on the pillow case, holding him up. The cutter switched, from an underhand; grip to an overhand grip and began stabbing Clyde in his neck and head repeatedly. Each swing drew more blood from Clyde and sweat from his attacker. Clyde tried to double over into a fetal position to minimize the damage, but the holder of the pillow case would not allow it. Clyde quickly became too weak to fight back or raise his arms to ward off the attack, and the essence of his life pooled around his knees and stained his body.

What did I do, he wanted to know, as faded into unconsciousness? Delirium began to creep up on him as someone finally yelled to the officers for help. But Clyde knew that help would never arrive in time to save him. Flashes of his life boomeranged into his view, dominating the dark red cast of the bloody pillow case. Clyde Rush could no longer hear the lonely drum of the water against the cold concrete floor of the shower. No longer could he hear the mumbling, shouting, or moaning around him, as the two inmates pushed Daddy Bo over, his smacking against the unrelenting concrete. The attacker whom Daddy Bo had elbowed felt the growing knot on the side of his head. The knot was beginning to close his right eye. He spit on Daddy Bo and kicked him in the head one last time before jumping into the water to rinse the blood from his body.

Clyde went into convulsions as his brain began to shut down. He saw the face of his beautiful wife as she sat on the bench in front of him, looking down at him sadly. "I tried," he told her. "I tried to raise them so that they would know and understand life and the hearts of their fellowman," he said as tears of blood leaked from his eyes. His wife just smiled brilliantly at him and held out her hand. She heard me, Clyde thought, and then, and then he knew it was time to go.

Chapter 76

Qwan awoke from his sleep hungry after his bout of freaky sex. He rolled over in the bed of the hotel suite fully awake. He was lying between two gorgeous young groupies who he'd brought to the hotel after the party from the concert the previous night. Mister was in the adjoining suite with girls of his own. Qwan started to look for K—flex, then remembered he'd decided to go off on his own instead of with Qwan and Mister.

Qwan looked around the room with a smirk. It was a disaster area, with drug paraphernalia, clothes, furniture, glasses, empty bottles, and food containers strewn everywhere. He looked around, the room for some weed to smoke but couldn't find any. He stepped over a naked girl who must've rolled out of the bed last night. He found his boxers and put them on before he knocked on the door to Mister's suite.

The bodyguards were asleep in the living, room of the suite with females of their own. It was a mad house, the same as it was after every concert. One of the naked females was on a cell phone in the living room as Qwan walked out of the bedroom.

"They're all asleep," she was saying before she saw Qwan.

"Who's asleep bitch?" Qwan asked. "Who you on the phone with anyway?"

"I, uh . . . I was talking to my friend asking her to pick me up because I got to . . . uh . . . go to work. I told her that, I didn't want to wake anyone up to take me home because y'all were sleep," she lied nervously.

Qwan was too much under the influence to notice or even give a damn. "Oh," he said as the girl got up to look for her clothes. She hurried to, the bathroom after finding her clothes in the pigsty.

Qwan walked to the door of the adjoining suite and barged into Mister's suite unannounced. Mister's was a carbon copy of his fucked up suite. He stepped over the mess and naked bodies, making his way to the bedroom. Mister was laid out with a girl of his own in the bed. Only one, Qwan thought. She must be a bad muthafucka! He'd probably be in the pussy before the day was over anyway. That's how they rolled. Any bitch in "Their room was fair game to the whole crew. It was understood before any of' them stepped across the threshold.

Qwan shook Mister from his sleep. "Fool, fool," Qwan whispered. Mister opened his bloodshot eyes, clearly agitated from being awakened so early in the morning.

"Nigga, leave me alone . . . What tha fuck ya want?" he asked groggily.

"Man, I'm getting ready to jet. I'm hungry."

"So what the fuck you tellin me fo, take ya ass on!" Mister said.

"Man, ya know that Amin said we should stay together cause -of what happened at the park," Qwan said.

"Damn, nigga, order room service or sumpthin," Mister snapped.

"They ain't got shit. All they have is a Continental breakfast, plus it cost too much."

"Listen, man. You actin like a bitch. Eat that and leave me the fuck alone," Mister yelled.

Qwan knew that he was wasting his time fucking with Mister so he turned to go and wake one of the bodyguards. As he turned there was a figure clad all black, holding a pistol with a silencer attached. Clarity arrived an instant before the bullets did, which blew away his chest. "That-bitch!" he thought; she'd let the killer in. That was Qwan's dying thought as he fell across Mister in the bed. Mister jumped up ready to swing on Qwan when he noticed he was looking down the barrel of a gun. His shout never escaped his mouth.

Chapter 77

Precious sat up in Kiwan's arms as dawn peeked through the drapes of the hotel room. Kiwan had taken care of her again. He'd bathed her, dressed her wounds, brushed her hair and stroked her into an intimate mood. Now they sat snuggled under each other as Precious' Dru Hill CD played softly in the background. There was no television, no stress, and no more hard feelings by Precious toward the man; whom she undeniably loved. "Kiwan?" "Why did you fuck Ayanna? I mean, I forgive you, and I won't forget, but I can't really understand WHY?"

"Yo, P, it's hard to explain. Like I said before, it wasn't out of love or really lust; it was something that I had to make sure of. She and I had a strong history and you just can't stop and throw the past away, because the past molds who we are today. I needed to be sure that there was no chance for me and Ayanna," Kiwan told her truthfully. He was being totally honest with her, going out on a limb with his feelings for the first time since Ayanna. It hurt for Precious to hear the blistering truth from the only man that she'd ever given her heart and soul to, but she understood. At least she wanted to understand.

"Did you ever cheat on her?" Precious asked. Silence. She waited on his answer, but silence was all that Kiwan gave. She'd already known the answer to the question before she asked, but she wanted to hear him say it.

"Yeah, I cheated," he finally answered.

"You were her first, right?" Prescious asked, snuggling closer between his legs. She wanted him to know that he could trust her to be understanding. She didn't want to deprive, him of any intimacy on her part. Kiwan was a lot different from other men and she wanted to know why? Was it his prison experience? What was it? He was an enigma to her. Kiwan didn't clam up or put up his defenses when it came to her and her probing like other men did. He was open, an open book for her to read and in turn it made her reciprocate the favor. This was the foundation of their swift-paced love affair, she knew. Anything was everything, and everything was anything with them.

"Yeah," Kiwan said. Prescious felt the vibe of his fond reflection that generated his smile. Kiwan realized his mistake and fixed it, fast. Prescious rolled her eyes and shot him a dirty look before she slowly turned back around, resuming the conversation.

"You know that you are my first, too, Kiwan," she continued. "What makes me different from her, how do I know that you won't cheat on me?" she wanted to know.

"Damn, P, I can't answer that. All I know is that I don't have the desire to be with another woman. I'm ready to settle down. I've had ten years to think and decide what I want to and need to do with my life. My time behind the walls has humbled me. I don't give a fuck about balling, coming down, hustling, parlaying, or none of that other shit these fools out here doing. I have a vision. Everything else is either aiding me toward my vision or hindering me. And the things hindering me are the things that I'm going to cut off. Besides, I was balling, out of control and thugging before most of these niggas was leaving out of their front yards. I was hustling before hustling became cool. I know what Amin is just finding out, that the price of shame and fame are too high for a black man to pay and there's definitely no lay-away. But I will tell you, that if my thoughts start to stray, I'll tell you so that we can sit down and talk about it. Other than that, I can't see myself struggling with any other woman but you," he assured her.

"Prescious knew that he was spitting some real shit to her and she believed in him with all of her heart. She just prayed that they could maintain a prosperous relationship.

"Now I've got a question for you," he said. "What would you say if I asked you to leave Texas with me?"

"Prescious thought for a second. "Where would we go? Don't you want to be close to your family? I mean a new start would be awesome, but right now your happiness is my only concern because you are all that I have."

Damn! That was a bold statement and it shocked Kiwan completely. The simultaneous ringing of his and her cell phones broke the intimate spell that flooded the room. "Shit," Kiwan cursed, as Prescious did the same. She was comfortable and didn't want to move. But something told Kiwan that he'd better answer the phone. He tapped her naked leg for her to get up, and she did, reluctantly. Kiwan got out of the bed with his silk boxers and went to answer the call that would change his life.

Chapter 78

The unexpected phone call that Congresswoman Charlette Cunningham received had prompted an unscheduled plane trip back to Houston. As a mother, the news threatened to destroy her, but as a seasoned politician used to presenting a poker face to her opponents, she knew she had to summon all of her years of experience and keep the mother within settled. She fidgeted in her seat; smoothing her unwrinkled skirt. She fingered her gaudy diamond wedding ring, then as an afterthought covered her mouth with her left hand as she stared out of the window at the world rushing past outside. Although she appeared placid, her stomach was as roiled as the clouds they were passing through. She was sick with worry for her only son.

Federal agent Nya Phillips had notified her that Dexter's Mercedes had been found on fire, earlier that morning on the east side of Houston, and that his whereabouts were unknown. Agent Phillips had said that foul play was suspected, but there wasn't much to go on. Any evidence they could've had was destroyed by the fire.

Charlette prayed for her son's life, but she tried to prepare herself for the worst. A mother should never have to outlive her children; it wasn't natural. But, oh, somebody would pay! She didn't know the cause or people behind her son's disappearance, but she had a clue. For weeks she'd known of his association with Romichael Turner and his Ruff House crew, and she'd known of his dalliance with Prescious Daynette

Williams, and knew she was an executive with Murder One. She just knew one of the two parties was responsible for Dexter's disappearance, and she would go to her grave trying to destroy whichever it was, if her boy was harmed. She would use every bit of her power, exhaust every source and contact to come up with answers.

She'd had a feeling that she'd regret opening her doors to those thug ass niggers. Everybody her color was not her kind, she knew. She bent over backwards and turned cartwheels down the halls of Congress for her people though she knew that not all of them were worthy of her efforts. There had been countless debates, discussions, and forums held with the black elite on what could or should be done concerning black people in general. After all, that's how the N.C.A.A.M. committee had been formed. But she'd given a bunch of undisciplined, uncouth, no-vision-having, materialistic hoodlums a glimpse of her world and an opportunity to make a difference in their race that could possibly reverse the adverse effects of 400 years of racism and slavery here in America. And what do they do to thank her? They shit on her, that's what. Typical nigger shit, and it went to show that money could not make a man. Proper rearing does. Now she might be forced to let the raw and uncut nigger within her, out of the bag. It was a side that she'd buried years ago. She hated to admit it, but she would more than likely have to find other means and avenues, to reach the displaced youth of her race.

It was a sad, sinking feeling, and it prompted feelings of defeat where she'd never known the meaning of the word. "Damn rap music!" she cried unwittingly.

"Are you okay, Mrs. C?" her aide questioned, noticing her tears. In the ten years of working for the Congresswoman, Crystal Duncan had never seen her cry, not even when her husband died. "It's going to be all, right," Crystal assured her. "We'll find him. He'll turn up," she said, patting Charlette's hand. "Do you need a sedative?"

The Congresswoman just shook her off. Her thoughts were now centered on striking at the heart of all record companies that supported rap and hip-hop. She would hold them accountable if anything had happened to her boy, and she would start with Ruff House and Murder One Records.

Chapter 79

"Bitch, I know good and fucking well you didn't strike a deal with the feds about anybody in this family without telling me," Amin hissed in Nina's face.

Nina didn't know what had made her do it, whether it had been the overflow of emotions swimming through Black Jack's Third Ward home or the guilt she felt at losing her father-in-law. Was it an attempt to try and staunch the bleeding of her botched plans? Either way, she'd come clean to her husband in the living room while Black Jack, Felicia, Belinda, Kiwan and Tony were in the kitchen grieving. Why did she choose now, of all times, to tell Amin?

"I . . . Amin . . . Well . . . it wasn't like that," she stammered. SMACK! The blow to Nina's face rocked her from her seat. She could already feel the swelling coming on. "Okay! I know he didn't just hit me," Nina thought. "After all we've been through, after all I've sacrificed and have gone through for him."

Her ensuing reaction stemmed from a deep-seated, heart-wrenching sense of betrayal committed by someone who she'd die for. She got up off the floor and grabbed her purse, which had been by her feet. The look of surprise on Amin's face when she pulled the gun out would forever be etched into her mind. Her hands shook unsteadily as tears fell, pooling at her sandaled feet.

"I am not taking any more of your shit, Amin! Why did you hit me!?" she asked through quivering lips, her green eyes blazing.

Amin couldn't believe that he was staring, down the barrel of a gun held by his wife, his heart, his soul mate. His father's wisdom echoed, through his mind. "Boy, you need to straighten up and fly right and take care of your business with that girl. She's your right hand and needs to be cherished. If you make her happy, she'll make your kids happy and your kids are your future. And be careful, you got a woman who will do anything for you. So that means that she'll also do anything to you . . ." Now Amin could see what his father meant. He just hoped that it wasn't too late.

"You did not have to put your MOTHAFUCKIN hands on me!" she screamed. Out of nowhere, Tony flew into the room, causing Nina to flinch and fire the gun. The shot echoed as Amin hit the floor. The shot and report of the pistol brought Nina back to her senses. She dropped the gun out of reflex and rushed to her husband's side. She hadn't meant to kill him, she thought. Amin sat up unharmed, as the others came running into the living room.

"I'm all right," Amin said disgustedly, pushing Nina off of him. Suddenly, Felicia screamed!

"Tony!!"

Chapter 80

Ben Taub Hospital's emergency room waiting area was crowded with the Murder One family and friends. Amin Rush wanted to scream. His heart was a cave of despair over the violence that had been inflicted on his company and family the last seven days. Death and tragedy weighed on his broad shoulders like infinite gravity threatening to crush him. What had he done? Things had gotten drastically out of control, he knew, as he left the claustrophobic atmosphere of death in the waiting area, in desperate need of fresh air. He paced the walkway outside the emergency area, thinking of his poor judgement in dealing with the obstacles he'd confronted. His father used to tell him that a man's pride goeth before his fall, and Amin knew that his pride had slipped, through his fingers in his attempt to climb to the top of his game. Children's games, which had caused him to jeopardize the future of a multi-million dollar corporation. A petty vendetta had been the blindfold that had hindered his vision.

How could he have been so stupid? He was to blame for all of this, he knew. As much money as he had, he was still trapped in the pettiness of manly pride. If he would've' accepted Syon's offer in the first place, maybe his father would still be alive. Or even if he would've' just joined Romichael in an effort to obtain the committee seat instead of holding malice in his heart, over some childhood memory of blood and disrespect.

No; his actions had not been reflective of a man of his means or of the man he had always pictured himself as becoming. Once again, Amin felt the claws of guilt and failure tearing at his heart. But how could he undo death? How could he fix the shattered pieces of his family's future? How could he make the death of his father have meaning? As hard as he tried, Amin could not come up with any answers to his questions.

And his wife, he thought angrily. Here she was, running around playing lady mob boss with Moochie, killing up Houston in the name of the family. She'd explained everything to him. Although he could see the logic of her actions, he saw the ugly traces of his pride again; he was not so angry at her as he was upset at being kept out of the loop. It was sad, but he knew that his wife had more faith in him than he had in himself at the moment. He also knew that as sure as shit stunk, there would be consequences behind the death of Dexter Cunningham no matter how well Nina had covered up her tracks. With the way that technology was today, he would have to remodel the entire yacht to eliminate any DNA evidence of Dexter and Duck being aboard so as not to link the family to their disappearances.

Too many problems and not enough answers. It was time to put his pride aside and earnestly seek the help of his brother and mentor. He could no longer send Nina to see Daddy Bo to discuss a problem, seeking guidance. Death had overshadowed his ability to concentrate, formulate and overtake. Maybe that's what Romichael was counting on. Then again, maybe not. Who knew? The damage was done.

Now where did he stand? Not as a father, a brother, a son, but a Chief Executive Officer, responsible for thousands of employees, for the direction of a corporation that had standing, prestige and the responsibilities that went with that. He had two dead artists, two dead bodyguards, and a father who needed to be buried. The proper course of action would be to make arrangements with the families to assume all burial costs and hold a five-casket funeral. After that, how would Murder One rebound? Once again, too many questions and not enough answers. He didn't want to repeat his past by submersing himself in work, hiding his pain. Though it was good for financial growth, it was detrimental to his mental well-being.

Amin was so deep in thought that he wasn't aware of Black Jack standing behind him until he was tapped on his shoulder. Amin turned abruptly, startled. "Damn, man, you scared the shit out of me," Amin sighed. Keith was silent for a few seconds before speaking. Tears were in his eyes. Amin feared that Black Jack and the family would blame him. It was a deep-seated fear that was brought to the surface by the look upon Black Jack's face. Maybe they considered him inept and wanted him to step down? Amin couldn't blame them. As if reading Amin's thoughts, Black Jack finally spoke.

"It ain't your fault, young blood. Everyone knows that. They realize that shit happens. It's a part of life. Nobody in this family is new to tragedy. Just know that tragedy, while always being adverse, can lead to stimulation or to stagnation. A man can use tragedy as a time to look, within himself for strength to forge forward, or he can use it as an excuse to lie down and die. And as a leader of the family, everyone will be watching you closely, following your lead. It's time to utilize everything you've been taught, everything you've learned in life. You've still got me to help, but I can't and won't make your decisions for you. This is what you've wanted what you've been preparing for all of your life. Stand up. Hold your head up and move forward. We have too many people depending on us for you to fall apart. Wanna cry, cry! Ain't no shame in that, in grief. But don't let your pride get in the way of your progress any longer. Humble yourself and unshackle yourself from the vanities of what's worldly. We need you," Black Jack told him, tears streaming down his face. "Your father and I have always been proud of you. Always!"

Tears streaked down Amin's jaw. Black Jack had just given him something that you couldn't buy, something that you could never put a dollar amount on. He'd given him his confidence back. What more needed to be said? Black Jack knew that everyone needed to be consoled, even Idie Amin.

The two men embraced without shame. "We also have to get our story straight, young blood," Black Jack said after the embrace. "You know they report all gunshot wounds to the police."

"I know. We just have to stick with the story we told the paramedics. Somebody walked in and shot Tony. A crackhead from the neighborhood," Amin reminded him.

"All right," Black Jack said, trying to regain his composure. "I'll talk to Nina and everybody else to make sure they know what to say, make sure that there are no inconsistencies," he said before turning to leave. "Oh, yeah," he called out as an afterthought, turning back to face Amin. "You know that there is no pass for Romichael Turner. We find him, we kill him," Keith stated matter-of-factly, leaving no room for discussion in his tone. Amin nodded his consent, although he knew it wasn't needed. "He's a loose end. We finish what we started," Keith said.

Both men looked up to see Kiwan approaching with his head hung low. His hands were thrust deeply into his pockets, and his steps were tentative. "Damn, Black Jack said, gritting his teeth. Kiwan looked into Black Jack's eyes before speaking. Black Jack knew before Kiwan offered a word. "Tony didn't make it?" Keith asked, hoping the news would not be so drastic. Kiwan shook his head, and the men embraced as their shoulders racked from their deeply rooted sobs. The news hit Amin like a battering ram and made his knees buckle. The news cast an even darker cloud of sorrow over the entire family, as all the men in the emergency room began: to file out to shed tears and grieve together. Nina had to be sedated as Ayanna, Felicia, Tiffany, Precious, and A—Dray attempted to console her.

Sheba sat in the lounge, rocking Tony's two-year-old daughter to sleep. She would honor him by keeping their secret for themselves. Hopefully Kiwan would do the same, as he was the only person she'd felt comfortable imparting the secret to. Sheba vowed to herself to make sure that her daughter, Tony's daughter, would grow up knowing who her father had been in life.

Moochie took it the hardest out of all the men. He became inconsolable and left the hospital because it was just too much for him to bear. Moochie preferred to cry alone.

Amin felt in his heart that now was the time to rally his troops. If he was any type of leader, he needed to show that he was capable of leading under any circumstances. Black Jack was right; it was time to stand up. Business was business, it was never personal.

Kiwan stepped to Amin and pulled him to the side to speak with him. Now was the time that they needed to bond together and show a united front for the family. Kiwan searched for the words to articulate and convey his feelings, but couldn't find the right ones, and he kicked at the loose pebbles on the concrete, lost in his misery. He did not want to upset the balance of their relationship by seeming preachy at a time like this. He did not want Amin to feel like he was coddling him. He needed to choose his words carefully.

For the first time in Amin's life, he saw his older brother, his idol, at a loss for words. Being as extroverted and as charismatic as Kiwan was, Amin was shocked to see such a thing. But he knew what his brother was going to say.

"Yo, Ki, man it's going to be all right," Amin assured. "We gon put this behind us and move ahead for Daddy and Tony. We gon get the seat and secure our future. Man, we gon get major, major, Bill Gates money and realize our father's dream. We gon do more for the community and build the music enterprise back up to number one . . ."

Kiwan couldn't believe his brother. His ears had to be deceiving him. Kiwan grabbed the collar of Amin's shirt and yanked him closer so that he could understand every word Kiwan was about to say. "Nigga, I can't believe you," Kiwan hissed. "Is that all you think about; mothafucking money and the business? You wouldn't even begin to be able to comprehend the full concept Of Daddy's dream. Yo punk ass is too much into show. And how dare you try to attach Tony and daddy's name to some vain shit? Here we are with a major tragedy on our hands and you worried about a seat, and some chump change that you wanna throw back into the community. You overshadow that shit with your actions every time you roll in the hood with a new slab on fours or a new whip on dubbs, not, to mention that you get to write off any money you give, so you get it back at the end of the year. That ain't help, that's pacification to ease your conscience. Nigga, FUCK MURDER ONE!" Kiwan yelled. "Your gotdamn friend is laying on a slab in the morgue right now," he said with tears streaming down his face. "Who's gonna tell his mother? Who's gonna tell his daughter? Or didn't you even know he had one?"

Amin was decimated by his brother's outburst. Where had this come from? Jerking away from Kiwan's grasp, Amin asked, "What is all this shit, man?" The scuffle attracted Black Jack's attention.

"That's what I want to know, Amin," Kiwan continued. "You know what? Nigga, I blame you for all of this shit."

"That's enough!" Black Jack yelled. "Get off the bullshit," he demanded, trying to quell the storm that he could see brewing. Kiwan ignored him and continued.

"My daddy wouldn't be dead if it wasn't for you. Hell, he wouldn't even be locked up. Tony wouldn't be dead if it wasn't for you, if you wouldn't have got caught up in your feelings and put your hands on Nina. Ever since I've been home, I've watched you try to live up to this bullshit Idie Amin image. That shit might work for the outsiders, but to try to push that shit on the family is some buster shit."

"Nigga, fuck you," Amin yelled back at Kiwan. He was growing tired of his brother's accusations. "You act like I'm out here living a young, black male's fairy tale. I put in work for you, for daddy, for the family." Black Jack stepped between the brothers.

Kiwan laughed. "You too selfish to do anything that won't benefit you also. You're full of shit."

"Gotdamnit, I said that's enough," Black Jack ordered. They were causing a scene at the worst possible time and place. There had been enough drama to last him two lifetimes.

"Naw, fuck that shit, Keith. That's what wrong with him. Can't you see, he's a baby, and we've been burping and pattin him on the ass too long now."

That was it! Amin had had enough of Kiwan talking down with that hater shit. Maybe Kiwan was bitter that he hadn't visited him in prison? Or maybe he was jealous of his success? Either way he was going to swell his mouth up for him and see what his boxing game was like. When Black Jack turned to motion for the rest of the crew to separate the two men, Amin took off. BLAM! Out of nowhere, while Kiwan was still ranting, Amin socked him in the mouth. Kiwan staggered dazed from the blow. He instantly felt two of his teeth loosen. Just as suddenly, Kiwan shook the blow off and squared up with Amin. Amin shoved Black Jack out of the way.

"That's what I'm talking bout," Kiwan said. "Now you're caught up in your feelings and about to get your ass tore up," Kiwan said, feinting at Amin with his right, setting him up for the left jab that thundered Amin's way. Amin ducked slightly, anticipating the right-handed blow, not realizing until it was too late that it was a setup. Kiwan stepped into the left-handed blow as Amin tried, in vain to over compensate for his mistake, weaving directly into the blow. It landed directly across Amin's eye, splitting his eyebrow and dazing him.

The rest of the Murder One crew rushed over to break up the fight, grabbing both brothers in an attempt to restrain them. It took four grown men to hold each brother down as they struggled, cursed, spit, and screamed obscenities at one another. The conflict drew the women, who sprinted out to see what was going on after someone yelled, "Fight!" It was sheer pandemonium as the women began screaming, yelling, and arguing with the men to break up the fight, adding confusion to an already confused group of men. Felicia went so far as to jump on the back of one of the arbitrators, screaming for him to let her brother go. She pelted the man with blows to his face, causing another skirmish to break out. Pent-up frustrations were given the green light as total hysteria broke out. Fists flew from women who started out wanting to break up the fight but took advantage of the situation to release pent-up emotions. Pop shots were being given from old grudges long since forgotten to unsuspecting victims. Hospital staff and security guards rushed out to intervene. In the confusion, somebody bopped Precious in the back of her head as she tried to make her way to Kiwan. She looked back and could only see the side of A—dray as her brother Jamarcus had her lifted off the ground trying to get her to safety. An ambulance driver was accosted by Tiffany, who'd turned her anger on him when he grabbed her. A security guard, an off—duty HPD officer, took out his baton and began swinging, adding fuel to the already raging inferno. He was immediately swarmed, disarmed, and stomped for his actions. Amongst the commotion, no one took notice of the four dark unmarked sedans that came to a screeching halt outside of the emergency room entrance.

Nya Phillips stumbled out of the leading sedan, took in the semi-riot and screamed, "Everybody freeze!" The battle raged on. "I said FREEZE!" She yelled again. The melee continued. Felicia was now biting another one of the men holding Kiwan down. "Ow, bitch!" the man yelled, trying frantically to push Felicia off of him.

Boom! Boom! Boom! The gunfire blasted the riot into shock. "Gotdamnit, I said every one of you muthafuckas freeze!" Nya shouted into the silence.

The rumble stopped as abruptly as it started. Nya stood there, commanding everyone's attention. "Cuff him, him, and him," Nya ordered the other federal agents, pointing out Black Jack, Amin, and Kiwan. Agents immediately slapped handcuffs on the men, anxious and not knowing how the crowd would react. "And her too," Nya said, pointing at Nina.

All four were rushed into the waiting sedans and the convoy hurtled away, leaving the others looking at each other in confusion.

Chapter 81

After watching the midday news, Romichael began to put the pieces of the puzzle together and knew that it was time to get out of Dodge City for awhile. It didn't take a rocket scientist to figure out what the hell was going down. His jubilation after receiving early-morning confirmation of the hits he'd contracted was short-lived after finding out that Duck had mysteriously disappeared last night. His mind had been reeling all morning at the different possibilities for Duck's sudden disappearance. After last night's altercation in Club Flip Mode, Romichael had taken Duck's advice and caught the fourth quarter of a Houston Rockets game. After the game, he and Monica established alibis by hanging out off the Westheimer Strip at S.R.O.'s, an eclectic sports bar. Then the two of them retired to a hotel downtown in the wee hours of the morning. Since the early morning phone calls, Romichael had been wide awake plotting, planning, and scheming. Clarity overwhelmed him after watching the breaking news on the midday report. He knew that there would be consequences for the murder of Daddy Bo, but Romichael had planned on having time to counter whatever Murder One could throw his way. He instantly knew that he was on borrowed time after the news reporter announced that Assistant District Attorney Dexter Cunningham's late-model Mercedes had been found on the east side of town, charred and burned. Though the police had not found Dexter, Romichael knew that he was dead. Right along with Duck, Corey, Felicia and himself if he didn't skip town for awhile. But how? How did they get to Corey, to Dexter? What did they know, he wondered, as he stared out the passenger window of his Hummer? Flip was driving Romichael and Monica to Hobby Airport to catch a flight to Vegas, and he couldn't get there fast enough for Romichael.

"Damn, man, you can't drive no faster than that. She can drive faster than you," Romichael told Flip, referring to Monica.

Flip looked as if he didn't have a care in the world, which irritated Romichael. "Your plane doesn't leave for another hour, man, chill out. We're almost there," Flip told him as they exited Broadway Blvd off of 1—45. Monica was asleep in the back, high. Romichael wondered why he even bothered with the bitch. He missed Felicia, he thought, rubbing his crotch.

"Damn!" he shouted. Flip looked over at Romichael like he was losing his mind. That was okay, Romichael thought. If he only knew like I know, Romichael told himself. Murder One would be on the hunt for him for awhile and anyone close to him was subject to be snatched as a means to get to him, or for information. That's why he was leaving Flip behind and allowing, him to drive his vehicles. Flip thought that Romichael was headed to Cali to meet with a famous director about a movie deal, and so did Monica. But little did Flip know, he would be the bait. This would buy Romichael time to figure out his next move. Maybe now Murder One would know that he meant business. Maybe they would leave him alone, maybe not. Romichael knew that he was wishing for the pot of gold at the end of the rainbow. Murder One was not likely to leave him alone, but they would be in disarray for awhile after the death of the old man. Who would've known that the old man was calling all of the shots for the company from prison? How did Duck know, Romichael wondered, as they neared the airport? He could see jumbo jets coming in low for landing.

Suddenly, the Hummer died. Everything in the truck cut off and the doors locked. The music, the tv, even the radar died. "What the hell?" Flip asked as he eased the powerless truck out of traffic while it coasted to a complete stop.

"What are you doing?" Romichael asked Flip.

"That ain't me, man."

"Get off the bullshit. You the one driving," Romichael pointed out.

"Yeah, but it ain't me. For real," Flip bellowed. Romichael looked around disgustedly. The damn airport was right up the street and his truck breaks down. What kind of luck was that? Shit didn't make any sense, he thought, as he tried to get out of the truck, only to realize that the doors were locked.

"Unlock the mothafuckin door!" Romichael yelled. "And pop the hood!"

"I can't," Flip yelled back. Both men were frustrated. Especially Romichael, who didn't have time to deal with this shit. He would just have to leave the problem for Flip to deal with.

"Fuck this shit, I'm walking to the airport. Call Triple AAA and have the truck towed to the dealership and let them find out what's wrong with this bitch."

"How you gon get out?"

"Give me your gun and watch," Romichael told him.

Just, as Flip handed Romichael his pistol, the truck was surrounded by three unmarked sedans with flashers in their windshields.

Romichael knew they were feds before they even got out of their cars. "Fuck!" he yelled, startling Monica awake. He was almost at the airport, he thought, as the locks popped on the doors. When the locks popped and Romichael was instructed to exit the vehicle with his hands up, he realized what had happened. OnStar, he thought. The feds had cut the vehicle off using his own OnStar service, the question was, why?

* * * * * * * * * * * * *

Moochie had to turn the music down in his Chevy Avalanche to make sure that he was hearing correctly. Yep! He heard it again. He thought his phone had been ringing, but he wasn't sure. He was tempted to let the voicemail pick it up, but it could be Tony's mom calling from the Virgin Islands, where Tony had been raised. He picked up the phone and saw there was a strange number calling. Who could this be, he wondered? Lord knows that he wasn't in the mood for any bullshit right now. "Yeah!?" he answered, in an agitated tone so the caller would know that he didn't feel like being bothered. "Oh, hey,

what's up, girl?" he asked, wondering why she would be calling him.
"NO SHIT!? When did that happen . . . I tell you what, where are
you now? . . . All right, I'm on my way to scoop you, don't move. I'm
pretty sure I know what they are questioning them about. Especially
if you, say that Tisha was notified that they were being detained at
the Congresswoman's house. If they were going to jail, they would've,
already been there. Stay put!" Moochie hung up the phone and exited,
the freeway to head back to the hospital.

$*$ $*$ $*$ $*$ $*$ $*$ $*$ $*$ $*$ $*$ $*$ $*$ $*$

   Romichael was escorted up the cobblestone walkway by two beefy
federal agents. As they climbed the steps to the double-doored entrance
foyer, Romichael could feel the tension that surrounded the home like
a pack of gunpowder—fed dogs. Nya Phillips stood at the top of the
steps and instructed the agents to remove his cuffs. Her greeting wasn't
as warm as it had been on his last visit, but for Romichael it was a
start. Something was fishy about the entire situation. For one, how
did the feds have the authority to disable his vehicle with OnStar?
Two, he hadn't been read his rights before being taken into custody
so he couldn't be arrested. And lastly, what the fuck was he doing at
Congresswoman Cunningham's home?
   The, two agents had been deaf to his questions and ignored him in
the car the, entire way over. He needed answers to what was happening
and he wanted them now. "So that's how y'all do it now? Y'all just gon
yank a nigga off the streets? Just kidnap me," Romichael prodded. Nya,
knowing the two dummies wouldn't speak. He'd already failed with
them.
   "Shut tha fuck up!" Nya hissed, shooting him a look that could
start a fire with her icy blue eyes.
   "I want my lawyer. I thought you people were supposed to wear
suits and ties, look neat, and be courteous and professional," Romichael
joked. No one laughed.
   "Take this clown to the dining room and baby-sit him. If he gets
out of line, down him," Nya instructed, shoving Romichael in the back.
The two agents roughly grabbed him and ushered him into the house.
   When Romichael entered the dining room, he stopped dead in his
tracks.

Amin, Kiwan, Nina, and Black Jack sat silently at the mahogany table with somber looks of defeat on their faces. All eyes in the room turned to Romichael as he entered. Now what part of the game was this, he wondered? He couldn't help the snide, menacing smirk that involuntarily spread across his face when he made eye contact with Amin. Thoughts of their phone conversation played back through his mind. "Suit up, bitch, because we are going to war," were the exact words Amin had spoken. To him exactly eight days ago. Now look at you, Romichael thought; your precious father isn't here to hold your hand anymore, tramp.

The tension between the two men was thick enough to choke an elephant. It seemed as though Amin read Romichael's thoughts through the windows that were his eyes. Amin couldn't help it; he erupted from his seat in fury, ready to kill Romichael with his bare hands.

The agents took immediate action. One of them grabbed Romichael in the choke hold, lifting him up off his feet as another agent, who'd been seated near the Murder One family, rose to his feet to grab Amin. Kiwan grabbed his brother hurriedly to avoid an ugly altercation with the agents. He didn't want them to handle his brother like they were handling Romichael. Black Jack also stood. He halted the progress of the agent by holding out his hand for him to hold up. "We got him, we got him," Black Jack told the agent, who felt cheated out of his right to kick some ass, so he settled for talking some shit instead. They had been warned beforehand about the beef between the two men and had been instructed, to keep the peace by any means necessary.

"You better get him before I hurt him," the agent told Black Jack. "One more outburst like that and the cuffs go back on." Romichael wanted to say something about the lopsided use of force, but he could scarcely breathe.

Finally, the agent let him go, forcefully slamming him into a chair. Amin shot Romichael looks of hatred from across the room as he willed himself to calm down. "Baby, sit down, please?" Nina begged.

"I'm all right," Amin said, brushing his brother's arms from around him. He straightened his rumpled clothing before he sat. Nina scooted close to him and put her hand on his inner thigh. It was a reassuring gesture meant to calm him but it only aggravated him even more. "I'm cool," he assured his wife, removing her hand from his lap to hold it. Amin knew that he needed to exercise patience in this situation, especially if he wanted his brother to know that he could handle the pressure like a man instead of throwing a fit like a child. "I apologize, y'all. It 'won't happen again," he told the family. Now was the time to act instead of react. They were in a precarious situation and no one knew what to expect. The words of his mentor came rushing back to him, calming him. "Your father and I have always been proud of you." Amin sat up straight up in his seat and ignored Romichael's presence. It took every ounce of his will to do it, but he did it and immediately felt better about himself, more in control.

Nya Phillips entered the dining room, followed by Congresswoman Cunningham. Black Jack took one look at the Congresswoman and instantly knew they were all in deep shit. Gone was the Congresswoman's graceful manner. Gone was her poise and dignified look of a seasoned dignitary. What Black Jack saw was the shell of a strong woman, a woman filled with agony and grief, a woman scorned by the vicious bite of tragedy. Welcome to the club, he thought.

The Congresswoman's silver-streaked hair flowed past her shoulders as she stomped into the dining room. Her elegant, but out-of-place, silk Oriental house robe was pulled tightly around her body unevenly as if it was thrown on at the last second. Her eyes were sunken and bloodshot, like she'd been drinking or crying, or both.

"I'm going to be frank, people," she started as she plopped down in a seat at the head of the table. She fished a cigarette from a pack in the pocket of her robe. She lit the long, slender cigarette with a gold Zippo before slinging the lighter atop the table. Kiwan watched the lighter spin on the glossy table and wondered how ironic it was that he felt the lighter symbolized his life at that exact moment, just spinning with aimless direction and not knowing how or when to stop.

The Congresswoman inhaled deeply, pulling on the cigarette as all eyes watched her. She leaned back in her chair, blowing a cloud of smoke carelessly into the air through her pursed lips. Suddenly, she slammed her free hand on the table, startling everyone to attention.

"Where is my son, Dexter?" she asked in an icy, matter-of-fact tone that sent chills down Nina's spine. "Where is my son; where is my fucking son?" she screamed, shaking her head as if she couldn't believe or, accept the fact that he was missing. Her hair flew in different directions, personifying the unkempt image she was unwittingly portraying, adding to the unease all present felt.

Damn! Romichael thought; this bitch is really coming unglued. Somebody better tell her something, anything, he thought, looking at Kiwan. The looks around the table were accusatory, from the Congresswoman to Black Jack, from Black Jack to Romichael, from Nina to Amin, to the Congresswoman and back to Romichael, who, was now staring back at her. No one spoke a word.

"I'm not going to ask you simpleminded muthafuckas again. As you can see, I'm not playing with you people," the Congresswoman spoke forcefully, stressing her point. "General counsel for both companies have benefited already. I'm two seconds away from throwing all of your asses in jail. And if you think that I'm toying with you, just try me."

Black Jack didn't doubt the validity of her threat, but he knew that if jail was where she wanted them, then they would already be there. No, she was searching, reaching for any glimmer of hope for her son, just as confused as they were. "Mrs. Cunningham, what makes you think that any of us had anything to do with the disappearance of your son?" Black Jack asked, his face a mask of stone.

"Let's not play games, Mr. Vincent, hmm? My son was intricately involved with both companies up to his eyeballs," she spat. "Now I don't know the extent of either company's dealings with Dexter, but somebody knows something and somebody needs to fill me in NOW!" she demanded.

Black Jack didn't know who in the hell she thought that she was dealing with, but nobody in this room was even remotely stupid enough to incriminate themselves. "Listen, Mrs. Cunningham, we didn't deal with your son as a company. One of our employees carried on an intimate relationship with Dexter, but none of us dealt with Dexter on a business level," Black Jack tried to reassure her.

"Mr. Vincent, you must really think that I'm stupid," Charlette snidely remarked.

"No, that's not what I was . . ."

"Shut your lying mouth!" she yelled, cutting Black Jack off. "I know how you people deal, how you people live," she hissed, flailing her arms as cigarette ashes flew everywhere. "I know your so-called street codes and I know about your false 'sense of loyalty to one another.

You muthafuckas think that you run the streets of Houston with your slabbed out rides," she exaggerated by leaning back imitating a gangster, lean as she grabbed her crotch, cigarette still between her fingers. "You with your drug money, your blood money. Preying on the same people you call yourself trying to help with your bullshit programs and foundations. You people think sponsoring a Little League team, putting your company's name on the back of 12-year-olds, means you're giving something back. You muthafuckas wouldn't know the first thing about community, sense of self, or clout if it reached up and bit you in the ass. I made a grave mistake in thinking that I could allow some simple-minded, two-bit hoods into my legacy."

Nina looked to Nya, who seemed as if she was staring into outer space. It was a look of detachment that said she was hands-off. If only she could speak to Nya privately, maybe together they could clear this mess up. But that was wishful thinking and she knew it. She realized she had gone too far in ordering the death of Dexter, but it was too late to bring Dexter from the dead.

Black Jack had heard enough. His understanding only went so far. She could dish it, but could she take it, he wondered. "You talk that almighty shit from up on your throne, Congresswoman, but you don't really know the struggles I've faced and have overcome in more than fifty years of living. Yes, it's easy for you to sit and judge because you haven't had the misfortune of coming up hard like we have. What do you know of waking up in poverty with dope, death and deceit as things to over come on a daily basis? What do you know of making something out of nothing by any means necessary to survive, to keep a roof over your head, to keep your children fed?"

"Hell yeah I've broken the law to get where I'm at today but laws only apply to the lawless, and by no means am I or have I ever been without laws, morals or values in my heart. And I've raised my kids to be the same way. Life isn't fair, it's what you make it. My way may not have been right, but my ends have more than justified their means. All of my children have graduated high school and three of them have degrees. Let them find a better way. Let them blaze a path down the road less traveled. Why in the hell did you think we came to you in the first place? Huh?" he screamed. "Did you really think that it was solely to be independently distributed? Or did you really have the audacity to believe that we needed the committee to operate freely of Syon? Because if so, than you are not near as smart as I gave you credit for, lady. We wanted change, a real change. These boys' father and I never wanted to do what we were doing to make it. But we understood one thing about life and the streets. They don't discriminate, and they don't love nobody. So we vowed to hold each other down and raise our kids to be wise about life as a whole, not just in the streets. But it's hard for a black man to reverse the adverse effects of 400 years of slavery and brain washing. Especially when that man is still learning himself. So frankly, I don't give a fuck what you do. Send me to jail. My conscience is clean, my company is clean, so do what you do," he said, standing up, signaling that he was leaving with or without her permission.

"Mr. Vincent," the Congresswoman said exasperatedly. The past twelve hours of worry and grief were plain in her eyes. "My condolences on the loss of your friend. I heard about his death shortly before you arrived," she said, taking a long pull from a new cigarette. "We are all, in the same struggle, just in different fights," she pointed out. "I understand that you must stay true to your way of life, as must I. But I do want you ... I want you to know that I am very disappointed in the senselessness of your two company's rivalries and that behavior will not be tolerated as it has caused so much avoidable tragedy. Yes, I am familiar with the goings on in the record industry in Houston and else where and I frown upon the fact that we cannot come together as a people to overcome our struggles no matter how big or how small . . ."

Nya's cell phone interrupted the Congresswoman. Nya stood up, excusing herself to take the call out in the hall. Stepping out of the dining room, she answered her phone. "Agent Phillips," she answered. "What?!" she yelled. "When?"

Nya strode back into the dining room and headed straight for the Congresswoman. Her body language told everyone that something had happened. Nya leaned over and whispered into the Congresswoman's ear. When Charlette's eyes shot to Romichael, he knew that something wasn't right. When the tears started flowing again, he knew that he was in trouble. His mind reeled, trying to think of what could've happened. Had they found Duck and learned of the contracts that he'd taken out against the Murder One family? No, not possible. Duck was very likely dead, he knew. Had Flip or Monica betrayed him? Couldn't be; they didn't know anything. At least Monica didn't. What? Romichael wondered nervously.

Nya raised up and looked at Romichael suspiciously. "Mr. Turner, can you tell me how it came to be that my son's dead body turned up inside your gentlemen's club?" the Congresswoman asked, her voice cracking with emotion.

"BULLSHIT!" Romichael screamed, shooting up out of his seat. He glared at Amin and Nina, who were just as confused and surprised as he was, with more reason. "Them bitch ass muthafuckas are trying to set me up!" he pointed at Amin. "That's bullshit!!" he repeated, becoming dangerously agitated.

"Really?" Nya asked. "Well, why were you on your way to the airport when you were apprehended? Where were you headed? What are you trying to hide? Why are you running? Don't you also have another murder investigation currently pending against you in Louisiana?" Nya asked, firing off questions, the accusations piling up. For a moment, the room seemed to shrink to the two of them; Nya as inquisitor and Romichael as cornered criminal. She broke the spell by barking contemptuously, "Cuff his goddamned ass!"

But Romichael wasn't going out like that, not without a fight. He'd struggled too long, and too hard, for it to be snatched away from him like this, over something he didn't do and knew nothing about. He reached for the pistol that Flip had given him to shoot out the Hummer's window with. They had made a costly mistake and not patted him down before putting handcuffs on him. He'd stashed the gun in the small of his back, not having the time to do anything else with it when the feds rode down on him and Flip.

Nya saw the motion and screamed for every one to get down. In the momentary confusion the two agents hesitated, costing them their lives as Romichael shot the nearest one first, then the other, who died still trying to pull his gun free, a panicked expression on his face. Amin figured that he was next to die and he helplessly watched as Romichael gunned the two agents down. Kiwan reacted the quickest and slammed his body against his brother's chair. Nina was sitting next to Amin and all three were taken to the floor by Kiwan's momentum. Black Jack hit the floor and scrambled to the head of the table. He snatched the

Congresswoman's chair by the legs and yanked it, flipping the chair and causing her head to bounce off the carpeted floor. Better that than a bullet, he thought, scrambling on top of her, covering her body.

Romichael was on automatic now. He knew he was as good as dead, either now or within moments. He was determined to kill the one person who had been the focus of his hatred for decades now, the one man who had been his nemesis at every step - Amin Rush. He ran around the table, searching for Amin among the jumble of bodies trying to hide behind the overturned chairs.

Nya, in her first taste of armed battle, finally pulled her pistol free. She made an almost—fatal error by screaming at Romichael to throw his pistol away. He whirled and pulled the trigger twice, one of the bullets catching Nya high in her non-shooting shoulder. She slammed against the wall, slid to the floor and steadied her pistol against her knee. As Romichael turned to look for Amin again, Nya carefully fired off three shots, each centered on Romichael's head.

The room went quiet as the smell of cordite, gun powder, and the acrid coppery odor of blood filled the air. The eerie silence was broken by a groan from the Congresswoman, who shoved Black Jack away, struggling to her knees. The movement attracted the attention of a trembling Nya, who trained her pistol at the Congresswoman. Charlette saw the fear, shock and uncertainty in Nya's eyes. Put the gun down, honey. It's over."

She stood, looked at the carnage surrounding her and said quietly, "Someone, please call an ambulance."

Epilogue

A week later:

"I may be just a foolish dreamer ... but I don't care/cause I know my happiness is waiting out there, somewhere. I'm searching for that silver lining ... horizons that I've never seen/oh, I'd like to take just a moment and dream my dream ... ohh, dream my dream. Whoa, ohh Zoom! I'd like to fly far away from here/where my mind could be fresh and clear!/and I'd find the love that I've longed to see/where everybody can be what they wanna be!!!"

Kiwan blasted his theme song, "Zoom" by the Commodores as he followed the funeral procession down Cullen Boulevard to Paradise Cemetery. Tears flowed easily and unashamedly down his face as he remembered his father in life. He looked over at Prescious, who sat demurely in the passenger seat, holding his hand. She looked as radiant as ever and had been his comfort and sole support over the past week. He let the music sway him any way it pleased as he surrendered himself to his emotions. Prescious smiled at him, squeezing his hand, letting him know that they were going to make it, that everything would be all right.

The procession entered the cemetery behind the motorcade, a two—mile long line of cars holding people ready to pay their last respects to a well-respected man of many means and. friends. The line snaked its way to the burial plot, which had been prepared to receive Clyde Rush's corpse. Mourners, family members and friends began to file from their cars and gather around the canopied gravesite where chairs were setup for the immediate family. The rear doors of the hearse were opened and the pallbearers gathered around. Kiwan stood next to his brother and again felt a flush of pride at how well Amin had held up over the past week. Amin had stepped up like a man and had done his suffering without complaint and for that, Kiwan was proud. Yesterday they had buried Mister, Qwan and Punch, one of the two dead bodyguards. The families of Tony and Jack, the other dead bodyguard, had requested that their bodies be shipped home for burial there, and Amin had handled everything with grace and dignity. And now, today was Daddy Bo's funeral. A man should never have to attend back-to-back funerals on consecutive days. Yet Amin had done so and had held it together in the process. It seemed to Kiwan that his baby brother had grown up after all. Though they still communicated well since their fight, Kiwan knew that they had not lost love for each other.

The men silently carried the ornate casket to the burial plot from the hearse, slowly. Carefully. Methodically. With love and respect. The crowd that circled the burial site was enormous. There was barely enough room for the reverend to stand and deliver the final eulogy.

The preacher dynamically immortalized Clyde before he was lowered into the ground. Felicia sat next to her mother in the front row, sobbing on her shoulder, remembering her last glimpse of her father, as he quietly kidded her that last day as a guard. She was moved by the preacher's words, as was everyone who heard them. But each person remembered Clyde in their own way, and those who didn't know him personally were made aware of the legacy that he left behind. It was an emotional and overwhelming experience, that left everyone present drained.

After Clyde was lowered, into the ground, the crowd began to disperse. An announcement was made that there, would be a banquet held back at the Wheeler Avenue Baptist Church for those who wanted to attend. Kiwan pulled Amin aside as Nina and the kids hugged Kiwan, showing him love and support.

Kiwan said when they were out of everyone's earshot. "I wanted to tell you that I really didn't mean to blame daddy's death on you. I know that we were all born to die and when it's our turn to go,

then it's just that time. But I wanted to let you know how sorry I .
. ." Kiwan said, breaking down, sobbing onto his brother's shoulder.
Heartfelt, wrenching sobs escaped from the brothers as they embraced
one another. The scene caused a chain reaction as a fresh flood of tears
started to flow from every watching eye. Moochie had to turn away. He
didn't want to cry anymore.

"It's cool, man. I understand how you were feeling, man," Amin
said. "I started out all wrong when we were talking. I was nervous and
my words wouldn't come out. I didn't know that I had only one chance,"
Amin laughed, trying to inject some humor into the situation.

"Ahem . . . Gentlemen!" Nya Phillips said, not wanting to interrupt
but her orders had been specific. Kiwan was to be taken into custody
right after the funeral. His bond had been revoked. "I'm sorry," she said
nervously, shifting her weight from one foot to the other, vainly trying
to ignore the pain from her bandaged shoulder, which itched madly.

The family saw Nya waiting and knew what it meant. They swarmed
Kiwan and jockeyed for position to get in their last good-byes. "Bye,
baby," Precious said, kissing Kiwan on the lips. "Call me, I'll be at the
house waiting," she told him, lightly brushing her fingers across his
face.

"Bye, negro," Nina said, also kissing Kiwan on the lips, holding her
and Amin's youngest child so Kiwan could give her a kiss, too.

"Hey, hey!" Amin said, laughing. "Enough of that shit," he joked.
They all laughed to keep from crying.

"Shut up, Amin," Nina said as Black Jack and the rest of the Murder
One crew stepped up to give their love and support. Even K—flex had
tears in his eyes but tried desperately to stand strong and give his love.

"We gon keep it real, they were saying. Poo—Poo and the rest of
the boys gathered around for a group hug and pictures. Finally they
handed him over to Nya, who was still waiting impatiently.

As Nya escorted Kiwan to a waiting car, she received all kinds of
dirty looks and under-the-breath 'bitches' and 'hoes' from the family
and friends. A-dray was the one who shouted it out at the top of her
lungs. "BITCH! Just couldn't wait to take him to jail, his daddy ain't
even in the ground good!" she yelled.

Yep! Nya thought. This was it for her. Monday she was turning in
her resignation, for sure. "Wait up," someone called. Nya and Kiwan

turned to see who was calling them. Amin was trotting across to catch up to them. When he caught up he was. huffing, trying to catch his breath. "Damn, I didn't think y'all had walked off this far," Amin said, breathing heavily. He looked at the bottom of his 'gator' shoes to see if he'd scuffed them.

"What's up?" Kiwan asked, wondering why his brother had run over.

"Oh, I just wanted to tell you that I'll be up to see you as soon as you fill out your visitation list," Amin told him, smiling!

*   *   *   *   *   *   *   *   *   *   *   *   *

Moochie brushed Felicia on the shoulder as they watched Kiwan being driven away. "Don't be sad, baby girl. If it hadn't of been for you, we all would've been in deep shit," Moochie told her.

"Me?" Felicia scoffed. "You're the one who hadn't gotten rid of the bodies fast enough. If you would've dumped them when Nina told you to then we all would've been in deep shit."

"Yeah, but it was your idea to set up Romichael by putting the body in the club."

"Yeah, but you bypassed the alarm and got us in."

"So I guess it's safe to say that we make a good team?!" Moochie asked, hugging Felicia to him.

"Maybe!" she said, blushing.

*   *   *   *   *   *   *·   *   *   *   *   *   *

Beaumont — F.C.I. Medium — Three months later

Kiwan sauntered into his unit after the 8:30 count was clear. He was beat. Having to get up at 3 in the morning to go to work was draining him.

He liked being a cook in the kitchen, he just wished he could do it on another shift. He went straight to his room and got out of his funky clothes, heading straight for the showers. Thank God for small favors, he thought, happy that his roommate had already left for work, allowing him some much needed privacy.

After a quick ten-minute shower, Kiwan felt rejuvenated. He went back to his room, took care of his hygiene, then started washing his clothes. As he was gathering up his dirty laundry for the wash, he saw his unopened mail still lying on the desk from yesterday. He had been meaning to read his mail last night but fell asleep before doing so. He flipped through his three letters. He smiled when he saw one from A—dray. Knowing how brazen she was, he decided to read that one later for a good laugh. She was probably talking about not dropping the soap in the shower or some booty bandit shit like that, the way she always did when she came to visit him. Last time Kiwan had to tell her straight up to stop watching OZ. He was tickled when he saw the pink envelope that smelled of perfume. He knew who that was from before he even opened it or saw the return address on the envelope. To his surprise, Precious had been down for him like 18 flat tires on a tractor trailer... But he wasn't in the mood for a lovey dovey letter right now. Maybe later. The third letter caught his undivided attention because it was heavy and 'the front of it said, "Photos! Please do not bend!" He ripped the envelope open excitedly and began reading the letter before flipping through the pictures. It was a one-page letter from K—flex. It read:

Dear Kiwan:

I know that you are shocked to hear from me, but I had to take time out of my busy schedule to write you and hit you with some flicks. The tour is going great and we are sold out in every city. These are the first set of pictures of the 50—city tour in the states. You should be getting some everyday for about three weeks straight. You are going to be sick of pictures when I get through. I'm also sending you some when we go to Europe. All of the fellas send their love, even Poo—Poo. He's my new road manager! As you know, I got mad love for you and the Murder One family. I look at all the success we are having and I thank God! Especially for you I will always feel that I owe you my life. If you hadn't given me the keys to your truck and the house that night, I would've been dead along with Mister and Qwan. Anyway, Amin is giving me a label deal under the Murder One umbrella that will allow me a lot of creativity. When you get home, I hope that we can do some work together. I've learned a lot about the business being around your brother.

Well, I hope that everything is all right with you in there, but then again I keep forgetting who you are (smile.) Your violation will be up soon and I'm looking forward to you coming home. See you in six months. Keep ya head up!

One, Flex!

P.S. Check out the pictures of me and Eve. As you know we are dating now. These boys out here hating me, but baby girl is cool and down. Just make sure you don't hate and I might let you holla at her on the phone, so don't trip! Ha!

Much love and Respect,

Peace.

You couldn't wipe the smile off of Kiwan's face if you dragged him face first going 100 miles an hour chained to the back of a motorcycle. He sat up and flipped through the pictures feeling proud and happy for K—flex. The only thing that bothered him was that he didn't know how to tell Flex that when he came home he would distance himself as far from the industry as possible. Speaking of which, that reminded him that he had a phone call to make.

Kiwan hurried to the dayroom, where the phones were kept, hoping to catch his friend before he left for work. He quickly dialed the number, punched in his PIN number and waited for the call to go through. The phone rang five times before someone picked up. The automated voice machine announced his call as Kiwan waited to be patched through.

"What's up, dude?" Carl Littrell, his computer hacking friend, who'd embezzled $30 million of federal money, greeted when the call was connected.

"Hey man, I thought that I might've missed you," Kiwan said, breathing a sigh of relief.

"Nah, today I'm golfing at the country club with some buddies of mine from New York. You know, the ones I told you about from Syon."

"Yeah, I remember. Do you think that the business deal might go through?" Kiwan asked, smiling.

"We'll see. You know how corporate America is. More deals are made on the golf course and in the bedroom than the boardroom," Carl said.

"Ain't that the truth," Kiwan replied. "What about our pigeon? We still got him caged?"

"Hell, yeah! I keep his ass on a short leash, and you know I can't help but fuck with him a bit. You know test the waters. Play with his credit, shorten his cash a bit, prepping him for the big chabang."

Kiwan smiled. Chad Stevens would be in for the biggest surprise of his life when they got through with him. "Awight, that's cool. Just don't go overboard so he don't get suspicious."

"Me, overboard? Come on, Kiwan, I would never do such a thing."

Kiwan heard his name being called over the P.A. system for a visit. "Well, look, Carl, I gotta go. I'll call you tomorrow to see how things went at the course."

"All righty, man. You take care."

"You too," Kiwan said before hanging up. Damn; who could this be popping up on me like this, he wondered? Fifteen minutes later, Kiwan walked out of the shakedown area for inmates into the visitation lounge. He didn't see any familiar faces amongst the waiting visitors as he scanned the room on the way to the check—in desk. He handed his ID card to the officer to be checked in, without speaking. It was the same officer he'd cursed out when he left prison three months ago.

"Oh, hey, Rush," she spoke cheerfully. This confused Kiwan, because this type of attitude was contradictory to her normal behavior.

"Sup!" he said.

"They're bringing, the visitors up now. Just find a table," she told him.

He was tempted to ask her who was visiting him but he passed, wanting to be surprised. "Awight," was all that he said. He picked a table as far away from the check-in desk as possible and out of the way of the security cameras. He figured he might need some privacy. The group of visitors all came through the door at the same time. Kiwan searched the crowd thoroughly trying to spot a familiar face. Felicia was the very last person through the door, but the shock was who she'd brought with her. Never had he thought that Ayanna would come to see him, not even when she asked to be placed on his visiting list.

Kiwan got up and met his two visitors in the middle of the lounge. He hugged his sister, then moved on to Ayanna. "Daaamn!" Kiwan said, smiling. "It's good to see y'all."

"You shocked, nigga?" his sister asked."

"Hell, yeah!" he said, rubbing Ayanna's swollen stomach. she covered his hands with hers and stopped him from rubbing.

"Let's sit down first, I have to tell you what the doctor said," she told him.

He searched Felicia's face to see if it was good news or bad news, but she didn't let on either way. Her features remained neutral.

Although they had been through a lot over the past few years. Romichael's death had brought them closer. But nothing had served, to strengthen their bond like their unborn child. Kiwan and Ayanna had been keeping in touch lately and agreed to maintain a respectful and mutual friendship for the benefit of their child.

"What's the deal?" Kiwan wanted to know, getting straight to the point.

"Hold on, I'mma tell you," Ayanna said playfully, as she sat down with Kiwan's help. "Let me at least sit down first," she laughed.

"Yeah, boy, hold your horses," Felicia chipped in.

"Maan, talk to me, Kiwan said impatiently.

"Okay, okay," Ayanna said, squirming in her chair, trying to get comfortable. "What are you and Prescious having?" Ayanna asked.

"Uhmm, a girl, I think."

"You're pathetic," Felicia said, punching him in his arm.

"Well hell! I think, yeah, she did say that it was a girl."

"You're supposed to know that type of shit when it comes to women, you fool," his sister scolded.

"Anyway," Ayanna said, scooting closer to the table and leaning over in Kiwan's direction. "How would you feel about a little boy?" she questioned. Ayanna couldn't see Kiwan's face light up, but she sure could hear it in his voice.

"We're having a boy? A baby boy?"

"Noooo," Ayanna said, smiling.

"No? Damn," Kiwan said. "Well, it doesn't matter, as long as the baby's healthy."

"I'm sorry I couldn't give you just one baby boy, Kiwan. But how would you feel about two of them?" Ayanna asked.

"No shit?! You're having twins?" Kiwan yelled, forgetting where he was. "Shhh . . . the whole world doesn't need to know," Felicia said, laughing at her brother.

"I'll be damned, like hell they don't," he said aloud. "Everybody, we're having twins!" he joyfully announced to everyone in the visitation room.

*   *   *   *   *   *   *   *   *   *   *   *   *

Charlette Cunningham looked up from her desk to the image on the television. She wasn't for certain if the set was on the correct channel so she double-checked to make sure. Yep! her TV was tuned to BET but she couldn't believe it when she saw Ed Gordon interviewing Amin Rush. She increased the volume to catch the gist of the interview.

"Let me get this straight," Ed Gordon was saying. Sitting across him was the always-immaculately dressed Idie Amin. "After all of the deaths, tragedy and mayhem that went on in Houston three months ago, the major beef between Ruff House and Murder One ended in the two companies merging after all?"

Amin smiled his charismatic smile, charming the public. "Yeah," he said, shaking his head. "It's strange, isn't it? But I guess it takes fire to purify rough elements, after all. And now that the paperwork has been finalized, we've officially renamed the company. We felt the name Murder One was inappropriate to what we wanted to do. Our company now is called One Luv Records. And all future profits from the company will go to fund a lifelong dream of my father's, may he rest in peace. It will be called The Village of Common Roots. This will be a multi-million dollar organization that's going to build a foster home-type preparatory academy for minority males in the United States. We're starting with ten-year-old orphans and are going to raise them in a secluded community to call their own."

"That's commendable," Ed told him. "I would like to know more about that. What kind of backing do you all have?"

"Well, we are just starting and as you know, the company is not hurting for capital. Right now we're just getting our money together and building the nest egg. No one else is helping, yet! But we look to see others get on the bandwagon once they see how serious we are."

The Congresswoman was shocked speechless. She buzzed her aide and instructed her to get Mr. Keith Vincent on the phone. Ten minutes later, Charlette was on the phone with Black Jack. "How are you doing, Mr. Vincent?" she asked.

"I'm making it. How about yourself?"

"Good, good. I'm very blessed," she assured him. "I was calling because I'm sitting in my office watching BET and I saw young Mr. Rush on the television. I know that we both have our differences and that we also have our commons. But ... well ... I had to call and tell you how proud I am to see what you guys are doing. I was wondering how long it would take someone in the South to see the, uh, Russell Simmons vision," she chuckled.

"I commend you all on your efforts, and I guess that, I, uh ... well, I would like to keep tabs on your efforts and I am offering you any assistance within my powers that you might need." There. She finally got it out.

Black Jack couldn't help but laugh. He knew how hard it must have been for a woman of her caliber, after everything that had taken place between them, to do what she'd just done. In Black Jack's eyes, she was a fantastic woman and a tribute to her race. And in return, he would repay her with the truth.

"You know, Congresswoman since we are on the phone, there is something that I must say to you," he said. She braced herself for a tongue lashing, but got only silence.

"Yes, Mr. Vincent?"

"You know, I owe you more than you could possibly realize. Three months ago, that terrible day in your study, Romichael did not possess the deadliest weapon. You did. Before he pulled his pistol, you had already trained your pistol upon me. What you said, about my behavior and my rationalizations for that behavior, deeply shamed me. You made me realize that the codes that we've followed all our lives in the street are not worth what I've lost, what those boys have lost. In my lifetime I've lost more than I could ever gain back if I lived another hundred years. None of the drugs, the violence, the money was worth one second of any of the lives that were lost. I've sold my soul to get where I'm at now. But hopefully the sacrifice of my life. will not have been in vain. Hopefully, with a little help, I can rewrite those codes for these kids and surround them with examples of true success. They need to know that true success is when you come to the realization of self, and I just wanted to say that I'm a better man now than I was before you helped me to acknowledge that!"

THE END